We Spend
Our Lives

Bernard J Sieracki

Order this book online at www.trafford.com
or email orders@trafford.com

Most Trafford titles are also available at major online book retailers.

Print information available on the last page.

ISBN: 978-1-6987-1376-2 (sc)
ISBN: 978-1-6987-1378-6 (hc)
ISBN: 978-1-6987-1377-9 (e)

Library of Congress Control Number: 2023900098

Trafford rev. 01/06/2023

www.trafford.com
North America & international
toll-free: 844-688-6899 (USA & Canada)
fax: 812 355 4082

Contents

To Mary Masterson, who
made this work possible.

I

Blue Hat

Finally, the brakes squeaked, the wheels skidded along the tracks, and the streamlined train slowly came to a stop. It was the Union Station of Kansas City, and the passengers hurried out of the cars onto the crowded platform of Track 16. Some carried a suitcase to one side of them. A woman came along loaded with a shopping bag, an arm full of boxes, and three little children straggling close behind her. However, most of the people carried nothing at all as they walked alongside the standing train toward the escalator leading up to the passageway through which the people proceeded on to the lobby.

In the lobby, a countless number of people waited at the doors. Some were eating popcorn or candy or drinking Coca-Cola out of a paper cup as they waited for the arrival of their friends or relatives. Upon the arrival of the passengers from the train, in all the excitement, there was much handshaking, embracing, and kissing of the loved ones. A short ways from the doors, at the bookstand, were two girls talking excitedly to each other as they looked on with the excitement of expectation. One was taller and appeared somewhat more mature than the other. The younger seemed to be more excited about something than her companion. They stood in one place, but they certainly looked about in all directions, with their faces filled with the excited emotions of the imminent recognition of someone.

As the people came pouring through the many doors on the passageway, a soldier slipped out of the crowd and stood by, with his eyes searching through the crowd. From his decorations, one could easily tell that he was an active man in the army, and the captain's uniform added a decided attraction to his entire self. He scrutinized the faces of women. Often he would raise his left hand to bring part of a letter to his eyes. He would study some girl's appearance as he referred to the letter. Soon, he began wandering about impatiently through the crowd.

The last of the people from Track 16 straggled into the lobby. The doors were closed, and the crowd at the doors began to dissipate. It wasn't long before most of them had left. The captain, with his back against the doors, still holding the letter in his left hand, looked about with signs of disappointment.

The taller girl of the two left, but her companion remained. She wasn't looking around so feverishly any longer. Her downcast eyes and slow motions of her body showed all the signs of a heart heavy with disappointment. Her thoughts were drifting far away, and her lips quivered as if she were about to cry.

The captain studied her several times before, but after referring to his letter, he turned elsewhere. She also looked at him several times but paid no more attention. As he watched her this time, he saw her disappointment and instinctively started toward her. He worked his way around to her back, and he drew up close enough to embrace her.

"Mary!" he cried out with delighted excitement.

"George!" she cried out in return.

She turned around and threw her arms around his neck, only to recover in time before she kissed him. Quickly, she withdrew her arms, but his arms were holding her fast at the waistline. Her face felt a sudden glow of heat, and so embarrassed was she that her chewing gum found its way down past her esophagus. She pressed his arms away and retreated a few slow steps backward.

"No, it isn't George—it's me," he said in a soft tone.

He smiled, so silly, as though he had known her a long time. He slowly stepped forward, after her, putting the letter in his pocket.

"So I see." She kept retreating, slowly, step by step.

"Johnnie is my name," he said. "Johnnie Jones."

"Your name does not interest me. Please go away before my aunt gets back," she remarked.

"Am I afraid of your aunt?" he jested.

"I don't know. Please go away. You see, I'm engaged, and she will talk if she sees me here with you." Mary pleaded with him and even took off her glove to proudly display the ring.

"You don't seem to like me very much." He followed her with every step; she retreated backward.

"I would like you more if you would leave right away. Now will you please go?"

"How is it you're not wearing your blue hat?"

"What blue hat?" This thought stopped her, and she looked at him in bewilderment.

"The one that matches your eyes," he said.

"The one with the feather in it?"

"Yes, the one with the feather in it." He smiled.

"Don't you like this one?" she asked.

"It's all right, but what about that light gray suit you're supposed to wear?"

"Who told you what I was supposed to wear today?" she questioned.

"I guess if I said I would be at the railroad station with a light gray suit and a blue hat, I'd be at the railroad station with a light gray suit and a blue hat. How do you expect somebody to find you if he's looking for a blue hat and you're not wearing one?" His smile never faded from the moment he first spoke to her.

Mary was embarrassed with this. She felt like a scolded child, although it came with a smile. *Some fresh guy who got hold of her letter somehow*, she thought.

"Look," she said, "here comes a policeman, and if you can't leave me alone right this minute, I'll ask him to help you."

She showed signs of anxiety while she looked about to see if her aunt was coming. She was nervous and frightened by this stranger who took it upon himself to make her acquaintance. He seemed so determined, and that constant smile meant to her that he had something on his mind.

"But why should you be calling on anyone for help when I wouldn't hesitate leastways to be at your service? I hope it will be my pleasure to escort you home," he said calmly with sincerity.

Mary's back was chilled, and her face turned pale. She realized what he had on his mind and that there would be no end to this. She noticed that her aunt was returning, and in her nervous anxiety to be rid of this character, she cried out "Officer!" to the policeman who stood a short distance from them.

"What is it, ma'am?" the policeman asked her while he looked at Johnnie.

"I assure you, Mary, this wasn't necessary." His smile disappeared, and he felt taken back.

"Officer, help this man to leave me alone." She faced the policeman when she spoke and immediately turned to leave.

Johnnie quickly turned to follow her.

"You heard what the lady said!" the husky voice of the policeman bellowed as he took hold of Johnnie by the arm.

All the people in the surrounding area were attracted, and they watched with interest. Some even came closer to learn what was going on.

Mary hurried away to her aunt.

"Mary! Come back! Mary! Don't leave me! I just want to talk to you! I want to talk to you about your brother!" Johnnie shouted louder and louder as she hurried farther away from him.

She came upon her aunt halfway across the lobby. She tried to compose herself to make it appear as though nothing of any importance had happened.

"What did you find out, Chris?" she asked with an air of innocence.

"The only information we can get at this railroad station concerns the train schedule and the tourist."

She spoke to Mary, but her eyes were straining far across the lobby where Johnnie tussled, verbally, with the policeman. It was not the size of the policeman that held him back; it was his respect for the law.

Of course, the policeman sympathized with Mary, and he waited for her to disappear out of sight before he would permit Johnnie to be on his way.

"Maybe we could get some information from the Red Cross office," Mary suggested impatiently in trying to get away from Johnnie.

"Yes, we may. What would you say is going on over there?" She turned to Mary.

"Where?"

"Over there." Christine pointed with her eyes.

"Where? I don't see anything." Mary looked in the designated direction.

"You know what I'm talking about," said Christine firmly.

"What?" asked Mary, feigning ignorance.

"That army captain you were speaking to." Christine confronted Mary with the fact that she saw everything.

"Oh, Johnnie?" Mary's face grew pale when she realized that there was nothing she could hide.

"So it's Johnnie? Take me there and introduce him to me," she said to Mary in the form of an order.

"Oh, but I don't even know him—I never saw him before in my life! Believe me, Chris, if you ever did," she pleaded.

Mary was frightened. She began to feel an unpleasant sensation in her stomach and her abdomen. For a moment, she thought it was caused by the chewing gum she swallowed. *There's no telling what this will lead to.* A feeling came over her, and her imaginations ran wild with the worst that could happen.

"You never saw him before in your life, yet you threw your arms around his neck as if he were your sweetheart." Christine disclosed her knowledge of the scene.

"I did nothing of the kind!" Mary recoiled.

"You would have kissed him too if you were sure enough that I wouldn't see."

"I wouldn't either!"

Mary was boiling with rage. She had no means of self-defense in this case.

"Come. Introduce me to the captain. I'd love to meet him."

Christine edged her on. She had a grievance with a heartache to settle, and although her words came forth smoothly, the bitterness from her heart always seeped through somehow.

"I'll do nothing of the kind. I'm going home, even if you're not."

"It so happens that I have the keys, and it is my car, Mary."

"I'll take a taxi." Mary began fumbling through her purse, in doubt of having the fare for the taxicab.

"Now you're being foolish. Come. Introduce me to him, or I will see to it that your fiancé knows about Johnnie."

"All right, let's go. I have nothing to hide. I never saw him before, and we embraced each other by accident," Mary conceded under a feverish nervousness of fear.

Christine was hurrying along while she looked forward to meeting Johnnie.

Mary had a sickening feeling and thought she was going to faint. Reluctantly, she tagged a step or two behind Christine. She couldn't figure out what was coming up next. She couldn't see through the moves that Christine was making. Anyhow, she felt that no good would come of all this.

They came upon Johnnie still wrangling with the policeman.

"Hello." Johnnie broke out with his silly smile as he almost sang his greeting.

"You're making trouble for me, Johnnie," Mary cautioned with all her seriousness.

"I am?" he asked, displaying signs of satisfaction.

"This is my aunt, Christine," she said to Johnnie, "and this is Johnnie." She turned to Christine. "He calls himself Johnnie," she added.

"That's the way my mother would like it to be, so that's the way she wrote it on my birth certificate. Could you think of any reason why I should have it changed?" he asked.

"Oh no! Of course not . . . Under the circumstances," replied Mary in an apologetic way.

She felt a need for a formal apology, but her mind was already so enwrapped with the incident that she had a dazed liking for him. She wanted him, yet she tried to be rid of him because of Christine's presence.

"And I'm the law. Remember, young lady? I'm the law," the policeman added with emphasis.

"Oh yes. This is the officer that I asked to keep Johnnie company so I could go home with you. He wanted to take me home," Mary complained.

"I don't see any harm in that. Do you, Christine?" Johnnie made eyes of understanding at Christine.

"Johnnie, tell Chris that I never saw you before in my life," Mary almost demanded, but she was begging.

Johnnie looked at the policeman.

"This is interesting—and more interesting as we go along," the policeman implied as he looked into Johnnie's eyes.

"But, Mary, how could I say such a thing after all that time in the park we spent together? All the plans we made before I left with the armed forces? Why didn't you write me that there was someone else?" Johnnie's smile disappeared, and he spoke with seriousness of a broken heart.

"You lie!" Mary cried out with fear in her mind.

Mary's eyes popped wide open, and her mouth was open for a few seconds before the words came out with full force. *How could he be saying this? Why should he?* She had the feeling that she was going to break down and cry and run home to cry some more, but she couldn't do that, especially in front of Christine.

Christine was happy with the sight of Mary suffering before her very eyes. She was amused and took special notice of everything that was going on.

"You see how much simpler it would all be . . . if you would only have worn that blue hat with the feather in it?" Johnnie spoke softly with caution. "Like you said in the last letter you wrote to me."

"She's been writing to you?" Christine questioned, with her eyebrows rising high.

"Oh yes," Johnnie admitted affirmatively.

"Lies! Lies! Lies!" Mary cried out.

"Here's the last letter she wrote to me. See?" Johnnie said, producing the letter. "Could you recognize her handwriting?" he asked Christine.

"That is her handwriting." Christine confirmed Johnnie's statement and returned the letter to him.

Mary couldn't stand any more. She broke down in tears and turned away for them not to see. She took a few steps away, and then she hurried, almost on the run.

Johnnie started after her, but with a tug at his arm, the policeman jerked him back.

"You're staying with me, Johnnie, my boy," the policeman whispered in his hoarse voice.

"It's all right, Officer. He can come with me," Christine assured the policeman.

"Seems to me like something's wrong somewhere, but if you want him, you can have him," the policeman remarked, freeing Johnnie, walking off to another part of the lobby.

"You don't mind coming to our house for dinner, do you, Johnnie?" Christine asked, taking hold on his arm.

"Is Mary going to be there?"

"Yes, she will. She and her folks are living with me," Christine said, watching his eyes.

"Of course, I don't mind." He smiled to her with some understanding.

He had a feeling that he had something in common with Christine. Of course, he would never pry into her affairs. She did not interest him from any other viewpoint than the fact that she would bring him closer to Mary. That was all important to him, and that was all that mattered. Christine looked to be about twenty-eight or maybe thirty. She didn't have the youthful charm of Mary, but she made up for it in many ways. She was amiable, smooth, and mature in her thoughts. She seemed to be leading him on. She had something on her mind. It seemed to be some plan or scheme or something, but whatever it was, it would do her no good as far as he was concerned. His mind was on Mary, and he was determined that Christine would not divert his affections onto herself.

"What came over Mary? She's acting strange," asked Johnnie.

Johnnie slowed his steps to needle out as much information from her as he could before he would meet Mary again.

"I don't know. She's engaged now. I guess that is what makes the difference."

"I guess I've been away too long—that's what makes the difference." Johnnie interpolated his own thoughts into her reasoning.

"Oh, I wouldn't say that. If she was writing to you, at least you had a chance. Maybe you slipped up somewhere?" explained Christine.

"But she never told me about the engagement."

"She's got her mind set on that orchestra conductor. Won't be long before she marries him."

"How long?" Johnnie almost snapped out.

"Another year—as soon as she graduates. She's got a crush on him that simply ties him up in knots. Every time her fiancé comes over, there they are—her sitting at one end of the sofa and him sitting at the other end. Or else she's hammering away on the piano while he's sitting there twiddling his thumbs in complete ecstasy. She says he's going to make her a great concert pianist, but I don't think so. She never had an interest in music until she met him. He also has some classes in music at the college."

"What about yourself? A beau waiting—maybe?" inquired Johnnie.

Her eyes watered, and she turned her face away from him. She pressed back the tears with her fingers, and it was all over. With a smile, her eyes returned to his.

"I have a home and a place in my heart for a man, but what chance have I got? Can't go anywhere, can't do anything—that's the life of a teacher, especially in college."

"Well, you never know when somebody is going to pop up somewhere." He laughed encouragingly for her benefit.

"Waiting isn't as bad as losing someone," she said.

"Whatever happened to Mary? I suppose she took a taxi home." Johnnie tried changing the subject.

"I don't think she went anywhere. When we left home, she didn't have enough money to buy a package of chewing gum. She's probably waiting for me in the car," Christine explained.

They came to the parking lot. Soon, they were beside Christine's car, and there, behind the steering wheel, sat Mary with her head resting on her arms, supported by the steering wheel. She straightened up slowly when Johnnie opened the door. Christine threw the car keys to her.

"You might as well drive as long as you're behind the wheel." Christine laughed and motioned for Johnnie to get into the coupé, but he helped her instead. It would be better that way—with himself to the opposite side of Mary.

"Is he coming too?" Mary asked in disgust.

"He's coming to the house for dinner. Any friend of yours is a friend of mine," Christine implied.

"Believe me, he's no friend of mine—even with that uniform on." Mary spoke with tight lips from the bitterness in her heart for him. She knew she would never forgive him for the act he put on at the railroad station.

As Mary drove along the road, she did not speak to Johnnie or even glance in his direction. Her mind was preoccupied only with the thought of getting home. What she would do when she got home, she did not know, but anyhow, it was a consoling thought. The one thing she was sure of was that she would not eat at the same table with Johnnie. What a mess this would be if she could not justify herself before her fiancé! With all that Christine would add—to Johnnie's ready-made lies—it could set her wedding date further off or eliminate it entirely.

"How did you happen to be at the railroad station all by yourself? With no one to greet you on your happy event of returning home? No mother . . . No father . . . No sweetheart?" Christine inquired as she looked into the rearview mirror for Mary's reaction to the question, with the emphasis on "No sweetheart."

Johnnie's eyes blurred, and he felt a choking sensation at his throat. For a few seconds, he could not utter a word. He swallowed as though his throat had an obstruction in it.

"Mother was there . . . Father was there . . . Mary was there," he said, turning to Mary.

Mary looked at him. She noticed the tears in his eyes. Her attention went back to the road. Somehow she did not feel angry at him now. Her sympathy was aroused, and she felt that there was something deeper than the blue hat with the feather in it. She felt that there was some connection between Johnnie and her brother.

Yes, there must be. She wasn't listening when he was yelling after her at the station. What did he say? Where did he get hold of her letter? Conflicting questions were popping into her mind, and her curiosity called for a quick solution. She loudly cleared her throat.

"You know my brother George?" she asked without looking at him.

"Yes. In a way," he replied.

Christine looked at Mary with surprise, and her head turned back and forth as each one spoke. She seemed to be left out of the conversation now.

Johnnie was delighted to hear Mary's voice again—and in a friendly tone. He decided to hold back for more. It was a natural thing for a woman to do the talking, and the more she talked, the better the chance was of meeting her on her own terms.

"Were you with him in the service?" she prodded him on.

"I have a uniform, haven't I?" Johnnie laughed softly.

"I mean, did you see him often? What I really mean is were you two together in the same outfit?" Mary tried to alleviate the pressure of embarrassment out of her failure to express herself.

"Sometimes close together, sometimes very far apart. Haven't seen him for several years up until lately," he said.

"Did you see him before you left?"

"As a matter of fact, I did," Johnnie acknowledged nonchalantly.

"How is he? Tell me all about him. Has he changed much? He was supposed to come back with you—wasn't he?"

Mary was bubbling with questions. The answer to one question opened the way to a dozen other questions. There could be no end, she thought, to the things she had to talk over with Johnnie. At one point, she couldn't turn her eyes back to the road. At the moment, she completely forgot she was driving.

Christine was silent but listening carefully. Suddenly, the car swayed as the wheels on one side of the car went off the road and dug into the soft shoulder alongside the road.

"Hey! Watch the road!" Christine yelled.

Christine grabbed the steering wheel, holding onto it hysterically tight with both hands.

Mary struggled with the steering wheel while the car swayed crazily, half on the road and half off the road, making a snake-like pattern in the soft ground between the concrete road and the drainage ditch.

"Chris! Let go of the wheel!" Johnnie yelled instantly at the top of his voice.

He was trying to wring her hands off the wheel, but with one look at the drainage ditch on his side, he took a firm hold of the steering wheel with both hands and helped Mary steer the car back to the road again.

"I was so frightened," Christine confessed, with her face white and her lips blue, as though it were drained of all its blood. Her shaking hand rubbed her forehead, and she was getting ready to faint. After a moment, her weakness left her. "Perhaps you would like to have someone else drive the car?" she asked Mary.

She knew she was not in a condition to drive, so she wasn't referring to herself. There was Johnnie sitting to the other side of her, and she was referring to him.

"We'll be home soon," Mary defended herself.

"As I was saying about your brother," Johnnie cut in as though nothing had happened, "he's fine. Hasn't changed a bit for the worse. We were supposed to return together, but his papers weren't quite in order, so he'll be coming on the next boat."

How could he tell her that her brother was lying in the hospital, seriously wounded? Why should he be the messenger of bad news? Why should he cast upon her the misery of anxiety? They would send word home if George was not making any progress. He had a feeling George would write as soon as he regained consciousness. However George would come out, he could not tell her the truth for her own good. She would find out for herself—it would be better that way.

"How long will it take for the next boat?" Mary asked.

"Three weeks. Maybe a month. There's nothing to worry about, Mary. Before you know it, he'll be back. I would bet he is worried more about his girl than he is about you or your folks. You see, when he comes back, he will still have you and your folks, but will he still have his girl? That is the question keeping his insides grinding and his mind disintegrating."

"George? A girl?" Mary was caught in surprise.

"A sweetheart," Johnnie corrected, and he felt everything was bringing Mary closer to him.

"But he always talked like a confirmed bachelor. He had nothing to do with girls, ever," explained Mary.

"This war has done a lot of things. It has made men out of boys, and it has done a lot of other things, but most of all, it has destroyed many lives and much property. You know, when a fellow is lying out there in the foxhole, digging his hands into the ground at the bottom in trying to pull himself closer down into it, while the bombs are bursting all about him and the earth is trembling from the force of the heavy bombs upon it, life itself takes on a brighter hue. He begins to see life from an entirely different standpoint than he ever did before."

"Wait till I see that brother of mine when he gets home. Seems to me like he's keeping a lot of things to himself lately," said Mary in a threatening tone.

"Don't be too hard on him," Johnnie cautioned. "George may have his reasons for what he's doing."

They turned off the road, and they reached a cluster of modern homes, one of which was the property of Christine. Christine bought the home for her own purpose, but living in this big seven-room house made her more lonely.

II

Favor

$\mathcal{M}$ary's mother and father were awaiting the return of George. There wasn't room enough in Christine's coupé for the folks to go along; besides, Mary's mother was quite busy arranging and rearranging everything for George's homecoming. Her father put in his share of helping with everything. By this time, everything was in order, and the folks leisurely passed the time away by the window from where they could see the car returning.

Several years ago, Mary's father lost his business through some high financing. All he had left was his trousers and what was in them, and there wasn't any money in them with which to start over again. This affected his mind. He spent a lot of time brooding over his loss. He was a businessman, and he knew his business—only he slipped once, that's all. He couldn't gather up enough courage to work for a salary and save week by week until he could start with a business again. He lost faith in himself, and he lost faith in religion. He had many friends from old times who pitied him and treated him with drinks until he could not walk off in a normal way. Then they would take him to a taxi and pay his fare home. He always accepted with the understanding that he was not a pauper looking for handouts but that he would reimburse them for every penny—someday, sometime. He got drunk when he went out, and he went out when sitting at home became monotonous.

"It is too late. It's all over. What's the use? I'm too old," he would say whenever someone tried encouraging him to start a small business or go to work for a salary.

Although his wife held a secretarial position, he never would accept money from her. She thought that by his doing the heavy work about the house, there was some hope of his recovery. She was graying fast from worry.

She could have married her employer by merely divorcing her disintegrating and degenerating husband. Her employer begged her and often tried to buy his way into her heart, but she was strong in her heart's desire.

She never mentioned the change in the family's life in her letters to George, her devoted son. She advised Mary and Christine to do likewise. *Everything would be so much easier for George to see and to understand when he returns home.* She was afraid George might fall into the same state of mind as his father, and now George was returning home. When she saw the car come with the figure in uniform inside, her heart was filled with joy and sorrow at the same time. The sorrow tried to weigh her heart down, and the joy tried to buoy it up and make it light while she struggled somewhere between the two—first to one side and then to the other. She hurried away from the window, out through the door, and out to the gravel road where the car stood. She was overjoyed with the fact of seeing her son back, but how was she going to tell him about his father?

She was stunned speechless and arrested in her stride when she realized that the figure in uniform was not her son. Worry had crowded out the joy in her heart, and it joined with sorrow to make her heart ache painfully.

Mary saw her mother come bursting out of the house, and she was afraid her mother might suffer a terrible letdown. She hurried out of the car as soon as it stopped, and she ran to her mother. When she saw her mother stop, she knew it had happened.

"He's all right, Mother. George is all right. He's got some trouble with his papers. This is a friend of George." Mary embraced, hugged, and kissed her mother until she recovered from her disappointment.

Mary's father wasn't more than a few steps behind her mother. Soon, everybody gathered around her. After a minute, she blinked her eyes several times, swallowed her sorrows, and turned to Johnnie with a smile.

"I'm glad to see a friend of George," she said.

"This is Mr. and this is Mrs. Masterson. My dad and my mother," said Mary to Johnnie. "This is Johnnie—he was with George," she explained with pride.

"George will be home in four or five weeks," Johnnie reassured her. "His papers didn't get through yet. He'll be back on the next boat. I'm sure of it."

"I'm so glad to hear you say that. Won't you come in? I have dinner almost ready, and the table is set for five." She looked to him, in doubt of his acceptance.

"I wasn't planning on it, but I just can't resist home cooking," he replied.

They sat about in the living room and listened to what Johnnie could tell about George, but always, he would trail off the subject and talk about the pleasant experiences of army life and the system of demilitarization.

Soon, Mary and her mother served the dinner. They intended to have Johnnie sit at the head of the table, but he wasn't informed of the intended seating, so he chose to sit opposite Mary's mother. The folks were seated to one side of the table, the girls were supposed to be on the opposite side, and Johnnie was to sit at the head of the table, with Mary and her mother at his elbows. This arrangement was made under the expectation of having George back home. When Christine returned from her dressing room, she occupied the chair adjacent to Johnnie, and the seat at the head of the table remained for Mary. When she finally came with almost a complete makeup and her hair brushed, she hesitated and was reluctant on occupying the position. It was not the way she had intended it to be. She looked to her mother for an explanation.

Johnnie glanced from Mary to her mother.

"Won't you sit over on this side with us?" Johnnie asked. He rose to help her with the chair, and everyone rearranged their position to balance the two sides. Johnnie was centered between Mary and Christine, and although he looked more often to Mary than to Christine, he carried on a general conversation as best he could.

After dinner, Johnnie offered to help with the dishes—under the expectation of doing them with Mary—but he was voted down, three to one. He spent the time talking business with Mr. Masterson.

"I'm going to start a business of my own when I get through with college," he said.

"On what capital, my boy?" Mr. Masterson implied gently.

"I don't need much to start a small business of something or other."

"Johnnie . . . If you start with a small business, you'll die with a small business . . . Those days of building a business are over. They're gone . . . In this age of sharp competitive markets, you're working pretty close to the line of breaking even, if you can break out even on all your gambles . . . Ask me, I know!" Mr. Masterson raised his voice.

"I wasn't figuring on big business. That is not within my reach at the present time . . . Besides, all I have in mind is a home, a family, and a small business with an income to meet the needs of my family."

Johnnie also raised his voice to the level of Mr. Masterson's, and it wasn't necessary to raise their voices to be heard in the kitchen, where the women listened as they slowly worked on the dishes.

"You're not a businessman! You have no ambitions!" Mr. Masterson cried out emotionally.

This seemed like a bitter remark to Johnnie, but he listened with an open mind. He was ready to learn from the mistakes of an experienced man. He was beginning to understand this man of ambitions and high ideals. Everything fitted together so nicely—his heart attached to Mary, his interests parallel to her father's, his liking for her mother and for Christine, and her brother being a buddy of his.

"I cannot speak of ambitions at this time other than those which I have just pointed out to you. Somehow I feel that by the time I complete my college training, I may change my mind about the future and return to the service for the Stars and Stripes."

"Are you serious about going back?" Mr. Masterson questioned.

"I cannot say that I am not serious. Are you serious about starting a business again?" Johnnie countered.

"If I had the capital, I'd be back there pitching again like I was before," said Mr. Masterson emphatically.

"Of course, you would. I believe you will," Mrs. Masterson said, coming from the kitchen.

She came around to his back and took hold of his chin in the palm of her hand, and she turned his face to kiss him on the cheek.

"What's that for?" Mr. Masterson asked his wife.

"Let us play some cards," she said to him with a smile that was meant to be the answer to his question.

All five played gin rummy till late at night.

Realizing that it was already past eleven, Johnnie made known his intentions of going home, and he excused himself for keeping them up so late. When everyone left the card table, Johnnie caught Mary alone at one part of the living room. "Would you drive me to the streetcar, Mary?" he asked in a low, soft tone.

"I couldn't do that. I'm engaged. See? But I'll ask Dad to drive you." She raised her hand to bring the ring before his eyes.

Christine noticed the quiet conversation between the two, and she had her suspicions as to what was going on between them. Impulsively, she strolled over to them.

"You're welcome to stay, if you like, Johnnie. You can double up with Mr. Masterson, and Mrs. Masterson can sleep with one of us. Then we can all go to school together in the morning," said Christine.

"You two go to the same school?" Johnnie asked out of surprise.

"Why, yes. The difference is that I am a professor. Good old Elmhurst!" Christine cried out joyfully.

"Wouldn't it suffice to merely say that you teach there?" Mary looked at Christine. She felt as if she was deliberately run down by Christine.

"I have a sincere appreciation for your hospitality, but at the same time, I cannot stay tonight. There are things that must be done tonight, and besides, it's liable to become a habit. If you have a telephone, I'll call a taxi." He worked his way out of the invitation.

"You need no taxi. You came in my car. You shall leave in my car. Come—I'll drive you home," said Christine, taking hold of his arm.

"I want to go too," Mary added.

"Mary, it's past your bedtime," Christine informed.

"It's past yours too." Mary laughed.

Christine gave her a mean look, but she couldn't do any more than that, so she put the car keys in Johnnie's pocket, and when they reached the car, she brushed past Mary to sit next to Johnnie.

They talked about school most of the time, and Christine continually reminded him that he was a month behind the other students already, and whenever he would need any help, she would be glad to have him call on her. Mary was on her fourth year at the college, and she pointed out the professors who were too conscientious in trying to teach everything pertaining to their subject. They painted him a gloomy picture, telling him how tough it all would be on him for being away from his studies for so long and for enrolling late. When they arrived at the city limits, Johnnie noticed a taxi parked at the end of the car line. He stopped the car alongside the taxi.

"This is as far as we go," he said.

"But we don't mind taking you all the way home," Christine protested.

Mary looked on with disappointment. She was hoping to see Johnnie's home. She would have a much better understanding of him. She liked everything she knew about him, but her interest did not stop there. Her curiosity had no end.

"That would take you almost an hour and a half to get back to your house. It's past midnight already." He looked at his wristwatch. "Good night," he said. "See you on the campus in the morning."

"Good night!" Christine cried out after him.

Mary was behind Christine and felt left out of the conversation. "Good night," she said slightly above a whisper. She felt sorry for something or other, but she did not know what.

Johnnie dreaded the thought of going home. He could not go home yet. He was hurt once before, and he was afraid he might go to pieces if old memories took hold of him. He rode to the campus in the cab, and after a few stops, he found a rooming house where he could stay. If it were not for his uniform, he would get a good cussing from every housekeeper for calling at this early hour of the morning.

He thought he needed something to shake him out of his dreaminess for Mary. He took a hot shower and shampooed his hair with some shampoo that belonged to his snoring roommate. Of course, he would tell his roommate about it in the morning and promise to make up for it anytime his roommate would need something. Quietly, he crept into bed, and after a yawn, his body relaxed and slowly drifted into slumberland.

When he awoke in the morning, it was after nine o'clock. He intended to get up with the other students, but he had not heard the slightest sound to break his sleep, and they were all gone. He snapped out of bed and looked at the hat tree where he had left his uniform when he undressed to take the shower before going to bed. The hat tree was there, but his uniform was not—even his shoes and socks were gone. He looked about in deep thought.

Surely, these could not be jokers living here, or is this the beginning of a nightmare, he thought. Without any more concern over it, he went to the clothes closet and opened the door. To his amazement, there it was, and it appeared as though it had just come back from the cleaners—everything so neatly put away. There were a number of other clothes put away in the same fashion. He looked down, and there were his shoes—polished better than he would think of doing it himself. He looked through his pockets and didn't find a penny missing. He hollered down the stairs for the housekeeper.

Soon, a gray-haired gentleman, bent with age, came shuffling up the stairs. He was thin and pale from age. His wife passed away, and his daughters married off, so he invested whatever he had in the rooming house. He insisted on being self-supporting, and he had a great desire for a son, but unfortunately for him, destiny endowed him only with daughters. His daughters made him very happy, but there was still something missing in his life. He spent his time with the boys—"my boys," he called them—and did everything he could to make them feel comfortable.

"In my hurry to get to bed, I left my things on the hat tree. When I got up, I found my suit brushed and put away in the clothes closet and my shoes shined. This couldn't be a service of the house, could it?" Johnnie inquired with a touch of humor.

"That's not a service of the house. That's the kind of roommate you have. He's sensitive as a child and bashful. Why, he'd run if a girl would come after him. He's always studying, always studying."

"Well . . . always studying? That would mean good grades."

"Oh, he's not doing so well with the books. That's why he's always studying," the old gentleman explained.

"I see. In that case, I may be able to help him along. At first, I thought I would be getting the help."

Johnnie realized he was still undressed. He hurried to the washroom while the old gentleman began making up his bed.

"How is this college?" Johnnie asked.

"Fine. How was the army?"

"Fine. How is the football team?"

So the conversation went on between one trying to wash and shave in a hurry and the other working on the bed, while their voices traveled back and forth from one room to the other. It wasn't long before Johnnie was dressed and on his way to the registrar of the college. He intended to get up early and buy a suit of clothes that he could change into, but it was late, and he had many things to do this first day at school.

"I doubt if you should start this late in the semester," the registrar said, eyeing Johnnie's uniform, "but under the circumstances, you may be permitted to take one-half the number of hours in the regular course. This will enable you to do the work you will have at present and also the work you have lost by the late enrollment. The following semester, you will be a regular student."

"But in that case, I may not qualify for football this semester, and it will be a whole year before I get to play football," Johnnie protested.

He had to play football, not merely because he wanted to but because of the effect it would have on Mary. He couldn't wait a whole year after all that time he had spent in the service figuring out new plays and studying the different games of the great teams.

"You played football in high school?" the registrar asked, with his interest rising.

"Yes, sir, I did."

"Well!" the registrar let out enthusiastically. He was bubbling with excitement. "You go on over to see the head of the physical education department. When you get back, I will have your adviser here, and we will work out a program for you."

"Thank you," Johnnie replied, and he walked away with a sense of lightness in his head.

As he walked across the campus, he was sure to use the walks as a city-bred student would. The worn paths across the lawn called to him for a shorter route to his destination, but he was more interested in the walk that led him by some buildings he wished to see. He studied the pictorial map of the campus while he gazed at every building he went by. At every building, he wondered if Mary was in one of the classes. He passed a student here and there going to or from the library. One student was reciting, aloud, his assignment for the speech class as he sat on a bench, under a tree, holding his script in his hands, staring blankly into space. Johnnie began to wonder how it would be to start studying again after being away for almost five years. Whatever it would be like, he knew that the school days would be the happiest days of his life.

The head of the physical education department recognized Johnnie, and it wasn't long before he wrote out the schedule for football practice that Johnnie would have with the team. Soon, Johnnie was on his way back to the registrar's office with his football schedule. At the office, they worked out a full program that would not conflict with his football schedule. They said he need not go to any classes that day since it was Friday noon but to start with his first class Monday.

Johnnie took football because it had been on his mind since the day he had left school for the service. Of course, Mary would see him play. He took music to have a subject in common with Mary. He took dramatics for self-expression and so that Mary could see him upon the stage. He majored in commerce partly because those were his intentions and partly because Mary's father was a businessman. His mind was occupied with Mary, and she came first in all his thoughts.

With his registration completed, his first thought was to locate Christine. Looking through the college catalogue, he noticed that Christine had an office, and in the office she was when he got there. She was flattered to have Johnnie see her at the desk, with all the surrounding shelves full of books. He remarked about the books, to her delight. They went over his program, and she informed him of the courses with which she could help him. All this time, Johnnie was thinking of asking about Mary, but he couldn't get around to the question without making his intentions of the visit too obvious. After a while, classes were dismissed, and Christine had a class for the next hour.

"You will find Mary in the library at this time." She smiled as if she knew the purpose of his visit, and they parted.

"Thanks. I'll be seeing you," Johnnie whispered before he turned to leave.

Christine was teaching third- and fourth-year rhetoric and literature, so that put him out of her classes. Anyhow, she was planning to help him with some of his courses that were in the field she was teaching.

When he arrived at the library, he realized Mary could be most anywhere depending on what she had to study. He wandered about on the main floor and then on the second floor, where he finally found her studying at a table with a group of students, most of whom were girls. When he sat next to Mary, everyone looked on with surprise. They knew Mary never spoke to any boy and especially now that she was engaged to the orchestra conductor. They wondered if he was her new heart attack. His uniform attracted much attention. Mary flushed with pride. Without saying a word to him, she gathered her materials, leading the way out of the library. He remembered the bench under the tree where the speech student recited, and they strolled over to it, with Mary asking all the questions about him and his program.

They went for his books first to one bookstore and then to another, and they stopped at the soda fountain before returning to the library. They met again after Mary's afternoon class. Then Mary went to the music hall to practice the piano and more so to see Percival, her fiancé, the orchestra conductor who also held classes in music.

Johnnie immediately went to see Christine.

"Johnnie," she said, "would you do me a favor?"

"I would if I could," he replied.

"Believe me, you could if you would." Christine looked deeply into his eyes.

"All right, I will. What is it?" he submitted.

"Tonight Mary must go downtown for her private piano lessons. She's taking lessons on the side so Percival would think all the benefit came from his instructions. Do you follow me?" she asked, looking into his eyes.

"So far," Johnnie replied.

"Well," she went on, "here are the keys to my car. I'll be working late on this semester's play with the dramatics department. The car is yours for the weekend—only let it be known to Mary that you needed the car to get around, so you borrowed it from me."

"But I have a car at home."

"Then keep it at home. It will do you more good. Here," she said, handing him the keys to her car and telling him where he'd find it.

Reluctantly, he took the keys. He had some suspicions that she was trying to get Mary out of the picture. He left the office after expressing his gratitude. How would his car do him more good by keeping it at home? Still, he had the keys to Christine's car. For a while, it seemed like a riddle to him. Then it dawned on him. Mary had to go home; Christine had to stay. He had the keys to the car that was Mary's means of getting home. *That's it,* he thought. Christine was actually setting Mary right into his lap. How easy it all turned out when he put the pieces together! When would Mary be going home? *That's simple. She would be going home after she had dinner with Percival.* Then it came to him in a flash that Christine would call on him when Mary would be ready to go home.

III

Tomorrow

Johnnie had his dinner and loafed about the rooming house, getting acquainted with all the nine other boys and men of the house. He noticed that his roommate was timid and weak and everybody picked on him with practical jokes and remarks or puns. There was not much that Johnnie could do about discouraging the others from picking on his roommate, but there was a lot of encouragement he could give his roommate to stand up under it all and to fight back, at least some of the time.

A short time later—it was after six o'clock—the telephone rang, and Johnnie ran to be first to answer. It was Christine, and she was asking if he could drive Mary home because she was working late and Mary had to go home.

"I'm coming right over for her!" he replied with excitement.

Returning the receiver to the phone, he walked on air cushions to the car. His head was crowding with ideas as to how he could spend the evening with Mary. He was not acquainted with the new places about town, but he remembered some of the old places, and they might still be there.

"Will you please drive Mary home?" Christine asked. When he got to them, Mary and Percival were standing beside her.

"How will you get home?" Johnnie asked out of sheer innocence.

"Oh, I can take a cab." Christine brushed him off.

"I hope to be back before you leave," Johnnie said.

He walked away with Mary, leaving Christine with Percival to rehearse the cast of the semester's play. Since the following day was Saturday, they could rehearse and improve till late into the night—without any sad thoughts of getting up early in the morning.

Mary was happy to be riding alone with Johnnie instead of having Christine cut in on her conversation all the time. She was overjoyed with the fact so much that she told him what road to take. Then they came to a dirt road out in the country.

"Turn to the right over here for about half a mile," Mary directed.

"What's out there?"

"You'll see." Mary smiled.

He turned and followed the dirt road per Mary's direction. At first, he thought Mary had some friends or relatives out in this direction—what else could there be?

"Right over here." Mary pointed out an old farmhouse. He turned off the road past the shabby fence. The gate was open, and it lay flat on the ground—about fifteen feet from its hinges. The yard was well overgrown with weeds. The house was not painted. By the sight of its wood, one would think it never was painted. The shutters were mostly torn off, with a few still hanging on. The porch fence was lying on the ground, but the stairs were still in place.

"I just wanted to see this place," she said.

"Well, let's go inside and look it over."

He led the way to the house. The door of the building was not locked. He walked into the living room, and Mary followed close behind. After one look at the heavy dust covering everything in the room, he looked to Mary.

"This place is abandoned," she said in explanation. "But I heard that some of the boys and girls from the college come here. See? There are footprints." She pointed them out on the floor.

They followed the footprints about the floor, and they discovered the first floor had only two large rooms—the kitchen and the living room. Of course, there was the washroom, the pantry, and a clothes closet too, but these, they did not consider rooms. They followed the footprints up a stairway leading to the second floor, which was more like an attic than anything to live in. Three feet above the floor, the roof began to slope upward to a point for the entire length of the house. The second floor looked as crude as a hayloft, with no finishing of plaster or hardwood flooring. There was an old wooden bed by each of the two windows at the front. Close nearby stood a dresser, with the mirror missing.

Mary admired the patchwork on the bedspread, and Johnnie took hold of it and flipped it to the other half of the bed. Then he scooped Mary off her feet with his arms and gently set her down on her back upon the bed. She looked at him in fright as he sat down on the bed beside her. Slowly, he bent down and placed a gentle kiss upon her quivering lips.

"I have to go now," she said softly, bound in fear.

Her hands were shaking, and she seemed to be about to cry or scream, if necessary. She thought she gave him the impression that she had brought him here for sinful association.

"Whatever you say, Mary," he said, looking down into her eyes as she covered her lips with the back of her hand to keep him from kissing her again. He helped her up to her feet and replaced the bedspread. Slowly and silently, they retraced their steps to the car. The sun was already beginning to set on the horizon, and its orange and golden colors were cast upon the clouds above as darkness was creeping along from the opposite direction.

"I'm sorry," he said as they settled in the car.

Mary seemed to have lost her speech. She merely shied away to one side, turning her face away from him. She said nothing; her face was solemn, and her eyes were downcast.

Johnnie sped away from the abandoned house. His mind seemed to be somewhat dulled, and he couldn't find anything to say. Then he returned to the paved road.

"Which way? This way?" He pointed to the right.

Mary looked at him and nodded in silence.

He drove down the road for what seemed like a long time. Each one said not a word and looked directly forward. Finally, he stopped by a Snack-Shack, and he turned to her, taking hold of her hand.

"Would you care for a bite?" he asked.

Mary turned her eyes from his holding hand to his eyes and silently turned her head from side to side with a slow motion meaning no.

"Mary." He gripped her hand tight with one hand while he leaned on the steering wheel with the elbow of the other arm and looked for her to meet his eyes before he went on. "I want you to know that my intentions at the abandoned farmhouse were entirely honorable. I couldn't stand to have you think otherwise. I was going to ask you to marry me. Will you marry me?"

He looked into her eyes, and she looked as though she were in a trance. He wrapped one arm around her neck and his other arm around her waistline and pressed his lips upon hers. Her eyes opened wide, and then they closed and remained closed. She remained like this even after he withdrew his lips.

"I have to go now," she reminded him, with her eyes still closed, and she opened them only after Johnnie withdrew his hands and started the car.

"Yes, I think we better go," he said with a downhearted tone.

"That was the house of Tomorrow," Mary said.

Suddenly, when Johnnie started the car and she opened her eyes, she took on a new life. She had lost her silence. She was happy and gay with a sort of effervescent personality. She smiled to him, made faces and silly imitations.

"The house of tomorrow? Ha ha! What a house of tomorrow!" He joined her smile with a laugh.

"You won't be laughing long," she warned. "Tomorrow is the name of the man who owned it."

"Oh." His laughter sank into seriousness.

"Well," she started out, "Tomorrow inherited the farm from his uncle who lived on the farm like a hermit. When Tomorrow was notified of the inheritance, he married the prettiest girl in the countryside and moved into the house. Every time she asked him to do something, he'd say, 'I'll do it first thing in the morning.' Or he'd say, 'Tomorrow I will get it done.' But he never did anything about it.

"His wife tried to do everything. They were married in the fall, and she managed to keep house because the uncle had a winter's supply of food stored away in the cellar. During the winter, the livestock died away one at a time from lack of care and lack of food. When planting time came, there were no horses to pull the farm machinery. Tomorrow was going to get a tractor tomorrow, but when that day finally came, they told him he needed money for a down payment, so he was going to get a job in town tomorrow. And when that day finally came that he went to town for work, they told him they needed skilled help, not laborers. So he sat in his rocking chair, smoking his corncob pipe, trying to think of something else he could do tomorrow to get the money to buy the tractor, to plow the field, to have some food for next winter.

"The food was gone, and his wife was expecting a child. In spite of the fact that she carried a child, she still tried to do the work, and she came down with a miscarriage. It was late into the night. He carried her to bed, and she begged him to bring a doctor quickly, but he said to her, 'I'll get you a doctor tomorrow—first thing in the morning.' And he meant it too. He left her to go down to his rocking chair, to smoke his corncob pipe, and to figure how he would get the money to pay the doctor tomorrow. She cried after him in pain, but that didn't help to bring a doctor to her.

"Tomorrow smoked and rocked in the chair throughout the night, and when he went to see her in the morning, she was dead. He buried her in the garden and went back to his rocking chair and his corncob pipe. He rocked in the chair, eating his heart out and smoking his pipe. He never left the chair or his pipe very long. When he was too tired to stay awake, he slept in his rocking chair. He had little to eat and never any good sleep. He got thin and haggardly looking.

"One day, when a neighbor saw him pass down the road, she became frightened over his appearance, and she called on her husband and her neighbors to help him with the planting, which was already late. They gathered at Tomorrow's farmhouse, and they waited and waited for Tomorrow to come home, but he never came—and nobody knows if he ever will." Mary finished with a sigh.

"So the moral to the story is don't put off for tomorrow what you could do today." Johnnie laughed.

"But that is nothing to laugh about." Mary said to him in a serious tone, without a smile on her lips. "That is a true story as I heard it, and just think of what the poor girl went through."

"I'm sorry. I haven't looked at it from that angle," Johnnie said, changing to a somber seriousness.

On arriving home, Mary said, "I'll be ready in a few minutes," as she went on to her dressing room.

Johnnie sat in the living room with Mr. Masterson. Mr. Masterson began his conversation with the subject of big business and what he would do once he could get hold of some money somewhere. He talked big, and he had the facts to back all his statements. He claimed he didn't need more than a hundred thousand dollars. He could even get started on a little less than that. Johnnie listened with interest, and he received many good impressions from Mr. Masterson. He could listen to the big talk with an open mind. He was learning from the explanations by this gentleman who had all those years of experience in the back of him.

Mary didn't take long to change and put some makeup on her face. She seldom put any makeup on when going to school or in her associations with Percival. He would be terribly upset if she had not retained her natural beauty. This made her seem under the pressure and control of Percival.

As she was leaving with Johnnie, Mr. Masterson and his wife grinned their approval of Johnnie. They wondered if this was the introduction of a change in their prospective son-in-law. This, they emphasized by looking to each other and hurrying to the window. They watched gleefully while Johnnie opened the door for Mary and then close it after her, to walk around to the driver side and drive away. They had a feeling that Mary's makeup had meaning to it, a meaning that they thought they understood.

Mary was quite talkative all the way to the studio.

Johnnie stayed in the waiting room, while Mary had her lesson by one of the greatest teachers in Kansas City. When she returned, she expressed relief of having it over with.

"Let's go to the concert at the Municipal Auditorium," Johnnie suggested, looking at the time on his wristwatch.

"Okay," Mary broke out with a grin of agreement.

"We're late, but at least we'll be there for a good part of it." He grinned back at her.

While they sat through the concert, Johnnie held her hand. Every time he squeezed her hand, she looked at him with a shy smile, while he seemed to have a smile on his lips all the time. Then the concert came to an end, and they stopped in the foyer on their way out.

"Let's go to a movie," Johnnie suggested.

"Okay," Mary brightly agreed.

They went to an all-night theater, and of course, Johnnie held her hand all the while. They stayed for the second show. As the second show was about to end, he shifted her hand to his outside hand, and he put his inside arm around her neck, and he kissed her.

She swallowed her gum and said, "I have to go now."

"Yes, we'll go home now," he said. "But first, we'll have to stop somewheres for a snack."

He stopped at a hamburger stand, and they had some wheat cakes. Mary didn't care for anything more than a glass of milk. When they returned to the car, Johnnie took hold of her cheeks between the palms of his hands, and he kissed her. Then he said, "I have to go now," and he kissed her again.

When they stopped in front of Mary's home, he coiled his arm around her shoulders, and with his other hand, he turned her cheek so that her lips could meet his with a prolonged kiss. Mary had her hands on her lap, and she clutched at her purse.

"I have to go now," she said as soon as she could, and she brushed his arms away to leave the car.

He followed her to the door, where he took hold of her head between the palms of his hands. "Good night, Mary," he said with a kiss, and he waited till he could see her no more.

"Good night," she said as she looked out through the partly closed door.

The light of the early morning sun began to light up the sky. Johnnie settled behind the steering wheel, stepped on the accelerator, and sped back to the rooming house. He shed his uniform in a hurry and hopped into bed for a few hours of sleep, but as fast as he had hopped in, he hopped out again. It was the most uncomfortable bed he ever was in. It was like lying down on a roll of barbed wire unexpectedly. He raised the bed sheet, and under it was a mess of metal clothes hangers. He laughed at himself and at the joke someone pulled over on him. After removing the hangers, he reclined and pulled the blanket over him.

He tossed about in bed and could not fall asleep. He thought it was the wheat cakes and coffee that were keeping him awake, but his thoughts were rambling around about Mary. Her image kept appearing before him, and it kept softly repeating, "I have to go now." Then he was thinking about the clothes he was going to buy. None of his old clothes would fit him anymore. He wondered what kind of clothes would impress Mary the most.

As he kept on thinking from one thing to another, he heard footsteps softly shuffling up the stairs. He listened to the footsteps trail off to one of the rooms and back down the stairs again. Then one of the boys came by, rubbing his eyes on his way to the washroom and yawning without end. He was the one who started work at six-thirty in the morning. He worked part of his way through college at the cafeteria. Two others worked at the cleaner's and one at the gas station. So they lined up for the washroom with one wash basin in it. In five minutes or less, each one was out of the washroom and on his way to wake the next in line. Johnnie watched and took the end of the line. By seven o'clock, all the working students were gone, and Johnnie was on his way to breakfast with the rest of them. They painted him dark pictures about some professors and bright ones about others.

After breakfast, he drove downtown and bought several suits of clothes and plenty of shirts, socks, ties, and shoes. He put everything away, changed into civilian clothes, and was ready to see Mary that Saturday evening; all he had to do was wait till the time came.

Upon arriving at Mary's home, he received a very warm welcome from Mr. and Mrs. Masterson, whereas Mary was in her dressing room. Johnnie impatiently kept looking for her to appear while he tried to carry on a conversation with Christine and the folks.

Christine liked him in uniform, but she was fascinated to a much higher degree by his smooth appearance in civilian clothes, his shy disposition, and his perpetual smile. She looked at him from the corner of her eyes. She squinted at him, and every time his smile would appear, she seemed to be getting closer to him than she was before.

Mary made no appearance until Percival came, and he seemed to be upset when he saw Johnnie present.

"Oh, Johnnie came to see Christine," she blankly said to Percival.

Johnnie looked at her with his smile disappearing. So this was her fiancé—the college orchestra conductor. He had to outshine this rival—but with what? All he had was his army pay. What was she trying to point out to him when she told him the story about the house of Tomorrow? He began to imagine some connection between himself and his position and the story she had told him. Surely, there couldn't be any similarity between himself and Mr. Tomorrow. He was studying and preparing for the future. His mind was becoming confused with a lack of understanding.

Mary looked in Johnnie's direction, and she smiled to him, when Percival could not see, as she was about to play the piano. Percival sat in an armchair about three feet at the back of Mary, while Mary struggled with the difficult exercises. She wasn't able to concentrate on the piano and looked toward Johnnie ever so often.

Johnnie caught a stare coming from Percival. It gave him the chills. It actually accused him of something without saying what it was. He turned away from the stare to face Christine.

"Would you care to see a stage play?" he asked her.

"How do you think of those things?" Christine asked. "I'll be ready in a minute," she said, turning away for a look into the mirror.

When Johnnie and Christine were getting ready to leave, Mr. and Mrs. Masterson showed signs of disappointment, while Mary stopped playing and looked on as they left.

Percival immediately called her attention back to the piano, and he pointed out a few errors.

As she played on, her number of errors increased; the music seemed so boring, and the keys seemed so hard to handle. She wished Percival hadn't come; then Johnnie might have asked her instead of Christine. Mr. and Mrs. Masterson retired from the living room, and the evening seemed so empty to Mary. There was Percival sitting in the armchair to the back of her, keeping time with his arm and extended index finger. At every mistake, he would call her attention to it and give some instructions—always giving instructions, always. He always did before, but today it was so different. It bored her from within, and it irritated her mind till she felt a dull frontal headache. Her thoughts continually wandered off. She was thinking of how she had spent last night with Johnnie, and she was wondering how Christine would spend the night with him, when they would be back. What troubled her most of all was would Johnnie kiss Christine like he had kissed her? The instructions came so frequently that she finally left the piano and sat down at one end of the sofa.

Percival put his armchair away and sat down at the opposite end of the sofa.

"I'm much too tired to play the piano today," she said.

"I knew that makeup would affect your music. You look like a girl from the burlesque show." He displayed his upper teeth and rolled his eyes in every direction. He pulled on his tie and his collar, and his arms were in continuous motion.

Mary could not take this as a compliment. She could only imagine a burlesque girl as a loose woman who advertised her profession openly with indecent exposure. Johnnie told her she looked pretty, and he kissed her when he said that. Johnnie kept buzzing in her mind, bringing back memories of everything he did from the time she had met him. There was a silence while her mind roamed around among her memories of yesterday. Then she turned to him.

"Percival," she said with wide-open eyes, "do you go to the burlesque show?"

"When I was a student in college, I went to the burlesque show . . . four times in one week." Saying this seemed to derange his physical emotions, and he pounded the sofa with the palms of his hands.

"Percival!" Mary looked aghast. "You didn't."

"Uh-huh." He opened his mouth. "Once, we went to a nightclub, and we stayed all night, and we drank a whole glass of beer."

His emotions carried him away as he pounded on the sofa and raised his legs off the floor, twisting one around the other and back again.

"Percival, have you seen any good movies lately?"

"Oh no, I wouldn't care to."

"Percival, have you seen any good plays lately?"

"Oh no, I wouldn't care to."

"Percival, have you been in the park lately?"

"Oh no, I wouldn't care to."

"Is there anything you would care to?"

"I would rather sit at home with you."

Mary was getting restless. She lost all hope of going out for the evening. She envied Christine for going out with Johnnie, and she hated Johnnie for taking Christine out for the evening. Percival never took her any place. Everything to him was music.

"I drove Christine home yesterday," he said.

"Did you take her anywhere?" she asked with improper curiosity.

"Oh yes, I took her home," he said.

"I mean did you stop anywhere along the way?"

"Oh no. She asked me to take her home, so I took her home. She didn't have any way to get home. She said Johnnie was using her car."

"Did she say anything about me?"

"Not last night, but she did this morning," Percival informed her.

"What is it?"

"She told me about you and Johnnie, and if you see him again, I'll have my engagement ring back," warned Percival.

"What about you and Christine?"

"She asked me to stop several times along the road, but I didn't want to."

"Percival, I'm so glad you didn't," said Mary, expressing relief.

"I drove her home as fast as I could. Even in the dark. I went twenty miles per hour all the way home," boasted Percival.

"I don't know what to say for myself, Percival," she said.

"Then don't say it," he replied.

"I'll try not to." Mary was serious.

"I love you," he broke out, displaying his upper teeth, rolling and blinking his eyes without control.

"I love you too, Percival," she replied as an echo, "and we must never let anything come between us."

"Put your hand over there." He nodded to the empty space between them.

Mary placed her hand to her side.

He looked and said, "A little closer."

She placed her hand at the center of the space between them, and he put his hand on top of hers. He giggled and trembled with twitching muscles.

"Ahem," she cleared her throat before she spoke. "Once, I went to a movie with a boy."

"You did?"

"And we stayed for two shows."

"You did?"

"And he held my hand all the while . . . and he squeezed it . . . now and then." She looked at him shyly.

"He did?" Percival questioned, getting furious.

"And he kissed me in the theater," she said.

"He did?" Percival snatched his hand away from hers.

"And he kissed me good night," she said.

"You've been unfaithful!" he snapped out, looking down upon her.

"Oh no, Percival . . . But the way he kissed me," she said.

"How?"

"He just took hold of me, and he kissed me," she said.

"He didn't ask you?"

"Of course not," she said.

"I'm so glad he didn't ask you. Then you could have said no." Percival felt somewhat relieved.

"But the way he kissed me good night." Mary looked at him out of the corner of her eye.

"How?" Percival was infuriated with curiosity.

"He just grabbed me and kissed me," she said, glancing at him and alternately looking down at her fidgeting hands in her lap.

"How?"

"Well," Mary said, rising to her feet, "I was standing by the door like this."

She stood before him, looking down into his eyes, and he got so uncomfortable that he stood up to one side of her.

"And he grabbed me, and he kissed me like this," she said, actually taking hold of his head between the palms of her hands and kissing him hard.

When she drew her hands and lips away and looked at him, his eyes were bulging, his mouth was gaping open, and his hands were pulling his tie. He broke his tie off, tore it to shreds, and used it to wipe the perspiration from his forehead. His face got pale, and he sank down to the sofa in a fainting spell.

"Oh, Percival!" she cried out and ran for the smelling salts.

Percival took a few whiffs of the smelling salts, and he came back to his senses. He moaned a few times and sat up straight to look at her.

"And what did you do?" he asked.

"I almost did what you just did," she said.

"You didn't see him anymore—did you?"

"I saw him, yes, but I didn't let him get close to me anymore," she said.

"I'm so glad. What a tiresome day this was!" he said, rising and going for his hat.

Mary followed him to the hat rack and then to the door. She looked at him with anticipation of a good-night kiss, but he put his hat on and turned to the door.

"Good night, Mary. And don't neglect to spend more time on your piano more often," he said, and he walked out, closing the door quietly behind him. He didn't even hold her hand in saying good night.

Nervously, she broke down and cried. Then she ran to the sofa and cried some more into her elbow. Was this her fiancé, her lover—or was this her piano teacher? She could certainly get more music out of the piano than she ever could out of him. She wanted him, yes, but why couldn't he be at least a little bit like Johnnie? Here, it was nine o'clock on a Saturday night, and she was all alone. She was the loneliest girl she could imagine. She promptly went to bed, where she buried her face into the pillow, and she cried some more when she couldn't fall asleep.

IV

𝒫laying 𝒷ackgammon

𝒥ohnnie came home with Christine immediately after the play ended.

"Looks like Mary's gone," he said to Christine.

"Probably went to bed," Christine said. "Her fiancé doesn't believe in 'late to bed and early to rise.'"

"We should have stopped somewheres along the way for a bite to eat. I'm thirsty," he said, trying to moisten his lips with his dry tongue.

"Would you care for something to drink?" she asked, eyeing his face.

"What's your best offer?" He smiled.

"A scotch and soda?" she said in a questioning tone.

"Coming from a teacher, I'd say yes—anytime."

"Mr. Masterson keeps his supplies in my room for good safekeeping," she mentioned in a slight sense of self-defense as she left for the drinks.

First, she went to her dressing room and came out with a bottle of scotch in one hand and a bottle of cream soda in the other. Then she went into the kitchen, where she made up the drinks, with an ice cube floating in each one. Then she carried the drinks to the living room, one in each hand. Johnnie had the card table set with chairs opposite each other.

"I'll play you some gin rummy," he said as she handed him a glass.

"I'll play you some backgammon," she replied, walking off for the game.

Mary could not sleep. She tossed about, yawned, kept her eyelids closed, and prayed to God to bring her sleep, but she remained wide awake. When the light was turned on in the living room, she knew that Johnnie and Christine had returned, and she became more restless than before.

The longer the light in the living room stayed on, the more curious she became. It must have been past one o'clock. *What could they be doing all this time? Are they holding hands? Is he kissing her?* The more she thought about it, the more she tossed around. Finally, she slowly set her feet on the floor and straightened up into a sitting position. As though she had been put into a trance by her curiosity, she walked to the door and slowly worked her way down the hallway. As she came close to the living room, she crouched against the wall and peeked around the corner. There was Johnnie playing backgammon with Christine and sipping on his drink. She became nervous, and she began to feel uneasy on the inside. She slipped away and into the Mastersons' bedroom.

"Johnnie is back," she said, waking her father gently out of his sleep as she knelt beside the bed.

"What of it? Christine will keep him company," he groaned in his sleepy state of mind.

"They're playing backgammon."

"What of it?" he mumbled.

"And they're drinking something," she whispered to him just in case her mother was awake and listening.

"Scotch!" he let out, springing out of bed.

He stepped into his sandals, wrapped his bathrobe around himself, tying it at his side, and was gingerly strolling down the short hallway to the living room. In the meantime, Mary retired to her room. She thought the rest would take care of itself.

"Well, well, well!" Mr. Masterson exclaimed, clasping and rubbing his hands together. "I had a dream that I was thirsty, and the thirst drew me out of my sleep. I happened to see the light. So here I am."

"There's another light in the kitchen," Christine replied.

"Don't let me hold back your game. I won't have any trouble finding the kitchen."

Christine smiled to Johnnie, and he smiled back to her with understanding.

Mr. Masterson was overjoyed when he got to the kitchen. He mixed three drinks and took them into the living room on a tray. His drink was half-and-half with no ice in it; the ice took up too much space, and if it wasn't strong enough, then he would drink it like that much lemonade instead of sipping it. He sat there and drank with them while Johnnie and Christine played backgammon. He was just as excited as they were, and he rolled the dice for Johnnie every now and then. When the glasses ran dry, he would take the tray to the kitchen and refill them. When the bottle ran dry, it was past two o'clock in the morning.

"Time to go back to bed," he said, getting up.

Johnnie rose from the table also.

"Because I'm going to bed doesn't mean you have to go to bed," Mr. Masterson explained, patting Johnnie on the shoulder while his vision was beginning to sway like the rolling motion of a ship at sea.

"It's about time I should be going," replied Johnnie.

He walked slowly to the door, with Christine trailing close by. At the door, he kissed her as Mr. Masterson looked on.

"Good night, Christine," he said. "Good night, Dad. It was a wonderful evening."

"Good night," Christine replied softly with sleepy eyes.

"Good night," Mr. Masterson replied, steadying himself on his feet as he tried to wave good night.

The next morning, Sunday, Mary approached her father when he was alone.

"Did he hold her hand?" she asked, referring to Johnnie and Christine of the night before.

"Of course, he held her hand. Why, every time he'd reach for the dice, he'd take hold of her hand instead."

40

"Did he kiss her good night?" She looked on with fearful suspense.

"Of course. How else would he say good night?"

"How?" she asked inquisitively.

He looked at her and sensed a crying spell coming to her.

"Like a chicken would peck on a corncob," he said.

She felt greatly relieved and smiled, saying a sweet "Thank you, Father" before leaving.

Her father watched her walk away to study for her Sunday school teaching. She felt greatly relieved of the pressure from last night by knowing that Johnnie had kissed Christine good night "like a chicken would peck on a corncob."

While she was returning from Sunday school, she was caught by surprise on finding Johnnie waiting for her outside the church building. She refused to budge from the place when Johnnie offered to drive her home.

"Johnnie," she pleaded, "you mustn't come to the house anymore. You know I'm engaged to marry Percival."

"I didn't think that Percival would mind since you're wearing his ring."

"He said he'd take it back if he would discover that I was with you again." She explained her predicament and the cause for her request.

"Oh, he did? Instead on battling it out with me, he picks on you. How do you like that?"

"Please don't come . . . Please . . . If you do, I'll be in more trouble than ever," she begged sincerely.

"What's this? Trouble?" he inquired.

"I can't eat, and I can't sleep, and I'm always worrying about Percival. If I don't marry him and get to be a great concert pianist, I'll die." She informed him of her profound love for Percival.

"Well"—Johnnie looked at her seriously—"I wouldn't want Percival to take his ring back. That would be a mean thing to do . . . And I don't want to see you in trouble, Mary."

"I was hoping you would understand," she said, looking at him.

"Mary, drive me to the bus?" he asked.

"Why?"

"Then you can drive Christine's car back home so she would have it for school tomorrow."

"Okay," Mary conceded.

Mary drove him to the streetcar line, and this time, there was no taxi. When Mary stopped at the curb by the streetcar, Johnnie reached over with his arm, and he kissed her on the lips very passionately. She sat there, looking after him until the streetcar moved, and she saw him waving goodbye out of the rear window, so she waved too. The streetcar left, minutes went by, and she sat there behind the steering wheel, feeling sorry for herself as she looked at the engagement ring. Her thoughts wandered off into dreams, and before she knew it, the motor had been running for more than a half hour already. She shook the dreams out of her head and made a U-turn to start back home.

When Mary returned home, she found Christine alone. Mary still had that dreamy look when Christine spoke to her.

"See Percival?" Christine asked with anticipation.

"No, I drove Johnnie to the streetcar," replied Mary.

"One look at you, and I should have known it was Johnnie."

"Why? What's the matter?" Mary asked in an air of innocence.

"He probably came to see me, and you turned him away. That's what it was. I can see it all now. That's why he returned the car to you instead of to me."

"It isn't true. He met me by the church." Mary defended herself against the frontal accusation.

"It's my car, isn't it? He borrowed it from me. Why didn't he return it to me?" argued Christine with a tint of jealousy and bitterness as she never displayed before.

"I don't know!" Mary shouted back.

"First of all, you took Percival away from me, and now you think you'll take Johnnie away from me. That's the gratitude I get from you for taking you into my home and providing for you."

"You never went with Percival. That much, I'm sure."

"I'm old enough to be your mother, and Percival is old enough to be your father. Percival attended the same college as I have. We've been working together here for years before you ever came to college. I bought this home so we could spend some time together. Then you came along and wrapped him up all for yourself!" Christine talked with a hoarse voice rising with indignation.

"But I didn't know!" Mary complained in tears.

"Then leave Johnnie to me!"

"But Johnnie loves me! He said so himself!" recoiled Mary.

"Then give back Percival to me!"

"But Percival is my fiancé!" insisted Mary.

"Listen, child! You can't marry both of them!"

"You can't have Johnnie because I love him . . . and you can't have Percival because I want to marry him." Mary drawled through her bawling while heavy tears blurred and rolled down her eyes. She promptly ran to her bed, where she flopped and buried her face in the pillow.

Christine could not understand why Mary could not leave either Johnnie or Percival, why she was tied to two different men who were years apart. She couldn't understand why Percival had turned away from her and taken up with Mary. He was at least seventeen years her senior. Patiently and silently, she bore her grievances until now, and she felt that she had done something wrong by having this quarrel with Mary, but she couldn't hold out any longer. Mary should have been told at the very beginning. If Mr. and Mrs. Masterson should hear about it, then there would be more trouble. She wondered about George, who was still in the army and who had a serious number of disappointments awaiting him upon his arrival home.

V

A Delicate Sunshine Yellow

Johnnie retired to his room. Saturday and Sunday, most of the students were gone—they left Friday, after the last class, to go home for the weekend. He sat on the edge of his bed. He was tired mentally and physically. He hadn't slept much on the train or since the trip home. He became drowsy as he sat there trying to figure out Mary. He lay back across the bed with his feet resting on the floor, and his thoughts about Mary withered away into peaceful slumber.

His daydreams took possession of his mind. His mind projected himself into his daydreams. He courted Mary to her satisfaction, and finally, when the wedding bells were ringing, he stood before the church and couldn't move his feet. Mary was waiting at the altar, but he was in front of the church, struggling in vain efforts to move his feet, which seemed to be cemented to the pavement. He looked up from his feet, and there, he saw Percival laughing, laughing with all the vigor of his lungs. Percival was going into the church to marry

Johnnie's girl. As Percival ascended the stairs and clasped the handle of the door, he turned to Johnnie and looked down upon him.

"I will get married today, and you will get married tomorrow," he said to Johnnie in a scornful manner, pointing an accusing finger down at him. "Goodbye, Mr. Tomorrow!" Percival shouted as he disappeared behind the doors of the church.

Johnnie struggled, and as he struggled, he was startled out of his sleep. Sweating, shaking, and nervous, he rose to his feet and took a step toward the washroom but fell to the floor like a tree that fell at its base. He sat down on the floor and looked at his feet to find his shoelaces tied together. Who could have done this? Certainly not he himself in his sleep! He looked about and realized that no one was in the house. While he was still sleepy, he slipped his shoes off and went back to bed again so that he might continue with the same dream to see how everything would turn out.

He fell asleep shortly after finding a comfortable position. Soon, he found himself in uniform again. He was leading his men across the enemy lines when they were stopped by the enemy with a heavy bombardment. He hugged the earth at the bottom of a crater when a huge shell exploded nearby and buried him alive. He struggled to work his way to the surface, but it kept pressing down on him. Then the bombardment stopped, and all was quiet. Out of the quietness, in the darkness, he heard his mother calling in a slow and distant voice—"Johnnie." Then his father alternated with a slow and distant masculine voice—"Johnnie." He struggled to break through the earth to the surface from where they seemed to be calling.

When he awoke again, his heart was beating hard, and sweat soaked his clothes and the pillow under his head. His hands were shaking from the strain. Immediately, he went to the washroom, ran the tub full of hot water, and toned his nerves down with a hot bath. Quickly, he dressed in dry clothes and took a taxi home to his mother and dad.

Upon arriving at his home, he tried the door, and it was locked, as he might have expected. Then he knew that the kind old lady next door would have the key. He hurried to her and found her most enthusiastic about seeing him again.

45

"Since your folks went away, I took good care of the place," she said.

"It makes me very happy to see you again," he said. "How was Mother and Dad before they left?"

"Oh, fine! Fine. They left quietly, and each one had something written for you in an envelope." She reached into her desk drawer and turned to him with the letter. "I would have mailed it to you, only they said I shouldn't," she explained.

"You did the right thing, Addie," he said. "By the way, I'm attending college now, and I expect to be very busy. You'll come and watch me play football, won't you, Addie?"

"You bet I will!" she cried out in her dry and croaky voice while she pinched his cheek.

He walked slowly for her to keep up with him as he was returning to his home. She had been a lonely creature whose marriage left her without children for her comfort during old age. When her husband died, he left the house and nine patches of land totaling 2,600 acres of good farmland. It was easily worth $130 an acre at the present listings. From this, she derived a substantial income, although she did none of the work on the farm. Hired hands took care of everything. She spent all her life living in the Country Club District, Kansas City's richest residential area and long accepted as a model residential district of America. Johnnie lived in a modest little home next door to her costly homestead with richly embellished furnishings. She came to love Johnnie from the day he was born, and she took him into her heart as her very own.

Her silver hair was cut short at the sides like a little girl's. Nothing ever seemed to bother her—not even the many relatives who needled her for a will to leave her property to them. However, they never thought of giving her comfort in any way—oh no. In spite of it all, she was always disposed to be cheerful and light. He was surprised to see how clean she kept the two homes.

"Just kept my hands busy and my mind occupied," she said. "I had a sneaking feeling you'd come back home when nobody would expect you."

"Addie, you know what? I have a girl! And her name is Mary," he said without thought.

"Good!" Addie cried out, clasping her hands and grinning with excitement.

"But she's engaged," Johnnie added in a low tone.

"Bad." She swiped the grin from her face with one sweep of her hand.

"But I'm going after her with everything I've got." He pressed his jaws firmly together.

"Good for you!" she cried out again with that grinning excitement. "Go after her with everything you've got!" She showed her clenched fist for emphasis.

They sat about and soon returned to her home, where she prepared some dinner.

"This is just like old times," Johnnie reminded.

Addie's smile disappeared when she thought of the old times with her husband, but he wasn't talking about her husband. He was talking about the times when he would drop in on her after school and she would feed him her home-baked cakes and cookies. With this adjustment of her thoughts, she regained her smile.

"We still have each other, haven't we?" She beamed at him.

"I'll be home for the weekends, if you'll do the baking like you used to. I might even bring Mary—if she'll come."

"Tell you what I'll do. I have a cake you can take to the boys."

"Oh boy! Pappy will like that!" Johnnie cried out with excitement.

"Who's Pappy?" she asked with an interest of curiosity.

"He's our housekeeper. Nice old gentleman. Kind of lonesome too. No wife . . . All the children married off."

"Can I ride over with the cake myself?" She looked at him, blinking wildly.

"We better leave right away so you wouldn't be coming back home late, Addie," he cautioned.

Johnnie tried to take his seventeen-year-old maroon Chevrolet sedan out of the garage. It has been standing for some time. From a five gallon drum, he added two quarts of oil to the motor, a pail of water to the radiator, and some distilled water to the battery. The battery was discharged from long standing, and it wouldn't turn the motor over. What's more, it wouldn't even give a peep out of the horn.

"I could use a new car instead of troubling with this antiquated contraption." He laughed to Addie, who followed him around everywhere he went as he worked on the car.

"Then Mary would really come running after you," she pointed out to him.

"You think so? I never thought of it." He looked at her with the picture of Mary riding with him in a new car clearly in his mind.

"That would be your best investment in Mary—if you really want her. A yellow convertible would be just the thing," she said. "A sunshine yellow," she added. "A delicate sunshine yellow," she corrected with some emphasis on the color it had to be.

"My first class starts at eleven tomorrow, and I'm quite sure that by then, I'll have my new car."

"Are you sure? What about the waiting list?"

"I don't think there will be a waiting list for me. I have some friends from the service who are back in business again."

He paused before he gave the engine a turn of the crank with his hand. He cranked and cranked, and the motor finally popped, sputtered, popped, and then roared at high speed. Addie looked on, and all the while, she was thinking how much more convenient it was for her to call a taxi than to trouble with the ownership of a car.

They arrived at the rooming house, and Addie strutted along with Johnnie, holding the cake high before her. He took her directly to see Pappy—after all, it was her cake and Pappy's house. Pappy was dusting, as he always did when he didn't know what to do with himself. Upon introducing them to each other, Johnnie retired, leaving Pappy with Addie and the problem of distributing the cake. The boys were back from their weekend visit home. Some would be back in time for their first class on Monday. Soon, all the boys were invited for a cup of coffee and a piece of cake. Addie and the boys were introduced, and with the cake came many compliments that filled her heart with the energy of joy. After it was all over, the boys retired to their rooms—some to study and some to loaf—and Addie washed the dishes while Pappy wiped and put them away. They sat about, talking of things from their past, and when she decided to go home, she kindly brushed off Johnnie's offer to drive her back.

"How silly it would be for you to drive away over there and then back here again when I could take a one-way ticket on a taxi," she said.

"Hurry back!" Pappy cried out, waving goodbye as the taxi sped on its way.

Johnnie found it very difficult to fall asleep again. His thoughts were centered on Mary's actions. He was worried about his further progress with her since he could not visit her at home anymore. The question bothering him most of all was should he appear at her home regardless of the fact that she had asked him not to? Christine would invite him anyhow, or he could see her at home under the false pretense of seeing her father. What effect would the car have on his progress, and why would it have to be yellow? He tossed about as his thoughts roamed from one thing to another—but always related in some way to Mary.

He was up early Monday morning and out of the washroom before the first one of the long line of students had arrived. He hadn't slept much that night, and when he did sleep, it seemed like he was half awake. He was anxious about getting the car because he didn't know how much it would help his purpose. He wasn't sure he liked a yellow convertible. He'd much rather have a black sedan.

Before his friend, a buddy from the service, opened shop, Johnnie was out there waiting for him. He had used cars and plenty of them. He had them in window displays, in his huge storage garage, and on the lot. Johnnie was standing at the center of the display window, admiring a light-gray Buick convertible, when his buddy noticed him.

"Johnnie!" he yelled, hurrying to Johnnie.

"Roland!" Johnnie yelled, hurrying with outstretched hand.

After a warm handshake and a few excited pats on the shoulder, Roland invited him to look over the place. Johnnie told him that he actually was on the market for a car.

"I have a girl. What kind of car would you suggest that I get?" asked Johnnie.

"Engaged to her yet?"

"I'm not engaged, but she is. You see what my trouble is?" Johnnie explained.

"I know just how you feel. I would suggest that light-gray convertible with the black canvas top. The one you were looking at. That's a brand-new car!"

"Think I can afford it?"

"I'll see that you can—would a discount help a friend?"

"That isn't exactly what I was thinking."

"So what? A hundred dollars down, and the car is yours. Pay me the rest when you get it."

"Five years from now?" Johnnie asked in hope. "By then, I'll be through college and working."

"Ten years, if it takes that long—I'll still be a friend of yours in business. You'll send me a lot of customers during that time."

Roland drove the car back through a door to the garage. He marked it "cash, paid in full" and turned the title with the keys to Johnnie.

"Don't forget to bring the girl around!" Roland shouted as Johnnie drove away with the gray convertible, leaving his old car with Roland on the used car lot.

Johnnie's first impulse was to rush over to Addie and see about her approval of the car. It was only nine o'clock, and he had till eleven for his first class. It wasn't a yellow convertible, and he didn't see any reason why it had to be yellow.

"Uh-uh," she said. "Nothing doing. I said a yellow convertible with red leather upholstery and a black canvas roof."

"But why does it have to be yellow?"

"Because I'm superstitious, and if I'm not mistaken, so is Mary superstitious," she explained with a wink.

"Then I'll have it repainted."

"Make it a delicate sunshine yellow." She rolled her eyes.

Then he told her about his friend, Roland, and how the car came into his possession.

"Uh-uh," she said, simulating a fainting spell. "Now you're in some real trouble. Come into the house quick."

She took hold of his hand like a sweetheart at sixteen. They hurried together into her house, where she opened her wall safe and took out a stack of hundred-dollar bills.

"Here's twenty-six hundred and another two hundred for the paint job."

"But why? I can pay for it in five or ten years from now," he protested.

"Don't you expect to have Mary as your wife in less than five years from now?"

"Well . . . Yes . . . But . . ."

"Well, you'll be courting your girl on borrowed money, and that means trouble," she warned.

"I still don't see it at all."

"You would if you were superstitious. Did you ever see the house of Tomorrow?" she asked.

In a flash, he pictured the house of Tomorrow with Mary, Addie, and himself in a triangle around it. He did not see the connection directly, but Mary was holding out on him about the house of Tomorrow. Addie was trying to give him that which Mary was holding out about the house of Tomorrow, and he was at the third point of the triangle.

"No, I didn't," he confessed falsely to weed out the necessary information.

"Well, there was a Mr. Tomorrow who bought a farm with a down payment. He bought it specially to court his girl, and when he took his girl over the threshold on the wedding day, she cried and cried for days and days. She worked hard in trying to help him pay for the farm. Then she was carrying an unborn baby and working as hard as she ever was, and that killed her. He lived on the farm for a short time after that and died from a broken heart at her grave.

"Then his nephew took over the farm, and he got his girl by waving the farm before her eyes. She came from good folks and a nice home. They sent her to high school to get an education. She was the prettiest girl in school. Then this lowly nephew comes hanging around the schoolhouse like a stray dog, looking for the prettiest girl he could carry off with him. When he waved the big farm before her eyes, she left school and followed him to the minister. He had no education, but he was cunning as a fox, in his own way for himself.

"When he brought her on the farm, she discovered he had lied to her all that time. He lied when he said to her the house and farm were paid for. The day she got on the farm, she looked through the papers and then checked with the real estate office. She found that with the new equipment he bought on payment to show off to her, the farm was worth less than what he owed. He meant good with the new machines—that would be less work for her—but he lied to her, and she knew that he would lie again and again, so she left him and went back to her mother. She could not bear deceit and misrepresentation.

"The nephew's name was Tomorrow too. He couldn't eat much, and he didn't sleep well after that. One day a neighbor saw him talking down the road, and she got scared. He looked like a scarecrow. She got some of the neighbors to help him, but they never saw Tomorrow anymore. The last I heard, he was in the state asylum for the insane.

"Now the bank has got the property, but they can't sell it because it's cursed."

She looked at him with the seriousness that convinced him every word she said was true, but what was the connection between the favor Roland extended to him and the house of Tomorrow? It all seemed so strange that Mary's story differed from Addie's in many respects. Of course, Addie's story must be more accurate because it happened about the time Addie was a girl. Mary had the story as it was handed down to her, as it traveled from many lips to many ears, with many ears leaving out something and many lips adding on something—depending on the disposition of the one whose ears or lips they were.

"I'm not very much inclined to be superstitious," he said, "but I believe every word you say."

"Then I'll go back with you to the dealer."

"Talking about superstitions, what about this money I'm borrowing from you?"

"You're not borrowing it. I'm giving it to you. It's yours to keep forever," she said.

"I don't understand how I ever got to deserve a gift like this," he replied with amazement.

"Let's say it's a welcome home gift," she said, reaching up and kissing him on the cheek.

"But I don't really deserve a gift such as this," he said in an expression of the modesty in his character.

"Don't let anyone fool you. Nobody will ever give you anything which you have not already earned," she warned.

"But you might need this money," he tried, pointing out to her.

"At my age, friends are worth more than my income of thousands. From my friends, I can get what I cannot get from my income. My income gives me false friends and thereby false security."

"You're a girl of wisdom," he said. "Back to the dealer we go!"

He hurried to the dealer and arrived there in a short time. Addie would sit tight with excitement as he squeezed through the tight spots and turned the comers at a high speed. The canvas top was folded back, and once more, Addie felt like a schoolgirl on a joyride.

"Here she is—back without a splotch!" Johnnie cried out while he hopped out of the car, hurrying to Roland.

"Is that your girl?" Roland asked with a dumbfounded look masking his face.

"It's my girl, all right—but not the one I'm going to marry." Johnnie winked to Addie.

"You have girls in all age brackets?" Roland glanced at Addie and then scrutinized Johnnie. "You've got the girl that you're going to marry, and you've got girls that you're not going to marry?"

"Here's the money I owe you for the car, and how much would it cost to change this light gray job to a yellow?" said Johnnie, changing the subject.

"You nuts? Want to start a riot at the college? Yellow, he wants on a convertible!"

"That's right!" Addie cried out with determination. "And I want to see it before you put it on!"

"I give up . . . Fifty dollars for the paint job for a friend. When do you want it?"

"As soon as you can get it on," Addie put in. "We don't have any time to lose."

"Well, we won't have to take this old paint off. We'll just take the dust off and cover it with yellow by the day after tomorrow." He removed his hat, scratching his head with the same hand that he held his hat.

"Don't say the day after tomorrow—say Wednesday," Addie corrected.

"Okay, lady—Wednesday."

"Can I see the yellow?" she asked.

"Sure. Why not? You want a delicate sunshine yellow, so we'll give you a delicate sunshine yellow."

He showed her a great number of samples on some metal plates from which she picked out the one that resembled the kind of delicate sunshine yellow she had in mind. The yellow almost dazzled Roland's eyes, and his exclamations put the emphasis on the bright color she picked out.

"And put a spotlight on each side," she said.

"Okay." He looked at her.

"And a horn that goes *to-too-to-too!*" She sang the sound of the horn with excitement.

"Anything else?" Roland asked in search for the end of the line of accessories.

"Oh yes! One of those birds for the nose. The one with the red wings almost straight up that light at night." She was getting more excited as the questions came on.

Now Roland looked at her without asking.

"And, and, and . . . and that's all," she said, with her excitement receding.

"I hope to repay you for all this," Johnnie said to Addie, waving for a taxi as they left.

"Like I told you before, you've already paid me for it. Now let's go and see what Pappy's doing."

The taxi driver let them off at the rooming house. Johnnie took Addie to Pappy, and leaving them, he scooped up his books, rushing off for his eleven o'clock class. Addie had much to talk about with Pappy. She prepared lunch for two, and they spent the afternoon together.

Johnnie went to his classes and then to look for Mary in the library. He looked carefully throughout the main floor and the second floor, but nowhere could he find Mary. His next thought was to see Christine.

"Just dropped in to say hello," he said, closing the door of the office slowly behind him.

"Have a seat, Johnnie," said Christine, turning away from her writing at the desk.

"Can't stay but a few minutes," he said. "I'm about due for football practice."

"Mary won't be in school for a few days."

"Why? What's happened?" He looked at her with great concern about Mary's absence.

"She went to St. Louis for a meeting on the coming Christian Youth Movement Program."

Johnnie let out a sigh of relief. "For a moment, you had me thinking she met with some accident."

"She'll be back in school Wednesday afternoon or Thursday morning."

She knew that he had come to ask about Mary. For what other reason would he come? She had her doubts about him ever since she first met him. For what reason would a boy his age court a girl her age? She didn't show the slightest sign of being misled by his attentions, but she loved him and welcomed the faintest opportunity to come into contact with him. All the time, she felt and she knew he loved Mary and that, in some way, she was bringing him closer to Mary.

After football practice, Johnnie had his dinner at the college cafeteria and returned to the rooming house, where he found Addie still with Pappy. He couldn't decide whether she was waiting for him or enjoying her stay with Pappy.

"Did you see her?" she asked with a few blinks.

"She's gone to St. Louis. A meeting related to her work at church."

"Oh, she's a good girl," Addie commented, coming to a realization of the situation. "Once them kind get engaged, no boy could ever cut in on their fiancé. To them, a promise is not merely a promise—it's something sacred."

"That's right," Pappy added. "And you would save yourself a lot of grief by starting with some other girl."

"He isn't starting with no other girl," Addie corrected him with a stern look on her face.

"Addie's right. I'm putting all my stakes on Mary. If I lose, then at least I will know that even with my best, I was not good enough.

I'll never have peace of mind until I succeed or fail in my efforts—anything in between would give me a long life of unrest."

"Well, a man is bound to do what he thinks he can." Pappy put in some encouragement with his bit of philosophy.

"I can borrow a car from one of the fellows if you're ready to go home, Addie," said Johnnie.

"Oh, don't bother," she said. "I can take a taxi, and besides, Pappy and I will be playing some cards. I can hardly wait to see your new car." She turned to Pappy, telling him all about the new car Johnnie would have.

Johnnie left for the library with his roommate, William. When William didn't study in the library, he studied in his room. He wasn't making good grades, but wherever he was, he was studying. He never attended the social functions of the college. He would rather study than enjoy a football game—so he said. Everyone regarded him as a queer one since most of his studying came to naught, and his behavior could not be understood. When they returned, Addie had gone home already.

Tuesday was a long day for Johnnie. He was kept busy with all his school responsibilities, but that wasn't what troubled him—it was Mary. Constantly, she was on his mind wherever he was. He went to see Christine two times that day. Each time, he left with some degree of satisfaction from his visit.

VI

Ta-Taa-Ta-Taa

On Wednesday morning, he went for the car and only met with disappointment when he found them installing the accessories. He returned for another long grind through his classes and football practice. By this time, he knew his car would be ready and was wild with joy as he drove it back to see Mary.

He hurried to the library, hoping to find Mary, and he found her in the same place he had the last time. She was studying her back work with some of her girlfriends. When she first saw him, she turned away. He came to her and rested his hands on the back on her chair.

"Hello, Mary," he whispered softly into her ear.

"Hello." She turned, glancing at him.

Immediately, she rose from her chair and picked up her purse, books, and notebooks, leaving the library. She turned to him in all seriousness.

"Johnnie," she said, "please don't speak to me anymore. Don't even come close to me. Let it be as if we never met."

"Mary, my heart takes this with great pain. I don't understand it at all. First, you ask me not to come to your home. Now you're asking me not to speak to you, not even to come close enough to look at you, to wipe you out of my mind completely . . . Let us sit down on that bench over there and straighten out a few things."

He talked from his subconscious mind. Since he first thought of buying a new car, he started accumulating heartfelt phrases that he wanted to recite to her. He had everything set in his mind as to what he would say first, what came next, and what followed in order, but now his conscious mind was stunned. He lost all the pretty phrases he had stored for her. He felt like an actor on the stage who had lost his memorized script, which he had clearly in mind until he had come upon the stage. He was lost, with nothing but darkness about him. What would he do if he couldn't speak to her—not even to see her or to ignore her presence if it could not be avoided?

"We don't have anything to straighten out. I'm engaged, don't you see?" she explained.

"Mary, I'm terribly in love with you. If you'll cut me off like that, I'll die," he said, trying to impress her in the language she understood.

"But I can't be seeing you anymore. You're not a gentleman," she said in earnest.

"Now what have I done? I can't see it," he moaned.

"You kissed me seven times that day we spent together, and you didn't even ask me once," she said.

"Was I supposed to ask my girl for a kiss?"

"I'm not your girl. See this ring?" she said, flashing the engagement ring before his eyes.

"I see the ring. It's not the ring—it's what is in your heart," he explained.

"In my heart is music—and mostly piano music." She set him back.

"If I would have asked for a kiss, then you would have held the ring before my eyes in answer to my asking," he reasoned with her.

"Percival never kissed me without asking."

"Did he ever ask?"

"No, but I expect he will on our wedding day."

"*Huh!* On your wedding day? Are you sure you will like his kisses then, or will you get used to them? Because it will be too late since you will already be tied to him for the rest of your life."

"Percival is a modest gentleman."

"Not only is Percival a gentleman, but also, he's a modest one, she tells me," he said, clapping the palm of his hand to his forehead.

"Now you're being hidebound, Johnnie."

"Why, it's a crime for a man to be modest. The virtue of modesty belongs to women."

"Percival is going to make me a great concert pianist, and I will be grateful to him as his wife."

"But you're going to marry him before he molds you into a great concert pianist—like that much putty in his hands." He effected his remark with motions on squeezing putty in his hands.

"Why not?" she remarked.

"What a tragedy! Supposing he doesn't turn you into the supposedly great concert pianist?"

"Oh, he will," she replied with confidence.

"Look, Mary," he said, taking hold of her hand, "let's take a ride somewhere and talk things over."

"But there is nothing to talk over. I'm engaged, and I want to be a great concert pianist, and that's all there is to it."

"When did he first tell you of being a great pianist?"

"When he saw me playing the piano for the first time. Christine brought him home that day. Before he left, he recommended that I enroll in his class."

"And when was that day?"

"Last semester."

"Come on, let's take a ride somewhere," he insisted.

"But I don't want to take a ride anywhere," she protested.

"You must come with me, Mary," he pleaded.

"But I want to study in the library," she said.

"The library can wait, Mary. I bought a new car, and I want you to see it."

"All right. But that's as far as I'm going," she warned.

The delicate sunshine yellow convertible, with a spotlight to each side and a bird with outstretched wings setting on the tip of the hood, was parked at the front of the library with the roof down, waiting to take them riding. As a matter of fact, it stood there, not fifty yards from them, watching their every move.

"This is it," he pointed out upon approaching it. "Isn't it a beauty?"

"Is this your car?" she asked with disbelief.

"Of course, it is."

"All yours?" she asked, smoothing the fender with her hand.

"All mine. Every bit of it—no payments, no lien, no nothing. All mine," he said, showing her the clear title to the car.

"I can't believe it. This is something like Dad used to have when he was in big business," she said.

"Let's take a ride by the river somewhere and try it out. Will you, Mary?" he said, taking hold of her hand to lead her to the door.

"But I can't. I want to study the lessons I missed while I was away," she complained, shying away from him and the car.

"Mary," he pleaded, "I want you to be the first one to ride with me in the car."

"I don't have much time. Besides, it won't matter who will be the first one to ride with you."

"But it means so much to me for you to be the first to ride with me, Mary. It won't take long. We'll go for a short ride and be back in less than twenty minutes." He felt her physical resistance waning as he held her by the waistline.

"All right—but make it a short ride," she said as her determination weakened into passive resistance.

He led her to the door and closed it after she was well seated. All excited, he hastened into the driver's seat and sped away from the campus. He had no idea where he could take her in ten minutes so as to be back in twenty. He looked at her and smiled. Then again, he thought, why should he hurry back with her? She would let him know when she wanted to go back to the campus.

When Mary first got into the car, she was completely entranced, and she seemed to be beyond the door locking out her own freedom. She smoothed the red leather upholstery, played with the gun-grip spotlight, adjusted her hair in the mirror on the sunshade, and rummaged through the glove compartment. The luxury of the car swept away her memory for Percival and his engagement ring. She even forgot about being back in twenty minutes. She talked so freely and was so gay that it seemed like her heart was not tied up with Percival.

We Spend Our Lives

Her music ambitions seemed so unimportant; she didn't give them a thought.

Johnnie sped toward a parking spot by the river. They talked about the river, and she never thought of the time. While they were parked, he took her in his arms.

"Now may I have the pleasure of a kiss on your lips, Mary?" he asked softly, and he kissed her before she had a chance to say no.

"You shouldn't have asked me," she said, turning away from him.

"I was only trying to be gentleman."

"A gentleman does not ask when he sees an engagement ring, and you knew about Percival."

"I'm sorry. You will teach me to be a gentleman—won't you?" he asked in seriousness.

"I'd like to," she admitted.

"Then I'll drive you home tonight, and we can start with the first lesson."

"Oh no! I have to be with Percival this evening."

She was suddenly well aware of the time that had lapsed since she got into the car. It was almost an hour since they started out, and Percival was to come for her at the library at six o'clock. Nervously, she looked at her wristwatch.

"I have to go now. Please hurry back," she said to him with fear written on her face.

Percival was to drive her home for dinner, as he always did on Wednesday. He had some strange power over her that Johnnie could not understand. He wasn't presumptuous in his actions like Johnnie. He was extremely sheepish in the presence of the opposite sex—especially in close contact. He was like an artist living in a world all his own. His conversation was strictly from the contents of music outside of the regular routine about the weather. In the presence of a group, he usually found the topics so boring, his mind would wander off into his world of music, and he would piece together new compositions with which he could experiment.

On arriving close to the campus, Johnnie made a roundabout return to reach the library by way of Percival's regular route from his apartment to the library. He knew Percival walked to the library. It was only a short distance, and Percival had an excuse for inviting Mary into his apartment to show her his new compositions. He judged his time to reach the library a minute or two before six since Percival was punctual about his time as he was accurate about his music. When Johnnie approached the library, Mary was facing him and telling him how mean it was of him to stretch the twenty minutes out into an hour and a half. As she was talking to him, Johnnie sounded his horn—*ta-taa-ta-taa!*—and he waved to Percival, slowing down as he passed by him.

Percival was attracted by the musical notes of the horn. He turned briskly and saw Johnnie in the car, with Mary sitting alongside him. He stopped in his tracks, knowing not what to do. He was taken over with a flustery surprise. When he saw them stop at the library, only then did he proceed on his way.

When Johnnie sounded the horn and waved his arm, Mary's attention naturally followed his eyes. She became so frightened with the sight of Percival that she promptly pulled her head out of sight like a turtle, but she realized it was too late, and slowly, she straightened up again. When they parted at the library, Mary opened the door, and without another word, she hurried to Percival. Johnnie wasn't slow to follow, and the three of them stood there on the walk for a moment, wondering what the others would say.

"Percival, I would have been late if Johnnie wouldn't have given me a lift," she explained, remembering his concern over punctuality. "I was at the other end of the campus, at the music club, and I overlooked the time."

She talked slowly, half frightened and half searching for a logical and appropriate excuse. She realized she struck the right one when she impressed him with the thought of her interest in the music club and of her efforts to meet him on time.

Percival smiled to her in acknowledgment of her excuse. Then his smile turned to a frown for Johnnie in resentment to Johnnie's pleasure of driving her.

Johnnie noticed the confident smile changing to a frown when Percival turned to him, and he strained his mental faculties in a vain effort to establish a justifiable relationship with Mary to fit the occasion.

"Mary was almost running when I noticed her," he finally added to her excuse.

Johnnie had a good notion to tell him off. He wanted very much to tell him the truth, but in so doing, he would point out that Mary was lying, and he could never sink so low as to call her lies. *Let him find out for himself, if he ever will.* Percival was the type that could swallow a lie much more easily than he could the unpleasant situation that it covered. He was credulous to the extent of self-deception. Anyhow, they were white lies that would not set upon her conscience, as Mary would say.

"I'm so glad she came on time. Nice weather we're having," he said, turning away, with Mary walking not closer than two feet at his side.

"Yes! Nice weather we're having," Johnnie repeated.

Johnnie remembered what Percival had said. "I'm so glad she came on time." That was what he had said, and it irritated him as he remained on the same spot, tossing it about in his mind. Maybe Percival meant that he was glad Johnnie had given her a lift to get there on time, but why didn't he say it that way? Percival seemed to be more concerned about the time than he was about Mary. Why was it necessary to be so punctual?

Mary told Johnnie once that Percival said, "A person who is not punctual is not worth associating with." Percival was on time every time, everywhere. The timing in the music probably had a stranglehold on the timing in his life. After all, notes played at the wrong time did not make music for him.

Whenever he was in trouble with Mary, Johnnie's first thought was to see Christine. Somehow he always thought he could get to Mary through Christine. So he found himself opening the door to Christine's office. The translucent glass in the door showed that a light was on, and without hesitation, he walked in.

"Working late again?" he asked.

"It's not again—it's always," she said from what seemed like frustration.

"You certainly are attached to those books."

"That may be what they call an escape from reality. You seem kind of happy today. See Mary?"

"Yes, I did. Just a few minutes ago," he confessed. "She left with Percival."

"Must be something else," she said, looking at him from the corners of her eyes.

"Well, yes . . . I bought a new car . . . If yours should ever break down, I'll be glad to drive you home."

She wrinkled her forehead with a movement of her eyebrows. Then she looked at him with understanding.

"Come to think of it," she said through a smile, "my car just broke down."

"Good!" he cried out. They spoke the same language, and they understood each other. "One of the fellows at the house works at a gas station. Could you give me the keys to your car?"

"Here you are," she said, handing the keys to him.

"I'll be right back for you as soon as I get it to the gas station."

He was at the door, and away he went before she could say, "Hurry back." He knew where she always parked her car, and in fact, he saw it when he was driving Mary. He settled into the driver's seat, inserted the ignition key with a twist, turning the switch on, stepped on the starter, and gunned the motor, and away he went to the gasoline station.

"Jim," he said, "can I park this car around here somewhere?"

"Sure, Johnnie . . . I'll park it right by the wall."

"And, Jim, if anybody wants to know, tell them that the car is eleven years old already, and it should have a complete overhauling—got it?" he said, handing the car keys to Jim.

"Anything you say, Johnnie."

"I'll let you know when the overhauling is done." Johnnie laughed. "I got myself a new car. I'll be seeing you," he said, leaving Jim with Christine's old Ford V8.

"You bet you will!" Jim cried out, overjoyed.

Johnnie returned hastily to Christine to find her waiting for him. When he showed her the car, she was taken aback.

"Is it yours?" she finally asked.

"It sure is," he boasted.

"All yours?" she asked in a want of belief.

"Every bit of it," he emphasized.

It came to his mind, as he held the door open for her, that Mary had asked the same questions. *Everyone else will most likely ask the same questions.* They seemed to be the standard questions for every new car—especially an expensive one. Blondes were usually attached to the more expensive cars around the campus, but he would attach Mary, a brunette, if he could—not because she was a brunette but because she was Mary.

She talked with him freely, gazing about as he drove on. She had a feeling that he was not driving her home, but she didn't know why, and at first, she didn't care. He was not driving along the regular route home, and she had no idea as to where he was taking her, but she appeared amiable, as ever she was. When she caught sight of the river, her feminine instinct told her that he would park somewhere along the river—but why? She loved him, yes, but she was not in his age group, and she was not his type. Throwing her suspicions and her suppositions overboard, she went along with him in an atmosphere of being a college girl once again. At last, he parked the car in the same place as when he was with Mary. She was looking at him, and he was looking at her.

"Christine," he said, "I'd very much like to kiss you for all the happiness you've brought me, but I'm afraid it's liable to go to your head."

So that's what it was. *He would like to shower me with his affections, but he wouldn't want me to fall in love with him,* she reasoned. Her thoughts seemed to be unrelated to the present situation.

"If you're afraid, then don't," she advised.

"I'm not afraid to kiss you for the sake of the kiss itself. You see, I had Mary here earlier in the evening, and I kissed her."

"Oh!" she let out. "Why tell me about it?"

"What I'm trying to say is that I like you very much, but I don't think I could live without Mary," he said, turning his eyes away from her.

"That's a beautiful way of saying that you like me and that you love Mary," she said.

"If I'd kiss you, I'd only imagine that it was Mary that I'm kissing—that's why I brought you here. I hope you will forgive me," he begged.

"Of course, I forgive you—who wouldn't?"

"Christine," he said, "I wouldn't hurt you for anything in this world."

"Let's go home, shall we?" She made it as a casual suggestion.

"That would be the best for the both of us," he said.

While he drove her home, he told her about the trouble Mary almost got into when he drove Mary back to the library, how Percival believed every word they told him.

Christine was beginning to see everything adding up now. She began thinking that it was a rather cunning way of putting things up to her. First, he impressed upon her that he liked her and that he could not live without Mary; then he gave her a confidential piece of information that she might be able to use to her own advantage.

When Johnnie drove up to the house, he sounded the horn—*ta-taa-ta-taa!*—and he waited for Christine to leave, but she had no intentions of leaving by herself.

Christine spent her time in her office, working late because Percival was at the house, and she couldn't stand thinking of the years going by while someone her age was courting Mary. She felt lonelier than ever when Percival was with Mary.

"Would you care to come in for the evening?" she asked with questioning eyes.

"I don't believe I could—it's forbidden territory," he explained unintentionally.

"Johnnie," she said, "you can't take me home and then drive off like a cab driver."

She took hold of the horn ring, and when the horn blew its tone out onto the countryside, he had no choice but to abide by her wishes.

"We'll play some backgammon," he said, closing the door after him.

"I keep hearing some nasty notes blowing in my ears," Percival remarked, referring to Johnnie's auto horn, upon Johnnie's arrival into the house with Christine.

"I sounded the horn. Did it disturb you any?" Christine asked blankly.

"Not only does it disturb me—it aggravates me since it takes Mary's mind away from the piano," he complained.

His complaints came to naught when the dice began to roll and the excited voices of Christine and Johnnie came into full play, sounding above the notes of the piano.

"Quiet, please!" Percival would shout.

Still, Mary lost her interest in the piano from the moment she heard the horn. Her mind wandered off to the riverside or to the movie or to the Snack-Shack where she had stopped and eaten with Johnnie. With him present, she could not concentrate on the piano or the music sheet—especially when he started playing backgammon with Christine.

Within the hour, Percival became discouraged to such an extent that he left without a word to Christine or Johnnie. He made no audible signs of anger, but his conduct betrayed his inner feelings.

"Would you care to join us, Mary?" Johnnie asked.

"No, thank you. I'm going to bed," she said.

Christine and Johnnie stayed with the game until ten o'clock, when the Mastersons returned from one of the neighbors'. They were never around when Percival came to see Mary, unless their staying could not be avoided.

"Where is Percival?" was their first question.

"He's gone," said Christine.

"And Mary?"

"She said she was going to bed," said Johnnie.

"Just as well we retire too," Mr. Masterson replied.

When Johnnie was leaving, he kissed Christine good night, saying, "I will be back for you in the morning."

So he came in the morning, early. Mary and Christine were still in bed at six-thirty when they heard the already familiar sound of the horn—*ta-taa-ta-taa!* Mary buried her head under the pillow at the sound of the horn. Would she ever get away from it? She began to wonder, and her heart began to burn with the desire to be with Johnnie, but at the same time, she was thinking of Percival and her promise to him not to see Johnnie again.

Christine jumped out of bed at the sound of the horn. She opened the window, shouting, "Just in time for breakfast! Come on in!"

Johnnie waited in the living room for almost a half hour while Mrs. Masterson was preparing breakfast in the kitchen, Christine and

Mary were dressing, and Mr. Masterson sat in a robe, keeping him company.

"Mighty fine car you've got," he commented.

"Just got a notion to get one, and there it is," Johnnie said.

"There was a day when I had one like it, but I guess I'm too old to get another one," he moaned.

"I wouldn't ever say it's too late," Johnnie encouraged. "How much would you need to get started in business again?"

Mr. Masterson looked at him skeptically. "More than I could save in a whole lifetime," he said. "But I could make a good start with anything near a hundred thousand."

Johnnie thought it over for a while and repeated in a low tone, "A hundred thousand. Why, I was figuring on starting something with a few hundred."

"You can start that way if you want to—but not me. My wife and I started like that the last time but couldn't stand the grind of long hours and small returns again. My wife and I worked hard, and we're not young anymore. Nowadays, you start with a small thing, and that is what you end up with. I'm just too old. It's too late for me," he said.

"I'm looking forward to some advice from you when I will go into business," said Johnnie.

"I would offer you all the advice within my knowledge anytime you're in need," he said.

At this time, Christine appeared and disrupted their conversation.

"Breakfast is ready," she said, patting Mr. Masterson across the shoulder and then turning to Johnnie.

When Christine arrived at the table with Johnnie, Mary and her folks were already seated. The conversation carried from Johnnie to Christine to Mr. Masterson to Mrs. Masterson, but Mary could only speak when spoken to. Even then, she was nervous and said no more than was necessary. Her eyes revealed what mental activity was going on behind them. She was powdered and rouged, neatly making herself very attractive, and she looked to Johnnie for attention. Her eyes remained fixed on him or her plate of bacon and eggs with buttered toast in her hand.

Johnnie tried hard not to look in her direction. He faced Christine most of the time, looked to the Mastersons in speaking, and only glanced into Mary's expectant eyes. He didn't speak to her since her eyes reminded him of the fact that she had asked him not to come to the house anymore, but it was Christine's house, and he was there by Christine's invitation. There was nothing Mary could do under the circumstances, unless, like Mary would say, "if you were a gentleman, you would not have come here." Since Mary had no smile or words for him, this was what her eyes had actually said to him.

The Mastersons did not pay any special notice to Mary since their interest was centered on the guest, who spent most of his time talking business with Mr. Masterson. He told him of how he expected to start with some small business and asked Mr. Masterson how it would be possible to start with a bigger business. Mrs. Masterson was delighted to hear of Johnnie's plans since they pointed out a way for Mr. Masterson to get back on his feet. With Johnnie as an example of courage and confidence, she hoped to shake her husband loose of his frustration and to arouse his ambitions once more.

Mary and Christine had classes at nine o'clock, and they made it a habit to have an early breakfast and to appear on the campus at eight o'clock. When seven thirty came, they left the breakfast table and were on their way to the car where Mary brushed past Christine to seat herself next to Johnnie. She couldn't bear to have Christine in the center. Anyhow, with Christine at her side, Percival could have no reason to let his imaginations run wild.

Christine was doing some heavy thinking for herself, however. She would get even with Mary for this and for taking Percival away from her. As she was thinking, it came to her that Percival wouldn't like it a bit if he knew the truth about the incident where Johnnie took Mary for a ride, how Mary lied about the ride, how Mary sat next to Johnnie this morning. Her first intention was to see Percival. Her desire to make trouble was intensified by the act of Johnnie going with Mary to study in the library instead of coming with her to the office. She could help him more than Mary could.

Mary completely forgot about Percival, and the ring reminded her of nothing. The moment she first saw the car that morning, she became a jolly talker, and on reaching the campus, she hadn't remembered that she asked Johnnie not to speak to her. "Don't make it necessary for me to be where you are not," she told him. Now and then, she encouraged him to study with her and would try to help him.

VII

Percival

Christine looked on while Mary walked off with Johnnie. There was a time when she walked off with Percival. Now she was walking off with Johnnie. She shook her chills away and started out for the music hall instead of going to her office.

"Percival," Christine said to him, "I heard some rumors about you and Mary."

"Rumors?" He looked scared. "What could they be?"

"Well, I heard Mary is going to drop you for Johnnie. Could that be true?"

"No, it can't. She can't do that to me! I'm the college orchestra conductor. I'll be the one to drop her! What else did you hear?" He whispered the question with the blind curiosity of a closed mind and itching ears.

"Well, yesterday he took her for a ride to a place by the river," she said.

"He did?"

"And he kissed her."

"He did?"

"The roof was down, and everyone could see."

"They could?"

"And he almost didn't bring her back by six o'clock."

"Is that so?" he remarked with disbelief.

"And he drove her to school this morning."

Percival could not speak anymore. He stared into space with his hand over his open mouth.

"I'll bet, if you went to the music club, you'd find out if she was there." Christine whispered the thought into his mind with the power of a psychologist.

"I'll go right now," he said, turning to go, but Christine clutched him by the arm.

"Be sure you don't tell anyone that I know about this." She looked him sternly in the eye.

"Oh no—I'm very grateful to you for this," he said, hurrying away.

He went directly to see the sponsor of the music club, who was a music teacher in the same building.

"How did Mary do at the meeting yesterday?" asked Percival.

"I missed Mary yesterday. She probably forgot, or she might not have read the bulletin."

"You haven't seen her at all at the meeting?" Percival sickened.

"No, I haven't, but that's a beautiful car she is riding in lately."

"Car? Oh, yes . . . Belongs to a friend of her brother." Percival backed out of the vacant classroom.

He hurried to the library and was breathing hard from the fast walk when he reached the second floor. He turned pallid at the sight before him. There was Mary sitting at a library table with Johnnie, and they were studying close by each other. Without them seeing him, he came upon them from the back.

"Ahem!" He coarsely cleared his throat for attention.

Mary recognized the familiar "Ahem" and turned to see.

"Percival," she whispered.

She saw Percival briskly walking away. Her open mouth was covered with the fingers of her hand as she stared at Johnnie with fright in her eyes. Without another moment lost, she hurried after Percival and caught up with him outside the library.

"Percival," she pleaded, "you misunderstand."

"I will see you at your home tonight," he said, turning away, refusing to listen to another word while Mary tugged at his arm, begging for an ear.

Mary was confused, and she stopped to watch him disappear around the corner of another building. She acted as though she were hopelessly ruined. Her shoulders slumped, her feet seemed to be so heavy, her head drooped, and her eyes were blurred, with the corners of her smile sinking toward a crying spell. Johnnie was at her side, but he could do nothing for her comfort. She gathered her belongings from the library table and slowly walked to Christine's office, with the color gone from her face. Johnnie was still at her side; he tried to carry her things, but she wouldn't have him.

"I don't feel well," she said to Christine. "I'm going home."

"I will drive you home, Mary," Johnnie popped.

"Oh no, Johnnie. I'm taking a taxi," said Mary, leaving the office as slowly as she entered.

Johnnie was with her until he closed the door of her taxi at the cab stand.

"Goodbye, Johnnie," she said through a daze.

"Goodbye, Mary," he said with pity in his heart.

Christine had struck a new spark in her life when she saw Mary in her mental dejection. She felt that some of the wrong Mary had done to her had been compensated for. There was a time when she was going through the same throws of despondency as Mary was at this time, and that was when Mary wrapped up Percival all for herself. She began looking at life in a new light, with Johnnie in the picture with her.

Johnnie returned to Christine's office to explain to her what happened to Mary. After seeing Mary in that condition, the blues turned upon him too. He told Christine the account of what happened at the library, and this made her happier yet to hear everything from a close witness. Unfortunately, it was about time for her first class; otherwise, she would have lulled herself into a dream of hearty satisfaction. With mention of her class and the approaching hour, she excused herself.

"See you at five," said Johnnie, turning off toward the library.

At five, he drove Christine out to dinner and then to see a stage play downtown. He knew that Percival would be at Mary's home, and he wouldn't like to be there for more vexation.

When Percival arrived at Mary's home that evening, she made sure to be alone. She induced her folks to play cards at the neighbor's, as they usually did when Percival was coming to visit. She took special care in arranging things, and she bought a package of marshmallows to keep handy. Marshmallows were a special delicacy of Percival.

"I have come," he said upon arriving.

He was standing in the doorway, and he looked at her with a feeling of indigestion.

"Oh, Percival. I'm so glad you came this evening!" she said, interrupting him when she sensed that he was going to say, "I have come for my ring."

"I . . . I . . . I . . ." he stuttered.

"Percival, I have some fresh marshmallows for you—see?" She led him with one hand and pointed to the marshmallows with the other.

"But I didn't come to stay," he explained.

"Percival, you just sit right there and eat your marshmallows while I play the piano," she said while bringing his chair and then leading him to it like she would a child.

His purpose of the visit was overwhelmed with all the attention and the handling he received. He could not think of anything cross to say; in fact, he could not think at all when Mary began playing the piano without him perceiving one error. He sat there munching on his marshmallows, floating in ecstasy as she played through one piece after another. When she stopped to rest, he pounced on her.

"Your marshmallows are fine, and your music is fine, but I still forbid you to see him," he said.

"Yes, Percival," she said meekly.

"The last time, I asked you not to see him, but this time, I forbid you to see him, and I believe you will adhere to the difference in the latter," he said with firmness.

Mary swallowed. That was quite an order.

"Honest, Percival. I will not see him again—upon my word of honor," she said solemnly, reassuring him.

That evening, Percival left in a much happier mood than he ever did before. He enjoyed himself with the pleasure of her handling him. He felt and acted as though he had the cards and that she could do nothing more than follow suit. He pictured himself as the master and her as the slave of his desires. He felt that as long as she belonged to him, she should be subservient to him. He felt that she was enslaved by his musical genius.

When Johnnie returned with Christine, Mary dashed off to her room. He had no intentions of staying, but as he lingered in the living room in his unwilling mood to leave, the Mastersons returned. They were glad to see him, and by this time, they were beginning to attach him to Christine, thinking that he was actually courting her. Once Johnnie started on the subject of business with Mr. Masterson, the time slipped by so rapidly that he failed to give Christine any attention.

Christine finally cut in on them. "I only regret that I am not a commercials teacher."

Johnnie was embarrassed over the fact that he had overlooked her interest in him. Shortly, he excused himself from Mr. Masterson and left in the usual way.

"See you in the morning," he reminded Christine at the door.

The following morning, he was sounding his horn at six thirty, but this time, Christine was at the door and already dressed. She had an apron over her dress, and it made her more becoming than her environment of books at her office. She waved to him and waited with open door.

"I'm cooking this morning—surprised?" she asked enthusiastically.

"Not surprised a bit," he said. "I always thought you could do anything with a book in one hand."

They laughed together, and merrily, they walked on to the kitchen table. Johnnie was hoping to see Mary at the table again, and he tried not to make it noticeable when he missed her.

"Mary is not feeling well, and she won't be going to school today," Mrs. Masterson explained, to his heartfelt disappointment.

Without being conscious of it, the conversation between Johnnie and Mr. Masterson drifted into the subject of small business. Somehow Mr. Masterson became interested and favored Johnnie's ambition to start with whatever capital he had on hand to develop into whatever possibilities might arise in the future. He toned down his big-business talk and spoke of starting something on a small scale.

Mrs. Masterson's hope was blossoming into reality as she listened to her husband speak of his intentions to start a small business. She never doubted him, but she couldn't help wondering whether he was carrying on a psychological conversation or whether it came from a genuine desire. She intuitively cast all doubt aside and lolled in the celestial bliss of recovering her husband from his world of frustrations. She treasured the presence of Johnnie more than ever, and she began to love him since he was the key to her happiness with her husband.

Johnnie commented on Christine's cooking, and he accepted her offer of a second serving, much to her delight. When breakfast was over, the Mastersons, with Johnnie and Christine, sat about in the living room until seven thirty. Then with a sound of his horn and a wave of his arm, he was off to school with Christine, while the Mastersons stood in the doorway, looking on.

Mary was quite disturbed with the sound of the horn on Johnnie's arrival. However, she had made up her mind not to have breakfast with him. She tossed about in bed from nervous anxiety. She wanted to be with him, but she was afraid of Percival and of herself. She gave Percival her word of honor, and she had no choice but to make good on her word. If she would keep her word, she would keep Percival, and so she thought as she watched with mental anguish while Johnnie sounded his horn, waved his arm, and drove off with Christine instead of her.

Johnnie accompanied Christine to her office, where he studied his lessons with her help when needed. When Christine mentioned her nine o'clock class, they parted, and he decided to see Addie.

Addie was fussing over cake recipes when he walked in on her. She had cookbook, newspaper, and magazine clippings scattered over the whole dining room table. It appeared as though she were sorting or filing them.

"I was going to toot my horn for you, but my tooting isn't doing me much good," he said in a discouraged tone.

"I was wondering if you got the car. I phoned you yesterday, and Pappy said he knew you had the car, but he didn't see you or the car yet. I kind of figured that you were busy looking after Mary."

"I can't understand that girl. She looks at me, smiles to me, and talks gayly to me, yet she won't have anything to do with me," he explained with a vivid picture of her in his mind. "This morning, she didn't even sit at the breakfast table with us. Of course, she could have been sick."

"Did you toot your horn in front of her house like I told you to?" she asked.

"Many times. Every time I got in or out of the car in front of her house. Yellow, red, or black car—wouldn't make any difference to her," he replied.

"Let me tell you something, Johnnie—but be sure to keep it a secret," she whispered as if the walls were listening.

"That, I can do. I promise," he stated.

"I always figured that a man was made of money and he is worth as much as he is made of," she whispered softly into his ear, and then she looked him in the eye.

"Made of money?" He looked questioningly to her.

"It takes a lot of money to build a good home, to give the boy an education, and to give him a good start in life."

"Oh, so I haven't got enough money invested in myself?"

"Don't get me wrong now. You see . . . Percival has a doctorate degree . . . He has a highly honorable position at the college . . . and no doubt, he has a bank account that speaks for him."

Johnnie puffed up his cheeks and blew the air out of his lips as if he were blowing out the light of a new candle. The candle, he had not noticed because the light, he did not see. The new candle had thrown more light on his affair with Mary.

"I'm afraid you'll have to work along those lines. You've got yourself some real competition," she warned.

"But it will be years before I get a doctorate—if I ever decide to go beyond the baccalaureate degree. She'll be married to my rival and have two or three children by then. In the first place, I was hoping to settle down. Although I don't have money in the bank, I have a home where we could settle down. I could work day and night to give her the things her heart desires."

"What you have, Johnnie," she cautioned, "you must compare with your rival."

"So I'm not worth as much as he is?" he sneered, thinking of Percival.

"It's not that way. You might be worth just as much to her as he is in other ways, only he got to her first."

"Thanks a lot, Addie. You've helped me a great deal. I must hurry back to class. See you tomorrow, okay?"

"Okay!" she cried out as he dashed out again.

Johnnie sat in the classroom, but his mind was smoldering with heated thoughts. *Money, money, money. I have to compete with money— the thing that I have the least!* he thought every time Percival came to his mind. He stared down into the book, and he moved his lips with what he was saying to Percival.

The professor looked at Johnnie several times, and he was sure that Johnnie was not out of his head, but he wasn't sure that Johnnie wasn't going. He was concerned over this and thought it might be due to some bumps on Johnnie's head from playing football.

At the first opportunity, Johnnie had a talk with Pappy—about women.

"Well," said Pappy, "in my life, there were always two kinds of women. The kind you want to marry and the other kind. The kind you want to marry are usually the kind who marry the first one who comes along. The other kind would shilly-shally around for the best they could get, never being satisfied—not even with whom they did get married. This kind, like good wine, could be taken in with pleasure, anytime, whether they are married or not."

"I don't follow you," Johnnie said.

"Well, ahem." He cleared his hoarse throat. "One girl will lead with her heart, and the other will control her heart with her mind. What kind of girl Mary is, you will have to decide for yourself. If she likes you and your company, then you're in—if she's the kind. If she's the other kind, she will make a comparison with everyone available, and if you want her, you will have to eclipse all the others. Then you are in, but the comparison with others does not cease—it goes on forever, in which case you will never have any peace or contentment, and your dream of happiness will merely be an illusion."

"I'll sleep on it tonight," he said, taking his books and going off to class with his roommate.

In the evening, he drove Christine home, and they spent all evening playing cards with Mr. and Mrs. Masterson.

Mary was quite determined to keep her word of honor. She remained in her room the entire evening and tried to study to have her mind occupied.

Johnnie could not concentrate on the game since his mind was on Mary until Mrs. Masterson mentioned that Mary was confined to her bed. When he went with Christine to see Mary, he found that they were locked out.

"She probably decided to sleep and does not wish to be disturbed," Mrs. Masterson explained.

Saturday night, Johnnie came again, but so did Percival. Although Johnnie was there first, he did not get to see Mary until sometime after Percival arrived. He was studying Percival, and he was beginning to formulate some facts about him that would make it easier to compete with him.

Percival declined Johnnie's greeting, turning his eyes away from him as he passed by. He had been extremely courteous to Christine since she informed him about Johnnie. He placed his chair in his regular listening position by the piano and waited for Mary.

Mary came, and she did not answer Johnnie's greeting. She did not even look at him, but her makeup showed that he was on her mind. She went directly to the piano, and with a smile to Percival, she proceeded with her music, to Percival's delight.

"What I could do to him if he were not on the college staff," Johnnie moaned in a whisper to Christine while he stared at Percival.

"Come," said Christine, taking his arm, "before you lose control of yourself."

They left for a movie, and soon, a taxi drove up to take the Mastersons out, leaving Percival and Mary in complete privacy. Percival, at once, asked her to stop the music.

"I'm so glad you didn't speak to him," he said.

"Oh, Percival," she said. "You are the one who was in my heart all the time."

"I'm so glad," said Percival with an intractable grin.

"Percival," she said, sitting down into one corner of the sofa while he followed into the other corner, "if we were married, I wouldn't have to go to school, and I could practice on the piano all day long."

Percival was abased into humility. His collar seemed to tighten all of a sudden. Cold perspiration began to appear on his forehead, while a sickening sensation in his abdomen drained the blood from his face. With a shaking hand, he reached for his handkerchief and nervously patted his entire face.

"We can get married right away, Percival. Would next week be too soon?" She talked with a fear of his rebuttal.

"I'll have no such thing," he said. "Not until you have graduated. Think of what people would say if I married a schoolgirl." He seemed to have frightened himself with this thought.

"But, Percival." She started out with intentions to express her reasons—her side of the question—but she lost her point when she realized herself as a schoolgirl and him as an orchestra conductor. He had actually put the thought in her mind.

"Oh, Percival." Her voice trailed off as she looked blankly into space.

"This has been a shock to me. I will need some rest this evening," he said, and that was the end of his visit.

Mary felt sorry for herself. For the entire evening, she sat about, thinking of Christine with Johnnie. When she tried to play the piano, the notes had no pleasant effect on her nerves, and she lost interest. She suddenly realized that she was biting off her fingernails. She had them tinted a delicate pink with white edges to make them appear more attractive. How attractive they would have been if Johnnie would only have watched her playing the piano! She was thinking of how Johnnie begged her to marry him and how Percival shied away. The more she remembered Johnnie's kisses, the more disquieting it became to her nervous system. She retired to bed with her sorrows, long before Johnnie returned with Christine.

Johnnie was becoming concerned over Mary's detachment from him. Every day he had seen less and less of Mary, and now she seemed to be out of his life altogether. The less he saw of her, the more his mind pondered over the situation. His thoughts were confusingly tangled with Addie's, with Pappy's, and with the behavior of Mary. He was too young to be a philosopher and a psychologist to handle the problems with Mary to a desirable conclusion.

Sunday was the day of the football game. His years of study and planning football strategy during his spare time in the army had come to the notice of the coach, and Johnnie was named the captain of the football team. Sunday noon, he was having dinner with Addie as he poured out his troubles with Mary.

"Are you tooting your horn loud enough?" she asked him.

"Even if I did, she wouldn't listen," he said.

He helped Addie, with her home-baked cakes, into the car and drove her to Pappy. The boys had special front-row seats reserved for Addie and Pappy. They declined the offer of a piece of cake, saying they would make it a celebration after the game.

At the game, Addie and Pappy cheered and yelled themselves hoarse while Johnnie maneuvered his team to a victory by a margin of a few points. After the game, he walked with helmet in hand when he met Christine.

"Where's Mary?" he asked.

"I don't know," said Christine, looking forward to a celebration with Johnnie.

The whole group of Christine, Addie, Pappy, and the boys walked a short distance when they came upon the Mastersons. Johnnie left the group behind as he hurried to meet them.

"That was a mighty fine game, Johnnie!" Mr. Masterson greeted him with a pat on Johnnie's bulging shoulder pads.

"Where's Mary?" Johnnie asked in excitement.

"Why, I thought she was here at the game," Mrs. Masterson explained.

"Excuse me. I have to go somewhere," said Johnnie.

With a wave of his helmet to the group, Johnnie began running to his car.

"See you at the house!" he yelled to his fellow roomers.

He raced his car along the street with Mary on his mind, and this time, he did not sound his horn on arrival. He burst into the house without sounding the door chimes, and he found Mary looking through some music sheets.

"We won! It was a tough team, and we won! And, Mary, they made me the team captain!" he cried out excitedly at the top of his voice.

"Johnnie! How dare you come into this house with those shoes! You're going to scratch the floor and dirty the rugs! I thought you wanted to be a gentleman," she struck out at him with her tongue-lashing.

"Oh, I'm sorry," he moaned, taking off his shoes before he took another step.

"You're always sorry after the damage is done," she said, being careful to keep her distance from him, sensing that he would kiss her from the joy of winning the game. "Don't you come near me with those dirty clothes."

"I would just like to tell you all about the game. It was one of the greatest games so far," he said, standing in his stocking feet, holding his football shoes in one hand.

"Well, I'm not interested, so you may leave promptly," she advised, turning away.

"But, Mary," he complained, advancing toward her.

Without further thought, Mary was running to her bedroom, where she quickly slammed the door, locking it excitedly.

Before Johnnie knew what she was up to, Mary was almost at the door to her bedroom. He ran too, but his late start prevented him from reaching the door before she turned the tumbler of the lock.

"Mary! Listen to me!" he shouted to send his voice through the closed door while his hand turned the doorknob impatiently.

"Mary! Do you hear me?" he shouted again, but she did not answer.

"Goodbye, Mary," he said, leaving.

He went to the front door, slammed it shut just loud enough for Mary to hear, and returned on tiptoes to Mary's bedroom door. He waited impatiently with his shoes still in his hand, but she did not open the door. She was probably looking through the window for him to return to his car, he thought, and with this, he left with a disheartened spirit. He closed the door quietly this time. When he reached his car, he threw his shoes to the floor, adjusted himself behind the steering wheel, and drove off, sounding his horn.

Why couldn't he ever think when he was with Mary? He felt that his visit had done more harm than good. Now he knew he should have cleaned up and changed his clothes before going to see Mary, but he wasn't thinking of his clothes, of the dirt, or of anything else. He was only thinking of Mary. He was following her blindly, with no thought of himself.

Mary was flattered as she stood by the bedroom door, listening to his shouting. Softly, she went to her bedroom window and was quite disturbed when she did not see him go to his car shortly after leaving her bedroom door and slamming the front door. For a while, she thought he would stay outside and wait for her to speak to him. At last, when she saw him return to his car, with the shoes still in his hand, and how he threw his shoes into the car, she smiled with a gleam in her eyes and a lightness in her head. She was impressed with the huge shoulders coming to a V shape at the hips, and the familiar colors of the college uniform erased all the thought of dirt upon them. She lay across the bed with her mind floating about in thoughts of Johnnie.

Johnnie had an exciting celebration with the boys at the rooming house. Instead of a cup of coffee and a piece of cake, they had a real feast. Some of the boys had prepared for this earlier in the day. They had a whole turkey broiled at the barbecue stand, and they also ordered everything that went with it. He enjoyed himself, although he was thinking mostly of Mary. He kept thinking that his joy would only be complete in the presence of Mary. At least if Christine or the Mastersons were there at the table with him, it would have made him that much happier.

In the evening, Johnnie was at Mary's home. Again, he had dinner, but this time, it was prepared almost entirely by Christine. He sat at the table with Christine, and Mary was seated directly across from him. Mary was dressed more neatly than ever, and her makeup showed careful consideration with a lot of time devoted to it. She was so alluring with her sweetness and her beauty that everyone couldn't help noticing him staring at her. When he talked about the different plays his team went through successfully to win the game, he looked at Mary, and it seemed that he was speaking to her. All the time, he kept wondering if she had told them about his visit after the game. Christine and Mrs. Masterson tried unsuccessfully to lead the conversation away from football, but Johnnie and Mr. Masterson held their ground.

Mary glanced at him a few times. Aside from that, her eyes remained fixed on her plate or some other object on the table, or she would look smilingly as she spoke to everyone but Johnnie. She laughed and giggled excessively but did not carry on any conversation with Johnnie—outside of answering a question of his that was directed to her. She quickly drifted away from a conversation with him to carry on with some other member of the table. She was impressively picturesque at the table with a behavior full of emotions.

Christine was highly commented, by Johnnie, on her knowledge of the culinary arts.

"I wonder if someone else could cook like this," he mentioned with a glance to Mary, who looked at him with enlightened eyes. She knew he was speaking of her.

While they were about to finish their dinner, Percival walked quietly into the kitchen. His face grew pale and stern as he stared at Mary, whereupon Mary slowly rose to her feet.

"Percival?" she questioned with a half-frightened voice.

"Good evening," Percival greeted immediately, retiring to the living room, with Mary hurrying after him.

Christine went after Mary just in case Mary could not handle Percival in this situation.

"Percival, we weren't expecting you till later in the evening," Mary tried explaining to him.

"I think I will go home. It won't be necessary to explain. My entire evening is ruined," he said, slowly retreating toward the door.

"Percival!" Christine called sternly, and she took him by the arm. "You can't leave—come and have dinner with us."

"Thank you," he said. "I'm not the least bit inclined to eat."

"Johnnie is having dinner with me." She explained Johnnie's presence in the house.

"Oh!" He was enlightened with understanding.

"Are you sure you wouldn't care to try my cooking?" she asked, releasing his arm.

He looked at Mary and then turned to Christine, saying, "No, thank you." He was afraid Mary would resent the acceptance of the invitation.

Mary looked at Christine with eyes of jealousy, which caused Christine to release Percival's arm.

"Anytime you're hungry, help yourself to the contents of the refrigerator," Christine mentioned cheerfully as she turned to the dining room.

When Percival left the dining room, with Mary and Christine following, Johnnie went through a spell of embarrassment when the Mastersons remained, quietly sensing the trouble with Percival. He didn't know what to say or how to start. The Mastersons seemed to be in the same predicament. Finally, Mr. Masterson began with the subject of business and how he was planning to start again with a small business.

Mrs. Masterson was taken aback with the incident that happened before her very eyes. She had a sickening feeling in her stomach. She wanted very much to leave the table, but she dared not to display her emotions to Johnnie. All the time, she thought Johnnie was courting Christine, but this incident, together with her sense of intuition, told her the purpose of Johnnie's presence in their home. She had welcomed him wholeheartedly into their home, and she had learned to love him with some wishful thinking of having him for her son-in-law. He had promoted a remarkable and highly desirable change in her husband. He had already restored her husband's ambitions, and also, he had restored her husband's confidence in himself . . . and now Percival reacted with a conduct totally incongruent to her happiness.

She tried vainly to hide her mental injury.

Christine returned to Johnnie's side. She was afraid that if Percival broke off with Mary, Mary might turn to Johnnie for consolation and thereafter be permanently infatuated with him. Christine felt that she belonged to Johnnie and that neither Mary nor any other girl should set her further away from his attentions. Christine pictured Johnnie falling in love with her—what else could it be with all that time and attention he was giving her?

Johnnie and Christine left for a movie, while the Mastersons took care of the dishes. The Mastersons didn't stay themselves after having the dishes done. They went visiting for the evening, leaving Mary with Percival.

Mary didn't know what else to do, so she spent the entire evening playing the piano, while Percival lolled in ecstatic imagination. Once, she paused, when she changed her music sheets, to speak to him.

"Do you think I will ever become a concert pianist?" she asked in a timid way.

"Oh, my dear!" he cried out excitedly. "But definitely!"

Maybe if he wasn't so sure, she could very easily return his ring and come running to Johnnie, but she loved her music, and she wanted to marry Percival because he seemed to be the key to her happiness since he was the orchestra conductor.

When Percival left about nine thirty that Sunday night, she began to feel lonely. She was beginning to think of how much more pleasure it would have been to ride in Johnnie's yellow convertible. She felt herself being drawn to Johnnie more so every day, but she could not wrest herself free of her ambitions in music. She could not associate with Johnnie because she was engaged to Percival, and she had declared upon her word or honor that she would not see Johnnie again. She sat in the living room, staring into space and nervously biting off the thick skin at the edges of her fingernails. Only until there was no more skin to bite on did she realize what she had done. She looked at her bitten fingernails and began to cry. She retired to bed, and she cried herself to sleep.

When Johnnie returned home with Christine, he said good night to her at the door. It was about midnight, and he said he wouldn't want to keep her up any later than it was.

"See you in the morning!" shouted Christine as Johnnie settled behind the steering wheel.

With a wave of his arm, it was the end of another day, but it was simply a matter of hours when Johnnie was back for breakfast with Christine and the Mastersons.

VIII

Forbidden

*M*ary intended to stay home again. When her mother woke her for breakfast, Mary sat up at the edge of her bed, and her mind was wandering about. She was nervously trying hard not to bite off more of her fingernails and the surrounding skin. Johnnie had her heart, and Percival had her mind, and she struggled within herself over the two lovers.

The table was set. Everybody was seated, waiting for Mary. Mrs. Masterson became restless, left the table, returning to Mary, and found her in this dazed, nervous, fingernail-biting condition.

"Mary," she said with great concern, "please lie down and rest a while longer."

Mary lay down, being covered and tucked in by her mother. She made no reply to her mother but kindly obeyed without a question.

"Mary isn't feeling well. She's going to remain in bed today," Mrs. Masterson explained at the table.

The breakfast was somewhat dull that morning. Everyone became curious about her illness. Mrs. Masterson was well aware of Mary's ailment, but she would not share the secret with anyone else. She might tell her husband, but it would turn out better if he did not know. She was constantly worried over a relapse after seeing him on the way to recovery. Mary would probably straighten everything out by herself. Soon, Johnnie and Christine left for school.

"What could be ailing Mary?" Mr. Masterson asked.

"We'll see when the doctor comes," Mrs. Masterson replied, shying away from any further discussion.

The doctor came later in the morning, giving Mary a complete physical examination.

"Give her plenty of fresh air, sunshine, exercise—and here's a prescription for some vitamin tablets, of which she is to take two with each meal," he said.

"Is that all, Doctor?" Mrs. Masterson asked in doubt.

"Keep her in bed for about a week, and I will be back next week," he said while he put his instruments back into his satchel.

"But I have to go to school," Mary complained.

"Mary," the doctor said, "in your condition, you would only be wasting your time at school."

The doctor left, and Mary cried into her pillow. She knew that she had to attend school and study her lessons regularly; otherwise, she would miss too many lectures, which would result in low grades. The most terrible thing she could do would be to get a low grade in music. She would never forgive herself, and Percival would forever be grinding the same old record of her low grade. She would never hear the end of it. Percival had almost all As in his college subjects, so Mary had to strive to accomplish the same.

Pity sank deeply into the heart of the mother. She had a feeling that she knew what was ailing Mary, but she considered it base to reveal Mary's troubles to the others. She knew that Mary was torn between two lovers, but she did not know how to remedy the situation without hurting Mary or one of her lovers. She knew of a psychiatrist in Kansas City who may throw some light on one of the lovers so that she could help Mary rid herself of the other.

"Don't cry, Mary," she said. "Dress yourself, and I will have something ready for you at the kitchen table. Then we'll go to visit a specialist in Kansas City."

"But I just had a doctor," Mary complained in suspicion.

"This one might send you to school much sooner," she said encouragingly.

"All right, Mother. I'll dress in a few minutes," said Mary, getting out of bed.

Mary had some breakfast food, her mother had a sandwich, and they left upon the arrival of a taxi.

Mr. Masterson, under the strain of trouble, went out on a binge. He was rather disappointed when Mary didn't drop Percival and take up with Johnnie from the first night she had spent with Johnnie. The developments had been gradually putting him under a nervous tension until finally, he sought recourse from the tension by resorting to drinking. The tension had reached its peak when he realized how much Mary was attached to Percival.

He was gone before the doctor arrived, and the doctor's diagnosis would have no effect on him anyhow—if he stayed.

Since Johnnie came into his life, he could not see what interested Mary in Percival. He could very easily picture himself in a business partnership with Johnnie, but he could not see himself together with Percival under any circumstances. He had no special interest in music; therefore, he could not find any point of conversation with Percival, and Percival didn't know the least thing about business. Percival plainly and witlessly stated that he did not know anything about business, that he was not interested, and that he was concerned only with musical compositions. This was what antagonized Mr. Masterson in a helpless way, but there was nothing he could do if his daughter wanted to marry Percival. He suffered frustrations from this fact, and they added on to his other frustrations from his business enterprise. He was going on his binges more often until Johnnie came, and now he was going back again with more fervor than before—starting early in the morning.

When Mary arrived at the psychiatrist's office with her mother, she became frightened, and she had come to the conclusion that her mother thought she was losing her mind, that she was mentally ill.

"Mother," said Mary hoarsely, "you told me you were going to take me to a specialist."

"This is a specialist," she said. "You have nothing to be afraid of. I know a number of girls that he has helped in a relatively short time."

Mary's thoughts didn't seem to give her any clear point for argument, and she went into the office like a harmless lamb guided by the shepherd. She watched her mother go into the laboratory first, and when her mother came out, the psychiatrist beckoned her to come in. He took her quietly by the hand, and Mary reluctantly submitted to his will.

"Please sit down on this table." He motioned to the treatment table.

Mary looked at him through suspicion; then she looked at the nurse.

"All right," she said in doubt.

"Now if you will tell us all your troubles with Percival and Johnnie, it will be much easier for us to help you."

Mary stared at him when he mentioned Percival and Johnnie. She knew that her mother had told the psychiatrist all about her. In a flash, she imagined that her mother told everyone else—her friends, her neighbors, Percival, and Johnnie—that she was mentally ill, that she was losing her mind. She slowly descended from the table, staring at the psychiatrist. She backed to the door and opened it, still facing him, to walk out backward.

"Don't be afraid. I'm not going to hurt you," he said.

"Don't be afraid, Mary," the nurse encouraged. "The doctor will put you to sleep, and then he will talk to your subconscious mind. It's all so very simple."

Mary made no effort to reply, but she kept staring at him. Then she hurried to her mother, while the psychiatrist and the nurse calmly followed.

"I'm not mentally ill, Mother. I'm not! I'm not! I'm not! I'm not!" she cried.

"Mary, we're going to help you," the nurse encouraged.

"I need no help! I'll take my vitamin capsule, and I'll get my fresh air, exercise, and sunshine!" Mary cried, taking hold of her mother by the arm.

"They will help you return to school very soon," her mother mentioned with hope in her mind.

"I'm going back to school without their help." Mary spoke with determination.

"Perhaps some other time," the psychiatrist said to Mary's mother with a smile.

"Perhaps it would be better," her mother replied, taking Mary back home.

She was discouraged with Mary's behavior. She sat about the living room, trying to decide whether Mary should have Percival or Johnnie. If she would send Johnnie away, she would lose her husband, and if she would send Percival away, she would lose her daughter. The more she thought over it, the more pain she felt in her heart. With a downhearted feeling, she went to Mary in the kitchen.

"Mary," she said, "do you want to marry Percival?"

"Oh, but I do, Mother!" Mary cried out. "Don't you see I'm engaged to him?"

"What about Johnnie?" she asked, studying Mary's eyes for hidden answers.

"He doesn't interest me!" Mary snapped out with irritation.

"Oh, I just wondered," she said, turning away. "You're going to school tomorrow?"

"Mother, I must," Mary said with firm determination.

Mrs. Masterson was somehow relieved of her worries when she realized Mary had her mind set on Percival. She had no dislike for Percival. He looked like a fine, cultured, modest young man, and the fact that he was the college orchestra conductor appealed to her. Johnnie's appearance crept into her heart, and she loved him for the encouragement to her husband, but she liked Percival and his music too.

At four thirty, Percival arrived, and he was raving mad. It was most unusual for such a quiet, bashful individual to be angry, but Percival has reached this point.

"This is the third day you have missed school," he said. "How do you expect to go on from here?"

"I will be in school tomorrow, Percival," Mary replied meekly. "I just haven't been feeling well today."

"If this keeps up, you may have to withdraw from school with an 'incomplete' for the remainder of this semester," he warned.

"Why is it so all important that I go on with school?" she asked with irritation in her tone.

"Because I won't have you unless you graduate. Just think of my position," he said.

"But I don't see how your position makes it so all important that I graduate. Whether I graduate or not, it will still be me. If I drop out of school, you will always remember that I could have graduated if I wanted to," she explained.

"Yes, I will always remember that you could have and that you did not," he moaned. "I don't think you realize the social standards I adhere to."

Mrs. Masterson was in the dining room, listening to every word that went on between them.

Christine came in, but Johnnie did not when he saw Percival's car parked in front of the house. As she walked in, Percival's rage had vanished, and once more, he was the weak and retreating type. Christine sensed that something had been going on before she arrived. It appeared to her that her presence was not desired at the moment. She received a noticeably cool reception from them. Mary turned to her piano, and Percival took to his chair. Christine casually shook them off her mind and left them to find Mrs. Masterson in the kitchen.

Mrs. Masterson tried to be warm to Christine, but she was so confused with the complicated relationships of the family that she was not in a condition to have a cheerful disposition. It was kind enough of her sister, Christine, to take them into her home, and she was afraid that any action against Johnnie would reflect against Christine—which might return to them in the form of an eviction notice by Christine. So her thoughts and worries swirled around and around in her head with no visible means of a desirable solution. She was beginning to think she needed psychiatric treatment more than Mary did.

No sooner had the door chimes resounded in the dining room than the front door swung open and a taxi driver struggled with the weight of Mr. Masterson as he half-dragged the unconscious figure to the sofa. The music stopped, and Percival stared wild-eyed at what looked like a corpse but what smelled like a brewery. Mary was shocked with the thought of the effect this incident would have on Percival. Mrs. Masterson and Christine came hurrying.

We Spend Our Lives

"Does he belong here?" the taxi driver asked, looking about at the assembly around the sofa.

"Yes, how did you know?" Mrs. Masterson asked through a mask of humiliation and fear.

"I looked in his wallet," the taxi driver said.

"You looked in his wallet?" she asked.

"Don't worry, ma'am," he said. "All he had in his wallet was his name and address . . . And it's a good thing he had that because if he didn't, I'd have to take him to the police station. Here's the bill, ma'am." He handed her the taxi bill.

Mrs. Masterson paid the bill, and the taxi driver left without another word. She looked sorrowfully at her husband and then turned to the others. She couldn't see how Percival would stay if she didn't get her husband out of the living room and to bed. When her eyes met Percival's white face, she knew that Percival would be leaving almost any minute now.

"I'm so sorry," said Percival. "I just remembered that today is Monday, and on Monday, I have a meeting to attend. I hope you will excuse me."

Mrs. Masterson let out a sigh of fatigue. She was tired with all her troubles, which seemed without end. Lately, all her troubles took effect on other things, which turned into troubles, somewhat like a chain reaction. The burden of the troubles was growing strangely unbearable, and she had a feeling that she would collapse under the strain. She nodded for Mary to take Percival to the door.

Mary was stupefied with the shock of seeing her father brought home in such a condition in the presence of Percival. She wondered why the taxi driver did not bring her father in through the back door; then he could have taken him directly to bed instead of spreading his unconscious form on the sofa in such a revolting sight when Percival was present.

Christine seemed to be glad, but at the same time, she was careful not to express her happiness with her facial features. She would not have them know of the happiness she carried inside of her. As far as she was concerned, they only crowded in on her happiness—after they had moved in to live with her, when Mary took Percival away from her—and now it made her happy to see them carry on in misery. She knew that when Mary's brother, George, would come home, there would be more trouble because George would come home under the illusion that his father was a big businessman. She thought of how simple it would be if the Mastersons had never moved in with her, if they had some other place to go, but they had no other place to go. She felt sorry for her sister, for the failure of her brother-in-law's business, for her nephew being in the war, for her niece's loss of the opportunity for an education, so under the circumstances, she took them in. When Mary became interested in Percival, she treated their affair with understanding, locking her heartbreak secretly in her own mind.

"We better get him to bed," Christine advised.

"Yes, but how?" Mary asked.

Without any further discussion, they took hold of Mr. Masterson's unconscious form by the arms and half-dragged him to the bedroom, where they put him to bed.

The following morning, Johnnie appeared early as ever. He had breakfast with Christine and the Mastersons as usual, but Mary failed to come for breakfast. Without any mention of Mary, they managed to have a pleasant time at the table.

Mr. Masterson was still feeling good from the binge of the day before. The hangover didn't quite appear yet, or else he had a swig or two on a bottle hidden in Christine's room. He talked in a tone full of merriment. Nothing irritated him, and his trigger for laughter was set very lightly. He mentioned the places he went to, with the characteristic jokes of each place.

Mrs. Masterson intended to leave her husband to his sleep instead of waking him for breakfast. She was thinking of remaining in bed herself until after Johnnie would leave with Christine, but she did not want to upset the regular routine of breakfast. She thought her troubles would become more conspicuous if she and her husband were not at the breakfast table with Johnnie and Christine. She imagined that her troubles were more unbearable when others would see her in helplessness.

When Johnnie left with Christine, Mrs. Masterson went to see Mary. Her worries about Mary would give her no peace of mind. She worried about Mary's future because she wanted to see her daughter marry well, and if Mary would carry on with her ailment, it might destroy her happiness as well as Mary's.

"Are you going to school today?" she asked Mary.

"No, Mother. I don't think I ever will go to school," Mary replied in a lackadaisical feeling while she remained quietly in bed, with her mind being concerned with something she would not reveal—not even to her mother.

"What seems to be ailing you?" She pried into Mary's troubles with pity in her heart.

"Nothing, Mother," Mary replied innocently.

"Then why aren't you up already and away to school?"

"I just can't go to school," she said.

"Perhaps you would better transfer to another school."

"Oh no! I couldn't, Mother. Percival thinks it is an inviolable rule that I graduate from his alma mater," Mary explained with alarm.

"In that case, put your clothes on, and I will take you to school."

"But, Mother! You have to go to work soon," Mary protested, not knowing what her mother had in mind.

"The work can wait, if it will. I must take care of my darling daughter first," she said, feeling Mary's forehead for a fever as she sat on Mary's bed.

She realized that Mary was possessed with some kind of fear that was disturbing her mind. She thought that Johnnie had something to do with Mary's condition, yet she could not see how he could have produced in Mary the fear of school. She had something to eat again, although she was not hungry—it would enable Mary to eat with more appetite.

They took a taxi, and Mary found her mother present with her wherever she went. It became very embarrassing when her mother would speak to the professor in whispers and then seat herself by Mary. She felt that everyone was staring at her, thinking that she was unfit to look after herself.

They came upon Johnnie but declined to speak to him any more than they could get by with.

Johnnie could not understand what it was all about. Why should Mary's mother be constantly with her wherever she went? He thought that his visit in the evening to Mary's home would help him understand what was going on. First, Mary was getting more and more distant from him; now it would be impossible to associate with Mary because her mother was with her all the time. He asked Christine about it, and she said it was news to her. She thought Mary wouldn't be in school again since Mary didn't ride with them.

That evening, when Johnnie drove Christine home, he found that Mr. Masterson was out again, and when Christine was in the kitchen preparing something for dinner, Mrs. Masterson quietly came to him in the living room.

"Where's Mary?" he asked.

"Mary is resting in bed," she said.

"What seems to be the matter with her?" He could not hold back on his mind full of questions.

"That's what I would like to talk to you about." She lowered her voice just in case someone was listening.

"It's rather odd to see a student on the campus with her mother following everywhere," he mentioned.

"I'm doing whatever is possible to help her. She is not feeling well, and she can't afford to miss any more days from school."

"She missed two days for the church meeting in St. Louis, and now she has missed three more. That is going to affect her examinations," he warned.

"Yes. Not only that, but she may have to leave school, Johnnie," she said. "I would like to ask you not to see Mary anymore—not to come here."

"But I don't understand," he replied, being dismayed with the request.

"Johnnie," she said, "it's quite important to her recovery that you not see her anymore."

"But I'm in love with her, and that's why I'm here," he explained, and suddenly, he realized that Christine as his alibi would be useless since he had given himself away.

She had fought hard within herself these last few days in trying to decide whether she should save her daughter or whether she should save her husband. Now since Johnnie admitted that he loved Mary and that Christine was his excuse for being at the house—so as to be close to Mary—she was more sure of herself than ever that Johnnie was at the root of Mary's illness. She figured that by eliminating Johnnie, she would eliminate the source of Mary's illness.

"Johnnie," she said, "I have come to love you as I do my own son, but since you have come into Mary's life, she has not been herself. Her mind seems to be confused."

"I never imagined having a bad effect on Mary," he said. "I was hoping to have her as my wife."

"I know just how you feel about it, but she's engaged to marry Percival. I know it's only a childish crush on her music teacher. If you will keep from seeing her, it won't last long. She will come to her senses, and I will be very happy to see you with her."

"I'll do whatever I can." Johnnie submitted to her wishes downheartedly.

Much to her relief, she thought Johnnie very understanding. She found it so soothing to her heart and her nervous system that she could not carry on a conversation with him. Her mind was simmering with gratitude.

"Thank you so much, Johnnie," she said, leaving him and turning to help Christine in the kitchen.

Johnnie was so stunned with Mrs. Masterson's request that he forgot all about Christine. He felt as if he came to see Mary and was turned away—forbidden to see her ever again. It was such a heavy blow that he was not himself. He decided to leave immediately, and without seeing Christine again, he went to his car and drove off. He had to turn to someone for comfort, so his first thought was Addie.

IX

Alma Mater

When Christine came to the living room for Johnnie, he was not there, and to add to her disappointment, his car was gone. Immediately, she began to suspect that her sister had something to do with it—had everything to do with it. Her sister was with him in the living room, and he left without saying a word. The dinner was all set and waiting for him. In a huff, she hurried to her sister.

"What happened to Johnnie?" she asked, scrutinizing her sister's face.

"What are you talking about?" Mrs. Masterson inquired.

"He's not there!" Christine cried out indignantly.

Mrs. Masterson was alarmed with the effect her request had on Johnnie. She was thinking that she had lost his friendship. Since she recalled that he said he loved Mary, she was afraid she had hurt him severely. She hurried frantically to the living room, where she had left him, and found herself voiceless in her startled mind.

"Well?" Christine edged her for an explanation.

"I don't know what could have come over him. When I spoke to him, I was sure he would stay for dinner at least," she said, shunning the eyes of Christine and turning to the window. "His car is gone," she said.

"Yes, I have noticed that too," said Christine with an angry tone.

"He will probably be back. He couldn't have left without letting us know." Mrs. Masterson spoke with an air of innocence.

They waited until the dinner got cold, and then they put it away without having any part or it themselves. Christine was suspecting that her sister was responsible for Johnnie's unexplained departure, and her sister was suspecting that Christine blamed her for the act without saying it. Quietly, they languished about the house, thinking of what the other could be thinking. The atmosphere between them became cool and distant.

Mary's being bedridden made the house a lonely place to stay. The absence of her voice and her music added to the effect that everyone had a mourning spirit. Mr. Masterson went on another binge, and there was no telling how many more, like the one he'd had yesterday, would follow. Mrs. Masterson had some hope that Percival would add some lire to the house, but when Percival came, he had signs of depression from the day before—from the sight of Mr. Masterson brought home in a drunken stupor.

"Mary is resting in bed," Mrs. Masterson informed him.

"Thank you. I shall go to her at once," he said.

When he came to the bedroom door, it was closed. He looked with fear in his mind. He was overcome with timidity upon the thought of seeing her in bed.

"Who is it?" came Mary's voice through the door.

"Percival," he managed to reply with a stifled voice.

By this time, Mrs. Masterson came by the door and led the way. She set a chair for him at Mary's bedside and lingered in the room, straightening out the bed sheets and Mary's dresser.

"I'm so glad you came," said Mary.

"I deemed it essential that I be here until you are well again," he said with a sense of importance.

"Oh, Percival. It's so thoughtful of you," she said.

"It is most unusual to have you accompanying your daughter everywhere she goes," he said, expecting an explanation from Mrs. Masterson in return.

Mrs. Masterson felt embarrassed with the way he had said that. Her mind fumbled with excuses, and she paused, not being able to find a suitable excuse.

"I thought Mary would recover much sooner if I was with her," she said. "Percival, do you think it would be advisable to have Mary transfer to another college?" She watched his face turn white and his hands tremble.

"No! I should say not!" he snapped out. "It is highly consequential that she graduate from my alma mater."

Mrs. Masterson cast aside her work in the room. She felt the need to leave since she could stand the enervation no longer. Now she knew that she must leave her employment until Mary would get well. She could only see more dependence on her sister Christine, more strain on their relationship, since she and her family were already a burden to Christine.

"You have no desire of deserting my alma mater, have you, Mary?" Percival asked.

"You know I wouldn't, Percival," she said, remembering the last time she spoke to him about leaving school.

"I'm so glad," he said, suggestive of a swoon. "I shall keep you in an atmosphere of music," he said, rising from his chair and turning away.

While she listened to Percival's classical pieces on the piano, her mind dawdled in memories of Johnnie, with little knowing that she would not see him anymore. Percival played almost continuously for the entire evening.

X

Poetry Stuff

When Johnnie left Christine's house, he went directly to Addie. He poured out all his troubles while she listened.

"If you're not going to see her anymore, you'll have to get to her through the postman," she advised.

"Through the postman," he repeated. "But how? I can't tell her any more in a letter than I have already told her. Besides, she won't answer a letter."

"Well . . . We'll figure out some way," Addie said, feeling sorry for the situation he was in.

Johnnie received no satisfaction, as far as his troubles were concerned, from his visit to Addie. So under a nervous anxiety, he hurried to see Pappy. Pappy was having a nap on the couch when he walked in on him.

"Well, Johnnie," he said, getting up into a sitting position, "how are you getting along with your lady love?"

"Not getting to see her anymore, Pappy," he said, and he spilled all his troubles in love before him.

"Well"—Pappy scratched his head—"I don't rightfully claim to know women when it comes to troubles like that."

"You surprised me that time. You always told the boys you could read a woman like you could a book." Johnnie reminded him of their bull sessions they carried on in the rooming house.

"But Mary's different," he said dreamily.

"In what way?"

"In every which way you want to look." Pappy opened his eyes like an owl and looked at him strangely.

"You're getting me all mixed up," Johnnie complained.

"A rooster crows a lot, and they say he never lays an egg, but if it were not for his seed, would ever an egg be laid? In consideration of the amount of work a rooster does to plant his seed and the amount of work the chicken does to produce the egg, the credit for the egg rightfully belongs to the chicken." He studied Johnnie carefully.

"Do you mean that I should—"

"Oh no! God forbid if I ever give you that idea." Pappy acted startled.

"Then I don't know what you mean," he said.

"If you want corn, you must plant seeds of corn. If you want wheat, you must plant seeds of wheat. If you want oats, you must plant seeds of oats, and if you want Mary, you must plant in her heart the desire to have you." Pappy looked at him with the old eyes of a philosopher.

"That's what I would like to know—how to make her want me," he confessed.

"The rooster crows a lot, and the chicken lays the egg," he repeated as his eyes probed into Johnnie's facial emotions for the answer he was expecting.

"I'm all mixed up. How can I even see her with her mother standing by?"

"If you'll write to her—"

"If I write to her, her mother will intercept the letter, and then where am I?"

"I guess you're in a tough spot," Pappy admitted, reclining to his former position, which put an end to their conversation.

Johnnie returned Christine's car with a complete tune-up and a simonize. She was delighted with the new appearance of the car, and she said it ran like new.

Since he had not been going to Christine's house, he did not see much of Mary anywhere outside of the library. He sat there, looking across the library at Mary, and as she went to the book counter, his mind was fixed on the boy at the counter. It was a friend of his, a buddy from the football field. He saw his buddy go back among the stacks and come out again. He saw him hand a book to Mary, for which she signed, and his buddy stamped her card. That sight struck a spark among his troubles in his mind. He was sure that his buddy could help him, yet he knew not how at this time. He was thinking of having this fellow to serve as his postman, but he could not think of what to write or how to write it. There wasn't anything that he hadn't already told her. Like Pappy said, "you plant corn, you get corn," but he had to plant in her heart a desire to want him; that's also what Pappy said. It was on his mind the rest on the day.

After football practice, he went to his room. There, he was attracted by some scribbling that his roommate had done and unintentionally left on his desk. Johnnie immediately noticed it was some kind of poem. There were quite a number of sheets scribbled up with some kind of poem or other that did not make any sense to Johnnie. He went through the whole mess, and at the bottom, he found a poem that pleased him.

> I study, and I study,
> > and it makes me frown,
> More so than my buddy,
> > For I have no backgroun'.
>
> I envy my buddy.
> > He's never so busy,
> And he'll be somebody
> > 'Cause he takes it so easy.
>
> But I cannot study,
> > And it takes me so long,

Fore unlike my buddy,
    I take everything wrong.

That's why I study and study—
    Because I'm not like my buddy.

He read the poem, and then he read it again. From these simple little lines, he felt himself brought closer to his roommate than he ever thought he could be. These few lines brought him an understanding that warmed his heart with pity. The poor devil always studied and never learned much. The more he studied, the less he knew—because the more he had to remember, the more he forgot.

This incident struck another spark among his thoughts in his troubled mind, but he could not write poetry. He never tried. Then again, he thought of Christine. Of course, she would be glad to help him write poetry or anything else that would bring him to her. He rushed to her office, but it was locked, which told him that he was too late and that tomorrow was another day.

Mary was practically wasting her time at school. She was present in all her classes, with her mother accompanying, but she did not learn anything. All the lectures went in one ear and out the other without registering on her memory. She was mostly daydreaming about Johnnie until her mother would disturb the tranquility of her dreams. Mary's mother could have helped her if Mary was in a condition to be helped with her studies. She missed Johnnie and his fervent, forceful ways of making love to her. In his absence, her mind became more indulgent in memories of him.

The next morning, he greeted Christine as she came to her office. She was happy to see him and surprised with his interest in poetry. They sat by the desk as she looked through a book.

"Now here. You see?" she said. "You can easily write poetry. A poem is a verse that produces a deep emotional response, and a verse is an arrangement of thoughts according to some conventionalized rhythmic repetition. You could have the rhythm of ta-*tum*, the iamb, or the rhythm of *tum*-ta, the trochee, or *tum-tum*, the spondee, or ta-ta-*tum*, the anapest, or *tum*-ta-ta, the dactyl, or ta-*tum*-ta, the amphibrach, or *tum*-ta-tum, the amphimacer, or ta-ta, the pyrrhic."

"Gosh! I had no idea there was so much to it." He explained emphatically, "I would merely like to express my thoughts in a way more interesting than prose."

"That's fine," she said. "You can write free verse or polyrhythmic poetry. For instance, in your verse, you might have six feet of one accented syllable only, three trochees, two iambs, four anapests, four amphibians, one spondee, one foot of four syllables, three or five—or you can write unrhymed iambic pentameter."

She was eagerly trying to help him. She pointed to the rhythms and examples as she turned the pages of the book. If she had looked at his face, she would have noticed him losing interest in the subject from the beginning as she went along.

"I think I'll just write a letter," he said, getting up and ready to leave.

Immediately, she realized that for his first lesson, it was too much for him to digest. He had already lost interest in the subject, and she could not think of a way to revive his interest at the time.

"You can begin with the simplest and go on to the others whenever you like," she encouraged.

He stopped and smiled to her.

"I'll keep that in mind," he said, turning to leave again.

He had no class till eleven o'clock, so he wandered aimlessly about the campus. *I can't just write a letter*, he kept repeating to himself. That wouldn't arouse her desire to be with him. That would destroy his only opportunity if he did not strike the first note right. He had to write a verse—better yet, a poem. He had to write something that would produce a deep emotional response in her. He recalled the poem written by his roommate. He got such an impression from the poem that he had to read it again.

Returning to his room, he found the papers still on his roommate's desk, only they were neatly stacked into one corner. He took the papers and sat down on his bed. First of all, he read the poem; then he looked through all the scribbled papers. He noticed that his roommate had written several pieces about studying and many individual lines, but that one was the only poem that was complete. There were other incomplete poems too. He straightened out the papers and returned them as neatly stacked as he had found them. Then he reclined on the bed, looking at the ceiling while he had his hands under the back of his head.

As he was thinking about writing poetry, a ping in the radiator disturbed his thoughts, and they turned him to Mary. His thoughts trailed back over his experiences with Mary, to the first day he met her. He recalled how one minute, she was hot, and the next minute, she looked at her engagement ring and became cold. Soon, he imagined her as the heating system and himself as the janitor. In this frame of mind, he began to scribble. When Mary was cold, he would like to see where the janitor was, what the janitor was doing, and he guessed that the janitor was lackadaisical or might even be dead—meaning ineffective. Then he concluded that the janitor was on a bender— not giving Mary the attention that he should. Finally, he thought of himself as the janitor, with disgust.

> Piping's cold, piping's hot—
>> Not a janitor on the lot.
> "Oh, where can he be?"
>> Is what I'd like to see.
> He might still be in bed,
>> Or he might even be dead!
> But here is what I'm thinkin'!
>> He is on a bender drinkin'!
> Piping's cold, piping's hot—
>> What a janitor on the lot.

He read it over to himself. Coming to his senses, he realized that it was not exactly written for her to understand as he intended. He was about to throw it into the waste basket when he thought it would be better than nothing. He copied the poem on another sheet of blank paper and hurried to the library. At the library, he turned the poem over to his buddy from the football field who worked at the counter, with instructions to slip it into a book that Mary would ask for.

He still had a half hour of time before his first class. Could there be any better place to spend the time than to sit and watch Mary in the library? He seated himself a distance to the opposite end of the library and in such a position from where he could see Mary. He waited and watched under the pretense of studying a book before him and was rewarded as he was about to leave. Mary had called for a book, and when she was on her way back to her seat beside her mother, his buddy casually saluted him. Johnnie saluted back, but he had no more time to stay.

Mary sat down beside her mother. On looking through the book, she found the poem. She was amused upon reading it and displayed it to her mother. She thought someone had accidentally left it in the literature book, and since it had no name or the poet, she could not return it—so it was hers to keep. She put it in her portfolio with happy thoughts of having it in her possession to read again and to show to her friends.

Johnnie was back during lunch time, but his buddy only worked at the library from ten to twelve in the morning and from four to six in the afternoon. Johnnie was back about four o'clock, right after football practice, before he had his dinner. He settled down into the far corner of the library with the problem of writing another poem for Mary. He had not much time before his buddy would be leaving, so he wrote what came first to his mind.

> I set me down
>> To write a sonnet.
> I set my mind
>> To dwell upon it.
> I say, in vain,
>> I racked my brain;
> I shall not spend
>> No more time on it.
> I could not write
>> This thing, a sonnet.

He looked at it; then he read it and looked at it some more. It didn't look to him like a verse, and it had not the effect of a poem when he read it, but whatever it was, it was for Mary, and it was a message from him to her. He meant to write that he would like to do something for her, but in vain, he racked his brain and could not. He transcribed it on a scrap of paper, unlike the first poem, and decided to leave his name out—like he had on the first poem. He was afraid she might get suspicious if each poem was written neatly on the same kind of paper, and he wanted her to fall into the illusion that someone had accidentally left it in the book.

Mary called again for a literature book before she left the library at six o'clock. Since Christine was driving the car again, she and her mother accompanied Christine to and from school. She was thinking of doing her literature at home that evening, if she had the time.

As she sat in the center of her bed, leaning on her elbow, that evening, she looked through the literature book for some material to use in her class, and she found the little scrap of paper wedged in between the pages. Not only did she read it with interest, but also, she reread the first poem. She began wondering how it was that she happened to get the particular book with the poem in it. After she read them over again, it came to her that both were written by the same pen in the same handwriting. Being puzzled over her discovery, she tried to reason things out, but the more she reasoned, the more bewildered she became when her thoughts absorbed too many imaginations. She finally discounted the facts and decided it was a coincidence.

That evening, Johnnie thought he would spend some time in the library looking through various books of poems. The more serious the poetry he read was, the less he liked it. He couldn't see how Mary could be interested in serious poetry since it would not entertain her—at least, he thought it would not. As he began writing, his imagination looked upon the walls of the library as prison walls that imprisoned those who sought knowledge, those who had ambitions of getting up in the world. They were prison walls because they kept one from doing the things one would like to do at the time. They were prison walls because there, one had to serve his time to do the research work to accomplish something. The library was a prison because there were sent those who tried to accomplish something and were caught in the act. This, he gathered from the fact that the library was empty during the school holidays. He wrote as though he were speaking to the library.

> Every book is a teacher—
>   So thin, so thick.
> So dull as a preacher,
>   Of words won't stick.
> From catacombs come they,

Whose thoughts unfold,
Within these pages gray
To minds enrolled.
Twice bless'd are those
Of mind so dark and dreary,
Who slave or browse
Within these prison walls
of thee, library.

With this poem and getting samples of his other two, he went to see Pappy. As usual, Pappy was lying on the couch.

"How are you coming?" Pappy asked, raising his head without getting up.

"Well, I'm getting notes to her," Johnnie said.

Pappy watched him reading the contents of the papers in his hand and became curious enough to sit up.

"What have you got there?" he asked, reaching out.

"The notes," said Johnnie, handing them to him.

"Poems?" he questioned, and then he swung his head slowly from side to side. "Boy! You must have it bad when you get to writing her some poetry stuff."

"I thought it would be more interesting," said Johnnie.

Pappy looked at him and turned to the poems in silence. When he was through reading, he returned them to Johnnie with a smile.

"'Interesting'?" He looked at Johnnie for a pause. "Why, if you write that kind of stuff to her, she'll crumple to pieces—you'll drive her out of her mind."

"Don't worry," said Johnnie. "She would come back to her senses after getting married."

"I would have never thought you could write the stuff," Pappy said, lying down again on the couch.

"Neither did I," said Johnnie, leaving, and he was on his way to pay Addie a visit.

"The man had no trouble till he found himself a woman—a woman that belongs to another man," Pappy said, stopping Johnnie in his steps.

"Pappy," Johnnie said, going back to him, "let's keep in mind that she belongs to me—only that she considers herself bound in a sacred promise to him."

"I don't mean it the way you're thinking, Johnnie," he said, sitting up again. "First thing you know, you'll have me all wrong. If people like you, they will like your writing too. What I'm trying to say is why do you go deeper and deeper into darkness when there are so many pretty girls just hanging around your car?"

"Well, Pappy," he said, "I always figured that if you attract people with your money, they will come to you for it."

"Now, son"—Pappy called him "son" for the first time as though he were lecturing to his own boy—"you're getting some sense into your head. Why don't you settle this thing for once and have it over with? There are a lot of things which I don't understand, and there are a lot of things which I do understand but that I cannot accept. Why do you keep banging your head against the old apple tree? There are a lot of easier ways to bring the apples down. It's better to get hurt once than to keep going back for more and more. Don't you know it's there? Don't you know it hurts? Why don't you sign your name to those poems? Why don't you write her in plain English that you love her and that you want her for your wife?"

"Don't tell me you got married when leap year came around." He looked into Pappy's eyes with a smile.

"Course not—I was quite a devil when I was a young one. Got married when we went on a hayride."

"Well, Pappy," he said to him, "you had no choice. It was a case of 'or else.'"

"That's what you think—she probably had the same thing on her mind as I had. I used to give her the worst licking she ever got from anybody. Why, I used to beat her up so bad, my folks got into trouble with her folks . . . I never did like her. She used to tattle on me to my mother, to the teacher, and to the preacher. Then when I married her, it turned the stomachs of everybody in the village. Why, we were so happy after we got married, we could tell the rest of the world to go run its course without us."

"Sometimes I think I should do the same," Johnnie said in deep thought.

"It takes a good man to make up a woman's mind. Otherwise, she'll be changing it and changing it and changing it. If you don't treat her like a man would, you'll find yourself sitting on your tail, like a bear in a zoo, waiting for her to throw you an offering." Pappy was raving and his face turning red from anger.

"I'll keep it in mind," said Johnnie, getting ready to leave.

"Love is a funny thing—deal as you find it necessary, but never lose sight of your measure," Pappy warned.

"You're quite a philosopher, Pappy."

"You'll get as much for it as you desire, providing you don't sell for less."

"Pappy, I admire you," Johnnie remarked with a grin at getting him started on all this.

"I admire you too! We're going to be great friends as long as we admire each other." Pappy laughed. "You see what I mean? You admire Mary, and Mary admires Percival. All I can say is take the girl that follows you. You'll find more happiness that way, and if you're so daffy about Mary, then force the issue. Make up her mind, either yes or no, and be done with it. If you want her bad enough, then take her—and pay no attention to what she or Percival has to say about it!"

"Think I'll take a ride over to Addie. Thanks for the advice, Pappy," he said, turning to leave.

"Advice from a friend doesn't cost a thing, and sometimes I think it's worth just as much—in other words, use your own head." Pappy laughed and leaned over to his lying position. "When you got time to lie around like this, you got plenty of time to philosophize," he said.

"Like you say, the head on my shoulders should be turned by me." Johnnie laughed back.

"I'm afraid you won't be able to say that if you keep on writing poetry stuff!" he shouted after Johnnie, but Johnnie was already gone.

When he arrived at Addie's house, she was washing dishes, and she set them aside, but on his insistence, when he took a towel and began wiping, she resumed her washing. They talked while they worked, and they stopped when they had something important to say.

"How are you getting along with Mary?" She started out on feeling out his troubles.

"Addie," he said, "I'm terribly disappointed with myself. I can't even see her anymore."

"That's bad," she said. "Are you honking your horn like I told you to?"

"I don't even use the car anymore, except when I come to see you."

"Oh, I see," she said in a low voice. "Listen—my mother always said a woman's attitude is a reflection of a man's attention."

"Would you say that in my case?" He smiled.

"No, I wouldn't. Come to think of it, she's a queer one. Maybe she's in love with you. My mother always told me, 'Run from your lover, but be sure he's following. Then when he catches you, you know you've got him.'"

"If she is in love with me, then why won't she have anything to do with me?"

"It might be a mystery that she herself cannot explain."

"Do you think she would make a good wife?" he asked.

"Well," she said before a pause, "there are two kinds of wives— one that looks up to her husband as the object of her happiness and the other who looks down upon her husband as the subject of her happiness—and God help the subject because nobody else could! He needs somebody to tell him what to do and when to do it and what not to do and when not to do it. Some lovers are like pieces of furniture— they are convenient but not indispensable. They don't move unless you move them." She looked at him from an angle. "You don't look to me like a piece of furniture," she said with a grin.

"I'm all so confused," he moaned. "Pappy said I had no trouble till I found myself a woman—a woman that belongs to someone else."

"Johnnie, pay no attention to that Percival fellow," she said. "Just apply some *heat*, and you'll have yourself a girl—Mary or any other."

"Some heat?" he asked in bewilderment.

"Girls like to be 'helped, encouraged, amused, and thrilled,' and if you can think of anything else, then add that on too."

"She has a heart of stone that no heat or flame can change for me," he moaned.

"You've got to get to her somehow. If you're capable of applying the *heat*, then she wouldn't be interested in another man regardless of his social position or the number of figures in his bank book."

"I don't know how else I can get to her except by writing notes." His face was expressionless, and his mind was blank.

When they had the dishes put away, they retired to the living room. Addie said she had the habit of putting the dishes away after each meal without washing them. Then when they stacked up high enough, she started to wash them.

"Just look at my hands," she said, showing him the enlarged knuckles of her fingers. "And my muscles just ache and ache every time we're going to have rain or a change in the weather."

"As I was saying, I'm writing notes to her," he reminded Addie, taking her mind off her old age.

"Would you tell me about them?" she asked excitedly.

"You may read them, if you think you'll get any pleasure out of them," he said, taking the poems out of his pocket and pausing for her answer.

"Can't you see I'm all a-twitter?" she cried out.

She took the poems and read them twice over. Then she looked at him with surprise.

"That's very nice," she said. "I'm proud of you."

"I thought it would be more interesting than writing a letter." He sought to excuse himself.

"Mary's going to like that," she said. "Let me see some more when you get to write it."

It was getting close to eleven when he left Addie's house. His visit to Addie was more comforting than his talk with Pappy. He was beginning to think that Pappy was edging him on to violate her maiden wreath and to trust that she would be happy after they were married. Addie was helping him in a different way. She was helping him to win Mary through courtship first before marrying. He intended to ask Addie about the way Pappy had gotten married, but it slipped his mind. The more he thought about it, the more apparent it seemed to him that Pappy was suggestive on the act itself. After all, it was the way he got married, and it was the only way he knew how, but since Mary was a prominent member in church activities, he realized that it would have been a darker sin than he could bear.

XI

Hot Stuff

$\mathcal{A}$s he neared the campus, he came upon the neighboring church, and the lights were still illuminating the translucent basement windows. Without giving it a thought, he stopped his car at the church and went to see the pastor. Being reminded of the fact that Mary was an active church member prompted him into this action.

He went down into the basement and found it to be a large hall where a church bazaar had taken place. It was a successful endeavor to raise money, and it was a complete sellout. The pastor, with the help of some men and women, was cleaning up the place. Johnnie asked one of the men, and the man pointed out the pastor.

"Yes, I'm the pastor," he said in a kind voice. "May I help you?"

He was an old gentleman with all his hair gone—except what was left around his ears and the back of his neck. His face was always uplifted with a continuous smile. Whenever he talked, he would hold his hands clasped or locked over his protruding abdomen.

"I have come to you with my troubles," said Johnnie quietly.

"Come with me, and I will listen to your troubles," said the pastor.

He led Johnnie to the church above the basement hall. There, with a beckoning gesture, he pointed out one of the pews.

"Sit down, and tell me about your troubles," he said, taking the pew ahead so that he could sit sideways and look back at Johnnie or turn his face to one side and listen with one ear.

"Well," said Johnnie, swallowing, "it's about a girl, and her name is Mary."

"That is nothing unusual—every Adam has his Eve," the pastor commented.

"But I happen to be in love with a girl who belongs to another man," explained Johnnie.

"That's bad," he said. "Look for some good in everything bad—it must be there."

"I was going to ask you for advice," said Johnnie.

"Out of the bad will come something good," he said.

"I love her, and I must have her," said Johnnie desperately.

"She belongs to another man?"

"She's engaged," replied Johnnie in a voice tinted with despondency.

"You must learn to share the bad things with the good things in your life. You say you're in love with her—that is good. You say she is engaged—that is bad. If she loves her fiancé, then it is good, and your love for her is bad."

"But I'm sure I love her more than he does," Johnnie protested.

"Would you say that she loves you more than she loves him?" The pastor studied Johnnie's face with every question he asked. His smile never faded from his lips.

"I don't know," confessed Johnnie.

"It is more blessed to give than to receive because it is more gratifying to receive than to give . . . In your case, since you love her so much, give her all the attention you could possibly find the time for and expect nothing in return. If you proceed in this way until she marries the other man, you will at least have the consoling thought that she does not love you and that you would be better off without having her as your wife."

"But how can I give her any attention when I can't even come close to her? She asked me not to see her. Her mother asked me not to see her, and her mother is with her all the time," explained Johnnie.

"Well"—the pastor scratched his head—"if I turned off these lights in this church now, what would happen?"

"Nothing would happen." Johnnie smiled. "It would only be dark."

"Ah! That is right," he said. "Darkness is the absence of light. Ignorance is a lack of light in the sphere of the mind. When the time comes, you will find your own light, but until then, you shall be groping around in darkness. When there will be a light, you will come to the light like a moth."

"You have made me a much happier man than I have been before I came to see you," commented Johnnie.

"Unhappy is the man who does not see his own faults to correct," he said. "As I have always said to the members of my church, plant your seed in sod and hope to God."

"Do you mean I should force her to marry me with my seed?" asked Johnnie. He had a heavy blush on his face. It wouldn't have been half that bad if he were not speaking to a man in holy orders.

"Lord forgive me if I gave you the slightest understanding in that direction," he said. "No, Johnnie. Give her all the attention you are capable of and pray that she will respond."

"I'm sorry for misunderstanding," said Johnnie in embarrassment.

"I am glad that you asked. That is the only way we can come to an understanding. Do you happen to be one of our members?"

"No. I'm sorry to disappoint you," said Johnnie.

"And what church do you belong to, may I ask?"

"Not any. You see, Mother and Dad never belonged to any church," Johnnie explained.

"Good heavens above!" The pastor clasped his hands, looking upward to the heavens. Then he turned to Johnnie with an absence of his smile and in grave seriousness. "Johnnie," he said, taking hold of his hand and squeezing it lightly, "you must come Sunday and be baptized."

"I won't be coming for some time. You see, Mary is an active member, and I hope to become a member of her church, and if she won't have me, then I will join the church of whichever girl will have me."

"But," the pastor warned, "if you were to join her ranks now, I'm sure the good Lord would be on your side. Come to think of it, that is just what might be keeping her away from you."

"I was thinking along those lines, and I just happened to drop in to have a word with you. I saw your light on while I was passing by," said Johnnie.

"And what church does she attend?"

"That, I don't know, but I would be glad to let you know when I find out."

"In any case, I will be very glad to take you to any church of which she may be a member." His smile took its place back again on his face.

They were leaving the church when he rested his hand on Johnnie's shoulder. Out of their conversation, a question popped into Johnnie's mind, and he turned to the pastor.

"What kind of letters do you think I should write to her?" asked Johnnie earnestly.

"Write them close to the Bible," he said. "It would make me very happy to present you with a Bible."

"Thank you." Johnnie reached into his side pocket. "I have a pocket size," he said, showing it to him in the handkerchief in which he had it wrapped.

The pastor was so astonished that he was at a loss of what to say. For a split second, his eyes popped wide open, and his smile disappeared when his mouth dropped open. His smile returned, and he beamed with admiration.

"I hope to see you Sunday, Johnnie," he said as they parted.

Johnnie burst in on Pappy, who happened to be sleeping on the couch, covered only with a thin blanket. It was about midnight, and Pappy would be getting up at one o'clock in the morning to look after the fire in the boiler, so he couldn't keep himself from waking Pappy.

"Don't go poking and fussing with me. I heard you coming. Don't you ever sleep?" complained Pappy.

Johnnie could have sworn by the Bible that Pappy was snoring when he came in—that was why he was so irritated when Johnnie woke him from his sleep.

"Just one little request, Pappy," he begged in a half whisper. "Tell me something close to the Bible."

"What could be closer to the Bible than the devil himself? Why, he roams around from page to page between the covers. The whole Bible is just a struggle between the good and the evil."

"Thanks, Pappy. You never helped me more," said Johnnie, turning away from him.

He knew that Pappy was shaken out of his sleep and therefore irritated, so he troubled him no longer. This spark had started a new series of thoughts in his mind. He was getting ideas about what he should write to Mary. That was all he wanted from Pappy.

Pappy was shocked out of his sleep with Johnnie's reply. He raised his head up and was about to shout after Johnnie when he realized he might awaken the other students. He sat up, trying to figure out whether Johnnie's reply was a comment or a bit of irony. Soon, he went to look after the boiler and then went to bed.

Johnnie lay in bed, thinking about Mary and her mother, about Addie, about the pastor, and about Pappy. As he was trying to piece the situation together, his thoughts turned to the Bible and what Pappy had just told him. He was sorry he had not thought of it before—to write something to Mary in a spiritual clime. He was sorry he had not thought of Mary as a religious girl. He belonged to no church, so it was very difficult for him to see these facts until they were pointed out by the pastor. In this sorrowful frame of mind, he fell asleep.

Early the next morning, he was in the library. It opened at seven thirty, and he was there. He sat in one corner of the library, at a table, and had the Holy Bible, *Dictionary of The Bible*, *The Holy Scriptures*, *A Commentary on the Bible*, *Encyclopedia of Bible Life*, and *The Book of Saints*. All these lay before him while he searched in vain for a theme to his poem for Mary. As the time went on, he thought of Pappy's words and of the devil himself. With the thought of Mary and the devil in mind, he wrote,

> Go away! Young devil.
> Go away! Old devil.
> Go away! All devils!
> For me to keep from evil.

He read his poem, and it had not enough emotion in it to please him, but it was difficult for him to write upon the suggestions of the pastor since he was not associated with any church. Regardless of his own opinions, he passed this on to his buddy in transition to Mary, and he felt that it was on the side of the Bible and against the devil, as Pappy said it should be. It was, to him, something like a prayer. He remained in the library, struggling in research for something new to write, and he was also waiting to see the effect his poem would have on Mary.

When Mary got the book with the poem in it, she was delighted on finding the poem. She became so happy on adding another to her mounting collection that she eagerly displayed it to her mother. Her mother was highly pleased on reading it, but she thought nothing more of it. She had no idea where Mary was getting the poems, and she never thought of asking since they seemed to have no motives other than to fulfill an assignment in the literature class. Mary read it over and over until she had it memorized and dramatized in her mind. The poem had such an effect on her that it crept into her plans for the Sunday school lecture. Already, she visualized how she would read it to her group of youngsters in Sunday school.

Seeing the pleasing effect his poem had on Mary, Johnnie was greatly encouraged. When he left for his class, all his thoughts were centered on the devil and the Bible. He would associate his mind with the devil if that would bring him closer to her. A confusing quantity of themes and ideas were coming to his mind, but he could not do anything more at the time than to hurry to class. In the class, the emotions in him were so great that he could not keep from writing. While he was writing his poem for Mary, his imagination carried him so far that his mind was not in the classroom at all. He had not the slightest thought of what was going on around him.

It was the rhetoric class, and the professor was lecturing from a book. She noticed Johnnie was not paying any attention to her lecture and that his thoughts were far away. She worked her way around to the back of the room to come upon Johnnie's back, from where she looked over his shoulder. With a glance, she realized he was writing poetry, and after reading his unfinished poem, she withdrew to the rear and back around to her desk, carefully trying not to disturb him.

He had finished the entire poem during this class time. At the end of the class, the professor called to him as he was on his way out, and Johnnie heard it, but he had the feeling that he knew why she was calling him. He couldn't let her read the poem simply because he had written it for Mary. At least Mary had to be the first one to read it. Besides, the professor might make it embarrassing for him by mentioning his poetry writing to the other members of the class. Of course, she, the professor, would be more understanding, but what would these young fools of his class think? What would they do? What would they know about love and letters of love?

Under the pretense of not hearing the professor calling to him, he left the classroom and went directly to the library. He had to read it over again, several times, in peace. He sat down at the library table in his usual corner, and taking the poem out of his book, he read it.

> Oh, Satan, he whispers,
>   He coaches, he brags.
> He sends me into shivers
>   Whenever he brags.
>
> Oh, Satan, he's black;
>   He's burnt to a cinder.
> At me, he takes a whack—
>   My work, he'll never hinder.
>
> Oh, Satan! He's got horns!
>   He's got a tail!
> He's worse than thorns—
>   For those who fail.
>
> Oh, Satan, a pitchfork, he's got;
>   He jabs you and jabs you well!
> All those who fall away from God,
>   He jabs you and jabs you down to Hell.

She's going to like this one. He came to this conclusion from the effect he had witnessed of his previous poem. He left the library for lunch, but he was back about three o'clock while on his way to the football field. He found his buddy studying in the library and gave him the poem to turn over to Mary in another book. On Fridays, they would practice football till it was too dark to see. He regretted that he would not be there when Mary would find a poem again. He was going to hold it off for another day, but that would not come till Monday, and he was itching to pass it on to her. One of these days, he would be signing his name to them, and she might write back a note to him. She could not be able to turn him down after taking his poetry to heart.

Early Saturday morning, he went to see Addie, and he showed his latest poems to her. He watched her as she read the poems.

"That's nice," she commented. "But why do you have to write about hot and cold pipes and sonnets and libraries and devils and Satan? Why don't you give her some sugar and spice? That's it—give her some *heat!* Warm up her heart for yourself. If I were Mary, I would appreciate getting these, but I would always be hoping you would write something about me, about you, about the both of us together. You want to write some hot stuff—straight from your heart."

She put the emphasis on "together" as if she were angry at Johnnie, but it was because she felt every word she said. She had gone through this feeling a hundred times, and she wanted so badly to teach him how to get his girl. She felt sorry for him. This was his first love. This was the only girl he ever had. He was deep in Addie's heart, and she felt everything that he felt—like a mother did.

Johnnie was becoming more confused by the day. Pappy was giving him ideas about forcing Mary into marriage—"Be a man!" he said. The pastor was giving him ideas about writing something that the pastor himself would like to read—"Write something close to the Bible," he said. Addie was giving him ideas about writing something she would like to have received herself, as a sweetheart—"You want to write some hot stuff," she said, "straight from your heart." How could he ever take the advice of any one of them verbatim when not a one of them ever saw Mary? He looked strangely at Addie and said to his heart, "One woman should know best what another woman needs."

He helped Addie with the heavy work about the house, and after having lunch with her, he took her with a cake back to Pappy. Saturday afternoon was football practice again, and Saturday night, he went to see a stage play with Christine.

He hadn't spent much time with Christine this past week. He paid her a visit two or three times a day for short periods. Sometimes she would help him with some difficulties in his studies. Sometimes he would just drop in to hear about Mary. Christine had invited him to dinner many times.

Apparently, she was not aware as to what was keeping him away because his excuses were so smooth and satisfying. He would meet her downtown, have dinner, and then go to see the stage play.

He enjoyed himself and entertained Christine without showing any signs of his love for Mary. He was very careful all evening not to let her know about his poetry writing. If he told her about it, she would not stop hounding him until she would read the poems herself. She might even tell Mary, and then Mary might give him more trouble. All evening, he held his own, as far as his love affair was concerned, and it was after midnight when he kissed her good night.

In the morning, he felt that he had to get some sleep and rest for the game, so after a heavy breakfast, he went to sleep again. He woke in time to have lunch at Addie's house and to drive her back to Pappy. She would come out there, in the grandstand with Pappy, to root for him and his team. This time, she had baked several cakes, and it looked like an improvement coming up over the last celebration. When they arrived, Pappy had the table and chairs all set. The boys had already brought some things from home and some from the store, but there was more to come after the game. Win or lose, they were going to celebrate, only their minds were set for a victory. They could not poke so much fun at their opponents if they lost.

Johnnie went through the game looking for Mary in the grandstand. Although he could not find her, he played as if he could see her out there rooting for him. His imagination carried the ball to victory for him. After the game, all the boys helped Addie and Pappy into Johnnie's car, and with him sitting atop, they crowded on and drove him to the celebration. They were everywhere—on the fenders and on the bumpers. They yelled and sang and blew the horn all the way. The dining room was full of laughter and rejoicing. Johnnie was happy. He knew that Mary would read about the game in the college newspaper.

During the time of the game, Mary was at the church giving a lecture to a high school group of youngsters. She was all in smiles after she read the two poems to the group, with highly desirable results. They asked her if she would be interested in some of their writings, which was not on paper yet, pending her permission to be read in class. This made her very happy since it aroused the interest of the group.

Sunday night, it was dinner and the movies again with Christine. He learned from Christine that Mary was unable to see the game because she was giving a lecture to a high school group. This eased his mind to a certain extent, but he was still hoping Mary would read about the game in the college newspaper.

Early Monday morning, he settled into his favorite corner of the library. Addie told him to write "hot stuff" straight from his heart— "hot stuff" about Mary, about himself, and about both of them together. Before him, he had a collection of books that might contain the type of poetry Addie advised him to write. He read sweetheart poems, poems of love and lovers, poems on courting, and poems on marriage, but he was still in doubt as to the kind Addie had in mind. While he was thinking about Mary, the house of Tomorrow came to his mind in vivid imagination. He could see Mary as clearly as he did on that evening they had spent together, and he could hear her voice saying, "I have to go now." In a trance, as if cast upon him by Mary, he brushed the books aside, and with his pen, he began scribbling. When he combined all his different thoughts into a poem, he read it with some satisfaction.

> "I have to go now,"
>   She said with an air so true,
> Yet he could not understand—
>   The why, the where, or when.

> "I have to go now,"
>   She calmly impressed on him,
> And she honestly urged him on,
>   While their hearts still beat as one.

He held her closer in his arms,
    While the dark was turning light.
The dewdrops rolled down the car,
    And his thoughts have ranged afar.

With a sparkle in her eyes
    And dimples in her cheeks,
She slowly brushed his arms away,
    Meaning she could not stay.

They strolled together to the door,
    And for the last, they kissed good night.
So she whispered with a twitch of her brow,
    "I have to go now."

Returning to his car,
    He slumped into the seat.
He glanced at his watch—"Wow!
    I have to go now!"

When he read the poem over again, he realized that it was not like those he had read in the books. He had only had in mind sending a message to Mary that would interest her, thereby creeping into her affection. He liked this one more than any of the others. It was something they both took part in. It was something they both had in their memories. He gave the poem to his buddy to pass it on to Mary. He waited, patiently watching and studying Mary.

When Mary found the poem, she shied away from her mother and read it, holding the book open so that her mother could not see the poem. The words were in her mind, but somehow she never connected them with the house of Tomorrow or with Johnnie. She was thrilled upon reading it. Without disturbing her mother, she carefully folded it and put it away, adding it to her collections. She began to think that someone was deliberately leaving the poems in the books after writing them. Then again, she wallowed in a dream of having the author or the poems for a lover. She began to imagine the pretty phrases he might say to her and the various courtesies he might do for her benefit. As far as her church activities extended, this poem was definitely out, but she treasured it more than the others. Her words were in it, and she considered it part of her dreams. She would read it over many times in her room after she would return home. She spent much time in her room after she would return home, lately studying for the mid-semester examinations. She was hoping to make her usual grades since she had been absent so many times. She was becoming anxious for the school day to end so that she could be alone in her room, but she would have to wait for Christine to drive her and her mother home again.

Johnnie watched her become happy and restless when she read his poem. He felt that his poems were taking effect, and he foreshadowed Percival being turned into an exile by Mary. As he left for his class, he envisioned thousands of poems being written by him for Mary.

In his rhetoric class, during the class period, the professor asked Johnnie to remain after class. Without guessing, he knew why she wanted him to remain. He was starting another poem when she called his attention about staying after class.

"I understand you have written a poem in class last Friday," she said when he came to her desk after the class was dismissed.

"Yes, I did," he admitted shyly.

"May I see it?" she asked with a smile in her eyes.

"I don't have it anymore—I disposed of it," he lied from fear.

"I'm so disappointed," she said. "I wanted to read it. Could you rewrite it again?"

"I don't think so because I didn't like it," he said, hoping he wouldn't have to expose himself—next thing, she would be asking him whom it was for.

"I don't mind if you should write some poetry in my class, but I do mind when you don't reveal your writing to me," she explained under a serious tension.

"I'm sorry. I won't do it again," he apologized.

"Oh, you may write in my class if you feel the urge." She smiled.

"I really meant that. If I should write in your class again, I will show it to you."

"You may bring any poetry to me that you write. I would like to put your poetry in the college paper or help you in your poetry writing," she said.

"I don't have the time to write poetry," he said. "It's just that sometimes I cannot resist the urge."

With this, he put an end to the session. He was working up a cold sweat when he was thinking of having his poems in the college newspaper. Some students would appreciate his poems, but others would only find something in his poems with which to laugh at and ridicule him.

He returned to the library before going to lunch, thinking he could snap out a poem and have his lunch too. He sat there in the library, thinking and dreaming up poems, but nothing was accomplished, and he had to go to his algebra class without his lunch. In his algebra class, he was suffering from pains of hunger in his stomach and frustration in his nervous system. He tried laboriously to think of something on which to write a poem, but it brought him no results. In his next class—which was his economics class on Monday, Wednesday, and Friday at two o'clock—with a pencil in his hand and a scrap of paper in his book, he scribbled with one eye on the professor.

> To go with you,
>   What I could do.
> I think of much
>   And could not such
> A thing a do
>   To you a woo.

> With you, I do
>   And do to you.
> I dream of so
>   And now my woe.
> For do a such
>   A very much.

Before he went to the football field, he left his poem with his buddy, who passed it on to Mary in a book she called for when she came to the library.

She was tickled with the theme of the poem. It was something like Percival would write if he could. Percival would like to marry her, but his wooing was something terrible. That was what the first part of the poem meant to her. The second part told her that Percival was going steady with her and that he dreamt of doing a lot of things with her, but he regretted his dreams because he could not carry out any part of his dreams. She recalled how timid and bashful Percival was, and she began to wonder if he had any dreams. She decided to keep the poems secret and conceal them from her mother.

XII

Woo and Woo

That evening, Johnnie went to see Addie.

"How am I doing?" he asked while she was reading his poems.

She paid no attention to him until she read the poems twice over and then reading them once more after giving him a look of contemplation.

"It's all right," she said, breaking out into a wide grin. "But I think you could do better," she added.

He looked at his poems, and after reading them himself, he was going to ask her what was wrong with them, but she couldn't tell him any more than she had told him before. "Give her some sugar and spice," she said. She wanted him to write "hot stuff"—so she said. She wanted him to write from his heart—how it felt and what it was doing. He was beginning to realize, first now, what she meant when she first told him that Saturday morning.

Although he had his dinner, she induced him to have dinner with her. She rambled over her childhood days, her likes and dislikes of the opposite sex, and what she had always been expecting from a lover. She

128

was sincerely interested in his affair with Mary. It made her relive her romantic days with her husband. She was lonely too, and she chattered on endlessly upon any subject that might interest him, thereby prolonging his visit. He helped her with the dishes and then excused himself by mentioning the coming mid-semester examinations.

That evening, while studying in his room, he looked at his roommate across the room. He was thinking of how fortunate he was in having Addie tell him all these things about girls. He had always been a nice, quiet boy who left the opposite sex to themselves, and he needed every bit of advice and fact that Addie had given him. He was sitting on his hollywood bed, leaning his back against the wall, and he held his book upon his knees as they were bent in support of the book. He looked across the room at his roommate, who was studying diligently at his desk, and he thought of how unfortunate his roommate was. He turned to the back of the book and took his pencil from his shirt pocket, and upon the blank back of the book, he began to compose and erase parts of his thoughts to make up a poem. He glanced at his roommate now and then, reinforcing his creative impulse.

> My roommate is a very bashful guy.
>> Even if a girl would ask him for a date,
> He'd say, "I don't see any reason why."
>> And so he'd just give her the gate.
> If she'd insist, his face'd turn red, his gills turn blue;
>> He'd stutter and stammer, saying, "No, thank you."
> So my roommate is one very bashful boy,
>> Who could make any girl's heart beat out great joy.
> Yet no girl has he ever kissed,
>> Knowing not what he has ever missed.
> I keep telling him of the day that I met you
>> And of the many things I'd like to do.
> Anything and everything, I'd like to do for you,
>> For when I met you, I have met my Waterloo.
> And my roommate has not met a girl as I met you
>> 'Cause he knows not where to go or what to do.
> So my roommate is one very bashful boy
>> That will not make a girl's heart beat out great joy.

He read the poem over to himself several times, looking for possibilities of improvements. He became hot with excitement. He could very easily have been looking at Percival and writing the same thing. It came to his attention that Percival and his roommate were very much alike, only Percival was almost twice as old. He was so excited over the poem that he studied nothing all evening. His mind was swirling around and around in happiness over his success in his poem, and it became intoxicating when he thought of the effect it would have on Mary.

Tuesday morning, he arrived at the library late—in time to pass the poem to his buddy.

"Don't give it to Mary in the first book she asks for," he cautioned his buddy.

"Okay" was the reply, and the thing was settled.

Johnnie watched Mary come to the library with her mother. He saw her get a literature book and gleefully watched her disappointment when she looked through the book over and over. He watched her return the book, asking for another. He watched her face alight with happiness upon finding the poem in the second literature book.

Mary did not read the poem for fear of interesting her mother to the point of asking for it. She was determined to keep the poems to herself and not to read them until she retired to her room, where they were safely all her own. There, she could read them over and over to her heart's content. She has been reading them over so many times, she had all of them memorized. They were so fascinating to her mind that they remained imprinted in her memory.

Johnnie was back in the library again before going to lunch. He had not so much thought of writing poetry as he had of pouring out his heart to Mary. This seemed to be an unblended message from his heart that he was writing. His thoughts of Mary flowed so smoothly that he completed the poem and still had time for lunch. He came back with the poem while on his way to the football practice. Taking it out of his pocket, he read it with a smile—a smile of accomplishment.

> Oh, a girl like you, I could woo and woo;
>   A thousand and one things, I could do and do.
> In the dark, a girl like you, I could caress
>   As I place my hand upon thy flesh.

And with kisses, you'd be smothered
    Until the moon would be bothered.
Oh, the moon would be a-watching close,
    But all we'd do is turn up our nose.
And the moon, she does not get frantic
    But encourages couples to be more romantic.
Oh, the stars would be a-watching too,
    As I'd keep on making love to you.
Oh, the stars, they'd blink their light
    As I'd grope 'round in my plight;
And the clouds would take mysterious shapes
    As you'd shed your needless drapes,
For until then would there be
    No barrier 'tween you and me.
In this way and that way, I'd express my love
    For you, my sweetie pie—my lovely dove.
If I were you and you were me,
    What would you do to I for the love of me?
And if I were you and you were me,
    What you would do to me! Oh gosh! Oh gee!

Johnnie could not resist the lightness in his head. After he read the poem, he wondered how he ever wrote it. He felt incapable of writing it, yet there it was, before his eyes. He passed it on to his buddy, who read all the stuff before passing it on to Mary.

XIII

Library Boy

*M*ary found the poem in the second or the third book, and she kept it a secret until she relaxed in her room at home. With anticipation, she slowly unfolded the first poem. As she started reading, she realized it could not have been written by Percival because it seemed to be about Percival—how his face would turn red, his gills turn blue, how he would stutter and stammer in trying to make love to her. Eagerly, she went through the second poem and conceived the fact that she did have another lover and that the poems were intended for her. She read all the poems over and over, and she lolled around in her room all evening—resisting the fact that she was supposed to study for the examinations. She only had another day, Wednesday, to study, and the examinations were Thursday and Friday after that. Never did she give the examinations a thought. Everything was so wonderful, and her books lay there so placidly; they did not bestir her slightest inclination to study. She was floating through the clouds in a luxury liner manned by Percival, by Johnnie, and by this mysterious lover.

All evening, Mary's mother and Christine thought that Mary was studying with perseverance for the coming examinations. Her father was out again. When her mother looked into Mary's room late in the evening, she found Mary fast asleep on the bed with all her clothes on except her shoes. She covered Mary with a blanket carefully so as not to disturb her sleep, and so Mary slept till morning.

In the morning, she read the poems again, and when she arrived at the library, her first impulse was to obtain another poem. At first, she asked for one literature book and then another and another, but in none did she find a poem. She took them out five at a time until there were no more literature books to look through. Her anticipations suffered a terrible letdown. She was nervous and irritable. Her mother had to quiet Mary's nerves often by speaking to her. Finally, she went to class.

That morning, Johnnie was in his room, studying judiciously for the examinations. He tried to write Mary a poem at first, but his mind was upset by the coming examinations. He had to pass the examinations because he had to stay on the football squad and also because he wouldn't have a chance with Mary if he should fail in one or more courses. Everybody was depending on him: Mary, Addie, Pappy, his fellow students, the professors, the coach, his team, and all those people in the grandstand—everybody! Everything was knitted together so closely that if he did not pass his examinations, everything would collapse on him, making it a lasting discredit to his name and his friends. They were coming to the important games of the season, and he had to pass the examinations.

At lunch time Johnnie's buddy came to his table with a hysterical look on his face. He tapped Johnnie's shoulder from behind and beckoned Johnnie to follow him outside. When they were outside, they looked at each other through a veil of disturbances in the mind.

"You got to do something quick, Johnnie," he said. "This morning, Mary took out every literature book in the library, and now instead of eating, she's going through the same process."

Johnnie's face flushed with embarrassment.

"I'll see you in the library this afternoon," said Johnnie, excusing himself.

He went back to the table, set his food back on the tray, putting it away, and hurried with his books to the library. There, he saw Mary framed in a pathetical situation. She drew out as many books at a time as her card would permit, and she went through the tedious task of looking between each two pages of the books where a poem might have been wedged. He had forty minutes left to write her a poem, and he pressed his creative ability to produce something before Mary would leave the library for her next class. He squirmed in his seat, and his mind was writhing in endless ways to compose a poem for Mary in time. When he was through, he looked up to find Mary gone and himself late for his next class. Since he was already late for his class, he had the time to read his poem.

> I must send you love that sets your cheeks aglow,
> > For since I've seen you last, it is so long ego.
> So to my love, I wish you would condescend
> > 'Cause I know you will like it in the end.
> I could not make my love so coarse
> > As to, before we are wed, end in divorce.
> I wish you would see my love follow through,
> > Just like successful couples always do.
> I'd take you to all the museums and all the parks
> > So that in your heart, I would leave some marks.
> I hope to travel in the future, I do hope—
> > Through North America, South America, and Europe.
> I'd travel through Europe, Asia, and Africa
> > And then come back to North America.
> And you will be with me all the time,
> > For you are that girl of mine.
> Life will take on a brighter hue
> > As I travel around with you.
> I will take you everywhere and show you all the light
> > To see your eyes shine for me like diamonds bright.
> We'll have a home like you have never seen
> > That will be fit for any king and queen.

He put the poem in his pocket and was on his way to class later than he thought it was. He returned to the library on his way to football practice, leaving the poem with his buddy of the library for transit to Mary.

When Mary came for a book, her eyes followed Johnnie's buddy into the aisle in the stacks where he went for her book. In his eagerness to turn the poem over to her, he got careless. She saw him take the paper out of his pocket, wedging it into the book she called for. Quickly, she stepped back to the counter, where she waited for him to return. Taking the book to her table and looking through it, she found the paper; she also found a poem in the same handwriting as the others were. In a waterfall, her bucket was filled with understanding—he was her mysterious lover. He was the poet writing to her directly by putting his poems into the books she requested.

She glanced through the poem casually and put it away before her mother noticed anything unusual. She was watching the library boy. When he looked her way, she smiled to him. She made eyes at him. She was exceedingly happy since she solved the mystery of her secret lover.

When Mary was in her room that evening, she found it more difficult to study than the day before. The coming examinations of the following two days seemed of no concern to her. She lay on her bed fully dressed with vivid imaginations of the library boy. She pictured the handsome features of his face—that blond hair of his with the wave in it as it was combed to one side and back. Her mind kept his companionship perpetually in her imaginations. She began dreaming of him holding her in his arms as Johnnie did. She had no control over her emotions or herself while she was in the room alone. She knew that she had to study for the examinations, but she kept brushing aside her studies for a few minutes more and more while she dreamt of her poetic lover until the entire evening was spent in dreaming without a bit of preparation for the examinations. The examinations seemed so unimportant that she went to bed without giving them a thought.

That night, Johnnie was arrested by the urge to write another poem, and he did. His mind was so preoccupied with the coming examinations that it became evident in his writing.

I got another date with a dream tonight,
and don't you be there late again! It might
turn into a nightmare, so then I would just
pull out my hair. I'm going to hug you and kiss
you as I squeeze you and feel you, here and

there—your bundles and your curves—and
run my fingers through your curly hair . . .
I'm going to caress you from head to foot
as I toss around in my bed—hugging and
squeezing the pillow from under my head. I
won't know what I'm doing, so it seems; fore,
all this, I'll be doing in my dreams.

More, I love you than I ever think I do.
I get up at night to scribble and scribe for
you, my lovely dove—the only one I could think
of. I don't know when to stop until I look at
the clock. And so it says it is half past two.
So, sweetheart, I send my love onto you.

I could forget my algebra. I could forget
my trig. I love the things you say that make
me feel so big. I could forget my education
for you and some relation. I could forget all
of my liberal art, but never could I forget
you, my dear sweetheart.

He was calling on her to respond to the purposes for which God
had created her.

In the morning, Mary was still so high in the clouds that
everything was bright and cheerful. At the library, she went to the desk
and looked at the library boy. She was all in smiles.

The library boy looked at her and smiled in return. He had a
suspicion that something was up.

"I would like to have a book," she said.

"Would you please make out a request on one of those forms?" he
asked, trying to avoid her eyes.

"Oh, that's all right," she said. "You may bring me the book, and
then I will make out the requisition."

"What book would you like?" he asked with a flush of
embarrassment.

"You know," said Mary, raising her eyebrows and then squinting coquettishly for his benefit.

Under his embarrassment, he could not think of a way out of this situation. He realized that somehow Mary knew that he was putting the poems into her books. Blindly, he gave her a book into which he placed the poem.

Mary flipped the pages of the book, expecting to find a poem, and she did find one.

"Oh, thank you," she said, taking a requisition blank. She smiled to him again in appreciation for his poetry.

At the library table, beside her mother, with the book, she shielded the poem from her mother and absorbed the contents of the poem. She put it away into her zippered portfolio and spent most of her time looking at and dreaming about the library boy.

When she got to the class of her first examination, her mind refused to concentrate on the examination; before she came to herself, she was only one-fourth of the way through when the time was up. In the class of the next examination, she had the same difficulty of concentration, but in addition to that, she was annoyed with the failure in her first examination. She wanted to toss her pen to the floor and run away from it all, but her mother was beside her. She was determined to do better in her next examination.

She struggled with herself, but her mind seemed to be blank. The answers to the questions were wiped out by the rhythmical flow of the words in the poems. Losing all hopes, she became nervous and bit her fingernails that she could. When the day was over and she returned to her room, she cried helplessly out of disgrace while her mother and Christine thought she was studying for the examinations of the following day. She cried into her pillow all evening.

The next morning, Mary was awakened by her mother. After Mrs. Masterson waited impatiently at the breakfast table for Mary, Mary was again confronted with her mother.

"What are you doing still in bed?" she asked in a tone of anger.

"I'm going to stay home, Mother," said Mary. "I don't feel well."

"Young lady! You're getting right out of bed this minute, and you're going to have breakfast with us, and you're going to school!"

Mrs. Masterson couldn't accept the excuse of Mary not feeling well. Her nerves had been irritated over Mary's behavior, and she was inflamed emotionally. Here she was, staying home from work to take care of Mary, trying to keep Mary in school so Mary wouldn't lose Percival, and Mary would not cooperate. Mary wanted Percival, but he would not have her until she would graduate from his alma mater.

"Mother," said Mary, "you can dress me and drag me to school if you like."

"Young lady," said her mother firmly, "you're old enough to drag yourself around. For this past week, I felt as if I were dragging you around the campus."

"I'm sorry, Mother," said Mary. "I don't feel well."

Mrs. Masterson felt Mary's forehead for a fever but found no fever. She drew her hand away slowly, trying to figure out what came over Mary. The last time Mary feigned illness, she thought Johnnie was responsible, but now Mary wasn't seeing Johnnie anymore, and she was having the same trouble with Mary. She became more confused and remained at a total loss of deduction. Maybe she had sent Johnnie away from Mary unnecessarily. Maybe Percival was at the base of Mary's troubles.

"Maybe you don't feel well—but what about Percival? He wants you to graduate this coming spring," she reminded Mary.

Mary could not reply; she cried, and it was more grief and confusion to her mother.

"Don't cry, Mary," she said. "I will call the family doctor."

When Mrs. Masterson went to call the doctor, she felt that she needed one herself. She was afraid that she could not bear much more of this suspense between the relationships of Mary and Percival and Mary's illness.

The family doctor came. He gave Mary a complete examination, and like the last time, he advised fresh air, sunshine—with plenty of sleep. He also left vitamin tablets and made out a prescription for a blood tonic.

Mary spent the day in bed, wondering about Percival and what he would say or do when he discovered her absence from school again. She imagined that he would break off their engagement, and it brought more distress to her mind. She lost all interest in her books and magazines and didn't even care for the comic strips in the newspaper. The future seemed to be so empty to her without Percival. She was so sure Percival would put an end to their engagement since she had a feeling that she could not continue her work in school.

Thursday, Johnnie went through his examinations with his colors flying. He didn't make any exceptional grades. He was satisfied with merely passing since his enrollment was late and he had spent so much time on Mary. Then on Friday morning, he went to see Christine, and she told him that Mary would not be in school that day. He was relieved to the extent that he would not have to write a poem for Mary since she was not in school and he had to study for his examinations. Friday, he also cleared a passing grade in his courses.

During the morning of Friday, Christine had gone to Mary's classes, telling them of Mary's illness. While she was about doing this, she came into contact with the professors from whom Mary took her examinations the previous day. She was astounded to hear that Mary had failed in all her examinations. Immediately, she telephoned Mrs. Masterson, adding that much more to the mounting troubles of Mrs. Masterson.

Mrs. Masterson was left so weak by the message over the telephone that she remained in her chair for some time. The day dragged on so slowly while she struggled with the burden of her troubles. Mary's responsibility was her responsibility. Not only did she like to have Mary graduate from college, but also, it was all important as far as Percival was concerned. All her troubles were grinding against one another, and she could do nothing about any of them. She couldn't think clearly. She worried over her husband, her job, and her son, who was coming from active service in the army, and most of all, she worried about Mary. She wanted very much to see Mary happily married, and she thought of Percival—with his position—as a desirable man. Time crawled along so slowly. Her regular interest at home seemed so boring and her work so tedious. Saturday morning, she decided to see the doctor herself.

"I would like to have something for my nerves, Doctor," she said. "There must be something we can do for Mary," she added.

"Nothing much we can do besides giving her plenty of fresh air, sunshine, exercise, and sleep," said the doctor.

"Doctor," she said, "I was thinking if we couldn't possibly maneuver into sending her away—with her accession to our plan without her knowing it. I have a sister in Corpus Christi, Texas, and she would be happy to have Mary till next fall, when Mary will be able to resume her studies. Out there, she could spend the time on the beach and at the resort, which will fulfill your prescriptions—but we would need your help. She wants to marry Percival, but apparently, he won't have her unless she graduates."

"I am glad you came up with the suggestion," he said. "That is what I really meant, although I tried not to make myself clear. Mary needs complete rest. She needs a vacation. She needs to leave her home, her friends, the school, and the city—to get away from it all and then come back for a fresh start. If she goes on her vacation, I'm quite sure I won't have to give you anything for your nerves. Once you go to work and get into the swing of your daily routine, your troubles will be over. However, I will give you this small container of tablets to take whenever you need them—but not more than three in one day."

"Oh, thank you, Doctor," she said. "You will come about seven thirty, won't you? Percival will be there by that time."

"I'll be there," he said, leading the way to the exit door.

That evening, Percival was in a terrible rage. He had heard of Mary's failures in her examinations, and when he arrived at Mary's house, she was sleeping.

Mary had no excuse that she could offer to Percival for her failures in the examinations, so she could not face him, and she pretended to be sleeping. How could she explain her failures to him? She could have been his wife, and he could have taught her the piano without all this ado about graduating. She was afraid that he would break off the engagement if he knew she abandoned her school career, and if she did continue with her school, she wouldn't be capable of accomplishing enough for a passing grade, and Percival wouldn't have her until she would graduate, and of course, he was expecting her to carry on with the same kind of high grades like she had been getting previously. The "ifs" and "ands" kept amassing conflicting thoughts, which put her reasoning powers into a jumble.

When the doctor came, he was properly introduced to Percival before he went on to Mary. He didn't even bother giving her an examination.

"Mary," he said to her in a low tone.

Mary could not resist opening her eyes to the call of this familiar voice—a voice that aroused her curiosity. She knew it was the doctor speaking.

"You seem to be sleeping rather well," he commented.

Mary pointed to the open door, and the doctor immediately apprehended her indication.

"Doctor," she confessed upon his return after closing the door, "I wasn't sleeping at all. I can't even sleep at night." She had faith in the doctor from childhood.

"That's bad," he said. "You really need a long vacation."

"But I can't be leaving," she complained. "What about my fiancé and our engagement?"

"That can be put off to a more favorable time."

"But I can't leave him—I won't leave him!" she cried.

"You love him?" he asked in doubt.

"I want him very much. He's going to make a concert pianist of me," she explained through her tears.

"Your aunt in Texas would be very happy to have you as long as you wish to stay," he said. "You'll have a wonderful time working at the resort, swimming in the salt water, and romping around the beach."

"But I can't leave—I can't!" She sobbed into her handkerchief.

"You're not really sick," he prompted. "What seems to be troubling you? Tell me. No one will ever know. Share your troubles with me, and I could help you."

"The heart has its reasons, the mind has its delectation, and the body has its ambition," she replied with almost as many sobs as words she put forth.

"I don't understand you, Mary," he said with an expectation of prompting further explanations.

"My heart argues with my mind, my mind ignores my heart and my body, and my body looks after its own comfort and security," she said, calming down a little.

"Mary, you're not doing justice to yourself," he said, inducing further explanation to get at the bottom of her troubles. "Let it go. Don't keep it pent up inside of you," he added.

"My body is with Percival, my heart is with Johnnie, and my mind is with the library boy." She sniffed, with her sobs dying away.

She was a prisoner of her secrets. After the disclosure of her secrets, she felt as if the gates were swung open and she was free again. Her confused mind seemed to regain its reasoning power, and now she could think more clearly. She felt as though she could smile again. There was a new day dawning with bright hopes of a future.

"Look your troubles in the face, stand up to them, and beat them down. Never keep anything secret unless you are in the service of your country. There is no use for secrets in our lives. A secret shrinks the heart, it curbs the mind, and it withers away the body," he counseled in her own language.

"Thank you, Doctor," she said with a smile.

"You must get away from all three lovers for a while. And then you will realize which one you cannot live without," he advised, patting the back of her hand.

"I want to be a concert pianist, so I know I can't be without Percival," she confessed.

"That is the point I am trying to bring to you. Percival won't have you until you graduate—and with high grades. So if I should recommend that you go to Texas for a vacation, you won't lose him, and you can make a comeback in your class work next fall."

"I believe in you, Doctor. It is the only way," she finally said.

"I will tell your mother and your fiancé that you must leave for a vacation, and I'm sure they won't object." He grinned to her with satisfaction. "And don't you worry about the secrets," he said, strengthening her confidence in him.

Mrs. Masterson, Christine, and Percival waited what seemed a long time. When the doctor finally came, they gathered around him.

"She must leave for some rest," said the doctor, looking directly at Percival. "That is the only hope for a cure of her illness."

"Gee! How long?" Percival asked.

"I would recommend till next fall," he said, turning away to leave.

"Next fall!" Percival gasped in realization of the length of time involved. It was almost a whole year.

"I expect she will leave Monday afternoon, but that will depend on Mary," Mrs. Masterson said to Percival, and Percival left for Mary's bedroom.

"I will play some music for you," said Percival, leaving Mary's bedroom almost immediately on seeing her lying awake in bed.

Percival played the piano, and everything he played was sad and gloomy. Soon, Christine left to meet Johnnie downtown again. Mrs. Masterson knitted while she sat listening to Percival's own compositions . . . Mr. Masterson was very seldom at home lately—especially evenings. He was drawn to the club, not by his former fellow businessmen but by his uneasiness with the troubles in his heart. All evening, it was so quiet, without a word being spoken, except for the peaceful and sad notes of Percival's endless number of musical compositions. Mary listened to the music with her mind wandering until she could not keep herself awake.

XIV

Intentions

Saturday morning, Johnnie went to see the pastor. He was bothered with some of his problems. Since he derived some satisfaction from his last visit, he returned to the pastor again. He felt that by speaking to the pastor, he might obtain a more accurate understanding of Mary because she also was very closely related to the church.

"I have come for counsel," he said to the pastor.

"Oh, I remember you . . . You're Johnnie—and have you found out what religion Mary is?" he asked with enthusiasm effervescing throughout his nervous system.

"Not exactly," said Johnnie. "You see, I believe that I am doing wrong to another."

"Out with it—out with it, my young friend, and be rid of those evils that weigh you down."

"You'll pray to God for me . . . to help with my troubles?" asked Johnnie seriously.

"But, my dear Johnnie, why don't you do your own asking?" he asked in the vagueness of perplexity.

"Well"—Johnnie swallowed—"to communicate with God, I would have to belong to His church."

"Then come and join us—you are welcome."

"Even if I did join your church, you would be closer to Him than I," Johnnie explained.

"God helps the man who knows how to use the help," the pastor countered.

"That is what I mean," said Johnnie. "If I could have you interpret God's help, then I would join your church and pray with understanding."

"Interpretations are very difficult in some cases. What did you have on your mind?" he kindly asked.

"Well," Johnnie started out, "here, you have two men who pray the same amount in the same church, yet one of them gets all the blessings, and the other gets nothing in return for his prayers."

"That can very easily be explained. If one is poor in reason, he is poor in money. Money can give us our worldly possessions, but there are a countless number of things that cannot be acquired with money. The poor man who thought he was getting nothing from his prayers must be overlooking something in his possession that money cannot buy." He looked at Johnnie, wondering if he had made himself clear.

Johnnie found himself in a mist of confusing thoughts.

"The rich don't beg, they never did—that's how they became rich," said Johnnie in his state of perplexity.

"The rich man works by day and night. The poor man works eight hours when he might," the pastor explained. "The rich man is independent and the poor man always a dependent. The poor man depends on his job, and his job depends on the income of the rich, and the income of the rich depends on the job done by the poor man. See how we are all tied together? One cannot exist without the other—that is how God has created us. One day might make the rich man poor, but many, many years may not make the poor man rich—that would all depend on the grace of God. The rich man is very poor indeed if he has no faith in the hereafter with God in heaven."

He drew a deep breath when he was finished with his exhaustive explanation. He studied Johnnie's face for any desirable reaction. He looked at Johnnie, and Johnnie looked for something to say.

"I'm really lost in a muddle," said Johnnie.

"One man became poor because he spent his money. The other man became rich because he invested his money in the place that the poor man spent his," he explained with forbearance. "In the same way, we spend our lives foolishly, or we invest our lives in the kingdom of heaven."

"Will you teach me how to pray?" Johnnie asked.

"The rich man prays for gold and silver and gets ulcers in return. The poor man prays for love and happiness and gets poverty in turn. To pray to God, one cannot beg for the material things as one would beg upon the streets—our primary objective is the salvation of the soul, the investment of our lives in the kingdom of heaven."

There were so many new religious terms and phrases emerging from the pastor's explanation that Johnnie's mind was groping about in its plight to follow the pastor's explanation. He tried very hard to think of some personal troubles in terms of religion.

"May all my sins be damned to hell so that I may go to heaven," said Johnnie in trying to speak with the pastor on a religious level.

"But why do you want to go to heaven?" the pastor asked in a prompting tone to get at the base of Johnnie's reasoning.

"Because Mary will be there, and I would like to be with her," replied Johnnie.

Johnnie was serious, and the pastor knew it.

The pastor looked upon Johnnie with a compassionate desire to save him. Here, before him, was a heathen within his grasp, yet he could do nothing more than to answer this heathen's questions, and for that opportunity, he was mighty grateful.

"He is part of hell who cares not for heaven," the pastor said. "Why don't you join us and prove to Mary that your lives will be happily and actively centered about the church?"

"I'm not quite ready yet," said Johnnie. "I must see Mary and talk things over with her."

"Ah!" the pastor exclaimed. "A good vessel floats by itself. A bad one sinks itself. You need not depend on Mary for the salvation or your soul. If you don't take on the qualities of a good vessel, then you shall sink into the depths of despair and degradation."

"But my trouble comes from women," Johnnie started, but he never got any further.

"Man was created on this earth for a certain purpose. Women have their own purpose also, and never should the two be compared. Maybe you try to get along with the opposite sex as you do with your own, but that cannot be so because she is not a man—she is a woman. We cannot say that one is inferior to the other, yet we cannot say that one is equal to the other—because each one has its own purpose as given by God Himself."

The pastor gloried in his explanations without being conscious of the fact. He could go on and on with many illustrations on his point, but he chose to be concise and impressing.

"But I meant that I have sinned against a woman," said Johnnie, losing all signs of restraint.

"Ah!" said the pastor. "Sin brings on sickness, and sickness brings on prayer. The closer we come to our grave, the harder we pray. I can see now your eagerness on learning how to pray. You have sinned, and now you are a sick man. He is a sick man who cannot find himself a woman—all his own. Come—indulge in penitence, and I will help you in every way I can."

"Well"—Johnnie swallowed—"I am going steady with the aunt of the girl I love. She doesn't know it, but I'm going steady with her because that's the only way I can keep in touch with the one I love. Do you think it would be a sin to go on deceiving the aunt in this way? She might have serious intentions in her heart."

"I'm afraid you have sinned twice, my young friend," said the pastor in grave seriousness. "First, you have sinned by permitting yourself to fall in love with another man's woman. Second, you are sinning with your pharisaical attentions to her aunt. When she discovers your purposes of associating with her, she will suffer deeply."

Johnnie's face flushed, and his hands were shaking nervously as if he had gone through a sudden chill. He had never realized how wrong it was and what effect it would have on Christine. Immediately, he resolved to amend his ways and to reveal his intentions for dating her.

"I see the error of my ways," said Johnnie.

"Now won't you join our parish and pray with us?" the pastor asked, calmly waiting for the answer in the affirmative.

"Not just yet. I will have to see Mary. Perhaps later on," said Johnnie, turning away to leave.

"It is rather late to repent and pray when death is at your tail!" the pastor warned in trying to impress Johnnie with the time flying by. "Now is the time—before another day, before another hour—fore, you never know when death will twist your tail and snap the life out of you."

"I'll see you again next Saturday," said Johnnie, leaving with his heart weighed down with his two sins.

When he arrived at the rooming house, he decided to see Pappy before doing anything else. Pappy was always bursting with plenty of philosophy of his own. For curiosity's sake, he would have to see Pappy. He found it rather disquieting to merely be thinking about giving up Mary and Christine. They both seemed to have a part in his life now—Christine as his friend and Mary as his sweetheart. He found Pappy lying on the couch.

"Pappy," he started, "do you think it is wrong to go steady with a girl with no intentions of marrying her?"

"Shucks, no!" said Pappy. "How do you know what her intentions are?"

"Well"—Johnnie swallowed—"do you think it is wrong to fall in love with a girl who is engaged to another man?"

"Shucks, no!" said Pappy. "How do you know that your girl would not fall in love with another fellow and give back your engagement ring to you?"

"I don't get it," said Johnnie out of disgust. Pappy was telling him things directly opposite of what the pastor had told him.

"You'll get it," Pappy forewarned. "Every man, like water, will seek his own level in life. Lately, my level in life is fourteen inches above the floor—in a horizontal position on this couch."

He laughed upon seeing Johnnie's puzzled look. Somehow Pappy and the pastor had the same vague manner of expression. Pappy's viewpoints were contrary to the pastor's and could be accounted for by Pappy's devilish conduct in his boyhood days.

"Pappy, I'm serious," Johnnie reminded him.

"So am I!" Pappy cried out without even raising his head up. "The older a boy gets, the less chance of him getting married. The older he gets, the more capable he is of selecting the right girl—until such a time when it is impossible for him to find the kind of girl that he is capable of selecting." Pappy laughed. "Ha ha ha! How did that one ever come out of me?"

Johnnie saw that Pappy was in a humorous mood, so he could not take his advice verbatim. Suddenly, he decided to see Addie. He was going to bring her over to the rooming house that evening, so it would be to his advantage to see her earlier. He would also have to practice football in the afternoon and then get dressed for his date with Christine.

He had lunch with Addie, and then they sat at the table after lunch, talking about nothing but men and women. He found valuable aid in her counsel since it came from the age-old experience of the opposite sex, and it was handed down to him like from a mother. He listened, gathering many impressions from her sincere advice, which he regarded as the words of the wise. Unlike Pappy, she was bound in thoughtful sobriety, which made things much more convincing.

"If you happen to fall in love with another man's girl, it isn't nice," she said, "but we can't say that it is wrong. After all, it is competition, and competition makes life more interesting. It often happens that a girl has many admirers, which gives her the opportunity for a happy married life. Whether she is engaged or not makes very little or no difference at all since it is only a promise, and she is not obliged to forsake her other boyfriends until she is married. The engagement ring can be returned as easily as it is accepted.

"If you happen to fall in love with another man's wife, that would be a white zebra with black stripes. It would be a wrong done to the other man and his wife. It would be a wrong done unto the good Lord, who has brought the man and woman together in marriage. It would have been a sin, a mortal sin that would smell to every corner of civilization.

"And about going steady with Christine, having no intentions on marrying her, I would say there is something to that." Her eyes turned away from his before she could go on. "You ought to let her know what's on your mind so that she wouldn't go and blow up her hopes like a bubble and then see her bubble burst one day with all her hopes gone." She looked in his eyes from the side. "You know," she went on, "sometimes a boy has no intentions of marrying the girl, but he goes steady with her for company. Then he gets to liking her, falls in love, and there you are—married!"

With the way she looked at Johnnie, he thought she meant him when she said, "There you are—married!"

Surely, he could not fall in love with Christine. All the boys at the rooming house referred to her as the intellectual that he was dating. She was good-looking with a fine personality, but she spent so much time studying, and she tried to teach her students everything she knew. They had to cram to get through her course. He liked her very much, and he liked her more every day. She was an exquisite cook and an excellent homemaker. Many times, he thought he would be better off with her than with Mary.

"Addie," he said, "you have given me some new light. Tonight I will see Christine, and I will tell her the purpose of my dates with her."

"Johnnie," said Addie, "I knew you could do it."

He took her to see Pappy. She brought the boys a cake—she always did. In the afternoon, he had his football practice, and in the evening, he met Christine downtown in the usual place. They had dinner and went to a concert, and instead of taking her home, he drove to his spot by the river.

"Remember this place?" he asked.

"Seems kind of familiar." She smiled.

"This is where I brought Mary one day."

"So you have told me once before," she recalled.

"I think I've also told you that I have no intentions of marrying you."

He looked into her eyes but could learn nothing from them. Her eyes remained the same all the time—cool and always smiling. She was much older than he, although she looked young and pretty, and she had the advantage of psychology over him.

"I remember that very well," she admitted.

"Then you know the purposes of my dates with you."

"That all depends," she said. "Supposing you tell me and I will confirm or deny my knowledge of your intentions."

"Well"—he swallowed—"I'm terribly in love with Mary, and you're the only one who can bring me close enough to her. If Mary wasn't engaged, everything would be a lot simpler."

He was sort of disappointed as he watched her face. He thought she was in love with him, and he was expecting some unfavorable reactions. Why would she be doing all those things for him if it were not so? She was such a conscientious and eager helper with his studies that he could not understand her motives. He watched her face, and in it, he could not see a bubble bursting like Addie told him there would be. He did not see any painful readjustment like the pastor said there would be. It was something like Pappy had told him it would be. This was what stunned him—to find out that Pappy was right. In spite of Pappy's devilish boyhood days, Pappy still seemed to know.

"I knew all the time that you were in love with Mary," she admitted calmly and without emotion. "I knew ever since that day at the railroad station."

"You knew all that time, and still, you went out with me?" he asked in trying to get at the root of her acquiescence.

"Well, Johnnie," she said, "when I was young and beautiful—as they say—I spent all my time studying. My studies seemed to be more important than any solicitor of happiness. That is how I never got to be married. So you see, Johnnie, you are taking me back through those days that I missed and that I cherish so much now."

"You have been my dearest friend since I met you at the railroad station," he said, kissing her softly on the lips.

"Talking about railroad stations, I almost forgot to mention the fact that Mary is leaving for a long vacation at my sister's place in Texas."

"Mary? Leaving?" he questioned with disbelief.

"Yes. This coming Monday—and she won't be back till the fall semester," said Christine, arousing his passion for Mary.

"What time Monday?"

"Five o'clock. You can be there if you get dismissed from football practice early," she said in a persuasive tone.

"Monday, at five o'clock," he said as though he were imprinting it upon his memory.

"You will be there—won't you?" she pried him on.

"Let there be no doubt about it. I'll be there if I have to skip football practice with my team. Thanks a hundred times—a thousand times over," he said, kissing her again.

He was supposed to ask her a number of questions pertaining to her and to Mary. He also wanted to know many things about Percival. His mind could not accept the fact that Mary would be leaving so suddenly and so soon. He couldn't visualize himself attending this college without her. She was the only reason for his presence at this college. Already, he was thinking of going to Texas after Mary. His mind kept foaming with a countless number of wild escapades.

Christine studied him silently. His insides ground against themselves, creating a sickening feeling. She began to envision the relationship of Mary to him. She realized that she could never take Mary's place in his affections. She was touched with his wound and felt her way through her thoughts for an appropriate lead in their conversation. She thought of the weather, the moon, the stars, and innumerable other things, but none of them seemed to be congruent with her desire to alleviate his present emotional disturbance. She studied him silently while he looked into space.

"I think I will have to be going home soon," she said, eyeing her wristwatch in the dim light of the moon.

"Oh," said Johnnie, being shunted from his wandering thoughts, "I'm sorry. I was so surprised with Mary's leaving. I fail to coordinate her reasons for taking that position."

"Well," said Christine slowly as if she were preparing an excuse for an unexpected query, "her aunt needs her at the resort."

"But why leave school at this time when she is so near to graduation?"

"Well, you see," said Christine, feeling that she was cornered, "Mary is really making a sacrifice. The graduation can wait, but her aunt is in no condition to wait much longer for assistance."

"Oh," said Johnnie, grasping the situation.

"You see, Mary's aunt is also my sister," said Christine with pride in her voice.

"That's a difference," said Johnnie, smiling. "Now I can treat the situation with understanding."

He drove slowly to Christine's home and kissed her good night.

"I hope to see you at the football game—yes?" he said before leaving.

"I will be at the football game—yes." She smiled, and they parted.

She remained at the partly open door to watch him wriggle behind the steering wheel, and she returned his wave of the arm while her eyes blurred and sent tears rolling down her cheeks. She tried wiping them away, but there were more coming. She quickly retired to her room and went to bed sniffling. She realized how fortunate it was for her that she held back her emotions until she was safely alone at home.

XV

To Texas

When the football game began Sunday afternoon, Johnnie saw Addie, Pappy, and the boys from the rooming house, but he fruitlessly searched the grandstand for Mary. He even failed to see Christine anywhere. Finally, during the last quarter, Christine appeared at the foot of the grandstand, and she was waving for him to come forth and speak to her. She was anxiously waving as if she had something important to say.

When Johnnie was tackled, he feigned injury and was benched from where he went to see Christine. It was the last quarter. The score was nothing to nothing, and his team was beaten physically but not in spirit.

"Mary has changed her mind!" Christine yelled against the competition of the crowd. "She's at the station now, and she will be leaving in about a half hour!"

Johnnie could not make any reply because the grandstand on the opposite side went wild. While he was standing there, listening to Christine, Peoria broke through their lines, and with some marvelous blocking, Peoria prevented any interception, and a goal was made, scoring six points for Peoria, but their goal kick went wide. Johnnie's team still had nothing.

There still were four minutes to play, but four minutes in a football game could last a long time—depending on the amount of time out for either side. He shook nervously on his feet out of his anxiety to leave for the railroad station. He had no doubt that the coach would not permit him to leave at this time. He looked at his team, and then he looked at the grandstand full of disheartened students. He looked at the opposite grandstand, and the crowd was going wild. They were throwing hats and programs into the air. They stood up from their seats, embraced one another, danced, and yelled with all the might of their lungs. Their band trebled its volume, and the cheer leaders raved, danced, and somersaulted before the cheering crowd.

Johnnie went to the bench and wrapped himself in a blanket with the feeling that it was his fault. If he had not left his team to see Christine, his team would have held up under the strain. He threw his blanket off and hurried to the coach.

"I can't let you in now . . . You're hurt . . . We've got more important games to play," replied the coach with a blank, expressionless emotion on his face.

Before he could make any formal negative reply, Johnnie was on his way to his team, and the coach immediately signaled for time-out. After the change was made, Johnnie's team was in a huddle for a change in strategy. They were deep in their own territory. With some wonderful blocking, Johnnie managed to hold the ball long enough for his right end to get out into the clear unnoticed. He threw a long pass, and it was timed with the running motion of his right end. The pass was completed, and the opposite team pounced on the ball carrier from all sides, forcing him to the ground and weighing him down with their bodies. They were about the center of the field.

His team got into another strategy huddle. With a short ten-yard pass directly past the opponents' line, one of his men got through a planned opening to intercept the ball, carrying it to the opponents' fifteen yard line. Johnnie looked at Christine and the grandstand and the band throwing up excitement. There was still one and a half minutes to play, but Johnnie was not so much concerned about the minutes to play as he was about the schedule of the train that Mary was leaving on. He was supposed to pass again, but with Mary and the train schedule on his mind, infuriated with the fact that he could not leave till the game was over, he boiled with undue strength and plunged like a rocket through a flimsy, unexpected opening in the opponents' line to set the ball under their goal. He was tackled from both sides, but he came through with such force, with his legs working like a tractor at high speed. The tacklers were floored to the ground.

He looked at the grandstand, and he saw Addie and Pappy behaving like the boys and girls of the college. Christine was overcome with excitement. As his team was lining up for a goal kick, he looked at the goal posts with cool inexcitability as cold sweat from the long dash rolled down his forehead. The outcome of the game didn't matter to him. He was inflamed over the change in date of Mary's leaving. If she would have left Monday, everything would be fine. He could have skipped football practice to see her off on the train, but now with all the time out from the football game for twisted legs and unconscious bodies, there wasn't enough time left out of the half hour that Christine brought him to reach the railroad station in time.

The football was set up, and with a few steps, he was upon it. With a swift kick, the ball went sailing far past the goal, but it had gone within the limits of the goal posts, making the score seven to their opponents' six. There was still a fraction of a minute to play, and their opponents tried several passes along the field, but they proved unsuccessful, and the gun went off, bringing the game to a close.

Everybody was wild with joy on Johnnie's side of the stadium, but when they looked for him to celebrate, he was nowhere to be found. He was on his way to his car with the full speed of his legs, and when he got there, Christine was sitting in his car so peacefully—waiting for him, with the motor running. He couldn't drive any faster than the traffic would permit, with cars hemming him in from all sides. At the railroad station, he hopped out of the car, leaving it for Christine to park—as she suggested.

"Track number six!" Christine yelled after him.

He arrived at the exit doors of the passageway to the trains. His hair was messed up, his face smeared with dirt and sweat. His clothes were completely marked with smudges of green from the grass and soiled with the dirt of the football field.

With one glance, he found no handles on the doors, and he sensed that he was locked out, but he saw a gentleman opening the door from the other side, which enabled him to rush through. The door attendant shouted after him and soon gave chase. Johnnie paid no attention to the door attendant. He came upon the escalator that led to the platform of track number six and ran down the escalator while the stairs were moving upward. The attendant couldn't make any progress against the motion of the escalator, so he turned to the stairway.

Johnnie saw the train standing, and he hurried, looking anxiously from window to window along the train. It flashed upon his mind to go through the train. On entering the coach, he found a porter at the door.

"Where you going, mister?" the porter asked.

"I'm looking for someone," Johnnie replied nervously.

"Who you looking for?" the porter asked, eyeing Johnnie's soiled hands and uniform.

"Mary! I'm looking for Mary!" he shouted when a bell began to clang and the engine began to hiss as it started on its way.

"Mary who?"

"Mary! My girl!" Johnnie tried unsuccessfully to gain entrance to the train. He had to get past the porter.

"Where she going, mister?"

"She is going to Texas, and I got to see her before she leaves!" Johnnie yelled more from frustration than to compete with the noise on the locomotives.

"She's not going to Texas, mister. She's gone . . . The Texas train left about ten minutes ago. It waits on track six—just the other side of this platform."

Johnnie looked on track six, and all he saw was the tracks. There was no train on track six. It was just like the porter had said—the Texas train left about ten minutes ago. No wonder he didn't see Mr. or Mrs. Masterson. All his excitement turned into gloom. He felt sick in his stomach, and his heart was pining for Mary. He walked slowly with a blank stare to the floor before him. What could he do now? He could write a letter, but would Mary answer the letter? He could telephone her if he knew it would help. He could leave school and go to Texas after Mary, where he could be with her. No one else would be there to interfere with his affair with Mary.

Soon, the door attendant caught up with him, and they walked back together.

On his return through the lobby, his heart was filled with sorrow. He promised Christine that he would see Mary off on the train, but Christine told him then that Mary would be leaving Monday—and Mary left Sunday instead. He felt so sorry for himself about getting there too late. He would have to see her soon—in fact as soon as he could figure things out. In his blue spirit, he felt a poem creeping up on him. He turned to the magazine stand, obtaining an old newspaper and a borrowed pencil. He had not a penny in his football clothes. Sitting down on a bench in the station, he jotted down the whole current of the poem as it came to him.

> I wish it were yesterday
>> And this would be tomorrow
> So that my heart would not
>> Be filled with sorrow.
> I promised I'd meet her
>> At the railroad station
> As she went off on her
>> Long, long vacation.
> On her vacation, she might
>> Meet another lover,
> And I might not even get
>> A letter from her.
> Oh, I wish it were yesterday;
>> Then this would be tomorrow.
> But now it is too late
>> For me some time to borrow.

He tore the part with the poem from the remainder of the newspaper—returning the pencil and newspaper to the clerk at the magazine stand. Folding his poem, he stuffed it in his shoe. On his way out, he met Christine. She had a difficult time finding a parking place at this time on Sunday, and when she found one, it was several blocks away.

"I got here too late," he said with discouragement.

"I don't see any reason why she had to leave today," said Christine, with her mind out of its place. "I told her you would see her off on the train tomorrow. She didn't even give Percival any consideration—just blew out like the wind."

"When did you tell her?" he asked.

"This morning—and she was supposed to give another lecture in Sunday school. I would like to see Percival when he finds out that Mary is already gone. He was at the football game with the band," she said.

Christine talked all the way to the car while Johnnie tossed in a question now and then. His mind was principally on his steps in the immediate future. When they settled in the car, he turned to her.

"Do you have the address she is going to?" he asked.

"I don't have the address," she answered, opening her purse. "But I know the address. It's my sister's resort," she reminded him again. "She lived there a long time. In fact, she was born there—and so was I."

She drew a little notebook and a pencil out of her purse, writing the address into the notebook, tearing off the sheet, and handing it to him with a smile. She watched him fold it and slip it into his shoe.

"Does that bring good luck?" she asked inquisitively as if she were superstitious.

"The good luck about it," he said, "is that when I will take my shoe off, I will find the note."

They laughed as Johnnie started out with the car. He drove to Christine's home. Christine claimed Mary had changed the time of her leaving to keep her mother from taking Monday afternoon off from work. "Anyhow," she said, "that's what Mary told me." He couldn't spend that evening with Christine because of the celebration at the rooming house and a shindig with the team that night.

On returning to the rooming house, he got the surprise of all surprises—nothing on the table had been touched, and they were waiting for him. This lightened his heart, and he was breathing easy again. He cleaned up the dirt with a hot bath, and he cleaned up the plates with his appetite after that game he had played.

Later in the evening, when the team was thoroughly satisfied with their celebration, Johnnie went off to his room. He recopied the poem and addressed an airmail envelope. After some consideration, he decided to leave out the return address on the envelope, and also, he decided not to sign his name to the poem. When he was driving Addie home, he mailed the airmail letter. On arriving at her house, he showed her a copy of the poem, which did away with her curiosity. After leaving Addie, he celebrated the victory again into the late hours of the morning with some members of his team.

When Monday afternoon came around, he started all over again, feeling sorry for missing the train. It was not his fault, but it bothered him since he did not see her before she left on her distant and extended vacation. After football practice, he returned to his room instead of going to the cafeteria with the boys of the rooming house for dinner.

He wanted to write Mary a letter telling how he felt about her, how much he loved her, and about the poems he wrote for her. He was contemplating on going to Texas to be with her, and he wanted to tell her so most of all. He had the envelope and paper on his desk, with pen poised in his hand, when he thought of marking the date of Mary's leaving on a calendar. In looking for a calendar, he found a tiny one above his roommate's desk. It was so small that he had not paid any attention to it before. In scrutinizing the picture of the calendar, he discovered that it was a picture of a beautiful nude sitting on her dress who lay across a chair. He decided the calendar was too small to serve the purpose he had in mind. He wanted a calendar with the date so large, he could see it from any part of the room or even when he would be half asleep. He made a note on his memo pad to get a large calendar and was about to write the letter when the nude came to life and urged him to write a poem instead. With zest, he scribbled and composed what finally took shape of the message he received from the barely visible nude on the tiny calendar. He read it to himself.

I have a girl in college too,
    One that looks very much like you.
She comes to my room in a manner,
    Not wearing a thing on her.
I always get so fluttered and elated,
    For she comes to my room naked.
Oh! She takes away my gloom,
    As she prances 'round in my room.

There, she sits on her skirt upon a chair
    And as she sits there, I think it is not fair
To you, sweetheart, who are so far away,
    So I'll write to you most every day.
I cannot chase this girl out into the hall,
    For she is only a picture on the wall.

He read it over several times. Then without signing his name to it, he slipped it into the envelope. He sealed it and left out his return address from the envelope. This time, it was not an airmail envelope; it was a regular white envelope. Immediately upon completion, he went out to mail the letter at the college station, and then he decided to have his dinner.

At the college cafeteria, he took notice of the head of the mathematics department. Johnnie was half through with his dinner when the distinguished-looking gentleman was about to leave.

"Sir, supposing you wanted to know something that you don't know. How would you go about it?" asked Johnnie upon approaching him.

"Well, Johnnie," he said, "the sum of something we know plus something we don't know is equal to that which we know. Now then to find that which we don't know, we merely subtract that which we know from the sum of which we know to give us the value of our unknown."

"Very simple, isn't it?" remarked Johnnie in such confusion that he felt embarrassed for asking the question.

"Yes," said the old gentleman. "It's just a matter of getting acquainted with the use of your knowledge."

"Thank you," Johnnie replied, and he returned to his table.

He sat at his table as though he had suddenly lost his appetite for food. He was thinking about what the doctor of mathematics had told him, but he couldn't see how mathematics could be applied to the problem Mary presented to him. After several more minutes on deliberation over his problem, he left the remainder of his dinner without giving a thought to his physical well-being.

Every day in the week, he would see Christine. He had to see her because he was anxiously awaiting the news of Mary's safe arrival in

Texas. He wrote no more poems. He could not settle upon writing a letter, and his mind was so troubled, he could not grasp the mood for a poem. He walked around like a man whose spirit was poisoned. His only interest was to see Christine, in quest of information about Mary, but mysteriously, Mary wasn't writing any letters—not even to her folks. He had his conferences with Addie and with Pappy.

"Leave her alone, and she will come home, wagging her tail behind her—didn't they teach you that in school?" Pappy lectured to him.

When he went to Addie, he got a different version of the same truth.

"You don't want to go leaving off to Texas. Why don't you sit back and relax? See what comes of it. You're following her too closely. You might even be pushing her around a bit. You're so close," she said. "If I were you, I'd wait two or three weeks before going after her."

She was convincing like a mother to her little boy. She eased his heart and put some spirit into him. He needed no one's advice. He could have done his own thinking and his own reasoning, but he was in the armed services for so long, he wanted to hear the viewpoints to his problems from civilians, and there wasn't a better source than from Addie, Pappy, and the pastor. He heard so much about this problem of readjustment. He felt in dire need of advice since Mary was his first associate from the opposite sex and he was not making any progress with her.

XVI

Resort

*I*t was like Christine said. That Sunday morning, on the day when Mary left, she told Mary that Johnnie would be at the railroad station Monday to see her off on the train.

Mary had her lecture ready for the church group that afternoon. She intended to be there, but her mind had lost its stability with the information that Johnnie would be at the railroad station, and she withdrew to her room. She cried into her pillow on the bed. Percival would be at the railroad station too, and if he would see Johnnie there, he wouldn't like it. He might even take some drastic steps, such as breaking off the engagement, if Johnnie would kiss her goodbye—and he would! She was sure of that.

"Why oh why does Johnnie have to be there?" she lamented over and over to herself, and it brought on a fresh flow of tears to her cheeks. Her radical desire to keep Johnnie from being at the station at the same time with Percival induced her to leave while Johnnie was playing football. She was all packed, ready to go, when she telephoned Percival, and Percival never did answer. She tried calling him again and once more until she was afraid to miss the train.

Christine drove Mary and her parents to the railroad station. Through Mary's confusion, they were at the station an hour earlier than the train was scheduled to leave, so Christine rushed to tell Johnnie.

Mary spent most of the hour in a telephone booth, trying to phone Percival. She had no idea that Percival would be at the game. He never took her to the game, and he never troubled with the band—his line was strictly orchestra.

Still, there was Percival presenting the bandleader with his own composition of a victory march, and he waited throughout the game, hoping that they would have the opportunity to play a victory march.

Mary was disheartened with the fact that Percival was not home. She began wondering where he could be, and she felt that he should have been at home because now she was leaving without his knowledge. She tossed the question of leaving without seeing Percival about in her mind, and she finally decided it would be better to leave without Percival's knowledge than to have Johnnie there at the same time with Percival—or maybe even the library boy too! The train carried her off while she waved goodbye to her mother and father.

During her entire trip to Texas, she sat restlessly and slept with difficulty. She kept wondering where Percival was at that time because she had known him to take a nap on Sunday afternoon. She arrived at Corpus Christi in a tired and disheveled condition. When Mary's train left Kansas City, her mother telegraphed Aunt Ellyn, and Mary was surprised to see Mr. and Mrs. Ellyn at the railroad station.

They greeted her heartily, after which they presented an airmail letter to her.

With one look, she missed the return address on the envelope, and she recognized the handwriting. She put the letter into her purse with some embarrassment.

"It's just a letter from my fiancé," she said. "He missed me at the train."

On arriving at the resort, she was shown to her room, where she immediately read the letter upon being alone. She put the letter away in her suitcase, being sorry she did not bring the other poems with her and feeling glad about leaving Sunday instead of Monday. She felt that she put one over on the library boy too. She was pretty sure the library boy would be at the station if he knew when she was leaving.

The following day, Mary was surprised to receive the second letter. Upon reading it, a peculiar feeling crept into her emotions, and she was bogged down in spirit.

The poem gave her the impression that other girls at the college might take her place and that when she would return, she would have no lover at all—instead of three. Quickly, she sat down at her writing desk and penned a letter to Percival, telling him how sorry she was about leaving without seeing him, how she tried to phone him, how disappointed she was when he was not home. She went off to mail the letter upon completion and sent it via special delivery airmail.

The following day, she received a letter from her mother. On the one side, she was happy to receive a letter from her mother, and on the other side, she was sad because the letter was not from Percival or the library boy. Her sadness fought with and outweighed her happiness. The next day, she had received no letter, and only the fresh air, sunshine, and work at the resort had kept her nervous system intact. That day, she was expecting a letter from Percival or at least a reply. She decided to wait another day, and when she did not get a letter, she packed up her things, leaving as unexpectedly as she had arrived.

XVII

Open Window

When Percival got the news about Mary's leaving, it was Christine who conveyed it to him in her own way.

"She left without any thought of seeing you," she said. "Mary could have told you Saturday night that she was leaving Sunday afternoon, but she didn't, or else you would have been there."

"She didn't even telephone?" Percival asked.

"Not that I know of," Christine answered, fanning his smoldering emotions. "If she intended to tell you, she would at least telephone for you to meet her at the station—wouldn't she?"

"Why, yes. I think so," said Percival, nervously biting the loose skin off his lips.

When Percival showed her the letter from Mary, he looked forward to an explanation because in her letter, Mary told him how she phoned at home and at the railroad station. However, Christine had a prefabricated explanation ready for him. She could twist everything before him and turn it to her advantage.

"I didn't see her phone, and I doubt it because she would have told me if she did."

"I will write to her and tell her how much I planned to be at the station Monday."

"No, don't tell her—don't write to her at all. She deserves to be punished for running off like this," Christine persuaded him. "Don't write to her. Show her that you're angry. Wait for her to write a few letters more pleading for your forgiveness."

"I'm so glad I spoke to you about it," he said. "I think you are right. She can't run off like that without letting me know."

He confided in Christine, and he seemed to be becoming closer to her until one day the phone rang, and it was Mary phoning him at his college office from her home.

"Well," said Percival, "it seems like you haven't been away at all. You go and come without letting people know."

"Oh, Percival." She sighed into the phone. "I missed you so much. I couldn't stand it any longer. Did you receive my letter?"

"Yes, I have received your letter," he admitted.

"Why haven't you answered it?"

"I'm angry at you—that's why. I'm really angry. You told me you would be leaving Monday, and you left Sunday," he said.

"Where were you all of Sunday afternoon?" she questioned.

"I was at the football game. I told you Saturday night that I composed a new victory march for our band."

It didn't sound like a question, but that was what it was in his sort of smooth tone of voice. He said he was angry, but his voice was the same as usual. The surprise of it all must have toned his anger down, and it remained only in his mind.

"Are you coming over tonight?" she asked in doubt. "I have so much to tell you."

"Yes, I will come over at the usual time," he said, and he went to tell Christine the good news.

"Is Mary home? I don't believe it." Christine was taken aback with the news. "Are you sure she wasn't calling long distance?"

"Well, I don't think so," he said in doubt.

"I'll tell you what," said Christine, concocting something new as she went along. "When I get home at six o'clock, I will phone you if Mary is home. If I don't phone you, then you will know the call was long distance from Texas."

She brushed his lapels, making eyes at him. He submitted to her, and this did away with his thought on using the telephone himself.

On arriving home, Christine was still surprised to find Mary had returned. Mrs. Masterson was working and Mr. Masterson was on his regular binge when the telegram from Aunt Ellyn arrived, so Mary had no reception at the railroad station. She came home by herself from the station.

"Percival is coming this evening, and I would like to have the living room for just us two," said Mary to Christine upon Christine's arrival.

"You need to worry no more," said Christine. "I am on my way to a movie."

Christine left promptly without having a bite to eat or to change her clothes. She merely took the time to set her books down and left. She felt that Mary was actually ordering her out of the house.

Mary felt this act worse than a slap on the cheek, and she could not say anything more. She watched Christine look at the grandfather clock and close the door quietly. How could Christine do this to her after the long journey home? Mr. and Mrs. Masterson left for the evening also. At this time, of all times, she could not have any interruptions—it was all important that Percival should be at ease and that they should be alone.

Mary waited for Percival. She had everything ready—even the matches for the marshmallows. She waited past his usual time of arrival. She picked up the receiver of the telephone, only to set it back without making the call. Maybe he was delayed, or maybe he would purposely come late with a mask on anger covering his face. He didn't say what time he was coming, so all she could do was wait in patience, which was rapidly dissipating. She waited all evening, and Percival did not come. Several times, she took to the phone, always in doubt, always wondering what had happened. She was afraid to phone again, shrinking from the thought that it would make her the beggar—and beggars were not choosers.

"Another day, and the tables will be turned if he doesn't come," she whispered to herself in her pathetic situation of terrible loneliness.

Percival did not come, and she did not phone him. She spent all evening alone, building up a nervous condition so that when morning came, she was under the care of the family doctor again.

The following morning, Christine went to see Percival. She was recklessly happy when she walked into his office.

"Oh, Percival!" she cried out. "Mary is back again!"

"She is?" Percival asked with digestive disturbance written on his face.

"Why, yes! She came yesterday afternoon."

"I told you she was home—didn't I?"

Percival's face was getting a sickly white when thoughts of Mary's telephone call came to his mind, especially when he recalled that Mary had asked him to come over for the evening.

"Come to think of it," she said, "you did tell me, and I was supposed to phone you at six o'clock, but I completely forgot all about it."

"How could you forget?" he moaned.

Percival tried, but he could not gather any ill feeling toward Christine. They worked together on the college presentations at the auditorium, and they had been together for so many years.

"You will forgive me—won't you, Percival? I was so surprised to see her back again that it slipped my mind," she begged pretentiously.

"I forgive you," he said, "but who will forgive me?"

"That's simple," said Christine with a quick reply. "Tell her that you had to work at the college auditorium with me."

"With you?" he looked at her.

"With whom else would you?" She looked him in the eye with a smile on her lips. "Phone her early this morning and tell her," she advised.

Mary was overjoyed with the telephone call. She forgave him before he had a chance to ask for her forgiveness. She pressed another invitation for the evening—only this time, she had to remain in bed.

When Christine returned from the college, her first move was to see Mary. She was expecting to be cross-examined by Mary, and she was already fabricating psychological answers to the questions she knew Mary would ask.

"Have you been working hard last night?" Mary asked at the first opportunity.

"Not working at all," answered Christine. "I was at a movie downtown."

Christine expected an undertow of questions to sweep her off her feet, but it had not come. Instead, Mary took on a gloomy atmosphere. Later, from the kitchen, she heard Mary phoning from the living room. She was phoning to the library, which was the only connection at this time.

Mary wanted to know if there was some kind of rehearsal at the college auditorium last night, and she was told that there was none—according to the college bulletin. She returned to bed with a suspicion that Percival went to the movies with Christine. Now she had to dig her nails into Percival's affections and cling to him with all of her strength. There might have been something doing at the auditorium, but she had no way to find out without phoning the music department, and she was afraid of Percival's knowledge of her mistrust in him. Again, her emotions were bound in her with no outlet. She bit her nails. She stared into one space for some lengths of time while the time ticked endlessly away.

Percival came, and Christine was disappointed because Percival and Mary seemed to be tied closer than ever. Mary had not made known her suspicions, and Percival dared not mention a word about last night. He played the piano while Christine and Mrs. Masterson sat about the living room. Mary was left alone in bed, and the music that reached her ears had no soothing effect upon her nerves. She lay quietly with no reactions to any of the stimuli in her environment. Percival came to her bedside before leaving.

"I will see you in school as soon as you are well," he said, concluding his visit for the evening.

Mary remained in bed, worrying all through the night without having any signs of approaching sleep. She worried about Percival, about school, about the examinations that she failed, about the poems that she was not getting from the library boy anymore, and about not seeing Johnnie. She wanted all those, and she could not have them. She was ailing helplessly, more so as the time went on from the day she met Johnnie.

Johnnie had discovered that Mary was home again on the second day of her return. His gloomy days of thoughtless wandering were over, but he had yet to solve the problem of getting to her.

"I told you to sit tight for a while, didn't I?" Addie proudly boasted of her advice.

"I told you to leave her alone, didn't I?" Pappy reminded Johnnie of his advice.

In his conversation with Christine on the third day of Mary's return, Johnnie plied Christine with questions concerning the layout on her house, and particularly, he asked about the location of Mary's room. He had to see Mary without her mother's knowledge. He wanted to get Mary on his side and then to approach her mother—in which way much more could be accomplished for his own purpose. He had no idea as to how he could reach Mary. His head was crammed full of wild plans of having Christine let him into the house during the night—to the lowness of picking the door lock himself.

That night, Mary lay in bed with her insomnious condition. She slept an hour or so after meals during the day, which, she thought, was induced by the doctor's medicine. As she lay in bed—so still, staring at the side wall of her room—she noticed a shadow flit across the moonlight shining through the window. She watched the window to see the head of a figure come into view slowly from one side. She braced herself up to a sitting position and watched unemotionally. Then a flashlight threw a beam of light into her face, yet she was not frightened and had no inclination to scream—she didn't as much as lift her eyebrows. Her internal conflicts had drained her nervous system, and her emotions amounted to nothing. Then the beam of light was turned back on the figure framed by the window, and she sprang out of bed to cautiously close the bedroom door. She hurried to open the French-type window because it was Johnnie on the outside.

"Mary," he asked, "why must I come like this to see you?"

"Perhaps it is the best way at the time," she said in a trance of happiness.

"Why have you turned me away like this?" he asked from his mind full of questions. "Why has your mother done likewise?"

"I guess it's because Mother does whatever I want," she said.

"But why must you send me away? I love you, and I missed you so much every day," he confessed. He begged from his heart, and then he set his foot upon the windowsill in preparation of climbing through the window.

"Oh no! Johnnie!" she cried out. "Don't you dare climb into my bedroom! You are not a gentleman," she said, almost feeling sorry for what she said.

"You were supposed to teach me to be a gentleman," he recalled to her from the past. "Why do you want me done away with?" he asked again.

"I don't know," she said in her daze.

The wind of the night was cold, and a draft was present at the open window with them. Mary was kneeling at the inside of the window, and Johnnie knelt at the outside of the window. She was in her cotton pajamas. Although she had just gotten out of the warm bed into the draft, she had no sense of the cold. They spent several hours there, sometimes holding hands and sometimes just resting their elbows on the windowsill. When he held her hands, he kissed them on the front and back until she giggled with excitement, but she would not have him kiss her on the lips or face. At last, he bade her good night, and she looked out the window after him until he disappeared into the night. She closed the windows again, opened the door, and went back to bed. She promptly sank into daydreams, which led the way to a deep and restful sleep.

When Johnnie returned to his car, he recalled that he forgot something—he forgot to tell Mary about those poems. *Oh, well.* Tomorrow was another day, and he could tell her then.

Mary awoke in the morning with a sharp cough. Her mother had been home, away from work, since Mary returned from Texas. She couldn't figure out how Mary had caught a cold merely lying in bed. The family doctor was called, and he acknowledged that Mary had a cough, a fever, and the chills. It seemed to Mary that she was eating pills all day long like she used to eat candy before.

At night, she fell asleep, only to be awakened by a tapping sound on the window. She was weak and feverish. On her shaking feet, she got a pencil and paper. She wrote the word "sick" and held the paper against the window to his flashlight; then she pointed to the flannel cloth wrapped around her throat and another upon her chest.

Johnnie read the note and watched her point to the flannel cloth, and then he pressed his lips against the windowpane. Instinctively, Mary pressed her lips over his against the windowpane too. He waved goodbye, and she watched him leave before retiring to bed.

The next day, Mary had lost her cough and her fever. She was well on her way to recovery. Percival came to visit her every night and spent all of his visits playing the piano.

This night, when Johnnie came, she was waiting for him as she lay awake in bed. When he came, she pulled the blankets off the bed, wrapping them about herself and over her head. She closed the door and opened the window.

"You look like a doll wrapped up in all those blankets," he said. "Like a beautiful doll with shining eyes, a smile of sweetness, and a voice of enchantment."

"Would you like it if I caught cold again?" she asked with a radiant smile.

"I couldn't bear to kiss you through a windowpane more than once in a lifetime," he replied, lending courage to her cheerfulness.

They talked for over an hour. He begged her to accept his presence in the household, to speak for him to her mother, and then it happened. The prankish weatherman sent a cloud of rain instead of snow.

"Hurry. Come in, or you'll get wet," she whispered.

He was on his way in before she thought of asking. This was an excuse made to order for him. In a few seconds, he was inside looking out at the rain, with Mary to his side. He suddenly realized that he was holding his arm around her waistline. The excitement of the sudden downpour had brought them together, and Mary didn't mind his arm.

"Mary," he said, reaching into his pocket, "I have something for you."

"You have?" she asked with eyes wide and her curiosity generating to a high emotional degree.

"Here you are," he said. "Keep it for me."

"What is it?" she asked, with her curiosity output slowing down since she was only to keep it for him and not for herself.

"It's something that will make you well," he said. "Keep it under your pillow, but believe in it, and you will become well."

She held the object in her hands while he pressed them together over it. He drew her up for a kiss, and she reached her arms around his neck, whereas the blanket fell to the floor while their lips were pressed together in a strong feeling of passion.

"Someone is coming," he whispered, breaking the kiss, leaping out the window into the rain, and sprinting out of sight.

Mary quickly closed the windows and was fumbling with the blankets when her mother opened the door.

"Mary, what are you doing?" she questioned, not being able to understand why the door was closed and the room so cold.

"I opened the window for a change of air," Mary said with fear that her mother would look out the window.

"When you need some change of air in your room, I'll see that it's done when you're not in the room," said her mother, tucking in the blankets of Mary's bed.

"All right, Mother," said Mary, closing her eyes to have her mother leave sooner.

Mary waited for a while; then she took the object from under the pillow to examine it in the moonlight. Her curiosity would not wait any longer. She unwrapped the large white handkerchief from the object and discovered that the object was an old and tattered pocket-size book. It was so small, it could easily fit into a shirt pocket. She turned on the bed lamp to find the book older than she had thought at first. It had a hole in it, and it was also stained with a dark color. She opened the book to one of its pages, and there it was—a bloodstain blotting out the print of the book. One glance was enough. She shut the book closed, wrapped it back into the handkerchief as fast as she could, and pressed it into her dresser drawer, closing the drawer quickly, and she was back in bed, leaving the light turned on.

She shuddered at the thought of blood. She lay awake all night, wondering why he had given it for her to keep under her pillow. It was the most nauseating sight he could present to her. It was blood, and it might have been human blood for all she knew. The mere thought of blood gave her the chills. *When he comes back the next time, he would explain everything to me,* she thought. He might have explained when he gave it to her if it were not for the interruption by her mother.

XVIII

Pocket Bible

In the morning, as if brought in by the rain of last night, Mrs. Masterson answered the door, and there, she found her son standing in uniform. She broke out in tears while he tried to kiss her tears away.

"I'm so glad to have you back. Your sister is sick in bed. Come see her," she managed to say through her choking sorrow.

She led him to Mary's bedroom, where she left him while she went back to the living room to have her cry. Here, he came, in such a surprise return, that she did not know how to tell him anything in a delicate way. She just sat on the sofa and cried from her misery and her happiness of his return. When he came to her, he was a hardened man, but the sight of her tears had softened him. He began to cry with her.

"Tell me all about it, Mother," he begged.

She sniffed for some time before she could speak, and even so, she found it difficult to keep from breaking down.

"Well," she started, "we lost everything . . . We even lost your father—he has taken to drinking . . . This is Christine's house . . . If Mary wasn't ill, I would have been working."

She broke out in tears again, and so did George. He embraced her, and they cried, cheek to cheek, while they sat upon the sofa. After they cried their sorrows out of their hearts, they could speak their minds without restraint. Soon, they were with smiling faces again.

In the afternoon, Mr. Masterson came home. He was full of good spirits—the kind that may be purchased in bottle containers. Upon his appearance in the house, he found his son standing in the living room, dressed in uniform.

"George! My son!" he cried out. "You have come at last!"

He approached his son with wavering steps and outstretched arms. He blinked his eyes to clear the vision for a better view. His lips were stretched out in a grin of exalted happiness.

George could not face him. He turned away from his outstretched arms. Could this be his father—the father whom he had left when he was called to service? It was hard to believe. It was painful to accept. Sorrow was choking his throat, and tears watered his eyes.

"Sorry," he said. "I thought you were my son."

He dropped his outstretched arms to his sides, and he turned to make his way toward his bedroom.

"Dad!" George cried out, hurrying after him. "Oh, Dad! I'm sorry!" he begged as they embraced each other with tears in their eyes.

"George! My boy!" he said. "Why be sorry? Let's celebrate!"

"Drunk or sober, you're still my father," said George. "I know how it is. I got drunk a lot at times when we were on leave from the army. I know what you're going through—you're eating your heart out over nothing."

"A rich man can be reduced to poverty in one day, but many, many long years may not bring the riches back again. I worked and slaved all the days of my life to have something for you and Mary, and now I have nothing—that's what hurts me. I'm too old. It's too late for me to start all over again."

"Don't say it's too late, Dad," George begged. "I'm not too old. I'll start all over again, and you can help me along."

He gave George a silent look of pity. He thought George was falling into dreams of fancy. He smiled to one side of his mouth.

"You'll start?" he asked. "With what?"

He turned away from his son to retire to his bedroom, where he flopped his tired old body across the bed. He left his son in a silence, stunned with embarrassment. He pointed out to his son that there was nothing to start with. All he could help his son with was his advice.

Mrs. Masterson came to the aid of her son.

"Dad said, 'There's nothing to start with,'" said George, turning to his mother.

"Yes, I know," she said. "I was in the kitchen, and I heard everything. Don't let yourself go to pieces. Start something. Go to school and start a new life."

"But it's just like being dropped from an airplane into a jungle—like being dropped without even any clothes on. First of all, you're hurt from the fall, and when you get over it, you've got the wild jungle to fight. Not until you have conquered the jungle could you begin to make yourself some clothes. Then you have to work bit by bit for the things essential to your way of life," he said gloomily with a clear vision of the dark future that lay before him.

His mother blinked her tears away and bit her lips while she looked at him searchingly with a loss of encouragement for him.

"Your father did it—why can't you?" she said in tears, turning away from him and hurrying back to the kitchen.

George realized that his mother was hurt, but in his melancholy stupor, it had no effect on him. He was like his father, and sitting in the lounge chair, he began brooding his loss. He thought his father hopeless. His sister was ill, keeping his mother from employment. So there was no income for the family. At this time, there was no source of income unless he would put himself up as one. He missed the luxurious comfort that he had left behind.

Mrs. Masterson sniffed as she worked in the kitchen. She started trying to prepare a special dinner for the homecoming of her son. She was sorry she had to send Johnnie away—she loved him, and he was the only one who was interesting her husband into starting a new life again. She worked for a salary when Mary was not ill, setting an example for her husband to follow. She kept the family together to the best of her ability.

She went to the living room to speak to her son once more, but he was not there—nor anywhere else in the house. She was hoping to have him present when Christine returned from school. She still had hopes that he would be back for dinner. Christine came home, and she had dinner with Christine. She couldn't rouse her husband from his spirited sleep, and she thought Mary should remain in bed, so there she was, eating at the table with Christine. George never did come for dinner.

At the usual time of seven o'clock, Percival came. When his piano playing started, Mr. Masterson awoke. He came to the piano with a groggy step and a spinning head. His hair was mussed. His collar was open, with his tie hanging to one side. His shirt was wrinkled, and his belt was open. To one side at the piano keys, he leaned on the piano with his elbows. He looked into Percival's face for attention while Percival was absorbed in the keys, producing the musical notes he had in mind. When Percival looked up, there was Mr. Masterson, staring into his eyes.

Mrs. Masterson and Christine were startled with the appearance of Mr. Masterson in his condition, and they were deeply embarrassed. They rose from their seats to ease him away.

"Stop it!" Mr. Masterson shouted, failing to obtain Percival's attention.

"Yes, sir," replied Percival in fear.

"That kind of music isn't going to cure my daughter!" he shouted again.

"Why don't you go and rest a while?" Christine asked, taking hold of one arm while Mrs. Masterson took hold of the other. "You're a sick man," she said.

"Sick like nothing!" He brushed them away with force. "You're going to marry my daughter?" he asked, turning to Percival.

"Why, yes—of course," Percival stuttered.

"When?" he sneered.

"Soon as she graduates," said Percival with a shaking voice.

"Then you will never marry her. She's not going to school until she gets well, and she's not going to get well until she gets married."

He had his say and left for the kitchen—for the food of the dinner that was put away. He twisted off the legs of the chicken. With a chicken leg in one hand and a slice of bread in the other, he paced the floor of the kitchen as he chewed. Having eaten the chicken legs, he took his hat and coat to leave the house again. He would be back for some sleep or something to eat. These were the only things that kept him interested in his home—if he could call it home since it was the property of Christine.

Percival turned ghastly white from what Mr. Masterson had told him. He was in Mary's bedroom when Mr. Masterson left the house. He felt that Mary's illness was due to his failure to comply with her wishes. He recalled how she had asked him about the wedding date.

"Mary," he said, sitting in a chair beside her bed, "we can get married anytime you like."

"Would a week before Christmas be too soon?" she replied, full of excitement.

"If you would like it then. You could start school again next semester," he said.

"Of course, I would, Percival. You've made me so happy. Bring Christine and Mother in here. I can hardly wait to tell everyone. I'll be sure and get well by the time our wedding day comes around," she said.

That night, when Johnnie came and flashed the beam of light upon her bed, she was not there. She was seated in a chair, waiting for him with his booklet, which was still on her dresser, wrapped in the handkerchief.

"Johnnie, please don't come here anymore—you mustn't," she begged, turning away to her dresser.

"What has happened now?" he asked in bewilderment.

"I can't keep this for you, Johnnie. You keep it for yourself—I'm getting married a week before Christmas."

The fact that she was getting married made him speechless. He was hurt where it hurt most. In deepest sorrow, he turned away from her while she stood by the open window. She watched him disappear slowly around the corner of the house for what she thought was the last time in her life. In closing the window, she was disturbed by loud voices—the voices of two men, the words of whom she could not make out. She listened, straining her ears through the open window, until the voices were no more. She stood there for almost a minute before her curiosity directed her to the living room window. Before she left the bedroom, she closed the window and opened the door wide, as it should be. She noticed the lights on in the living room.

When Johnnie left, he was carrying the booklet in his hand. On reaching the front lawn, somebody attacked him from the brush.

"So you're the guy!" he shouted, striking Johnnie with his fist to the jaw.

"Now wait a minute!" Johnnie cried out, taking a strong hold of his arms at the elbows.

"You're the guy that's making my sister sick! The next time I catch you around, I'll cut you to pieces!" he shouted from anger, trying to break loose of Johnnie's iron grip.

"You're not going to cut anyone to pieces, George," said Johnnie, lowering his voice. "You know I could beat you to a pulp whenever I get a notion to, but I'm not going to—you're my buddy from the battlefield, and so you shall remain as long as I live."

"Johnnie!" he cried out and they embraced each other like long-lost buddies. "Come on in—it's good to see you again."

"I can't right now. Maybe some other time . . . Here's something I'd like to return to you. I won't have any use for it anymore," said Johnnie, placing the booklet into his hand.

George took it, not remembering what it was. He didn't remember what he had loaned to Johnnie—it was so long ago since they were together.

"Thanks," said George. "Be sure to call me up sometime. We'll have to celebrate."

"I'll do that," said Johnnie, disappearing into the night.

George went into the house, turning on the lights of the living room. His patience demanded to know what was returned to him. He unwrapped the handkerchief to find the booklet with a hole in it. He got sick in the stomach, and all his muscles became so weak, he felt a fainting spell coming on. The booklet and the handkerchief dropped to the floor at his feet, and he flopped back into the sofa that he stood nearby. He leaned over to the armrest, burying his face into his elbows, and sobbed away his sorrows like an emotional child.

When Mary came into the living room, she saw him on the sofa and the booklet with the handkerchief on the floor at his feet.

"How did this get here?" she asked, recognizing the booklet as the one she had just returned to Johnnie.

"I brought it here," said George, lifting his head to answer.

"Where did you get it?"

"Johnnie, a buddy of mine, returned it to me—he said he has no use for it anymore," George explained.

George was sitting up now, wiping his tears and blowing his nose.

"What is it?" she asked out of curiosity.

"It's the pocket Bible you sent to me during the first few months I was in the service."

"This?" Mary implied with doubt.

She picked up the tattered Bible, and on the inside cover, she saw her name and address as she wrote it—beneath it was her sentimental note. It was stained with blood and covered with dirt, but the indentations were still there.

"What's this hole in it for?" asked Mary inquisitively.

"He carried the Bible in his shirt pocket over his heart like a smoker carries his cigarettes. He carried it with him all the time, and he used it whenever he had the time. Then there came a bullet aimed at his heart, and it made a hole in the Bible."

"And the blood," Mary anticipated. "George, tell me all about it," she begged. "From the very beginning."

"Oh." George sighed with indifference. "He was my buddy, and I struck him. Why didn't you tell me about him? At least that he had returned home."

"Tell me what you know of him from the army, and I will tell you what happened since he returned home," she said.

"Well, we spent the time together in training. He had the bunk next to mine. We had a great time together. Every time I got a letter from you, I would read it to him. He was a great guy—never too busy with his own responsibilities to help me. He asked me to send for your picture, but you never sent it to me. He waited for every letter you sent. He didn't have a girl waiting for him. He said he never was interested in any girl till he read your letters himself.

"One day he got a letter from his mother telling him how his father died in an automobile accident. Then about a week later, he got a letter from a lady who lived next door to his folks. In the letter, she told Johnnie how his mother couldn't stand the pain on losing his father, and she died of a broken heart. He didn't have anybody left except this kind old lady who was always like a mother to him. Every week she sent him a fruit cake or some other cake that wouldn't spoil for a long time. I never got any from home, so he shared them with me and the other boys.

"When his folks went away, he was a changed man. All the cheerfulness had left him. He never played cards with us anymore—he never did anything with us. He would always settle down someplace where he was alone, and he would read your letters. I gave them all to him. I told him he could write to you, but he said that if he did write to you and never came back from the battlefield, you would only suffer like he did when he lost his folks. I tried to give him some pocket editions to read, but they didn't interest him. He walked around as if nobody else was in camp besides himself. Sometimes he passed by an officer as if the officer wasn't there. Then you sent me the pocket Bible. I opened the package in front of him. He asked to see the book, and when he saw your name inside the cover, he asked me to loan it to him. He read it over and over with your letters, so I never asked him to return it. Then he started playing football on paper, but he was always by himself.

"When we were through with our training, we were separated and shipped to the islands. Then I got your picture, but it was too late to give it to him.

"About three years later, I met another soldier who was in the same outfit with Johnnie. He told me about Johnnie—how he carried the Bible next to his heart in the shirt pocket, how he took the most dangerous assignments, how he would filter through the enemy lines and direct our powerful long-range guns onto the enemy supplics. He told me how Johnnie roamed around behind the enemy lines, bringing back vital information to the outfit. He was promoted several times, but everybody didn't think he was doing those dangerous assignments for promotions—they thought he wanted to die.

"Then when we were cleaning up the islands of enemy guerrilla bands, my scouting party was ambushed by two guerrillas. One of them got me with three machine gun bullets in one thigh and one bullet in the other. My legs collapsed, and I fell to the ground. The others ran ahead, firing as they ran, but they were cut down by the guerrilla's machine guns. Then the two guerrillas came out of their hiding to finish the job. As they were standing among my buddies—looking to kill the living and to carry off the loot—I raised my rifle and shot one through the head. The other one turned around, and I shot him twice in the chest.

"I was scared. There would be more guerrillas coming. I couldn't use my legs. The bones weren't broken, but my thighs were numb with pain. I worked my way to the first-aid kit and bandaged my legs. With my hands, I dragged myself into the brush, and there, I waited. I didn't know what else to do. I just waited with my rifle ready. I waited all day and all through the night. The pain kept me from sleeping. By morning, I had a high fever, and my vision was becoming blurred. I lost a lot of blood. I was getting weak, so weak that I couldn't bring my rifle up to a firing position if I wanted to. By noon, I was getting delirious, and I knew it, but I couldn't help it. Then I heard someone coming. I couldn't see whether it was friend or enemy, and it seemed like I didn't care.

"'Having trouble, George?' he asked me as I was moaning about my legs.

"'Who are you?' I asked him, and I was trying to raise my rifle, but it wouldn't move. It seemed to be fastened down to the ground. I was so weak.

"'A friend,' he said. 'Don't talk. Don't even try to talk. I'll get you back to the base in a couple of hours.'

"The voice seemed kind of familiar, but he wouldn't talk to me anymore. He gave me a sulfa pill for the infection. He took hold of me and lifted me over his shoulder like a sack of potatoes—he had to. That was the only way he could carry me with his rifle ready. It looked like he could sense a guerrilla two hundred yards away. Twice, he set me down in the brush and warned me not to move or moan. Each time, I'd hear a few shots, and he came back for me.

"When it was getting dark, he threw me into the brush of a fallen tree. He told me guerrillas were coming fast, and he lay down in front of me. I could feel the heavy branches around us, and they made my legs hurt. Then I heard the pounding of feet on the ground. There must have been at least nine guerrillas running by. Then when

I thought they were all gone, I moaned—I couldn't stand those branches anymore. As I moaned, I heard a shot, and something fell.

"He said we'd be back in camp in a couple of hours, but he carried me all afternoon already, and it was getting dark.

"In my blurred vision, I could see that it was dark when we got into camp. They couldn't get a doctor to take the bullets out till morning, and by then, I was unconscious.

"I was lying in bed with a feverish delirium for four days before I came to my senses, the nurse told me. She also told me how lucky I was that somebody had brought me in. I knew I owed my life to the guy, but I didn't know who he was. She said that a Bible saved his life. He told her that when I moaned, there was a guerrilla trailing behind the others. When he heard the moan, he turned his gun, and Johnnie fired at the same time as he did. The guerrilla's rifle bullet went through a branch, through the Bible, and lodged in one of Johnnie's ribs over his heart. I couldn't find out who he was. Nobody knew. A boat dropped him off at the island, and another boat picked him up— the boat I was supposed to take home.

"When I recovered, he was gone. He was gone the following day after he had brought me in. Your letter was also gone—the letter that told me you would be at the railway station and what kind of clothes you would wear."

"So that's the way it was!" Mary cried out with understanding. "Johnnie took the letter. He knew what I was going to wear, but I wasn't wearing it. He came on the train that you were supposed to have come on," said Mary.

"It's just like him. He came on that train so that you wouldn't be disappointed. So that Mother and Dad would not suffer of worries over me," explained George. "I couldn't write to them saying that I was wounded."

"He told us you were all right, only that you must have missed the boat," recalled Mary.

"That's Johnnie."

"Oh, George!" Mary cried out. "I feel terrible after the way I treated him. Go find him and bring him to me. I would like to apologize to him. He is welcome in our home whenever he decides to come."

"But I can't go and bring him to you at this time of the night."

"Then please go early in the morning, George. Please?" She held her hands around his neck and begged like an innocent little girl.

"That's better," he replied. "Think of me going out after him at this time of the night."

"Why didn't you tell me that immediately upon returning? Then I wouldn't have sent him away like that," she scolded.

"How did I know?" he growled.

"Well, how did we know he saved your life? Why didn't you write us about it?"

"If I did write, it wouldn't help anyone, would it?"

"I'm going back to bed before Mother catches me out of bed. In case you forgot, she can lecture better than I can, and when she finds out that Johnnie saved your life, I can just imagine what you're in for."

"Oh, cut it out," he snapped back.

"Well, you should have written. Don't you think so?" She edged him on for confirmation of her reasoning.

"Yes, yes. I think so. Now go to bed and leave me alone," he moaned.

As he sat there alone in the living room, puffing rapidly and nervously on one cigarette after another, he tried to figure out how it was that he had never thought about Johnnie when the nurse told him about the Bible. It was so long ago since he had seen Johnnie, and receiving the Bible from Mary was such an insignificant item in his memory that it did not come readily to his attention. Why didn't Johnnie tell him his name instead of just telling him it was a friend? Why didn't he leave his name when he left the base? Then it came to him. It was just like Johnnie—helping everybody without asking for the credit for doing it. He would have to see Johnnie at the earliest moment for his own sake—not just because Mary had asked him to. He felt a surge of gratitude for what Johnnie had done for him and worked up a strong determination to see Johnnie early in the morning before Johnnie would go to school. He retired to bed, thinking about getting up early, when he recalled that he had not seen Aunt Christine. He felt a glow of shame settle over him, which kept him awake for some time.

XIX

Looking

When Mary went to bed, she couldn't very well fall asleep. All night long, she kept recalling the wrongful conduct she had carried on toward Johnnie—but why didn't he tell her about himself? Why did he give her the Bible to keep for him? Why did he return the Bible to George, saying that he had no more use for it? She didn't know who could be held responsible for this situation, and she felt there were a lot more details that she didn't know about. She was beginning to feel sorry for having the wedding date set. She began to wonder why she was getting married to Percival. In the face of things as they were at present, her aspirations to become a concert pianist seemed so empty of any excitement. She was trying to apply some self-analysis to her problems from the day she first met Johnnie until the present day.

She went over the memories on her associations with Percival, with Johnnie, and with the library boy. She realized that Johnnie was the most pressing of all. He was the most persistent. The more she turned him away, the more he persisted. She had realized, from the information she obtained from George, why Johnnie was not taking to any of the other girls in school. She was his first love, and she was rooted deeply in his heart through the letters she had sent to George and that he had read so many times. She realized that if she would have only turned the cover of that Bible, she would notice her inscription inside the cover, and everything else would follow naturally. She kept feeling sorry for Percival, for Johnnie, for the library boy, and, most of all, for herself because she was unable to help herself out of this situation.

Mary got out of bed in the morning, but her mother sent her right back. She insisted that Mary have her meals in bed until the doctor decided she was well on her way to recovery. In the daylight, Mary still looked pale and listless.

George was up early in the morning. Of course, he would not have been up early if his mother didn't drag him out of bed. She wanted terribly for him to meet Christine before Christine went off to school. He was so tired and sleepy; he felt he could very easily put in ten more hours of sleep. He was up at six thirty, and he remembered lying awake in bed at four o'clock in the morning. He was still exhausted from the long journey home. He had to ride in on a coach because all the sleeping cars of the train were reserved. He gulped down two cups of hot coffee first thing on arising, and that helped him in his desire to keep his eyes open, but his head was still groggy, and his limbs were excessively heavy.

At the breakfast table, Christine was happy to see George. She had heard about him, but it was different seeing him. Mr. Masterson stayed in bed. He didn't eat when the meals were served; he ate when he was hungry, and he got out of bed when he was rested. He came home to eat or to sleep. So George had breakfast with his mother and his aunt Christine. He mentioned nothing about Johnnie or the Bible. Upon completing breakfast, he drove Christine to school in her car.

At the dean's office, he obtained Johnnie's home address and the one of the rooming house at the campus. He arrived at the rooming house a little after eight o'clock since he had to wait in turn at the dean's office. He came up to Pappy, inquiring about Johnnie.

"I don't know what got into that boy," remarked Pappy. "I waited all night to see him, and he never did come in. He went to see his

Mary, and I guess he must have stayed at her house. You'll have to check with the office to see if he is in school today."

"Thanks, Mr. Pappipopulos," said George, turning away with disappointment.

George was on his way to see Christine. His conscience was heavy with fear that his attack on Johnnie was the cause of Johnnie's being out all night. It dawned on him to recall the "why" for of it all. Why was Johnnie seeing his sister at the bedroom window? Was he gaining entrance through the window, or was he merely seeing her through the window? The grass was trampled by the window, and a path was beginning to appear, leading away to the street. There were so many things that required an explanation, and his mind was so preoccupied with endless questions that he forgot he was on his way to see Christine. It came to him when he was halfway home, so he turned around, heading back again to see Christine.

He arrived at Christine's office after nine o'clock, and she had a class from nine to ten, so he had to wait in her office till ten o'clock. When she came, he told her about his visit to Johnnie's rooming house and that Johnnie wasn't home all night. He asked Christine if she could check if Johnnie was in school today.

"There is no way of checking right now. You will have to wait till after his first class. If he's not in his first class, then most likely, he won't be in at all today," she said, wondering why he was checking on Johnnie, why he was so anxious to see him.

"When is his first class?" he asked.

"From eleven to twelve today."

George moaned with discouragement of the long wait.

"Wait a minute!" she called as he was leaving. "You can check with the dean's office. If he won't be in school, he should have been excused by the dean."

George went to the dean's office, and the dean told him that there was no excuse in the office as to why Johnnie shouldn't be in school today. So George had to wait till twelve o'clock, and while he was waiting, he decided to look for Johnnie. He went back to the rooming house, but Pappy said he was still waiting for Johnnie. Then he went to the library. After failing to find him, he settled down to wait. He tried looking through some magazines, but his eyelids were closing. He left the library for some coffee in a neighboring restaurant, where he spent his time waiting, but it was all for nothing. He discovered Johnnie was not in his first class, and he was too tired to spend any more time on the campus. He gave the car keys to Christine and returned home via the bus.

Mary was out of bed and about the house despite the protests of her mother. She couldn't stand the slow pace of the hours while she waited for Johnnie. She passed the time helping with the housework.

"Why didn't you bring Johnnie to me?" she asked George when he came in without Johnnie.

"Simply because I didn't find him." George made his reluctant reply. He was tired and irritable.

"Why didn't you find him?" Mary asked in complete failure to understand.

"Simply because I don't know where he is."

"Why didn't you go to his rooming house?"

"I was there, but Johnnie wasn't in all night, and he hasn't come in yet. Johnnie wasn't in school today either."

"Why did you come back home? Why aren't you out looking for him?"

"Look," pleaded George. "Ask me no more questions. Give me no more troubles. I'm tired, and I'd like to sleep for twelve or fourteen hours." He turned to leave her for his bedroom.

"Wait, George." She stopped him. "How do you know what's happened to him? You struck him last night, remember? He gave you the Bible, saying he doesn't have any more use for it, remember? You've got to find him before he does anything to himself. He doesn't have anyone left besides me. He said he loves me, and I turned him away. You've got to find him. You've got to help him—don't you see? There's no telling what he will do," she pleaded.

"Well," he said, changing his mind, "I'll go out again as soon as Christine comes home with the car. In the meantime, I would like to get some sleep."

"I'll wake you when she comes," Mary assured him.

XX

Lot of Money

When Johnnie left George after returning the pocket Bible to him, he went home, parking his yellow convertible in the garage. He sat in the living room, nervously smoking his cigarettes, when there was a light knock on the door. Upon opening the door, there was Addie standing in the doorway. She looked as if she had left her bed and dressed in a hurry to see him. She shivered in her bathrobe, not being accustomed to exposure.

"I heard you drive into the garage. Are you all right?" she asked. "Are you sure you're not sick?"

"No, Addie," he said. "I'm not sick. I'm just . . . Oh, I don't know."

She sat down on the sofa beside him and watched him light a cigarette. She noticed how his hand was shaking. For a while, she didn't know how to approach him. She knew something was bothering him, and she was quite sure it was Mary.

"Your schoolwork giving you trouble?" she asked.

"No, Addie," he said. "I never have trouble with schoolwork."

She noticed he was rather reluctant to carry on a conversation. He had no smile for her, as he always did. He answered her question as shortly as she had asked it. She realized that a conversation could not be carried on in a question-and-answer fashion. She wouldn't get anything out of him unless she could break him into a conversation with a smile.

"You know," she said, "when I was a young one, I got stuck on a boy whom I never saw. I heard about him one day, and I couldn't get him out of my mind until I went out with another boy. Then I got to have a lot of boyfriends, and out of all these boyfriends I had, I learned all about my future. I learned that one boy was selfish, another was lazy, another was a troublemaker, and another liked to drink and so on down the line. So when I got myself a new friend, that was the end of the line. He was the kind that didn't have the bad traits of the others, and we lived happily as long as we'd been married. He's dead and buried, but I'm waiting to meet him up there." She pointed her index finger upward to the heaven above. "I know he's up there," she said with emphasis. "That's why I married him."

He smiled to her, and she thought she snapped him out of his morbific duskiness. She thought that she made life itself seem full of hope once again.

"I know you would like to tell me to go out with other girls, but I don't have any reason or interest in them. Like you say, I could marry another, but Mary would always be coming back to my mind, and I could not make a girl happy unless I was in love with her."

"I know just how you feel," she said. "If you buy yourself something cheap, you will have something cheap."

"Addie, do you think that I resemble Mr. Tomorrow in any way?" he asked.

"Well," she said in stalling for time to arrange her thoughts since this question seemed out of turn and she had to handle it delicately, "you don't have anything now, but you will have."

"Just like Mr. Tomorrow. He never had anything today, but he would have tomorrow—and tomorrow never comes," said Johnnie, losing his smile again.

"I didn't mean it that way," Addie apologized.

"What other way could there be?" He looked at her with expressionless eyes.

"Well," she said, "you're going to school, and you're preparing yourself for a future. You've got talent and ambition. You've got what it takes to get ahead."

"I have everything, and at the same time, I have nothing. If I don't have Mary, everything else will be worthless. I don't have a position, meaning I don't have an income to secure my future. I need some money—a lot of money," he said, showing signs of a desperate need.

"Where will you get your 'lot of money'—all at once?" she asked. She felt he wasn't telling her all he had on his mind.

"I got in touch with some men, and in a short time, I'll have plenty," he said positively, with determination in his words.

"What would you want all this money for?" she asked, with her intuitive sense working ineffectively.

"I've been seeing Mary this week," he said, "and the day before yesterday, I gave her a pocket Bible wrapped in a handkerchief. When I first gave it to her, she was happy and grateful. Then when I told her it was only hers to keep for me, she faded away with her happiness and her gratefulness. She probably thought it was some jewelry or some other expensive gift, and I don't have the money for expensive gifts."

Addie sighed with disgust over her own thoughtlessness.

"I completely forgot all about it. I hope you will forgive me," she begged. "I am old, and I don't think about those things anymore. You should have sent her flowers, and you should have given her something dear to her heart—something she would remember through all her life. It wouldn't have to be expensive. I could have helped you like I did with the car."

"That's no good," replied Johnnie. It was just like Mr. Tomorrow—everything he had was of somebody else's efforts and nothing of his own efforts.

"Why should Mary's little disappointment upset you so?"

"It's not only that I can't buy her anything. It's that she returned the Bible to me right the next day. In spite of it all, she went ahead and set the wedding date with Percival."

"The giving of the Bible couldn't have brought this misfortune," Addie cautioned him.

"I gave her the Bible because she was closely tied up with her church. It was the Bible I had loaned from her brother. She sent it to him, and her name was inside the cover. She couldn't have missed her name. It was the Bible that saved my life while I was saving her brother's life. I tried to prove to her that I believed in it and that it had saved my life. I also believed that it would bring us together in the holy state of matrimony, but she turned it back on me—and now I have no more use for it. I returned it to her brother."

"Get yourself some sleep, and I'll see you in the morning," she said, leaving.

She didn't know of anything else she could say. This matter required a lot of thought and consideration from different angles. She also thought that some sleep and rest may give him a chance to see a brighter picture with another girl in the future. She felt sorry for him. It seemed that now, with Mary's wedding date set, his chances of winning her were beyond the bounds of possibility.

"Good night, Addie," he bade her without the usual smile.

She lay on her bed, thinking about the situation Johnnie was in, thinking of the melancholy condition he had, and she tossed about, wondering how she could help him. The hours ran slower than her patience, and the hours were holding back her patience till it sometimes seemed like the clock was standing still.

With the break of dawn, she was out of bed after a sleepless night. She had in mind to prepare some breakfast for him when she heard several doors of a car being slammed shut. She went about preparing the breakfast until it came to her mind that Johnnie had mentioned getting in touch with some men. She hurried to the front window, and she saw Johnnie leaving with four men. They left in a big black seven-passenger sedan while she looked on through the window. She had a foolish notion to go out screaming after him, but when she opened the door to go out after him, the car was already on its way.

Poor boy, she thought. *Without someone to hold him, he is liable to get into bad company*. When she thought about the "lot of money" that Johnnie had said he would have in a short time, she also realized "clean money does not come from unknown sources," and already, she had fears that Johnnie was in bad company. She felt he was out of her reach now, and she began feeling sorry and lonely. She too had no one to rely on in her sickness or for the services after her death.

XXI

Fist of Iron

When Christine returned home with the car, Mary went to George's bedroom and roughly shook him out of his sleep. George opened his eyes and looked about as if he were still in the army camp—where else would they shake him out of his sleep like this? Realizing that Mary was standing over him, he sat up in his bed and began collecting his senses.

"Get up! Get up, George!" Mary encouraged impatiently as she stood over him.

"Aw, wait a minute!. I've got to wake up first. The way you wake somebody up, he'd think he's still in the army." He yawned and rubbed some circulation into his sleepy eyes.

"I have some fresh coffee for you," said Mary.

"If I drink any more of that stuff, I'll be a coffee man. I already drank so much coffee, it seems like I got coffee running through my veins instead of blood," he warned.

Mary paid no more attention to him since he was moving to leave the comfortable bed. She prepared some light food for him, and soon, she sent him out again in search of Johnnie. This time, she had more hopes than she did in the morning—she had more time to build up her hopes. She prepared some things for the occlusion, and she was memorizing the things she would say. When George would arrive with Johnnie, she would introduce the story of George's Bible to her mother. From that time on, Johnnie would be permitted to set foot upon the welcome rug at the door of their house.

George drove, in Christine's car, to the rooming house. He had his doubts about Johnnie being at the rooming house because Christine told him that he had not been in school all day. He had to make sure Johnnie wasn't anywhere around the campus. He talked with Pappy and the students, but Johnnie was nowhere to be seen about the campus. Well, that put out all doubt about Johnnie's presence on the campus. He drove the car to Johnnie's home, and after some pounding on the door, he decided to see Addie. Pappy told him that Addie would be the one to know where Johnnie was if he should not be at home.

Addie answered the door, looking at George with a strange feeling creeping over her.

"Could you tell me anything about Johnnie, who lives next door?" he asked without making any introduction of himself or his purposes for the visit.

"What would you like to know?" she cross-questioned, with her suspicions rising.

"I'd like to know where I could find him," he said.

"I don't know where you could find him right now," she said. "Who shall I say asked about him?"

"Oh, that isn't important if I can't find him. You could tell him George dropped in to see him," he replied.

Without mentioning Pappy's reference to her, he left without any further discussion. He figured on coming back again since he did not see Johnnie this time. He was still tired. He only had about three hours of sleep, in the afternoon, which wasn't enough to satisfy one eye. He returned home without bringing Mary any more news than he had at noon.

Mary was upset over George's fruitless efforts to find Johnnie. She was full of suspicions and jumpy conclusions. She listened to George, doubting his words and suspecting he did not put much effort into his search. Johnnie could not have disappeared without anyone knowing what he was doing or where he had gone. There must have been something, somewhere, that would let her know what was going on.

"I'll find Johnnie for you as soon as he gets back to school," George complained. "You won't have to find him then," she said. "Johnnie may be in need of help now, and now is the time to find him and to help him."

Mary had an urge to find Johnnie herself, but the doctor advised that she spend as much of her time resting in bed as possible, and her mother would not permit her to leave the house. Every day Christine came home with the same disappointing news to Mary—Johnnie had not returned to school yet. Mary's imaginations were adding up, and she was on the verge of doing something.

The days were passing by with no word of Johnnie until Saturday came along. Saturday night, George came home with a black eye and a swollen jaw. He was angry at Mary and was reluctant to talk to her. He sulked in his chair, paying no attention to her.

"What happened? Did you have a fight with somebody?" She repeated it several times.

"Johnnie is no friend of mine anymore." He finally turned to answer her persistent queries.

"I thought you said you two were buddies. You said he saved your life. Now you're saying that he is no friend of yours anymore? Why do you keep me hanging by my own imaginations? Why don't you tell me everything you know instead of sitting there in such sullenness?"

"Don't fire any more questions into me! Don't you think I've had enough with this black eye and swollen jaw for one day—not mentioning a hard kick in my rump? Go to bed and leave me alone! I have to straighten things out in my mind before I could understand everything in such a way as to explain it to you," he said.

"What happened? Did you have a fight with somebody?" She rang it up again.

"No, I didn't have a fight with somebody! I didn't even have a chance to fight," he sassed her back to still her questioning.

"Well, what happened?"

"I'll tell you in the morning."

"Tell me now!" she snapped at him. "I won't be able to sleep all night if you don't tell me now."

"So much the better," he said. "You got me into this. If you would have told me about Johnnie soon as I came home, this wouldn't have happened. Now I'll have to stay home all week, nursing my eye and swollen jaw and soaking my butt in a hot bath."

"Can't you even tell me who did it and why?"

"Don't ever ask me to bring Johnnie to you again. After this, I don't see how I could speak to him anymore."

"Johnnie did that to you? I don't believe it. You told me he said to you that he wouldn't strike his buddy and that his buddy would remain his buddy until the day he dies."

"Times change," said George. "He said that almost a week ago. Something got into his head, and *bang-bang*—a sock in the eye and a sock in the jaw, just like that. I didn't even have a chance to brace myself against the blow."

"Are you sure it was Johnnie?"

"Of course, I'm sure," he protested.

"Are you sure you weren't drunk?"

"Go to bed," he directed. "Trouble me with your troubles no more."

"But I've got to know, George," she pleaded, eyes blurred with tears.

"I'll tell you all about it in the morning. Now leave me alone."

"Couldn't you go back and ask him why he is not going to school anymore?" Her mind was bubbling with questions.

"Look, sis," he said. "Didn't I tell you that I don't see how I could speak to him anymore?"

"You could see him at least once more for me—couldn't you, George?" she begged.

"If you will leave me alone, I might change my mind by the time morning comes around."

"You're not the brother I used to have before you went into service, George!" she cried.

She hurried away to her bed, where she cried her tears away till there seemed to be no more. As she sniffed, she could not understand why she shed so many tears over Johnnie. She had never spent one tear on Percival. She realized that Johnnie was bringing her more trouble than Percival. Johnnie always gave her heart a twist or a turn, which sometimes would make it hurt and other times would make it pound with joy. She couldn't understand why she loved him so much—yet she could not marry him instead of Percival. The library boy was out of her life for the time being since her mind was concerned with Johnnie. Her troubles seemed to be directly associated with Johnnie because since she met him, she could not do as she pleased. Her troubles with Percival were an offspring of Johnnie's appearance in her life. Her troubles with the library boy had no indications of their source, but she felt that Johnnie could be held responsible for them as well as for everything else. She held no evidence, but her suspicions were of Johnnie. She could not understand why she was trying to help Johnnie when it would only bring more trouble with Percival. She tossed about in bed with her thoughts, and she fell asleep in the late hours of the morning.

George stayed up after Mary had gone to bed. He felt his swollen jaw, his blackened eye, and his hurting buttock while he was trying to think through what had happened between Johnnie and himself. He couldn't see why Johnnie would have revenge upon him. He twisted his thoughts about in his head, but he could arrive at no conclusion. He would have to know everything that had gone on between Mary and Johnnie, and that, he would have to ask Mary. She was supposed to tell him all about her associations with Johnnie, but she hadn't. He rested on one buttock because the other one was aching from the impact of Johnnie's shoe. He finally rubbed his jaw, looked at the clock, and retired to bed. He was tired and slept well till morning.

In the morning, Mary was anxiously waiting for George, and so was he waiting for her. Both were expecting to have things cleared up by the other. George was sleeping in the guest room, and when he awoke, there was Mary, sitting in a chair beside his bed.

"Are you awake, George?" she asked, seeing his eyes open.

"Yes, I'm awake," he said.

"Have you changed your mind about seeing Johnnie again—for me?"

"I haven't changed my mind yet, but I might if you tell me the whole thing between you and Johnnie," he said.

Mary told him everything—from the railroad station, step by step, to the bedroom window, leaving out not one kiss. She was sincere and begged him not to tell another.

"Now will you go to him once more?" she asked.

"Uh-uh," he said. "Not on my life."

"But why not? Last night, you said you will change your mind by morning," she reminded him.

"I said I might change my mind—but I didn't," he corrected her.

"Well, why didn't you?" she said in distress. "You've got to help me, and you've got to help Johnnie!"

"I'd like to help you, sis," he said, "but I don't like to have my face disfigured. He's got a fist of iron. Besides, what will happen when he kicks me on the other side? Then I won't be able to sit at all. This thing is strictly between you and him. If you want him, sis, go on after him. If you don't want him, forget him. You've got Percival. What more do you want—a spare lover?"

He looked at her from an angle as he supported his body with his elbow. The words "a spare lover" rang out in his mind when he saw her face take on a sadness, which told him that she was in love with Johnnie.

"George," she said softly, "do you have a girl?"

"Of course not. What would I do with a girl? No allowance, no clothes, no position, no nothing anymore." He felt irritated with every thought of his present financial condition.

"What about Lorraine?"

"Who told you about Lorraine?" He sprang to sit up in bed.

"A soldier at school," she said.

"And his name is Johnnie," he added emphatically.

"What of it?"

"That's so much the more for the reason why I won't see Johnnie anymore," he said with anger.

"Are you ashamed of Lorraine?"

"I'm not ashamed of Lorraine. I'm ashamed of myself. Here, I was telling her that my father had a big business and that I would be driving a big car, but look at me—all I have is what I brought back with me from the army," he said.

"Well, what are you going to do for yourself?"

"Nothing," he replied in seriousness. "What is there to do?"

"Mother isn't going to like this coming from you," she warned.

"What can I do?" he asked blankly.

"You don't get any more out of life than you put into it, and if you take life as it comes, then you will also have to take what comes with it," she warned.

"Me? Go out and work on a salary?" he questioned bitterly.

"If Mother can do it, then you can do it," she said firmly.

"I don't see Dad doing it."

"You forgot to tell me about your fight last night," she reminded him, changing the subject.

"There was no fight," he protested. "I just got beat up, and that's all there was to it."

"Oh!" she exclaimed with obvious understanding. "So you just stood there like a dummy, and you let him strike you first in the eye and then in the jaw. Then you turned around and bent over for him to kick you like a football."

Now she was using her wits in drawing the story out of him. It was to be this way if none other.

"I wasn't standing there!" he objected. "Every time he struck me, it threw me to the floor, and when I was getting up the second time—*wham!* I thought he kicked off one of my buttocks. That's all there was. Not a word to it—just two punches and a kick."

"You must have been pretty drunk, judging from the resistance you put up." She edged him on.

"I certainly was not—I'm telling you!" he cried out in anger. "We had a couple of drinks, but that was all."

"Who were the others?"

"What others?"

"You said 'we.' So there must have been someone else besides you," she reasoned.

"Aw, go away," he demanded.

"What will Mother say about your black eye?"

"That, I will find out when she sees me. Am I worried?" he asked.

"Those are unkind words," she said. "You don't seem to have any concern for anyone but yourself since you returned from the service."

"How do you expect me to feel? I didn't save my money while I was in service, so here I am, nothing more than a bum. I lose my girl, I have to ask Mother for spending money, and I'm supposed to go out begging for a job," he said in a despondent tone.

"Well, why didn't you? It's your own fault."

"Why didn't I do that? Why don't I do this? Why didn't I? Why don't I?" he complained.

"At least you can tell me what happened last night."

"But I did tell you! What more do you want me to say?"

"You haven't told me everything. Johnnie would never beat you up without a reason for it, and you're hiding it. If you don't tell me everything, I'll tell Mother and Dad about Lorraine," she threatened.

"You tell them about Lorraine, and I'll tell them about your romance with Johnnie. I'm pretty sure Percival wouldn't like it." He laughed.

Mary was startled with his counter-threat, and she quickly left the room in silence. She had lost her point for argument, and there was nothing more she could do. She retired to the kitchen to help with the breakfast, and she was thinking about going to see Johnnie herself. She knew not where she could find him since George wouldn't tell, but she had the feeling that she could if she would try.

When George arrived at the kitchen table, everyone was waiting for him. Mary had not mentioned the condition of his face. She wanted to make sure she would not provoke George into divulging her romance with Johnnie to them. When she saw George walk into the kitchen, she was laughing, and she tried very hard to keep her laughter on the inside from fear of George's retaliation for the embarrassment. George came in with a hesitant step. His face was covered with fear of their discovery, but there was no way out of it—they would know, if Mary hadn't told them already.

"Well—if it isn't my son, George!" his father cried out, rising from his chair.

"George! What has happened to your face?" His mother gasped, dropping the knife and fork on the plate on which she was cutting bacon.

"What happened?" Christine asked calmly. She and Mary were the only ones to take it quietly.

"Black eyes usually come when you go around peeking through key holes—but come, have a seat and tell us all about it," said his father.

He escorted George to the chair at the table. George couldn't sit straight because of the pain in one of his buttocks. He looked around and saw everyone staring at his face. He was totally uneasy, especially not knowing how much Mary had already told them.

"Well? Haven't you decided to tell us anything yet?" His father impatiently prodded him on.

George was doing some fast thinking as he looked at his audience at the table. He was under a nervous tension that he could not understand. He realized that he owed them an explanation and that he could not get by without one to their satisfaction—as was his experience with Mary. Last night and this morning, she was after him, and he realized what it would be like with the rest of them.

"Well," he said, stalling for time as he was thinking, "I was downtown to a movie, and as I was going out, I decided I needed a drink of water. I waited in line at the fountain, and when I got to be the fifth one in line, I was yanked out of the line just like that—by two men in army uniform.

"'Don't you know it's against the law to drink that stuff?' one of them said as I straightened up.

"I was surprised to see two of my buddies from the army. We went to one place and then to another. We only had one drink in each place. We were just looking for some entertainment. Later, we took in another nightclub and another drink for old times' sake. They were in the city only between bus runs, so I showed them around town, and I took them back to the bus station in time for them to catch their bus.

"Then I walked down Twelfth Street, and I saw him. He was on the other side of the street. I followed him to a tavern, and when I went in, I took a seat at the bar. I ordered a drink, and I looked around, but I couldn't find him at first. Then when I found him, he was at a table in a dark corner. There were three other men with him, so I didn't want to go to his table, but I watched for him to be going out. He would pass right by me at the bar, if he were going out.

"Then I saw him coming with the other three. I got up from my seat to greet him. He rushed at me and smacked me a hard one to the jaw. Naturally, it threw me off balance, and I fell to the floor. When I got up, I was going to paste him one, but he poked me in the eye. Naturally, I fell to the floor. When I was getting up this time, he booted me one on the butt, like I was a football. I sprawled to the floor, and I ran away. I don't know how. That's all there was to it—not one word between us," he finished with his eyes cast down upon his plate before him.

"What were you standing on? A pair of wooden legs? Every time he takes a swing at you, he knocks you down," his father growled with disgust. He was expecting to hear something of a battle with both fists flying, with George returning blow for every blow—at least.

"Naturally"—Mary cut in, not being able to withhold her bit any longer—"it threw him off balance, and he fell to the floor."

"Who was this 'him' you're talking about?" His father demanded to know.

George was burning with anger at Mary's insinuation. If she would only have held her tongue still, he could manage to work his way out of the question. He managed not to mention any name in his story so far, but now Mary had brought his dander up, and he had almost no control over himself. His only impulse was to retaliate for Mary's remark.

"It was Johnnie," he replied, looking at Mary's face with contempt.

"Are you sure it was Johnnie? Are you sure you weren't drunk and mistaken?" his father questioned.

"Of course, I wasn't drunk," George protested. "And even if I might have been, I'd still know Johnnie—even in the dark."

"But there must have been something between you two. There must be some reason. Johnnie wouldn't do anything like that to my son. He wouldn't do anything like that to anybody. There must be some reason." He looked to George for a further explanation—for the reason.

"But, Dad—I told you everything just the way it happened. I didn't get a chance to say one word to him. I got off my seat to greet him when he attacked me."

"Are you sure?" asked his father, growing pale on his face.

"Yes, I'm sure!" George snapped back at his father.

His father, hearing this, left all his food on the table and hurried to Christine's room, where his bottle of liquor was hidden. With shaking hands, he lifted the quart bottle from its hiding place. He screwed the cap off, and the bottle rattled against his teeth from the shakes of his hands. His heart was aching, and his alcoholic nerves called for a stimulant. He guzzled the liquor down into his stomach like a thirsty man would drink water on a hot day, and he went to lie down on his bed, but it wasn't long before he worked up another tension, and he fled from the household.

When his father left his breakfast on the table, George had no idea what was going on. Christine was innocent of the whole affair. Mary was beginning to sense that Johnnie and her father were great friends, that George should not have mentioned Johnnie's name. His mother knew what caused his father to leave the breakfast and to leave the house, but how could she tell George? Mary looked at her mother with understanding, and she left her breakfast too. She hurried to her room, and George followed her. Under the conditions, Christine decided not to eat, and Mrs. Masterson could eat no more. Half of the breakfast or more remained to be disposed of.

"What's going on in this house?" George asked Mary on approaching her while she sat on her bed.

"Don't you see what you've done?" she asked without raising her eyes to him.

"I have done something? What have I done?" he asked in complete innocence. "First, I get beat up by your lover. Then everybody walks away from their breakfast as if I gave them indigestion."

"That's what you did—you gave them indigestion, only I never thought of it that way," she said.

"Just what do you mean, sis?" he asked.

"You shouldn't have told Father that Johnnie struck you down. He loved Johnnie. He almost started a small business with Johnnie. Johnnie was the only one who made him happy, the only one who could bring him back to life. You hurt Father, and you hurt him deep in his heart." She struck at him with heavy words of truth.

"How could you blame me for it? It was Johnnie who struck me down, wasn't it?" He paced the floor before her.

"How do I know? Maybe you made up the story to get out of something. It doesn't make sense anyhow."

"How can you talk to me like that when you're at fault too?" he said with an accusing finger.

"Now you're going to point your finger at me?" she said, looking into his eyes.

"Yes—if it wasn't for your sassy remarks, I wouldn't get angry at you and mention Johnnie's name at all! I was doing all right until you wagged your tongue," he lectured, standing still before her.

"What did I say? I was only trying to help you!"

"That's your fault! You're always trying to help me when I can do better without your help," he pointed out.

"You're mighty free with your faultfinding—aren't you, brother George?" she sassed him back.

"That's right. It's your fault!" he stressed the point. "If you would have told me about Johnnie, then everything would turn out different. If you wouldn't have begged me to bring him back to you, I wouldn't have this black eye and this swollen jaw—and, if I didn't get beat up by Johnnie, then this wouldn't have happened today."

Mary could not sit there and listen to him any longer. What was he trying to do—scold her? She was too "maturescent" to be scolded. She realized that this attitude was part of the change in him since he returned home. Nothing could please him. He was suffering from the fear of going to work for a living. She knew there was no point in discussing the matter with him. She packed up her conversation and took it where it would produce a more pleasant atmosphere. She went to the kitchen to help her mother and Christine. After having the kitchen straightened out, Christine said that they would have to go to church without Mr. Masterson, and after looking around for George, Christine informed them that they would have to go without George too.

When Mary walked out on him, George did not have anyone to blame but himself. Like his father, he sought consolation for his heart along the side roads from the regular path of life—the side roads that had brought nothing but a dead end of respectable life. He was a very close resemblance to his father mentally, and he followed in his footsteps as they went on through life. The father was suffering from the frustration of losing his business, while the son suffered from the fear of starting all over from scratch. Nothing seemed to matter to George anymore. He discovered that he didn't have what he thought he had, and the disappointment was too great for him to conquer. It seemed as though he would be going out on benders like his father was—they might even meet somewhere and go down the road together.

Mary was so concerned about Johnnie without thinking of her brother or her father. Her father seemed to be beyond reclaim, and her brother seemed to be not within her dominion, but Johnnie seemed always to be within her reach. She had to save him. She would never forgive herself if something happened to him—about which she could do nothing at the present time. Perhaps in another day or two or three, she would have the doctor's permission to roam about by herself again. Then she would not have to depend on George for assistance, and she would once again be free—free of her doctor, of her mother, of her brother, and of her Percival too. Since her illness came on, Percival had been at her house, and he played the piano day after day—until lately, the music was more enervating than soothing to her. She couldn't visualize herself hammering the ivory keys of the piano the rest of her life, and she thought of being free from the perpetual grind. She was falling from her height as a great concert pianist to that of a housewife. However, she admired and she wanted Percival. She would also be free to see the library boy too, and there was no telling how many poems he had in store for her. She became intoxicated with the thought of leaving the walls of the house and of the many things she could do beyond them.

XXII

Heart and Mind

*A*s Mary waited for the doctor's permission, the days went long and many. It was almost a week before she had his blessing. Her first impulse was to head for Johnnie's home after driving Christine to school. She was sure someone in the neighborhood could tell her of his whereabouts. She heard of Addie from Christine and from George. When she found that Johnnie was not at home, she wasn't exactly disappointed because she didn't expect to find him in the first place she would try. Going to Addie's house was where she was bound for disappointment.

"I don't know what got into that boy," Addie said. "I haven't seen him for some time already."

Addie was careful not to give information to strangers. She was suspicious of everyone asking about Johnnie since she saw him ride away with those men. She was afraid Johnnie might be involved in a tortious scheme to obtain money, and she would like to help him out of it at the earliest possible opportunity of seeing him. She could not face Mary. She looked to one side or another and hoped that her guilty conscience would not force her to divulge any information about Johnnie.

"I'm Mary Masterson," she said, making the introduction. "You have probably heard about me from Johnnie."

"Oh yes," replied Addie.

She was gazing upon Mary from head to foot. She began to associate Mary with Johnnie's troubles—and hers as well since Johnnie came to her with his troubles. When she acknowledged Mary's pretty face and shapely figure, she realized why Johnnie could not be interested in another girl.

"Did he say anything about me?" Mary asked, her eyes beaming with excitement.

"Nothing, except that he loves you—isn't that enough to float on?" she asked, looking at Mary from the corners of her eyes. "Would you like to step in for a while instead of us holding a conversation out here in the doorway?"

"I didn't think I would stay very long," replied Mary, "but one never knows the length of an interesting conversation."

She guided Mary into a comfortable seat and asked Mary if she would like to try a home-baked cake. Mary was tickled with the thought of home cooking, and out came the whole cake with some hot coffee. She begged Mary to cut a piece for herself, but Mary shied away, so she cut a generous portion for Mary and one for herself. She was planning to hold Mary to a long visit and to pry into her side of Johnnie's troubles.

"I baked it for the boys at Johnnie's rooming house, but Johnnie didn't come for me, so we may as well eat it ourselves. I don't see how the football team will get along without their captain." She had a plug-in for Johnnie in almost every thought.

"I haven't seen a football game for a long time, and I haven't seen Johnnie for a long time too," admitted Mary.

"I believe you're going to see him one of these days soon," she encouraged.

"You think so?" Mary looked surprised.

"I know it. How do you like the cake?" she asked, changing the subject.

"I meant to tell you that it is very good." Mary blushed.

"I will give you the recipe, and you can bake one for Johnnie," she said.

She watched Mary for her reactions to the suggestion. She was studying Mary and working into her mental composition. Mary was quite unaware as to what was going on; otherwise, she would have reacted in the way she wanted things to be instead of reacting naturally.

"Don't bother," replied Mary. "I wouldn't know what to do with the recipe."

Addie was taken aback with the reply. Why, many people had begged her for the recipe, which she was so happy to part with. She always said, "It's better to keep a friend than to keep a recipe." She had acquired many a long friendship by parting with her most cherished recipe, but Mary bluntly declined to accept it. What Mary really meant was that she did not know how to bake a cake, and that conclusion finally made its way into Addie's mind. Addie was old-fashioned, and she was so surprised to find a girl of Mary's age who could not bake a cake.

"You don't cook either?" she asked Mary.

"For what reason would I need to learn the drudgery of a cook stove? I'm going to be a concert pianist," boasted Mary proudly.

"And whom do you expect to marry as a concert pianist?" she asked.

Addie could not get over the fact that here, before her very eyes, was a girl expecting to settle down and get married—yet she had no interest in cooking or baking.

"I'm going to marry Percival, of course—he does his own cooking."

"When you get married, who's going to do your cooking and washing . . . and cleaning?"

"Why, Percival, of course. All he needs to do is to cook twice as much, and there will be enough for both of us. He can do the washing and the cleaning like he always did when he was single. I won't have time for that when I get married. I'm going to practice on the piano from sunrise till sunset until I become a concert pianist." Mary parted with all her intimate thoughts as one woman would to another.

This was the end for Addie. She needed to pry into Mary's character no further. She had heard all she wanted to know, and she felt thoroughly convinced of Mary's character. She pictured Johnnie in the place of Percival—doing the cooking, washing the dishes, and keeping the house in order, while she would practice on the piano. She couldn't help bursting out loud with laughter.

"What makes you laugh?" asked Mary, thinking Addie was laughing at her.

"You just reminded me of a boy who was mighty glad he didn't marry a girl who wouldn't have him," Addie explained.

She was actually referring to Johnnie, who, she thought, would be mighty glad that he didn't win Mary if he would see the life Percival carried on after Percival would be bound to Mary in the holy state of matrimony. She laughed some more, and Mary joined her. Addie was of the opposite sex, but her heart and everything else was sided with Johnnie. She had a clear picture of Mary, and when Mary began to laugh, she laughed that much louder, feeling that Mary was laughing at her own self.

Mary told nothing of her associations with Johnnie. She was afraid Addie might carry the information on to Johnnie, and she didn't want to lose Johnnie's attentions. She didn't know why, but Johnnie's attentions were of equal value to her, as were Percival's or those of the boy from the library—but of the three suitors, she wanted to marry Percival, and oftentimes she was not sure herself that she wanted Percival for a husband.

Addie was careful not to give Mary any satisfactory information about Johnnie. She wanted to test Mary's love for him. She had led Mary to believe she was expecting Johnnie in a few days, and Mary disclosed her intentions of another visit by that time.

They bade each other a cheerful goodbye, and that was the end of Mary's first effort to locate Johnnie. She needed to satisfy her curiosity about Johnnie's mysterious actions. She didn't inquire at the college office, thinking that the source of information was right there in the neighborhood of Johnnie's home. She knew from Christine that Johnnie was not attending school, and it troubled her the more she thought about it. She could not resist the temptation to see the library boy. Anyhow, she had to wait at the college for Christine since she was using Christine's car, and she had to drive Christine home. She came to the book counter, all in smiles.

"I would like to have a book," she said coquettishly.

"What book is that?" He gave her a look.

"You know." She grinned and squinted.

"I'm afraid I don't know," he said kindly. "Will you please fill out the requisition?"

Mary was set back into her own self. Her smile vanished, and she looked at him with cold eyes. Slowly, she took the slip and filled in the name of a literature book. Handing it to him in doubt, she waited for his return. Her curiosity was weakened by his attitude.

He came and set the book before her. He looked on while she anxiously began looking through it.

"Don't be disappointed if you don't find any more poems," he warned.

"Do you mean I won't find any?" She gasped.

"I'm quite sure of it," He said without a smile.

She left the book right there, and she left the library. Her pride was whipped. Her hopes were rudely destroyed, and she was suffering within from the loss. It wasn't more than three hours of waiting for Christine, but she couldn't wait in the library anymore. She couldn't wait anywhere else either—she wanted to get away from it all. She returned the car keys to Christine and hurried home on the bus. She fled from disappointment to the comfort of her home, but her home held no comfort for her. Before, her heart beat with the intensity of pursuit by three lovers, but now she realized she had only Percival, and her heart was fettered with pain as it skipped two beats and struggled along on only one. She felt her lungs were resisting her efforts to breathe. Lying on her bed, staring at the ceiling, looking for the reason of her loss, she sprang from the bed to bring out the poems. There, she found her reasons; the ones she didn't find, she made up herself. "I have a girl in college too, and now it is too late—now it is too late!" She could see it all now. The library boy had another girl all that time she was away, and now it was too late for her to come back to him. As for Johnnie, she could only come to the conclusion that he had gotten married and had gone on a secret honeymoon. He never did care much for school, always proposing that she quit school with him to settle down.

Mary walked about the house with the same frustrated characteristics as her father and her brother—only she did not seek any relief through bottled spirits like they did. Her mother immediately noticed the difference in Mary, and so did Christine. Mary seemed to be helpless again, but she responded when she was asked to do something—like a faithful servant and no more. There was something cold and mysterious about her. She was not herself like the day before. She was not ill, as her mother would say; it was like her spirit had been drugged into a state of quiescence.

Percival seemed to be so ineffective in pleasing her since she believed she had lost her other two lovers. His courtship seemed to be so unexciting and even uninteresting. She was beginning to wonder what it would be like, being married to Percival. Maybe the career of a concert pianist was so much empty flattery by Percival, but taking everything into consideration, her career depended on her ability, not on Percival's management.

It took several days to work up the courage to look for Johnnie again. She was afraid to be repulsed, as she was by the library boy. Finally, one morning she was on her way to school with Christine. She had decided to begin her search at the other end this time, at the college instead of his home. Besides her brother, George, nobody knew what Mary was doing, and they didn't much care since they were happy to have her show interest in something.

She went to the dean's office, where she was told Johnnie telephoned one day that he wouldn't be in school anymore—that he left school for good. It weighed down her conscience heavier than before. She could see her brother's finger pointing at her while he was saying that it was all her fault. She was spurred into a feverish urge to find him. Obtaining the address of Pappy's rooming house, she was on her way in Christine's car. She didn't know whether to look forward to failure of expectation or to look for encouragement to her efforts, but she could not rest until she had reached her desired satisfaction of knowing that she was not the cause of Johnnie's mysterious actions.

"Mr. Pappipopulos," she begged, "could you tell me anything about Johnnie?"

"Maybe I could—who are you?" Pappy wanted to know.

His eyes were wide open, and his sense for youthful beauty was aroused. With the first glance, he had a suspicion that it was Mary— *the* Mary that Johnnie described so often, the Mary that Johnnie could not vanquish. It was interesting to see what Mary looked like, to see if she was really human or if she was from the heavens beyond as Johnnie flowered his descriptions. This was his opportunity to see what was dragging on the other side of the romance.

"I'm Mary," she said. "Johnnie told me a lot of nice things about you."

"So the boy has been talking about me?" he said, leading the way to the living room while she followed without hesitation.

"He said you have the nicest rooming house around the campus." She sat down on the couch with him.

"God help that boy," he said. "He was like a son to me. Now I don't know what to do with myself.

"Couldn't you tell me what he did or what he had in mind the last time you saw him?" She pressed him to shorten her visit.

"All I know," he said, "is that he went to your house, and he never did come back here. Didn't come back to school either. The football team can't come through without him. If anyone does, you should be the one to know where he is."

"But I don't know—that is why I'm here," she replied.

"What do you think of the boy?" He eyed her reactions carefully.

"Well"—she looked for an appropriate answer before she decided what to say—"I like him very much. Otherwise, I wouldn't be here, would I?"

"Why don't you say you love him?"

"I do love him."

"Why don't you marry him?"

"I do marry him," she said.

She was so engrossed with her thoughts of Johnnie that her mind was drifting, and at last, she answered without giving attention to his questions. Pappy looked at her with a "What's going on?" expression.

"You do marry him?" he asked.

"Did I say that?" She expressed surprise.

"Look, Mary," he said to her, "there's just you and me here, and I didn't say it—I asked it."

"I'm sorry," she apologized. "I must have been thinking about my fiancé."

"Let's just think about Johnnie," he said with something working in his mind. "Would you say you like him enough to go on a hayride with him?"

"I'd love that," said Mary, thinking it would be one way of finding him.

"Do you know how to cook hot dogs?" He beamed at her.

"I don't know—I never tried," she admitted.

She thought it was necessary to know as part of the hayride, but Pappy was only stringing her out, and she would be surprised to know what he had already strung out on the line.

"Well, you don't have to know," Pappy assured her. "Are you studying to be the same thing as Johnnie?"

"No," she said. "Johnnie is going to be a businessman, and I'm going to be a concert pianist."

"Then you won't be able to wash the dishes or do any housework," said Pappy, looking at her hands with an understanding of the delicate care they would require for the accomplishment of her ambition.

"Oh no. Nothing like that," she said. "When I get married, I'll be practicing on the piano from sunrise till sunset."

"Ohhh!" Pappy gave out in realization of her future. "Well." He paused. "I can't tell you anything about Johnnie. The boys say he quit school, but he never said so to me, and I'm keeping his room just the way he left it. If nobody else around here is expecting him back, I am."

"When are you expecting him back?" she asked in hopes of reaching the end of her search.

"Any day. He'll be back," said Pappy in low spirits. "He wouldn't leave me without telling me about it."

Mary was dissatisfied with the visit. She was expecting to learn much more about Johnnie's absence instead of being grilled by Pappy's questions. She knew that there was nothing more to come out of Pappy, so she made a move to leave. Pappy seemed tired and remained in his place on the couch.

"Thanks for your help, Pappy," she said as she was leaving. "I hope to see you again soon."

"Don't mention it," said Pappy. "I'm an old man, but I can still help people in some ways. I'll be expecting you."

She left him sitting there on the couch. When he was sure she had gone, he keeled over on his side, stretching out his legs on the couch. He was slowly closing his eyelids to fall asleep.

The transition from the illusion to the reality was painful to the heart and mind. She pictured herself being torn apart by the affections of three ardent lovers, and now she could only see Percival in the picture. She felt her ego taking a beating, and she felt herself being drawn to Percival for what little affection he may give.

She was out of the house and on the walk when it dawned upon her to look through Johnnie's room. Perhaps there might be a clue as to his absence. Regardless of what there may or may not be, she wanted to go through his belongings. She had to know more about him from his personal things. The boys were at school, and this was her opportunity to make a secret investigation. Johnnie told her he had a room on the second floor in front. *It wouldn't be difficult to sneak up there*, she thought, turning back to the house.

She opened and closed the door quietly. Then she slowly worked her way up the stairs quietly on her toes and looked into both of the front rooms. At first, she had some doubts as to which one she wanted to search. Looking into the closet on the first room, she discovered Johnnie's clothes put away neatly on hangers. She went through all the pockets but found nothing she was after. The handkerchiefs and loose change, she put back where she had found them. She looked through his books, his desk drawers, and his notebooks, but there was nothing to betray any reasons for his action. She expected to find some train or bus schedules with the journey marked, or at least, there could be some travel circulars, which might give her an idea, but there was not a thing. She turned to the other desk on the farther side, and in one corner, she found a stack of sheets, some of which contained finished poems, while the others had notes or poems in the making. In looking through these, she found one with familiar handwriting. She took it into her hands as the blood rushed to her face with the force of an astounding discovery. In wild excitement, she read it.

Oh, mighty rollers of the sea,
    Why do you pound and pound on me?
Oh, mighty winds of atmosphere,
    Why do you send the cargo here?
I ground and ground and broke in two
    The finest wood sent here by you.

Oh, mighty rollers of the sea,
    Why do you pound and pound on me?
Oh, mighty winds of atmosphere,
    Why do you send the cargo here?
I grind and grind and break in two
    The finest steel sent here by you.

Oh, mighty rollers of the sea,
    Why do you pound and pound on me?
Oh, mighty winds of atmosphere,
    Why do you send the cargo here?
I'm hard and tough and firm and real,
    And I will strike fire with steel.

Oh, mighty rollers of the sea,
    Why do you pound and pound on me?
Oh, mighty winds of atmosphere,
    Why do you send the cargo here?
I stand in water in ages.
    Man, he knows of me from pages.

Oh, mighty rollers of the sea,
    Why do you pound and pound on me?
Oh, mighty winds of atmosphere,
    Why do you send the cargo here?

When Johnnie had written this poem, he wasn't thinking of the sea, of the waves on the sea, of the wind and storm dashing the ships of wood and ships of steel upon the shore rock. This wasn't the prayer of the shore rock. This was Johnnie's prayer, and in it, the sea was the countless number of people in his life. The waves were problems of his everyday life, which were rough on his desires. There were times of peace and quiet in his life, but he was painting a picture of his troubles with Mary, where the mighty waves of trouble beat upon him, and yet they had not overpowered him. The ships of wood and ships of steel were painful experiences that drifted his way, that were cast upon him by influences beyond his control, but he was hard and tough, and he would maintain his ground. He had written this poem in a period of gloom when Mary was ill and she could not open the window to speak to him.

However, Mary did not see it as he thought he had written it. She saw the giant blue waves, with white caps, of the sea. They were crushing a ship against a lonely shore rock as the wind beat the waves into a greater fury and gathered more clouds of rain, thunder, and lightning about the unfortunate ship.

She also saw the resemblance of the writing to the other poems she had received. She quickly turned to Johnnie's notebook again, and there, she found the writing of the same pen and the same hand. When she looked through the notebook before, she had not noticed the writing since her mind was with Johnnie while she was searching for train or bus schedules or travel circulars. She smiled with satisfaction, folding the poem to put it away into her purse. Her eyes brightened again with the realization that she had not lost her poet lover. Now there was no doubt as to who the author of those poems was, and she was absolutely sure of it.

From the time she discovered who the one writing the poems was, Johnnie had two strikes on her, and she didn't know it. One more strike, and she would be helpless. She would be recklessly in love with him, but Percival had the third strike on her. At the present time, she could say, "My body is with Percival, but my heart and my mind are with Johnnie."

She would have been greatly embarrassed if she were caught rummaging through a room in a boys' rooming house. The news would spread like a forest fire, gathering heat and intensity as it spread. Fortunately, she left in the same way she had entered the room—on tiptoe, without being seen. That was the way she wanted it to be.

She was so happy on leaving Pappy's house in peace that she forgot about Christine's car, which she had driven to Pappy's house. It was standing at the curb in front of Pappy's house, but in her happiness, it did not make an impression on her mind. She walked along with the happy thoughts. She was on her way to Christine's office—and for what? She stopped in her tracks to turn the thoughts over again. Yes, for what was she going to Christine's office? Then it came to her that the car was at Pappy's house. She hurried back and drove off at a high rate of speed. She was going home to add another poem to her collection. The ride home seemed so long that she was speeding all the way home. This was her lucky day because again, she slipped by without being apprehended—this time, she slipped by a motorcycle policeman who had a handy book of tickets for traffic violators.

In her room, she compared the writing, and it was identical. This removed any doubt from her mind. She lay across the bed, facing the ceiling, and held the poems above while she read them over many times. Then she thought of Addie and wondered what Addie would know about the poems. With her curiosity reaching the point of satisfaction, she was able to control the speed of the car within the requirements of the police department. She was happier than ever before. The only thing that remained was for her to tell Johnnie how happy she was—which meant she had to find him in the worst way.

Addie was sleeping when Mary reached her house. When Addie came to the door, she looked tired—with her hair disheveled, her dress wrinkled and disarranged, and one stocking down to the ankle. It was afternoon already, and Addie had no cake to offer as she asked Mary into the house.

"I'm sorry," she said to Mary as she flopped into the lounge chair out of her weakness. "I haven't done a thing for the past week or so. I don't have anything I could offer you. I only keep hoping that Johnnie would return home."

"That's all right," said Mary. "I may have some good news for you."

"About Johnnie?" Addie popped out like an electric current was being sent through her body.

"Yes, he's been writing me some poetry, and I didn't know it until today. Do you know nothing about these?" Mary asked, showing her the poems.

"Oh no! No! My gosh, did he write those?" Addie flared up.

Addie denied any knowledge of the poems to give Mary the sensation of privacy in Johnnie's love affair. Addie was afraid that Mary might disapprove of having Johnnie show everybody the poems before sending them to her. Anyhow, she figured she was on the safe side by denying any association with Johnnie's lovemaking.

"Why, yes," replied Mary. "Aren't they beautiful? Each one like a flower to live in my memory forever."

"I'm glad you like them," Addie commented. "Only Johnnie could write something like that."

"It made me so happy when I discovered that Johnnie wrote them for me," Mary confessed.

"Don't let your happiness take you for a ride," Addie warned, leaning toward Mary. "What I have to say may not be so easy on your conscience."

"What have you to say? What is it?"

Mary cried out in excitement, almost without control. In a flash, she thought that Johnnie had returned and gone or that Addie was hiding something.

"I'm afraid for Johnnie," Addie said slowly and sadly. "Ever since he left, I have not been feeling well."

"Please tell me! Don't let me sit here waiting!" Mary cried out in a lower tone.

"I was afraid to tell you, but now I must. Are you sure your heart is strong enough? If not, then you must come another day." Addie talked with a hazy look in her eyes.

"Tell me now or tell me never! I cannot bear this suspense any longer," Mary protested.

"Do you remember the pocket Bible with the hole in it and the bloodstained pages? The Bible that Johnnie asked you to keep for him?"

"Yes—what about it?" Mary asked with signs of anxiety.

"Why did you give it back to him?" Addie talked slowly since she was ill and weak.

"I didn't know what it was. The sight of the blood had made me sick," Mary explained.

"It would have been better to bury it in your backyard or to burn it rather than to give it back to him. It was his blood, and the Bible saved his life. It was your Bible. It had your name in it. You hurt him when you gave it back to him. You hurt him as if the bullet, which was spent by the thickness of your Bible, had been sent through his heart by you." Addie's words were meant for punishment, and every word she spoke hit its mark.

"I didn't know!" Mary was crying profusely. "I didn't know until brother George brought the Bible to me and told me the whole story about Johnnie. Johnnie told him that he had no more use for the Bible."

"He came home straight from your house. I was surprised by him coming here at that time of night, so I went to see him. He said he didn't have the money to buy the kind of gifts for you that he would like to. He said he met somebody, and together, they could make a lot of money in a short time. Well, I didn't think nothing of it at the time, but I'm thinking of it now, and that is what makes me so weak." She paused to gain some strength.

"Go on—tell me!" Mary shouted through her tears.

Addie looked at her without the least bit of pity for Mary's tears. Addie felt that this would help her heart to beat with greater strength since it had the double satisfaction of being relieved of this secret and also since the knowledge was punishment to Mary.

"Early in the morning, I was making some breakfast for him when I heard a car drive up. I paid no attention to it at first, but when I looked out the front window later, there was Johnnie going into a big black car with four husky, tough-looking men." She paused for a rest, watching Mary closely and waiting for Mary's impatient ears, but Mary was wiping her tears away and blowing her nose.

"A few nights ago," Addie went on, "I thought I saw a burglar in his house. I threw my coat on in a hurry, and I peeked in through the window. I saw a man with a flashlight. I knew it was a burglar because he was searching through the bags that Johnnie brought from the army. I was going to call the police, but before I left the window, his flashlight fell down, and it shined on his face for a second or two. It was Johnnie—I'm as sure as I believe in God. I changed my mind about calling the police. I stayed there, and I watched him. He took out his pistol, his submachine gun, all the ammunition—and he ran out of the house into a taxicab before I got to the front. I know it was a taxicab because I saw it lit up going down the street." Addie paused, waiting for Mary to say something.

"It is hard to believe," said Mary, sniffing. "He was such a nice boy."

"Something is wrong, terribly wrong, and it makes me sick to think of it."

"I'm afraid you think that it is all my fault," said Mary, with the question on her mind.

"Faultfinding isn't going to help Johnnie," said Addie, shaking her head.

"Well—why don't you say it? Everybody else does!" Mary cried out, with tears flooding her eyes and sorrow choking her throat. She hurried out of the house without bidding Addie goodbye. She hurried home, where she could have a good cry on her bed. Any of her thoughts only brought her more tears as she lay across the bed on her stomach. Why did Johnnie give her so much trouble? She beat this question around in her head till the tears had flown away and there were no more. She had all the poems before her, but she could not enjoy them, knowing that Johnnie was involved in a dishonorable profession. That was the impression Addie gave her, and that was the way it remained. She had the Bible back from George, and she brought it out to keep with the poems. The Bible impressed on her that all was not lost that could not be regained with prayer. She read the bloodstained Bible, and she was not afraid of it. She had overcome the fear of blood itself.

Mary returned to the college for Christine, and after taking her home, she went downtown where George said he saw Johnnie when he got beat up. She looked into every tavern in her search for Johnnie. She walked the streets till late at night. Her legs were aching, and her feet were blistered, but she thought the time was well spent. Anyhow, the exercise was just what the doctor ordered. That night, she soaked her blistered feet, applying some salve to the blisters. She had her first restful sleep since she met Johnnie. She was not in a condition to do any more walking for at least a week, and this was all that kept her at home.

She related to George the incidents Addie had told her. She pleaded with him, and she begged him with all her heart. He listened with interest but shrunk away from her invocatory plea. Since he was the only one who could help her and wouldn't, there was nothing else she could do but to wait.

XXIII

Newspapers

efore the week was over, Addie came riding in a taxi. She was fearfully upset and on the verge of a breakdown. She had a newspaper under her arm. She asked to see Mary when Christine answered the door. Christine invited her into the living room, where Mary came to see her.

"Something terrible has happened," Addie said, fumbling nervously with her newspaper.

"Is it about Johnnie?" asked Mary, knowing that it could not be about anyone else.

"Yes, it is about Johnnie," she admitted, "but nobody knows it besides me."

"But you will tell me, won't you?" Good or bad, Mary had to know everything if it was about Johnnie.

"That's what I came here for," said Addie. "I'm afraid we can't help Johnnie no more—only God above can help him, so pray with me while there still is time."

"I will, Addie, I will—but tell me what has happened because I can't wait to hear," said Mary with impatience.

"You see this picture, in the paper, of the watch fob?" Addie looked for her reaction.

"Yes."

"Well . . ." Addie paused before she could go on. "I know that watch fob like I know the key to my house. It belonged to his father. His mother left it with me for her boy to have, and I gave it to him. It was handed down to him from his great-grandfather. Now they find it at the scene of a jewelry robbery where the watchman was murdered."

"But there could have been another one just like Johnnie had," Mary protested against the shoddy conclusion.

"I can't be mistaken. I know every nick and scratch on the fob. I waited a long time to pass it on to Johnnie." Addie insisted on her accuracy of identification.

"Couldn't there be some error in photography, or couldn't Johnnie have lost it?" Mary refused to accept the information.

"Then what about this elephant trinket that was found at the robbery of the other jewelry store? I remember that too. When Johnnie was a little boy, he found the trinket, and he kept it as a good luck charm on a key chain all his life. It was made of ivory, and it had a tiny compass set into it."

"Maybe you're right, but I still can't accept it as a true fact." Mary refused to take the identification as evidence against Johnnie.

"It is not a question of whether you will accept it but whether you will help him in the only way you can."

"Why must I be plagued with the troubles of this man?" Mary refuted the conviction of being tied to him since her wedding day was approaching rapidly.

"It is for you that he is doing all this—don't you forget it," Addie reminded her. "He went wrong in his desperation to please you."

"All right, Addie." She submitted. "As you said before, 'I will help him in the only way that is left.'"

Mary followed her to the door, bidding her goodbye. She watched Addie enter the waiting taxi, and she remained at the door until the taxi went out of her sight. Upon returning to the living room, there was her mother, Christine, and her brother waiting for her. George had the newspaper in his hands. Everyone looked to her for an elaboration of the mysterious visit, and she became embarrassed over the thought that they were eavesdropping and that they knew everything.

"Mary. You must tell us everything," her mother urged, feeling that it was Mary's duty to the family.

"But, Mother," complained Mary, "there is no more to tell. I'm quite sure you've heard everything."

"You didn't put the idea into his head of getting you some expensive jewelry, did you?" questioned her mother.

"Of course not, Mother. How could I even hint at such a thing?" Mary defended herself.

"You certainly did hint at it." George cut in. "Remember how disappointed you were when he gave you the Bible? You said you thought he was bringing you some jewelry."

"I didn't say anything of the kind," Mary protested vigorously.

"What's this about the Bible?" her mother asked, her curiosity aroused.

Christine was an innocent member in the house, and she listened to everything that was going on.

"Nothing, Mother—he's just babbling!" Mary almost shouted in her fury.

"Babbling? *Am I?*" George shouted back at her in anger.

"Will you two calm down so I can find out what's going on in my family?" Her mother had to shout to be heard.

"Mother, George has a girl, and he's ashamed of his family because they can't provide him with any money like they used to."

"Why don't you tell Mother everything about Johnnie?" George snapped back at her.

"Now is that the kind of conversation to carry on? Can't all this be straightened out and settled in a milder manner?" Christine shouted at first, and she ended in almost a whisper for emphasis.

"Mother, he's always saying everything is my fault. He makes me sick!" Mary cried out, hurrying away to her room.

George did not wait to explain anything to his mother. He couldn't bear the thought of all the questions she could think up. He took his hat and coat, snatched Christine's car keys from the dresser, and was on his way in his father's footsteps. Ever since George came back, Christine did not see much of the car except when she drove to and from school. He didn't even bother asking her if he could use it. He called her car a struggle-buggy, and she didn't like it because he had nothing to show for his witty-brained remarks.

Mrs. Masterson broke down with tears upon the revelation of the futility of her efforts to keep her family together. She saw her husband as lost, her son as drifting, and her daughter as carrying on in secrecy. She had always had a feeling that this would come since her husband lost everything, but she didn't know what it was like to be in the center of it all—to have her heart wounded from three different sides. She worked hard to set the family back on its feet when it fell apart, but all her work was for nothing. She was left helpless by the forces beyond her control. Her influence in the family seemed to have been nullified, and she had no judicatory power over any member of her family. She was only hanging on with whatever strength she had left, and she hoped and prayed for better times to come.

Her employer made it difficult for her to work for him. He was always knocking her husband and placing himself before her as an ideal. He was always proposing a divorce with her husband and a marriage with him.

Christine, on the other hand, had no husband or family to bring her mental suffering from bereavement. She had always envied the blessings of married life, and she expected difficulties at times to arise, but she knew not how painful they could be. She pitied her sister, and she shared all the heartaches with her. She gave her solace and a roof over her head. Sometimes she thought her sacrifice was too great since it delivered Percival into the hands of Mary, leaving her an aging spinster. Many times she thought that if she had her life to live over again, she would choose the course that her sister did. She shed her sympathy upon her sister, giving her comfort until her sister could gain enough strength to recompose her efforts to bring her family together.

Mary lay on her stomach across the bed, crying into a pillow over the fact that she had confided in her brother and he had turned upon her. He was such a changed man since he had returned from the service. Before he left for the service, through all their childhood days, they would share their secrets and their sorrows. They went to school together, and many times, they had seen a movie together, but now she felt as if she had no brother at all. He treated her with an overbearing demeanor, and he was thinking only of himself. She couldn't understand him or his motives anymore. She was never satisfied with his explanation of the blackened eye and swollen jaw. She was always wondering if he didn't have something to do with it. Judging from his conduct, she could almost be sure of it.

George, taking after his father, didn't spend much of his time at home anymore. His favorites were the pool room during the day and the tavern during the night. He couldn't see why his sister had to go and marry a fellow like Percival when she had Johnnie at her feet. There seemed to be nothing that he could do with a brother-in-law like Percival. He couldn't shoot a game of pool with him, he couldn't bowl with him, and he couldn't make the rounds of nightclubs with him. The truth hung over his head that he was not the one marrying Percival and that he was not the one to live with Percival—but why marry a fellow like Percival when she could marry one like Johnnie?

His sister, Johnnie, and Percival were not all that was on his mind. His father played an important part in his frustrations and his actions. He couldn't see how a businessman like his father could slip and make such a terrible blunder as to speculate and lose every cent he had. He felt this would change his entire future, and that future, from what he saw of it, he could not accept. He would rather roam about the country as a tramp than to be tied down to a job where he would have to punch the clock in and out. The bright days of coming to work after he'd had his uninterrupted sleep were over. That was a thing of the past. For the present, he could live off his mother's paycheck, and also, he could live off his aunt Christine's kindness. For the future, he had no thoughts since he could not see any pleasantry in it. Let it come as it may and bring him whatever it will. He could not help himself in his attitude, so he tried to implicate his father and his sister with the cause for the things he did.

Mr. Masterson became deeply rooted in his habit of drinking down his sorrows. The more he drank, the greater his need for drinking was. When he slept off the drinks, all his irritations took on greater proportions, driving him back for more in bigger doses. First, it was a matter of making a mistake in his calculations of advancing his business. Then came Johnnie into his life, exciting his ambitions, only for him to see Johnnie sent away beyond his reach by his wife and his daughter. Then came his son, who would not recognize his efforts to promote a greater business, who turned away from him—because he was eating his heart away with strong alcoholic beverages. He had it fixed in his mind that he was the father regardless of the condition of sobriety under which he may have been in. There was no one left who could steer him back onto the straight path of his regular family relationships. He had lost interest in all of his ambitions regarding his family and in his spiritual salvation. There seemed to be nothing left in his life but the urge to drink more and to spend more time in drinking with his colleagues of the same category in life.

Mr. Pappipopulos was taking life easy. His children came to see him often, bringing his grandchildren with them. He missed Johnnie, it was true, and he kept the room as Johnnie had left it, waiting for his return. There were no more victory feasts, no more cake-and-coffee parties, and the boys seemed to be in mourning. He had no one like Johnnie to talk to—to guide with his philosophy and his experience. He was not troubled with Johnnie's absence, although he missed him, and he knew Johnnie well enough to be sure Johnnie would be back—only he didn't know when.

Addie was stretching her imaginations with every little bit of news about Johnnie. From what she had seen with her own eyes and what she had read in the paper, she was sure that Johnnie joined up with a gang of jewel thieves. She was sure that Johnnie would shower Mary with some or the most expensive personal ornaments studded with jewels. She was going to tell Mary to expect a shower of the kind, but she didn't want to darken Johnnie's character—she just wanted Mary to know what Mary had driven him to. The more she thought about him, the less she could eat and sleep. She was getting thin and nervous. She bought the principal newspapers in town, always looking for something about Johnnie that she dreaded to find. She listened to the newscast on the radio, and her imaginations involved Johnnie in every jewel theft she heard of. She hoped and prayed that he would pay her a visit so that she may have the opportunity to straighten out his path and to save him.

Things went along quietly, with everyone looking after their own interests and thinking about Johnnie. They were gathered in the living room late one night, with Mrs. Masterson trying to quiet down her husband and send him off to bed. Mary and Christine were drilling George full of questions, but he only replied in some indignant manner. He wasn't quite in the condition his father was in. He made the rounds of the nightclubs with his buddies, but that wasn't his trouble. He got a flat tire on Christine's car, and he left the car right there—he didn't know where. They questioned him over and over until the monotony of it made his tired eyes so sleepy, he only wanted to close them and dream about his burlesque beauties shaking and shimmying at his own discretion.

Christine was worried about the car. It was an old one, but it was her only means of transportation to school. She could ride the bus, but that didn't practically appeal to her since she had driven her own car for so many years, and riding a taxi would only add another account besides paying out for the house and supporting the Masterson family.

There was a sharp hammering on the door, and everybody was startled into absolute attention. Mrs. Masterson opened the door, expecting to find some of George's army buddies in the same tipsy condition he was in, but it was nothing of the kind—it was a policeman. There was a push button at the door for the door chimes, but he hammered with his nightstick—*Bang! Bang! Bang!*—rapidly and heavily.

"What's going on here?" he demanded in a hoarse voice.

"N-N-Nothing, Officer. We're just— We're just— Just—" She was frightened.

She didn't know what to say. Her intuitive sense jumped to the conclusion that he came for her son or for her husband or for both of them. She was trembling with the fear of bad news.

Christine looked on, expecting George to be taken away. She could have bet on it. She thought it was something concerning her car. George might have run somebody down or collided with another car and brought home the story of the flat tire. How she wished the police would take George away and change his ways of thinking! George needed something just like this to shake him back to reality.

Mary looked on, suspecting that it was something in connection with Christine's car. She couldn't think of anything else because George changed his story several times. Once, he said the battery went dead. Once, it wouldn't start. Once, it ran out of gasoline. Once, the lights didn't work, and he was afraid to drive without them, and the rest of the time, he claimed it had a flat tire that he couldn't fix. Anyhow, his stories were so incoherent that they could not hold her belief in him. She, for one, wished that the police would take her father away and change his way of living. She wished that because she knew of no one else who could influence him into changing. She wished that because she yearned to see him return to life as a husband to her mother and a father to herself. She wished that because George followed in his father's footsteps, and once his father changed for the better, George would change with him.

The father looked on, thinking that his son got himself some trouble that the police took an interest in, while George thought the same thing of his father. They looked at each other with questioning eyes.

"Does Mary Masterson live here?" the policeman asked.

Mary was stunned for a second at first; then she quickly recovered when Addie and the newspaper articles came to her mind. Addie's words of the jewelry thefts came to her ears as she turned pale from fear. She expected to be taken to the police station for questioning in regard to Johnnie. She came to her mother's side like a little girl would for protection.

"I am Mary Masterson," she said in a low tone, her lips quivering from fear for herself and for Johnnie.

"Here is a message for you," said the policeman.

"Is that all?" asked Mary out of surprised relief.

"Isn't that enough? It comes from a dying jewelry thief. He's been shot, and we found this note in his pocket," the tough-looking, hoarse-voiced policeman rudely informed her, and he left them all looking at Mary as they had looked at the policeman before.

Mary knew she could not make this a personal matter as she looked back at everyone. She opened the envelope and found the note inside. It was written on a piece of old, wrinkled blank portion of a newspaper. The envelope had the return address of a police station. The upper half on the paper contained her name and address, while the lower half contained the message, with a line drawn between. The paper was only large enough to hold all the writing. It was torn with an uneven edge from the remainder of the sheet, and the other side had some printing, showing that it was a piece of a newspaper. She glanced at the address, and the message, she read to herself:

Dear Mary,

Do not lose faith in me, I love you, and I'm doing this for your happiness.

Love, Johnnie

She turned the note silently over to her mother. Her mother turned it over silently to Christine, while her father and her brother looked on. They were in such a condition that they couldn't read the note if they wanted to. They asked, they pleaded, they begged, and then they demanded to know. Mrs. Masterson, fearing that their demands would grow into threats, read it to them, word for word. However, they were disappointed with its contents, and they ridiculed Mary in their semiconscious state of mind.

Mary could say nothing. Her imaginations had no place to go. The information had fenced them in. It was like the policeman had said—Johnnie was a jewelry thief, he was shot, and now he had to be dying in sin.

"Mother," she said, "I must go to see him."

"You?" questioned her mother. "Go to see him? A thief? No, my dear Mary. I cannot permit it. How would you face Percival and the guests on your wedding day? If there would be a wedding after you did go to see him."

"Isn't there trouble enough in this house without you running off to jail to kiss a wounded criminal goodbye before he dies?" George cut into her heart, which beat for Johnnie.

"He is not a criminal! He is not! He is innocent, and I must go to see him before he dies!" Mary cried out.

Her father smiled when he heard these fighting words from Mary. He would like to say something, but all he could think of was some song to sing, and he moved out of the living room on his way to bed, mumbling a song that sometimes sounded off in full volume.

"But you can't go. The police are holding him, and no visitors could see him," Christine cautioned.

"If he is dying, they certainly will permit me to see him. Why did they send me this note?" Mary reasoned.

"What do you want to go and see him for? You want your picture in all the papers as the girlfriend of a punk jewelry thief? What for do you think the police came running to you with that note? Go ahead and go—that's where they want you for questioning!" Christine bellowed.

George was shaken out of his hazy feeling by the sight of the policeman, and it was transformed into anger at Johnnie. He still remembered the black eye and swollen jaw he had gotten from Johnnie. He was not yet in his sober mind, but his speech made sense as well as injury to Mary.

"Mary." Her mother appealed to her again in a different tone. "If you must go, please see Percival about it first. He should have something to say before you could be free to go."

Mary felt that everyone was against her wish to see Johnnie. She didn't know how to fight her way back, and she felt humiliated, standing alone in defense of Johnnie. Silently, she retired to bed, where she spent all night plotting how she could see Johnnie without the knowledge of the family.

The others didn't seem to have anything else to talk about after Mary left them. Georgic realized that Christine would soon be after him for her car, so he removed himself from her presence. Again, the two sisters found themselves facing each other and wondering what would take place next. Christine was always ready to help her sister, but there were times when she felt the urge to help herself more than the urge to help her sister. They remained for some time, with each one to her own thoughts.

XXIV

Police Station

*O*n the morning, Christine welcomed the day like a selfish, inconsiderate person. The weather was just right for another score against Mary. This was her opportunity to do something for herself as well. She went to Mary's bedroom, where Mary was still lying awake. Mary was surprised to see her.

"Would you like to go to school with me, Mary?" Christine asked in a suggestive way.

"Why, yes," said Mary. "I'd love to."

Mary did not catch the implications in Christine's tone because she was doing her own thinking, and this fitted perfectly into her thoughts. She believed that what went on in her mind was all her own. Little did she know that Christine was the spider and she the fly. Everything was so rosy, and she was percolating with the exciting thoughts of her plans laid out before her.

"You better hurry and be ready when the taxi arrives," Christine warned.

Christine was afraid that Mary would dally about the house and her mother would have the time to make a thorough inquiry. Christine had the breakfast ready, and they were through eating when Mary's mother came into the kitchen. Her mother suspected something, but before she made any progress with her protests, the horn of the taxi sounded, and Mary was off to school with Christine.

"You can have some rest and quiet around this place!" Christine shouted before she left the house.

"You may remain in my office if you like, Mary," said Christine on arriving at the college.

"If you don't mind," replied Mary, "I would rather be at the library. I may even go to see Percival later."

"Well"—Christine smiled—"come to see me if you should feel that you need any help."

"Thank you," said Mary happily. "I'll do that, and I won't leave for home without you."

Mary was happy since she didn't find it necessary to lie her way through. She was telling the truth when she said she wouldn't leave for home without Christine, but she could do anything she pleased as long as she would not go home without Christine. She could even go to see Johnnie without anybody apprehending her moves.

Christine smiled to herself, and she laughed in her heart about the cleverness of her ways in spinning a trap for Mary. She was free of it all, and Mary would tie the rope around her own neck—but who would kick the chair out from under her feet? Would it be done by Mary herself, or would it be Johnnie, Percival, George, her father, or her mother? Who would it be? She was not certain who it would be, but she was sure Mary would be strung up. That would derange everything for Mary's wedding. She entertained such silly thoughts as having Mary tell her how Johnnie was getting along, but a frontal inquiry may silence Mary, making her all the more cautious. She believed in Johnnie, and she would like to hear of him, but her position as professor at the college barred her from being associated with a known thief.

Mary went to see Percival, her former professors, and her girlfriends, and when the afternoon came, she was in a taxi—on her way to see Johnnie in the general hospital. She didn't spend much time at the hospital because the police officer in charge would allow no more visitors to see him that day. She returned to the college and rode home with Christine.

Christine talked of Johnnie, expecting Mary to contribute to the conversation with her visit to the hospital. Mary did not say anything for the simple reason that there was nothing to say. Christine sensed that there was nothing hidden in Mary's mind because if Mary had at least seen Johnnie, her nervous tension would have been released, and she would be happy and gay. On the other hand, there might be something seriously wrong with Johnnie, and he might be near death from the complications resulting from the gunshot wounds. She was not positive in either case as she weighed the two in trying to pass judgment on Mary's quiet mood.

When the taxi came to a stop in front of the house, the first thing that Christine did was to see if George brought her car back. Oh, well. If George wasn't home, she still wouldn't know whether he located the car or whether he was out looking for it. On entering the house, she was informed that George had left early in the morning and that neither he nor the car had arrived yet. They waited for George till late at night, but when he came, they couldn't get any more out of him than they had last night. The car was still somewhere; he knew not where.

The following day, Christine was disappointed since it was a repetition of the other day in all respects. Mary wouldn't talk about Johnnie. Her auditory nerves were itching for news. George didn't locate the car, and only God knew what hour he would come home tonight.

Mary had nothing to say about Johnnie as it had happened the day before—no more visitors that day, but maybe they would permit her to see him on the following day. The absence of the car didn't make much difference to Christine except that she had to wait for the cab, but it did make a whale of a difference to Mary. Mary had no income, and the taxi fares dug her savings out in no time to mention. That evening, when they reached home and Christine's car was not there, Mary was breathing fire in her heated desperation. She could run that brother of hers through a meat grinder three times over. How could he be so stupid as to leave the car somewhere and not be able to find it in three days? She would wait for him if it took all night. She wanted to know how he was going about it in trying to find the car. She had her mind set to wait for him; then she changed her mind before she waited five minutes. She reasoned that if the minutes passed on so slowly, she could not stand the crawling pace of the hours late into the night. She slipped out of the house, and a short time later, she was talking to the police department over the telephone at the fruit stand by the road. She talked with the air and said that it was her car. She gave Christine's name and the identification of the car. Then she was back in the house again without anyone missing her since her mother and Christine were busy in the kitchen preparing dinner. This made her happy with the thought that nobody knew of her telephone call.

They had their dinner and relaxed in the living room for the evening. Lately, they only served dinner for three, but they prepared enough for five.

George and his father would help themselves to the contents of the ice box at whatever hour they would come. They were getting into a regular schedule of coming in somewhere between three and four o'clock in the morning. Then they would raid the kitchen with their voracious appetites and go to bed by the time the sun brightened the sky. They were up again at two o'clock in the afternoon and out again by four. It seemed as if they shied away from meeting Christine, who was providing for them.

As they sat in the living room—quietly conversing on different subjects, trying to divert their minds away from the bad boys—a powerful spotlight was flashed past the front window, causing them to hurry to the window out of curiosity. Without a doubt, they guessed that it was a squad car looking for a certain address. When a plainclothes man left the car and headed for their door, they knew that it bore the certain address these men were looking for.

"Mary," her mother said, turning to her, "could this be another note for you?"

"I don't know, Mother," she replied. "Let us wait and see. It could be for George, you know."

Before there was any banging on the door with a nightstick or even the sound of the door chimes, her mother opened the door out of sheer anxiety at the mention of her son's name by her daughter. Maybe her daughter knew something about George that hadn't come to her yet.

"Does George Masterson live here?" the plainclothes man asked.

"Yes," replied Mrs. Masterson calmly.

"May I speak to him?" he asked, looking past her for George.

"He's not home right now," she said with growing fear.

"When will he be home?"

"About three or four o'clock in the morning."

"Working, is he?"

"No, he's not working at all. He returned home from the service a short time ago," she explained.

"That will be all, I guess," he said, turning away.

"Why do you want him, may I ask?" She had almost thought of it too late.

"We're just checking up on the boys that came home from the service. We'd like to help them if we can," he explained.

"Oh," she gave out with the relaxation of her nervous tension.

"Too bad he's not working, isn't it?" he said before stepping into the squad car.

"Yes," she whispered, and that was as loud as she could acknowledge the fact.

"How did you know they were coming for George?" She turned to Mary, who was shrinking away from answering the question.

"Because it couldn't be for me, and it wouldn't be for Father, so George was the only one left," she explained without implicating herself. This was a tight spot to wiggle her way out of, and in fact, she couldn't wiggle at all.

"How interesting," commented Christine. "Something going on in this house all the time. Never a dull moment."

Mary's fear was growing by leaps and bounds, so she hurried off to bed before any more questions could come her way. Only she knew that George must have had something to do with the car. She thought it would all be so simple when she had gone to the fruit stand to talk to the police about the missing car. She thought they would locate the car and deliver it in front of her house, and that would be the end of it, but she felt herself sinking deeper and deeper into the matter called trouble.

Christine again found herself with her sister. She knew what her sister was thinking. It was about George and what he could have done to have the police wanting him. That excuse, of checking on the boys, didn't get past her. It might have gotten past her if the plainclothes man didn't say that it was too bad George was not working. It was not a half hour later when the telephone rang. It was for Christine from the police station. They said that they had located her car and that she could get it any time she should decide to come to the police station.

Mary heard the telephone ring, and she hurried to the kitchen to listen in on the conversation. It made her happy to know that the car was within her reach. She slept lightly in her happiness until three o'clock in the morning, when the telephone rang again. In the hurry to answer it, she stumbled onto her mother and Christine in their anxiety to know who it was this time on the telephone. Christine was the first one at the receiver, so the others stood by.

"It's George. I think you better talk to him," said Christine, handing the receiver to Mrs. Masterson while George's voice could be plainly heard as he was shouting into the telephone.

"Hey, Mom!" he shouted, making it necessary for her to hold the receiver away from her ear. "How about bringing me something to eat?"

"Why can't you come home and eat?" she asked.

"Because I'm over here!" he shouted back.

"Over where?"

"Over at the police station!"

"What are you doing there?"

"Right now, I'm sitting!"

"How long are you going to sit there?"

"Till I can talk straight!"

"What have you done?"

"I haven't done anything! They just picked me up at the tavern and brought me in here! They say they won't feed me till morning, and I'm hungry! My stomach is turning over like a concrete mixer with no concrete in it! I—" The telephone was disconnected, and that was all for poor George. He had borrowed a nickel from the policeman, and he could borrow no more. He was led back to the cell, where he could sleep on the hardwood bench, and if he didn't like that, he could sleep on the cement floor.

After the squad car left last night, they had no trouble finding George. They radioed to headquarters, and headquarters put on several men to telephone the neighboring taverns. When they had George on the telephone, they asked him to wait for a long-distance telephone call. Then while he was waiting for the long-distance telephone call, the headquarters radioed back to the squad car, and they picked him up at the telephone.

Mr. Masterson came in happy as a skylark. He was singing and passed by them, standing at the telephone without noticing them. His eyes were concentrating on a straight path to his bed, although his feet couldn't find the straight path.

Mary, her mother, and Christine looked on with pity. They had always imagined the condition in which he arrived home, but this was the first time they witnessed the depths of his inveterate disposition. Mary and Christine looked to Mrs. Masterson, and they were sorry that they did since it only added that much more to her embarrassment. They tried to give her comfort, but the burden of troubles was becoming too heavy for her, and she could not be comforted. They went back to bed, but she remained sitting and worrying and praying. In the morning, she begged Christine to bail George out of jail and send him home in a taxi while they were on their way to school.

As they were riding in the taxi, Mary was involved in some deep thinking. There wasn't a word spoken since they had entered the cab. Mary turned slowly to Christine.

"Let him sit there for a while," said Mary. "Let him know where his meals are coming from. Let him try their stale bread and black coffee. It might give him a different picture of home life and what it should be like."

"You know"—Christine smiled to her—"I was thinking of the same thing, only I was afraid you would tell on me and it might involve me with your mother."

"Don't worry," Mary advised. "My head is working overtime to set him up on his feet. He's man enough to find an occupation and to pay his own way through life."

"I'm just wondering if you thought all that up by yourself." Christine flattered Mary more than Mary's outward emotions showed.

"You just leave everything to me," said Mary. "However it turns out, just say it's all my fault—everyone else does."

Mary was short on money, so she asked Christine for ten dollars. She was sure of getting it because of the understanding about George she promoted between them, and she hit the nail square on the head. No sooner had she asked for it than Christine drew the ten-dollar bill from her purse.

Of course, Mary was deceived with her own thoughts because Christine knew that the money was going for a good cause—and that was for a trip by Mary to see Johnnie. It was worth the money if Mary would only talk about her visit, and she was sure of getting it because of the financial difference between them.

Anyway, Mary wasn't talking on the way home. She went to see Johnnie, but she was too late. They allowed only one visitor per day, and someone else beat her to him. She felt like a silly fool, making all these trips for nothing.

"I keep wondering how Johnnie is," said Mary. "They are only permitting one visitor per day, and if one would get there first, one would get to see him."

"I think if one was not so secretive to see one, then one would see one much sooner than one thinks," said Christine, revealing her knowledge of Mary's actions.

"Then you knew all the time?" asked Mary in surprise.

"I was responsible for you since I brought you to school with me, so I was keeping track of your activities on the campus," Christine admitted.

"Spying?" Mary laughed.

"No, just looking." Christine laughed back.

When they reached the police station where they were supposed to bail George out of jail that morning, George was gone. Somebody had already bailed him out. Anyhow, Christine's car was still there, so they took that home with them. It was agreed between them that George should not use the car again. He himself had done away with his privilege of using the car. When they arrived home, there was George, waiting for them. He had borrowed another nickel from the policeman on the day shift, and his mother came down to the station to put up the bond.

"So that's the kind of aunt and sister I've got," he growled in anger.

"We were at the station this afternoon, and you were gone, George," said Christine.

"Why didn't you wait till next week before coming for me?" shouted George out of frenzy.

"That is exactly what you need, George," said Mary. "One week in the calaboose might put some sense into your thinking. They might rid you of your parasitic tendencies."

"Look who's talking. What about yourself? You never paid your way through one day in your life."

Christine stepped out of this argument for her own security reasons, while Mrs. Masterson stepped in like a good mother.

"Why can't you two forget the past and act like brother and sister?" she implored.

"It's all her fault!" George cried out.

"He's always crediting me with everything bad!" Mary complained indignantly.

"You phoned the police, didn't you?" he shouted.

"Whatever gave you that idea?" Mary asked with an air of sheer innocence.

"George, will you quit shouting?" Mrs. Masterson asked. She didn't want him to be quiet because then she wouldn't learn anything about this problem. She just wanted him to turn his volume down.

"The police captain said it was a young lady that phoned the station, and Christine is no young lady," he said.

"I resent that coming from you!" Christine broke her silence like a firecracker. "You're forgetting whose roof that is over your head. What was the matter with the food at the police station? You didn't like it, did you? You thought we should come running to you with food and money. Why, you don't have enough backbone to help yourself to a decent standard of living."

"What was the idea of Mary telling the police that the car was stolen?" he asked.

"I didn't say the car was stolen—I said it was missing."

"Aha!" George shouted. "So you admit you telephoned."

"So what if I did? I only asked them to find the car."

"Now you see, Mother!" yelled George. "See who's the troublemaker around here?"

"You ridiculed me when I wanted to go visit Johnnie in jail. Well, I believe he is innocent, but I cannot believe that in you even though you are my brother. So you left the car right there—you don't know where. Well, let me tell you something! The captain told me you rented the car to some soldiers, and it wasn't your car. That's why you spent that night in jail. It was an honest effort on my part to recover the car for Christine. It is her car. Could you say the same about your dealings? Now let's hear what you have to say, you faultfinder!" Mary glowed with pride.

Her mother and Christine marveled at the tongue-lashing she gave to George. With this accomplishment, she couldn't be ill anymore. All three looked to George for what he had to say. George became so hot under the collar from his embarrassment that he removed himself from them all and sulked in his own pride while he lay in bed. This struck him hard; he thought he wouldn't be able to face them, and he thought of leaving them all forever. Then he began some deeper thinking—if he would leave them, where would he go? If he had a place to go, where would he get the money? If he got the money and if he went wherever he got a fancy, where would he get the money for the room and board, clothing, and entertainment to stay there?

When morning came, he lay awake in the comfortable bed, and all his thoughts of leaving were gone with his embarrassment. He was a changed man, and his mother was surprised to hear him ask if there wasn't anything he could do for her. She was so taken by surprise that she couldn't think of anything. Even so, he took it upon himself to clean up the yard. His mother was so happy that she phoned her employer, saying she would report to work on the following day.

XXV

Insurance Company

$\mathcal{M}$ary couldn't figure out who that visitor to see Johnnie was. Her first thought was that the visitor was a girl, and any further thinking was stopped at this point. She had the use of Christine's car now and was determined to be the visitor for today.

The other visitor was a girl. She was not a young girl. She was more like a mother to him, always at his side and eager to help him—it was Addie. The police came to search his house the very same day he was taken by them. She helped them get into the house with her key, and she showed them around while they were in. They found his service papers but nothing else that might incriminate him. She wouldn't permit them to leave without taking her along.

"He's my boy! I'm a mother to him!" she insisted, and they took her to him, thinking she was Johnnie's mother.

The first day she saw him, he was in a delirium. He did not recognize her. She could only see him for a short time since visitors were not allowed that day. The following day, he was much better, but he still had a hazy recognition, not knowing her name or position in his life. Again, she could stay a short time, but when Mary expected to see him, Addie was at the hospital early in the morning and left before Mary had arrived.

"Johnnie, whatever happened to you?" Addie cried on the first day she could carry on a conversation with him.

"Oh, come on, Addie," said Johnnie. "I'll be home in another week—but the others won't. I was working for an insurance company."

Addie's face flushed red, not from embarrassment but from the sudden vigorous beating of her heart that rushed the blood to her head. Her heart was depressed by the succession of tragic events. This news was working miracles on all her ailments.

"What about all those things you left at the scene of the crimes?"

"I had to leave them there, and I'm glad you recognized them. It's going to be so much more valuable evidence with you recognizing the articles," he said.

"I'd like to hear your experiences," said Addie in an admiring tone. "Why didn't you tell me you were going to work as an insurance company agent? There I was, dying with every piece of bad news about you, and you were having a good time watching those thieves rob the jewelry stores."

"I'm sorry, Addie," he said. "That's the way it had to be—otherwise, my life wouldn't be worth a button which you have no use for. I was afraid that if I told you, you might slip up and tell Mary. Then she would undoubtedly tell her brother, and the news would sweep through every tavern in the city. It's not that I don't trust you. I'd tell you all my secrets. Haven't I in the past with this exception? I'm still not supposed to tell anyone until I get my instructions from the insurance company. Will you wait for me to say when?"

"Of course, I will," she said. "I understand those things better than you think I do. When Mary came looking for you, I didn't tell her a thing—until I recognized your things in the paper that were found at each robbery."

"Mary's been looking for me?" he cried out in joy.

"Now don't you go getting yourself well too soon," she warned. "I'm quite sure Mary will come to nurse you back to health again."

"Oh boy!" he shouted. "Tell me all!"

"You go on with your story first. Remember—first things come first," she said.

"Well," he anxiously started out, "I told you that I met somebody and that we were going to make a lot of money in a short time. The army intelligence turned in my name to the insurance company. The day before you saw me last, an agent from the insurance company came to see me. I wasn't going to take the job. I couldn't afford to leave Mary with Percival.

"Then when I saw Mary that night, she told me that she didn't want to see me anymore, that she was going to marry Percival, and that the wedding date was set. She even returned the pocket Bible to me. I got it from her brother when we were together in the service. The Bible saved my life while I was saving her brother's life. I gave it to her, and she thought it was some jewelry, so I asked her to keep it for me. I gave it to her because her name was in it, because I wanted her to know I believed in it as much as she does. When she returned it to me and asked me not to come to her anymore . . . When she told me of the wedding, I was so disappointed and angry at myself and the whole world that I almost reenlisted in the army—where they would knock some sense into my head.

"When I reached the front lawn after leaving Mary's bedroom window, I was attacked by somebody, and I discovered that it was her brother. He struck me in the face. He said I was making Mary sick. I returned the Bible to him, and I said, 'I don't have any more use for it.' What I really meant is that I was glad to return it to him since I had only loaned it from him.

"I telephoned the insurance company agent and said that I would take the job. When I got home, you came over, and you know how low my spirits were. The agent said he would come for me early in the morning. I got up before sunrise, and it wasn't long before the agent came. He brought three men with him. They would be my contacts in case I should need some help. I left as soon as they arrived, without having my breakfast.

"They took me to a swanky hotel apartment where they gave me some old clothes. They were the clothes of 'Shaky,' a crafty jewel thief whose hands would shake until he laid his hands on some jewelry. Then his hands would be normal until there would be another need for him to lay his hands on some jewelry—the more expensive the jewelry, the better the cure for his hands. Well, they gave me the whole history on him from the day he was born. They flooded me with pictures of his parents but not a one picture of him. He was a queer one, about my age, and he didn't associate with anyone—nor did he hang around in any place. Since he was fourteen years old, he'd been home only once, and we were going to start from there.

"This was our only chance of breaking into a gang that specialized in jewelry. They got the jewelry to a fence, and the fence would ship it out of the country where it never could be found. Two FBI men lost their lives trying to join up with the gang. We had to be careful. So we stayed in the apartment, and we studied Shaky's habits over and over during the whole day. During this time, we wore the same clothes and hats that we would on the job so we could recognize each other at a glance. The insurance company believed there was somebody in the FBI office that tipped the gang on the FBI men who were supposed to work their way into the gang.

"We started at the house of the parents of Shaky. They taught him the trade. I learned enough about jewelry to pick out the real stuff from the imitations. I learned how to get through any door and how to open almost any safe. I burst into the old house in the slum where his parents lived. They were soused up to the gills, and it was a good thing for me. It was that much less chance of them recognizing me as an impostor. The father had his lights out. His head was resting on his folded arms upon the table, and the mother was eating hot dogs. She must have bought them from the hot dog vendor at the corner. She gulped a mouthful of wine, straight from the bottle, after each bite. When she saw me burst in without knocking, she paid no more attention to me than if I were a little breeze coming through the door. I went straight to what was supposed to be my bedroom. Shaky brought home two suitcases full of clothes the last time he was home.

"'What are you looking for, son?' She came to the bedroom door with the hot dog in one hand and the bottle of wine in the other.

"'What did you do with all my clothes?' I asked her in an angry tone.

"'I took them all to the hock shop. What do you expect us to eat on? Business isn't so good,' she said.

"'Look, Ma,' I said, 'I brought you something. Remember that necklace you always wanted? Well, here it is.'

"Her eyes almost popped out. She belched and put the bottle of wine and the hot dog on the old, dust-covered dresser. She stared at the necklace with greedy eyes as her head floated in the wine. She squinted at me, but she couldn't keep her eyes off the diamond necklace very long. She couldn't recall ever wanting a necklace—especially this particularly expensive one.

"'Thirty thousand bucks! Any day!' she said. 'How did you do it?'

"'I don't work with small stuff no more, Ma,' I said.

"'Would this be a joke if I sold it to the fence and you got it back the same night? Ha ha!' She laughed.

"'What happened to my gun? Did you find it around here?' I asked her.

"'Yeah, we found it, and we took it to the hock shop after all your clothes,' she said.

"'How long ago?' I asked her.

"'A couple of weeks ago,' she said.

"'Have you still got the ticket?' I asked her.

"'You'd be wasting your time looking for the ticket,' she said, going to her bedroom dresser as I followed her.

"'Look all you want, but I don't think you'll guess what ticket it is.'

"There was a mess of tickets in the drawer. I started looking through them, and I noticed a 'G' marked on one ticket. The 'G' might mean gun. When she turned away, I slipped it into my pocket and dug through the tickets some more. Before I knew it, she was kneeling on the floor and pulling off the molding. Then she reached down into the hollow beneath the floor and brought up two guns. A .25-caliber Colt Pocket Model automatic and a .38-caliber Banker's Special Colt revolver with a short barrel.

"'Here's mine, and here's Pa's. We can't use these no more—with all those cops hanging around,' she said.

"'That's just what I need, the little one for the daytime and the big one for the night,' I said.

"'Be careful, son,' she said, 'and drop around soon. Your pa and I will need a lot of this kind of stuff to get out of this pesty hole and go back where we came from.'

"'I'll be back before the necklace runs out,' I told her, and I left as fast as I came in.

"As I was walking down the street, I noticed a man following me. I wasn't sure if it was an FBI man. They might have been keeping watch on Shaky's parents. When I took a better look at him, I knew it was the hot dog vendor from the corner. I headed for the newsstand, where my first contact man was selling newspapers.

"'I've got a tail,' I said, meaning that somebody was following me and I didn't know who. I gave him a dollar bill.

"'Camera department. Logan's store, two blocks down,' he said as if he were counting the change.

"'I've got a tail,' I said to the clerk at the camera counter of the store.

"'Washroom. Straight down the aisle. Spring lock.' He pointed in the direction.

"'The man who needs a shave,' I said and hurried off.

"As the man who was following me passed by the camera counter, a motion-picture camera was humming.

"'Hey, mister!' the clerk called to him.

"He stopped and turned to face the counter for a few seconds while the camera hummed on the counter, getting a front view of his face.

"'Care to look at our cameras?' the clerk asked him, but he hurried away after me without a word.

"I got to the washroom, snapped the spring lock, and shut the door. Then I opened the window and climbed out into the alley. I ran to the street and caught a taxi. He drove me around till I was sure there was no one following. Then I looked at the pawn ticket and asked him to go to that address. I got the gun, and as the cabby was driving away, I saw the dealer get into his car and follow me. I told the cabby to take me to Logan's store. I paid the cab driver, and I talked with the cabby, waiting for my follower to park his car. My follower seemed to be a complete beginner in this line. He followed me within twenty-five feet.

"'I've got a tail, with a gray hat on,' I said to the man at the camera counter.

"'Okay,' he said. 'Same place.' And the camera began humming.

"'Hey, mister!' he hollered again, getting a front view of my follower. The clerk held his attention for a few seconds, and by that time, I was on the street, hailing another taxi. Later in the evening, I walked up the stairs to our apartment. There, I gave the guns to my contacts, and they told me that they saw the motion-picture projection of the men who followed me. They said that according to the FBI records, these two men were definitely members of the jewelry gang. I asked them if they watched Shaky's mother, and they said she cashed the necklace at a jewelry store. I told them I would like to have the address of the store, so they telephoned the insurance company's office. I memorized the address and burned the paper.

"During the night, while my contacts were sleeping, I dressed and quietly slipped out of the apartment. I took a taxi to within three blocks of the jewelry store, and I walked the rest of the way. I hid underneath an old car across the street. I watched the store for about an hour and a half. It was two o'clock in the morning when I crawled out. I didn't think I had a chance to get in through the front door. It would be wired with an alarm—there was no doubt about that. I went to the rear of the house, and I made my way into the store through the apartment. I had no trouble picking the lock on the rear door. The rest was like filtering through the enemy lines, never knowing when I would get a bullet in my back.

"I made myself at home, packing into my pockets anything worth ten thousand dollars or more. I picked the tumblers on the safe, and there, I found the thirty-thousand-dollar necklace. From this, I knew that everything in the safe was hot stuff—I mean stolen jewelry. There wasn't much, but it was all in diamonds, necklaces, and bracelets. I'd say I cleaned up three hundred thousand dollars' worth out of the safe and about eighty thousand dollars' worth from the store. Then with my pockets bulging, I went to the bedroom. There was a man and a woman sleeping on separate beds. In the woman's dresser, I couldn't find any jewelry, but I found a small automatic. In the man's dresser, I found a .45-caliber automatic. I had no pockets for them, so I stuffed them behind my belt. I sprang the lock quietly and walked through the streets to Main Street, where I hailed a cab. I took the cab downtown and then another one to our hotel. When I got into the apartment, my contacts were still snoring. I woke them up, and when they saw the jewelry, they wanted to phone the office for an armored car to take it in.

"I was in a hurry to get this business over with. I was anxious to return to Mary before the wedding day would come around. I took the jeweler's automatic from behind my belt—and were they surprised! I gave them the smaller one too. Five guns, I collected already. I muffled the gun with a pillow and fired into the solid cotton mattress. Then I got the bullet out of the mattress for a ballistics test. I gave them the bullet and took two hundred dollars of the money that I got out of the jeweler's safe. I've already ruined the insurance company's plans by raiding the jewelry store. I packed the jeweler's gun behind my belt, and I told them I would be working alone from here on. They said they would stay at the telephone in three shifts in case I would need them.

"I got a room in a cheap hotel, and I stayed there until late in the evening. I hid the gun under the mattress. Then I went to the tavern where Shaky's mother bought her liquor. I sat at the bar drinking when two men got up from one of the tables and came to the bar. One of them looked like the hot dog vendor from the corner near Shaky's house.

"'You know,' he said to the bartender, 'it's too bad Shaky's ma and pa got bumped off. They got three hundred bucks for some ice, and they weren't satisfied—said they were going to sing to the cops.'

"I knew this was meant for my ears. I slid off the stool and headed for Shaky's house. They followed me to the house, where I found everything turned inside out. When I left, they were still following me. I went in through the front entrance of a tavern and out again through the side entrance. They were still following me, one on each side of the street, but I pretended that I didn't know. I went to my room and waited. Waited what seemed an awful long time, but it wasn't much more than an hour when there was a knock on my door.

"'Who is it?' I asked.

"There was no answer. I raised the window open so that they could hear it, and *bang!* They broke in the door. One of them had a gun pointed at me.

"'Inside, Shaky!' he cried out.

"I had one foot on the fire escape already to make it more convincing. He searched me for a gun, but it was still under the mattress. He put his gun into his pocket.

"'FBI,' he said, showing me the credentials.

"I took a good look at the name. I would have to remember that name. The one with him was the hot dog vendor. I was beginning to see it all now. This vendor was known to be a member of the jewelry gang, and under this information, the FBI man was an inside man for the gang. The vendor searched the room, and he found the gun under the mattress.

"'Is this your gun?' the FBI man asked me.

"'Didn't know there was a gun there,' I said.

"'Don't give us that malarkey!' the vendor said. 'You pulled off the job at the jeweler's. His initials are on the butt of this gun.'

"'Don't give me that malarkey!' I threw it back into his face like a tough guy. 'I don't know what you're talking about. I didn't know there was a gun there—you can't pin it on me!'

"'Oh, you didn't, aye?' The vendor was bracing himself to strike me on the head with the butt of the gun.

"'Look,' I said with a tight lip, 'I just moved into this place this morning. I haven't got any use for a gun, and if I'd have found it, I would sell it for a couple of bucks.'

"'I heard you worked alone, but I didn't know you worked without a gun,' the vendor said in surprise.

"'Who said I worked?' I asked.

"'What do you do for a living?' the FBI man asked.

"'I sell newspapers,' I said.

"'Where did you get all that money in your wallet?' he asked me.

"'I save so much every week, and I keep it all in my wallet because I don't trust any bank, see?' I said.

"'Be sure you don't move without letting us know,' he said.

"'Look, Mr. FBI Man, you better take this toy with you,' I said, and I gave him the gun. 'I don't want you to bother me anymore about it.'

"He took the gun, he looked at me, and they left. I watched through the window. I only saw the FBI man walk across the street, get into a car, and drive away. I thought this was my chance to convince them that I was Shaky. Shaky wouldn't stay in the hotel just because the FBI asked him to. I packed up my few things and left the hotel by the back way. I knew somebody would follow me. I got another hotel room a few blocks down, and I used a different name.

"As I was relaxing on the bed, I heard the lock click, and three men came into my room.

"'Hey! What is this?' I cried out.

"'Hello, Shaky,' the biggest one of them said.

"'You've got the wrong room. There is no Shaky here,' I said.

"One of them went to pull the shade down.

"'That was a clean job you pulled on the jeweler,' he said. 'We need a man like you in our outfit. There are a lot of places we can't get into—but you can.' He was angry, and he pointed his index finger at me.

"'I'm doing all right by myself,' I said.

"'So you think you're doing all right by yourself?' He laughed. 'We'll give you more for the stuff in one day than you're getting in a whole year,' he said.

"'I said I was doing all right by myself. I'm not looking for any trouble,' I said.

"'Your old man and your old lady died of lead poison,' he said, and his two henchmen pulled out their guns. 'I'm mighty glad you're not looking for trouble—that makes it much easier to come to an agreement.'

"'Sure, I'll work for you—I'll take whatever you give me,' I said. I was sweating while I was looking up the barrels of the two guns aimed at my face.

"'You know,' he said, 'I like you. You do a clean job, and you don't talk. You don't bother with the cheap stuff. We're going to get along fine. You won't have to live in any hole like this anymore . . . Okay, boys. Take him downtown and give him a treat.'

"He left in a big black car, and we drove downtown in another car. We parked it in a parking lot. While we were walking to the tavern, I noticed George across the street. Then when we were drinking at one of the tables, I saw him sitting at the bar. If he would only call out my name, he would be calling out my ticket for a one-way trip to some lonely spot in the country where I would get what they called a dose of lead poison. He was staring at me. I didn't know what to do. It was a good thing that my two gun-carrying friends were facing me all the time.

"When we were leaving, George was facing the bar and finishing his drink in a hurry to meet us. So I pulled him off the stool when he turned around, and I struck him in the jaw with my fist. He fell backward to the floor, and before he straightened up, I struck him in the face with my fist. I had to do it. It was either I shut his mouth for him or he gives my life away. When he was getting up the second time, his end was facing me, so I gave it a hard one with my foot. He sprawled on the floor again, and he scrambled out of the place pretty fast.

"My two gun-carrying friends were amused with all this, and they asked me what it was for. I told them that I didn't like the way he was sipping his drink. They laughed, and we left the place without anyone suspecting.

"They took me to their hotel apartment. It was like stepping into a mansion. There, we waited until Carter came in, and when he came, he brought the jeweler with him. Everybody called him 'Carter' because he resented being called 'boss.'

"'That was a mighty fine job you pulled at my place,' the jeweler said. 'Not a wire tripped.'

"'You're off your bean. I never was at your place,' I said.

"'How would you like to work for me?' he asked me.

"'Thanks,' I said. 'I'm already employed.'

"'That's fine—fine! Now we can go places,' he said, grinning to Carter.

"When we pulled the first job, I left the watch fob at the scene—which would give the insurance company the clue that I was there. My contacts knew of the fob, but the owner notified the police before he notified the insurance company. With the police came the reporters, and where would a reporter go without his camera? The same thing happened at the second place where I left the elephant trinket. Then both articles appeared in the paper, and it was lucky for me that none of the gang saw me with either one of them.

"I discovered that there were two gangs. One was the real outfit, and the other was a field from where they got their recruits. The field gang took their stuff to the pawn broker, while the real outfit took their stuff to the jeweler, who, in turn, got it across the border soon as they got enough of it.

"I was getting every bit of information as we went along. They liked the way I opened the safes, and I got to be one of the big three—Carter, the jeweler, and myself. I met and memorized the looks of every man connected with the outfit. They put me in charge of the warehouse. They had everything figured out—if there was a raid, I would get caught at the warehouse, and they would be in the clear. The warehouse was full of bootleg liquor with counterfeit government stamps on it. There were twenty-nine members of the entire mob, and seven of them stayed with me at the warehouse all the time. We shipped the stuff out, brought the new stuff in, bottled it, and stamped it, and out it went. The back end of the second floor had an apartment where we stayed. In a closet of the apartment was a ladder to the roof. I had everything figured out.

"When they got tired of staying in the warehouse, I would give them all the liquor they could drink. One time, while they were drunk and out cold, I wrote a letter to the agent who hired me. In the letter, I gave him all the information, including the name of every member of the mob or anyone connected with it. I had no postage stamp, and there wasn't any place to get one. I had to run a mile and a half to a mailbox. I didn't put a return address on the letter, so it would have to get there.

"The next time I wrote a letter, it carried the information about our first shipment of jewelry across the border. Carter was chiseling on the mob, and the jeweler was chiseling on Carter because the jeweler was the last to handle the shipment. I knew my letters were getting through without the stamps because something happened. I was called to Carter's apartment. There, the jeweler was on a hot seat. He was sweating and extremely nervous.

"'This guy's pulling off something funny!' Carter said to me with confidence. 'He's trying to tell us the FBI got hold of the shipment.'

"'Was it sent out already?' I asked in surprise. I couldn't make a slip here.

"'That's the question—was it sent out? Why, I got a good notion to give him some lead poison!'

"'But we can't do that,' I said. 'He's worth more to us than the shipment. Why not let him owe it to us? He can make it up with his share of the outfit, and if he pulls another stunt like it, we'll take his hide.'

"'I tell you, I sent the stuff across,' the jeweler moaned.

"'Well, why haven't I got any information on the FBI from my friends?' Carter asked.

"'Maybe the FBI stumbled into it. I'll pay you back with my work—every bit of it! You can even have the stuff I got in the store if you want to put me out of business.'

"'What do you think of it, Shaky?' he asked me.

"'We'll have to have a special meeting of the whole mob tomorrow,' I said. 'It's too late to call them together tonight.'

"'But we can't bring them all in here!' Carter cried out.

"'The best place would be at the warehouse,' I said.

"'I'll see you out there tomorrow night, and I'll see that this gentleman of ours has company until then,' Carter said.

"I left the apartment. I had a lot of work to do that night. I waited till they were all drunk, and then I gave each one a drink with sleeping powder in it. I had to make sure I had plenty of time to work. I went home for my guns. Along the way, I dropped into a radio store and borrowed a wire recording machine, speaker and all, complete. No trouble getting in or out. The cab driver waited for me. I told him it was for my uncle and that it was my uncle's store. I picked the lock so easily, I almost thought I had the key for it—and so did the cab driver. He drove me to within a block of the warehouse, from where I walked the rest of the way. The wire recording machine wasn't heavy, but it was bulky. My automatic pistol and the submachine gun were in a pillowcase in my other hand. If a squad car came by at this time, I think my whole plan would have been ruined.

"I hid the submachine gun, with all the cartridges, beneath a salt box by the railroad tracks. It was just right. It faced the door of the warehouse, which was the only way they would be able to come out, and I had the key to the door. Once the door would be locked, there would be no way of getting out except through the closet to the roof and down along the wall by rope. I started working fast. I hooked up the recording machine secretly at the place of our meeting. I hid the gun by the stairway to the second floor, and I got the rope tied to the elevator shaft. All I would have to do was to throw it over the side, and it would drop just beside the door. The door was for shipping and receiving. When I got through, it was early in the morning. I looked at the men, and some were beginning to shake off the wooziness of their head. As I watched them, I thought that I couldn't do anything more than I did in the time I had to do it in, and then I remembered that I left out something, but it was too late. I didn't let the insurance company know about the meeting. I forgot to telephone while I was outside, and now it was too late to write a letter. I was quite sure the telephone in the warehouse office was tapped by either the jeweler or Carter.

"The meeting took place, and the recording machine took down every word. The jeweler pleaded with the mob to give him a chance to prove himself. He flowered his speech with the things they went through together from the days they started the outfit. In my speech, I put in names and places for the recording. Carter called for a decision to either do away with him or keep him, but he was in favor of capital punishment for the crime that the jeweler committed. The discussions dragged on for almost two hours before a vote was called and the decision was in the jeweler's favor.

"They began celebrating with drinks. Then the pier of cases in which the recording machine was hidden was accidentally knocked over, and it exposed the recording machine. They stood there, looking at it with their senses of action stunned. They couldn't believe that they had been duped into this meeting for a special purpose. When their action thawed out, they looked among themselves for me, but I already had my gun from where I hid it at the stairs.

"If I tried to scale the open steel stairway to the second floor, there would be twenty-nine shots fired at me with every step I would take. Darkness was my friend, and I had my experiences with it from my wanderings in the jungles. I aimed and fired a shot into the light above them. I would have to keep them from the wire recordings. I didn't expect it to turn out like this. Anyhow, I knew the insurance company had an agent watching the warehouse day and night, and I felt that help would come from the outside soon as they heard the shots—but they couldn't hear the shots through the brick walls of the warehouse.

My first shot put the light out above them. My second shot put out another light, and that was the end of all the lights. The bullet caused a short, and it blew the fuse.

"This was all I needed. They all scrambled for the door. They thought I would try to get out that way, and they would block my escape. If I escaped, it would be the end of their activities for a long time to come, but I wasn't trying to escape. I had to get the reel of recordings of the meeting. From my wanderings in the jungle, my ears were trained for the slightest sound. But in the warehouse, there were no frogs or crickets or birds, so I would say I could hear a man breathing in the pitch-black darkness. I knew my way around the piers of cases in the darkness like a mouse, but I had to go slow from fear that I would bump into someone.

"At one time, I heard soft footsteps, and listening for the breathing, I located his head with the butt of my gun. I knocked him out. His gun dropped to the concrete floor with a metallic thud. There were four or five shots fired in that general direction, but I was gone with two guns in my possession. I came cautiously close to the recording machine when I heard a whisper.

"'Is that you, Carter?' somebody whispered, and I recognized it as the jeweler's voice.

"'I'm hit,' I whispered back, imitating Carter's voice.

"I located his head with the butt of my gun. He was sitting before—now he was lying, and I had three guns in my possession. I got the reel of wire recordings, and with it under my belt, I was working my way back to the stairway when the lights went on again. Somebody must have taken the fuses out and inserted pennies. It wouldn't last long before the wires would burn. But that might be long enough to get me. After that, they would need no more lamp light— they could light their way with cigarette lighters.

"I shot away the bulb at the stairway, and it seemed dark, so I made a dash up the stairway. There were only several shots fired at the stairway, which proved to me that only one man was firing blindly on suspicion of my intentions, but one of the bullets hit my left shoulder from the side. I caught the gun just before it slipped out of my hand. My left arm was limp with pain. Now I was only with half the chance of escaping if my right arm could maintain the half. I ran for the closet in the apartment, scrambled up the ladder to the roof, and threw the rope over the wall when a head appeared in the trap door, in the roof, to the closet. I held one pistol in my teeth while I handled the rope, watching for them to come. Snatching the pistol from my teeth, I fired a few times in exchange for the bullet that came my way. The head popped up, and I slid down the rope so fast, it burned my hand. At the time, I paid no attention to my hand—I had better not because I wasn't twenty-five feet away from the building when one of the gang was at the edge of the roof. I fired first, but before he went down, he sent a bullet into my left thigh. I hopped along, mostly on one foot. My left arm dangled in a paralysis, and with my burned right hand, I fired at every head that popped up above the edge of the roof. Many shots kicked up the dirt at my feet.

"When I finally got to the safety of the salt box, I still had one gun left—fortunately, it was my own. I reached under the salt box, drawing out the submachine gun from under the box. It was then that I wrote the note to Mary. I never expected to live and see Mary again. I wanted to let her know that I loved her till the end. I found the piece of newspaper in the bag with the gun, and I scribbled the note on it in a hurry. Before I had it completed, they started firing at the edges of the box, with chips off the edges spattering at me. I reached into the sack for a hand grenade. They were live souvenirs from the war that I was going to use on the Fourth of July. This would wake up the neighborhood and bring the police department to help me out of this mess. I pulled the ring with my teeth and counted till seven before I sent it sailing against the wall. It exploded a short distance from the rope. A man was about to slide down the rope when the grenade exploded, and he scrambled back on the roof.

"I finished the note, put it into my pocket, and poked my head above the box to realize the situation. I only had one drum for the submachine gun and one extra clip for my pistol. There was only one thing to do, and that was to use up the other three hand grenades and then to empty my pistol and, finally, empty my submachine gun. I tossed the hand grenades over the salt box one by one. It would give me that much more time to live and cherish the happy moments of Mary and me together.

"No sooner had the last hand grenade exploded than I heard the shrill, screeching sound of a siren. I hoped it would be help coming. Then there was another siren and another till the air was full of sirens coming from all directions. I peeked over the box, and I saw them sliding down the rope in their last panicky scramble for freedom. I opened fire with the pistol. One of them, sliding down the rope, fell to the ground. The other two were hanging onto the rope with one hand, firing with the other. As I was picking them off the rope and the roof, there was a heavy explosion, and the door was blown out of the building. I fired my last shot at the roof, and then there lay my last hope—the submachine gun.

"I peered around the side to see them pouring out of the gaping hole in the building where the door was before the explosion blew it out. Some men were headed for me in their mad plight for vengeance. Some were concerned only with their freedom as they ran to one side, while some turned off to the other. I popped up from behind the box like a jack-in-the-box, with my submachine gun bullets mowing them down.

"Before I emptied the submachine gun, somebody on the roof sent a bullet into my chest, and my gun fell to the ground as helplessly as I did. I lay there in the protection of the salt box when the screeching of one siren died out, to be replaced with the *rat-tat-tat* of a police submachine gun and the *bang-bang* of the police revolvers. A heavy body thudded against the box and fell within a foot of my head. Then the stars grew dim, and the shots seemed so far away until I closed my eyes as if I were falling asleep. When I awoke, I found myself here on this bed. The insurance company made out my identification, and the police department was finally convinced of my work when I directed them to the reel I hid on the second floor of the warehouse."

"Was that all there was to it?" Addie asked.

"Gosh! Isn't that enough? I almost died several times from the simple desire of seeing Mary," he said.

"I guess you would." She smiled. "I was wondering how you could keep from seeing her."

"Oh, that wasn't easy—especially when you're scared you're going to die without seeing her," he said.

"You know," she said in seriousness, "you better be careful with Mary. I have a feeling that she is no good."

"Addie—I'm surprised of you!" he cried out with clear surprise. "How did you ever run across that feeling?"

"Well, she can't even make coffee."

"Well, she'll have all the rest of her life to learn how to make coffee." He laughed as if in appreciation of a joke.

"But she even told me herself that her husband would do the cooking and wash the dishes and do the housework while she plays the piano from sunrise till sunset," she said in fear of hurting him.

"Oh, that? I wouldn't mind doing that for Mary—and anything else I could think of," he said, looking at her from the corners of his eyes.

"Are you sure you're not out of your mind with a fever?" she asked him, and she reached with her hand to his forehead to feel for the temperature.

"Anytime I think of Mary, I have a fever," he replied in smiles while she ran her fingers through his hair in a girlish way.

"Well, you just go on after her. She's very nice to be with," she said.

"Did you first find that out now?" He smiled. "I knew that from the first day I saw her—even before I saw her. When I read the letters she sent to her brother."

"She'll be here to see you—but let me tell you something." She leaned forward, closer to him, as if she were going to tell a secret that she didn't want the walls to hear. "Whatever you do, don't ever tell her that you were working for the insurance company."

"Why not? I thought she would be glad to know of my accomplishment," he said proudly.

"Take my advice. I never failed you, have I? She thinks that you went wrong on account of her, and she's coming after you to straighten you out onto the road of salvation. If you tell her that you were working for the insurance company, she won't have to work on you to straighten you out, and she's going to lose interest in you," Addie explained.

"But she's going to read the whole story in the newspapers anyhow." He didn't know whether he should question or merely present his points. "They're just holding back the papers till they intercept the contacts in the other countries."

"Let her read the newspapers, but by the time she does, you'll spend that much time with her, and you'll have that much time to work your way into her heart before her wedding date with Percival comes up," she said, making the eyes of a philosopher.

"I think you're the sweetest girl I ever had—besides Mom," he said. "You'll have to look after me like Mom did."

"Now you see what I mean?" she asked.

"How could I pass it up when you lay it out like that before my eyes? Of course, I see. I am blind to your guidance no more," he said. "But tell me. If I asked your advice before I went on the insurance company job, would you advise me to go?"

"That would all depend on how you would ask me and what you would tell me about it." She smiled.

XXVI

Hospital Days

The following day, Mary waited almost two hours at the hospital; with the use of Christine's car, she left the college immediately upon seeing Christine off to her office.

Addie wasn't surprised to see Mary at the hospital, but she was surprised to see Mary there so soon. She expected to be the one to pass the news on to Mary.

"You may have the visitor's card, if you wish it," said Mary kindly to Addie.

"No, my dear," said Addie. "You have it. You were here first."

"Were you here yesterday?" Mary asked with hopes that it was Addie rather than some girl.

"Yes, I was here yesterday and the day before and the day before that—in fact, every day from the very first day," said Addie proudly.

"But they told me there were to be no visitors on the first day," Mary complained.

"Well, they took me for his mother," Addie explained in a whisper before she left.

When Mary came into his room, she found him to be sleeping, so she bent over the bed, placing a very soft kiss on his lips, whereupon he opened his eyes.

"Oh!" she cried out, covering her mouth with the fingers of her hand out of surprise. "I shouldn't have done that."

"I was afraid you wouldn't. That's why I had my eyes closed." He smiled.

"Oh, Johnnie—Johnnie." She wept. "You must straighten out your ways. It was I who sent your soul into the hands of Satan. It was my fault, I know. I could have saved you, but you wouldn't listen," she said. "When you get out of jail, you must come to me, and we will partake of the sacraments, and I will lead you onto the road to salvation. You will come to me, won't you?"

"Well," said Johnnie, smiling in his heart, "you see, it's so difficult to find yourself again after being lost to the world—to return to the straight and narrow road, as they say. Once I strayed off from the straight and narrow, I found it easy to live. Everything was mine—all I had to do was to wave my magic wand, which spat little pellets of lead, to dispose of those who interfered with my wishes, wants, or desires. The whole world was mine as long as my magic wand did away with all interferences."

"Johnnie! Don't say such things!" Mary cried out. "You must have a fever. I'll call the nurse."

"I don't think you better," he cautioned.

Mary went out into the corridor for a nurse, but Johnnie was already sending his code to the nurse's office through the cord at his bedside. When Mary returned with a nurse, she found another nurse—cute and short with a sexy figure—at his bedside. She was straightening out the bed when Mary came up to her.

"Could you tell me if he has a fever?" Mary asked the nurse.

"I'll see," said the nurse, placing her hand on his forehead and then running her fingers through his hair in a playful manner in an effort to straighten it out. "I don't think he has any fever," she replied to Mary, and she left the room.

Mary looked at him through a daze as she said, "You have no fever, yet you talk like that. It means only one thing to me. Your mind is sick and confused in the leadership of the devil, and I have come unprepared. Tomorrow I will be back, and I will help you."

"Must you leave already?" he asked.

"That, I must. I am not prepared to fight the devil in you," she said, turning away from him.

"The devil always gives advice, doesn't he? But he never takes any, does he?" said Johnnie.

"Shun the devil and praise the Lord, Johnnie," she said.

"I may not live long enough to praise the Lord."

"It is better to die of sickness than of sin. Do not communicate with the devil, and I will be back to help you while there still is time," she said as she prepared to leave with disturbed emotions.

"Mary!" he called after her. "Have you forgotten something? I'll close my eyes if you say so."

"Oh, but I couldn't. I couldn't after what you've said. I'll be back, and I will come prepared," she said, leaving the room. She was gone for about ten seconds when she reappeared at the door.

"Does that nurse always take your temperature like that?" she asked in seriousness.

"Well," he said, groping around for an appropriate reply, "she never did, but I expect she will be back again soon as she knows you're gone."

Her face flushed rosy red when she realized that the nurse may be taking him away from her. She could not think of anything to say. To save herself from any further embarrassment, she left the room and the hospital.

The following day, she phoned Addie early in the morning, saying that she had to see Johnnie today in her efforts to save him. Addie submitted to Mary's wishes, saying that she would see Johnnie some other day, and she bade Mary good luck. Later, Mary came into the hospital room with a large Bible in her hand.

"Well, here I am," she said with a heavy smile on her lips and careful makeup matching her personality of trusting innocence.

"I see you've brought me a storybook. I hope it will be more interesting than my cute little nurse," he said.

"It certainly is more interesting—it's the Bible."

"Oh no!" he cried out, pretending to the contrary. "I told your brother I had no more use for it."

"Brother George gave me the Bible, and I'm going to keep it for you," she said.

"That's fine," he tried, appearing rough. "Now that I don't need it, you're going to keep it for me."

"Hush up, Johnnie," she said quietly. "You need it more now than you ever did. You must repent and pray for those evil days of your life."

"Oh, well—if you insist, then I shall repent." He submitted—but not without resistance in the tone of his voice.

"Poverty and shame shall befall those who refuse instruction," she said. "If your mind be evil, then it be full of dankness, and if no light penetrate the darkness, then you are lost to the cause of humanity— and you shall repent in hell."

"Trouble me no more. Read your chapter," he said in a commanding tone of voice.

"You are in danger," she said before turning to the Bible.

She was very discreet in her choice of the reading matter in the chapter. She did not attempt to put before him the evils of sin, imperfection, harm, injustice, malice, and its termination with retribution. Instead, she turned to the optimism of faith, hope, and cheerfulness with the philosophy of kindness, love, and labor. She took his wrongdoing as an ailment for which she held herself partially responsible and that she had taken upon herself to cure. She read to him, and he seemed to take more interest as she read along. She was back again the next day and the next until a week had already passed and he was able to get along on his legs. Mary's hopes mounted with his reclamation, and she telephoned Addie about it, asking Addie to put off her visit for another day.

Then came a time when some visitors appeared in his room while she was reading earnestly to him. It was one of the police commissioners and the president of the insurance company. They excused themselves before Mary and turned to Johnnie.

"In harmony with the police commissioners, it is a great pleasure to present you with a fair share of the recovered fortune for your work in the most extraordinary accomplishment," said the insurance company president.

Johnnie had the check in his hands with astonishment written over his face upon seeing the figures, while Mary broke out crying aloud. That was as far as the presentation speech had gone.

"You could have at least told me, you ol' meanie! I could never forgive you for this—never!" she managed to say through her tears before she picked up her things and ran out of the room.

Johnnie followed her in his pajamas with a noticeable limp in his step and the check waving in his hand above his head. He could not catch her—nor could he keep up with her.

"Mary!" he shouted down the corridor after her. "Come back! You must see it!"

Finally, several nurses and one intern strangled his efforts to follow her, and they held him until someone brought the wheelchair to ride him back to his bed.

"Too bad these things happen to me, and there's nothing I can do about it. I've just lost my girl again," he moaned before the officials.

"Your best girl? Again?" the commissioner asked in a joking way, trying to clear the dusty mood Johnnie was in.

"My only girl—again," replied Johnnie in despondency.

They extended their sympathy for his troubles. They invited him to a banquet in his honor before they left. They would have stayed much longer in a formal way had not the unexpected taken place. They felt that they had much to learn from and about Johnnie.

Johnnie tossed the check into the drawer of the bedside table. Mary always did seem within his reach, yet he could not manage to tie the knot that would bind them together under one roof. He lay back—staring at the ceiling, plotting his next move—when the doctor came to see him about the disturbance. He brought with him good news, saying if Johnnie was strong enough to run after his girlfriend, then he was strong enough to leave on the following day. He rolled from his side to his back after the doctor left, returning to rearrange his plot on the ceiling.

When Mary discovered that Johnnie had not gone wrong but that he had worked for the insurance company, she suffered a severe letdown in her efforts to save him. She felt as though she were deceived from the very beginning. It seemed like a trap door sprung open at the bottom of her heart, and all her affections for Johnnie dropped out.

So serious was she during all those visits at the hospital that it could happen no other way—not that she wanted it that way, but it was in her nature, and she couldn't help it. It looked to her like a pure form of deceit. Her heart ached as it shrank from disappointment. She felt that she would never see him again under any circumstances.

XXVII

Small Business

The following day meant kissing the nurses goodbye and blowing a kiss to the hospital as he was about to enter his cab. He went directly to Mary's home without seeing Addie, even after so long an absence. Mary was his first attraction, and everything else took its place in line after her.

He came to the door, and Mary couldn't help seeing him through the window, so she ran off to her room, locking herself in. Her father had finished his breakfast in the kitchen, and he was curious to see what had driven Mary to her room in such a hurry, while her mother was already opening the door. She was surprised to see Johnnie, and she still had fresh memories of the stories on jewelry robberies in the newspapers—plus the convincingness of Addie's visit. In her embarrassing disappointment, Mary could not think of readjusting the mental fixation about Johnnie in the minds of the members in the household. Mrs. Masterson was so frightened with the sight of him that she attempted to shut the door in his face—and she would have if he hadn't put his foot in the way.

"I'm not what you think I am!" he cried out.

He was trying to explain, but seeing his use of force, Mrs. Masterson retired to the kitchen. Receiving no reply, he put his hand lightly against the door, finding no resistance. It opened, and he found himself confronted with Mr. Masterson blinking his hazy hangover vision away. Johnnie was in doubt as to whether he should enter or not—he was not invited into the house.

"Johnnie!" Mr. Masterson yelled out in drunken excitement.

It had been a long time since he saw Johnnie at the house. He had no drink yet since it was only two o'clock in the afternoon, and he had just had his breakfast, but the excitement of seeing Johnnie again whirled his mind around with such force, he seemed to be loose in his joints and wavering in his steps as he blinked to see more than what was before him.

"How is business, Mr. Masterson?" Johnnie asked while shaking hands with him.

"Fine, fine! Come on in! We've got a lot to talk about," said Mr. Masterson with tremors of his muscles from the lack of a drink and under the excitement.

"Where's Mary?" Johnnie asked.

"I guess she's in her room. She ran out of here as if she saw a mouse. Just sit tight, and I'll see what I can do for you," he said, leaving for Mary's room, where he thought she was dolling up for Johnnie, but it didn't take long for him to return.

"Will she see me?" asked Johnnie.

"She's locked in her room," said Mr. Masterson, feeling sorry that he could not bring Mary to him. "She must be sleeping." He felt like a liar about the sleeping part; in fact, he knew he was, but it might help to ease the depression a little.

"Maybe I could see her some other time," said Johnnie, getting up to leave.

"Yes, you do that, Johnnie, but be sure to come. I'll have a talk with Mary when she gets up. She's getting married with that Percival fellow pretty soon, but don't let that worry you," he said, lending his encouragement.

"You know," said Johnnie, "I always wanted to go into partnership with you."

"I've always wanted to have you for my son-in-law. That's why I said don't let the wedding worry you. We'll stick together until the end—and even after the wedding, you still have a chance," he replied.

"I'm sorry. I'm not speaking of Mary. I'm really talking business. How much do you think you can get started with?" Johnnie asked, eyeing his face.

"A hundred thousand would be fine to start with." He laughed at the round figures; it had been so long since he talked big money that it seemed funny coming out of him. "You're not serious. Are you, Johnnie? About that starting with a small business?"

"Of course I am," said Johnnie with serious emphasis, reaching into his wallet for the check. "Will this be enough to get started on?" Johnnie was presenting the check to him.

Mr. Masterson shied away from it, thinking it probably was a week's salary that Johnnie had earned somewhere. He had talked enthusiastically with Johnnie about starting a small business some time ago, but his life and his habits had changed since then, and small business seemed like a waste of effort when he had big business in mind.

"You trust me, don't you? Even after I went broke on my own," said Mr. Masterson with a touched heart.

"I have a lot of respect for you, Dad," said Johnnie. "You always were a big-business man, and you always will be. There's a lot I have to learn from you. You've made all your mistakes, and I have not yet started on mine."

He folded the check once over and slipped it into Mr. Masterson's shirt pocket, after which he left without the exchange of another word. Mr. Masterson couldn't bear the thought of starting a small business with Johnnie, and he didn't have the heart to refuse Johnnie's serious efforts to start something. He stood staring at the floor, stupefied with his fear of small business. Johnnie left and was gone before Mr. Masterson realized it. He grew weak with the thought of the work involved in a small business, and he sat down at one end of the sofa, in serious deliberation, when his son, George, came into the living room after being awakened from his sleep by the voices.

"Hi, Dad," greeted George, seating himself at the opposite end of the sofa. "What's bothering you?" he asked, noticing the deep concentration of his father.

"We're back in business, son," said his father in a dazed tone. "Small business. Johnnie and I," he added.

George looked at his father. He saw his father in periods of melancholia—but never like this. He became suspicious when his father mentioned Johnnie. Johnnie was thought of as being a criminal. So what could he have to do with his father? Several times, his eyes were attracted to the greenish-yellow slip of paper in his father's shirt pocket before it came to him—the realization that it was a check. Casually, he reached into his father's shirt pocket, taking out the check and opening it before his eyes.

"A hundred and thirty thousand dollars!" George gasped, turning to his father while the figures shocked his father into sobriety. His father turned slowly to him and took the check slowly from him.

"We're back in business! We're on our way again!" Mr. Masterson cried out with joy.

He sprang to his feet and danced with his son in circles as they shouted, embracing each other. Then he ran to the kitchen and swung the missus around a few times. Her mind was spinning, and he kissed her, bringing the check before her eyes, which made her head spin so much the more. Mary came out of her room from curiosity as to the commotion. Mr. Masterson swung her around too, with a few accompanying kisses. When everything quieted down, Mrs. Masterson took the floor.

"Where did you get the check?" she asked.

"That's no secret—I got it from Johnnie. We're going into a business partnership!" said Mr. Masterson.

"You take it right back!" she snapped out at him. "First thing you know, you'll be in jail too."

"But a hundred and thirty—" he started out.

"Yeah! It might be a rubber check, Dad," George cut in. "You want to get pulled in for passing bad checks, Dad?"

"You be quiet, George! You and your suspicions. That check is good, and I know it." Mary fought back for Johnnie—not that she didn't like George anymore.

"Tell me more," George sassed her back.

"I was there when the president of the insurance company and one of the police commissioners presented the check to him," said Mary proudly, holding her head high, and her eyebrows lowered as she looked down upon George.

George and his father looked at each other and nodded in mocking understanding.

"But all those robberies in the papers . . ." Mrs. Masterson questioned Mary's statement.

"You'll read a lot more about it in the papers. Johnnie was working for the insurance company all the while," replied Mary with an air that she had all the answers.

In his happiness, Mr. Masterson took hold of Mary, and he waltzed her around the house. When he cooled off, he turned to his wife, saying that he would stay in the rest of the day and look through his books. He would study last Sunday's wanted and business sections, and by morning, he could have all kinds of ideas about getting into business.

XXVIII

House and Farm

When Johnnie left Mary's home, he went to the college and enrolled for what was left of the semester. The football season was about over, and of course, his team had a tough time without his leadership. They all admitted that they could have taken the trophy if Johnnie was on the field. This made him feel that he had let his team down, but taking into consideration the service he had done to the public, the team would soon take on a different attitude toward him. It was not for him to go about repeating his story to everybody on the campus.

From the campus, he went to see Addie, who was surprised to see him. Mary hadn't telephoned her that morning, and she thought that Mary didn't have the time. She expressed her great delight in seeing him on his feet again, and then she burst out into heavy tears.

"I'm a thief, Johnnie! I'm a thief!" She cried on his shoulder like a schoolgirl sweetheart. "I thought you went wrong, but all that time, I didn't know that I was the one. I'm going to the poorhouse tomorrow, sure as the day is to come."

"Poorhouse?" he questioned, thinking she meant that she was going to hell for her sins. Then again, he couldn't grasp the situation with what little she had told him. He led her to the sofa, where he sat beside her so that she could confess her sins to him.

"I have sinned against you, Johnnie"—she sobbed—"and I deserve to be punished for my sins."

"Punish you? That's a lot of nonsense. I don't see how even the Lord could punish you," he said.

"But I have sinned, and tomorrow you will see justice done unto me." She tried not to look into his eyes and covered them most of the time with her handkerchief. "Tomorrow they will take all my possessions away from me and take me to the poorhouse."

"Foreclosing?"

"Worse than that. They're taking everything—even my clothes that they could sell," she said.

"I can't believe it!" He gasped. "Why, you just bought me that expensive car, and I thought you've had loads of money."

"Johnnie," she said. "When your father went away, there was the insurance money left after him. Your mother gave him a very nice funeral. Then when your mother went away, there was the insurance money left after her. She trusted all her money and her papers to me. I gave her a very nice funeral like your father's, and she's lying there beside him. There was almost six thousand dollars she left with me. I kept nibbling away at it until you came back. Then I only had about half of it left. I only gave you a little over two thousand dollars that I had left. The money for the car really came out of your own pocket." She broke into heavy, uncontrollable sobs again.

"Don't you cry like that, Addie. You know better than that. Crying is for young little girls," he said, and she regained control over herself.

"But you haven't got the money you're supposed to have," she said.

"Money doesn't mean anything to me," he explained. "I almost got myself killed in the war and then again on the insurance job, and if I did, nobody would know the difference. But since I am here alive and since I know of your sin, it still doesn't make any difference to me. I know that you would have bought me the car anyhow, even if it were for your own money."

"The only time I cried like this was when my husband went away. After his funeral, I was sick, and the doctor said I only had fifteen or sixteen months to live. He said not more than a year and a half. The year and a half passed by, the doctor passed away, and here I am, still waiting to die after all these years. My muscles ache, and my joints give me pain, but the Lord doesn't want me yet," she finished with a tone of despondency.

"Don't you worry about anything. You can come to the rooming house and live with Pappy and me," he said, restoring her confidence.

"When my husband passed away, you were here, and you know how it was to get somebody to work on my farm. Then when the war broke out and you left with the boys, I couldn't get anybody to work on my farm. They all went to the city for jobs, and that's the way the farm has been ever since. The machinery rusted, so it can't be used anymore, and to hire somebody, I would have to get new machinery. I didn't have the money for the machinery, so everything remained as it was. The mortgage wasn't paid, the taxes on the farm weren't paid, the taxes on the house weren't paid, and last year, I signed a paper so they would let me stay another year."

"Do you have a carbon copy of the paper you signed?" he asked, wondering what its contents were.

"Oh, there was no carbon copy. The man just brought the paper, and I had to sign, or else he would move me out if I didn't," she explained.

"Do you have the papers for the house?"

"The man wanted the papers for the house, but I didn't give him anything," she boasted. "I have all the papers in a safe deposit box in the bank."

"How much would it take to straighten out your farm?" he asked excitedly.

"About seventy or eighty thousand," she said.

He paced the floor before her in his deliberation. He had to save the farm and the house. They meant so much to her. She would never be the same without them. He felt sorry for her as he would for his own mother. She was always like a good mother to him, even when his mother was with him. He had to do something, and that could only be done by reclaiming his check from the business partnership with

Mr. Masterson. He figured that he would have some money left over, and after the crops came in, there would be an income from the farm. What he had left plus the income from the farm might be enough for Mr. Masterson to start a business in the fall.

He set out immediately to the Mastersons' home. He felt that he had to see Mr. Masterson before Mr. Masterson would invest the money in some business enterprise. He waited a few seconds at the door of the house before it was opened by no one else but Mrs. Masterson.

"Is Mr. Masterson at home?" he asked meekly.

"No, Mr. Masterson left about ten minutes ago—but Mary is in the living room," she said. I'm very sorry about the way I acted this afternoon. Mary told me since then that you were working for the insurance company." She was really embarrassed at facing him again, feeling that she had hurt him, as had Mary.

"I have some very important business to transact with Mr. Masterson," he said, hesitating to enter the house.

"Mr. Masterson will be back very shortly," she said. "Won't you come in?"

"Why, yes, of course." His eyes caught the sight of Mary seated in the living room and looking out to him.

He took his place beside Mary on the sofa, and she smiled to him. He felt that he was making some progress in the relationship with Mary, and he realized that this was only the beginning.

"Would you care for a piece of cake?" she asked.

"Did you bake it?" he countered excitedly.

"No, but I watched Mother bake it," she replied.

"Oh," he gave out in understanding.

"Would you care for some marshmallows?" she asked. "I got them for Percival, but you're welcome to them."

"You always get marshmallows for Percival?"

"Uh-uh." She shook her head. "Sometimes I get a box of cherry centers."

"Cherry centers?"

"That's what Percival calls them. It's a chocolate-covered candy with white inside and a cherry in the center," she explained.

"Hmmm. Everything for Percival?" he marveled.

"Now will you tell me all about your work for the insurance company?" she asked with shyness.

"Is that what the marshmallows are for?" He turned to her.

"Of course not." She turned away from him.

"Can't you wait till you read it in the papers?"

"Why must I? Percival would tell me anything I would like to know," she said.

"Do I look like Percival?"

"No, but you could try to be just as kind. Will you tell me all about it, Johnnie?" she begged.

"Will you give back the engagement ring to Percival?" He felt greatly pleased with the thought as he blinked at her.

"I should say not! A promise is a promise, and this promise is a sacred one to me. You're being unreasonable in your bargaining when you know I could read all about you in the newspapers," she said.

"Where did your father go?" he asked, changing the subject since she cut him down with pain in his heart.

"He went to the club to see some of his friends. He was going to stay home tonight and study his books, but he became restless, and he went out for a while—so he said," she informed Johnnie.

They spent another ten or fifteen minutes in conversation on Percival and mostly on Mary trying her utmost to have him tell his story, while he skillfully wiggled his way out every time she thought she had him talking. Then it came to his attention that Mr. Masterson went to the club and that the club was nothing more than a tavern where businessmen congregated. Under the circumstances, Mr. Masterson would not come home till the late hours of the morning. He had to go after him to the tavern because the time element was important in reclaiming the check and in restoring the property to Addie. He rose from his seat and left abruptly. Even Mary couldn't understand his actions, for he said nothing to display his feelings or intentions.

"Johnnie left so soon? I thought he would stay to have dinner with us," said her mother.

"I don't know why, Mother. He asked me to return Percival's engagement ring, and I couldn't do that. Could I?" She looked at her mother with fear of the effect it had on Johnnie's feelings.

Johnnie knew where the tavern was. He was driving his convertible, so it wouldn't take him long to get there. On entering the tavern, he found Mr. Masterson drinking at the bar. There were at least nine men gathered around him, and it seemed like the drinks were on him. Johnnie stood by, looking and waiting.

"Is that your son?" one of the men asked, calling Mr. Masterson's attention to Johnnie.

Mr. Masterson looked back to see. Upon seeing Johnnie, his face became sickly pale. When the men saw Johnnie advancing, they made way for him, but they stood close by from curiosity.

"I've got to have that check, Mr. Masterson," said Johnnie. "Our partnership will have to be dissolved until another time."

Mr. Masterson could not say a word. He was sick in his stomach. He thought Johnnie had caught him squandering the money on treating his friends with drinks. His lips turned blue, and his face took on a bloodless appearance. He reached his hand across the bar to the bartender.

The bartender heard what Johnnie said, and he rang up the register, took out the check, and put it into Mr. Masterson's shaking hand.

Without a word, Mr. Masterson returned the check to Johnnie. In the embarrassment of taking back the check, Johnnie left without saying another word.

"Have a drink on the house!" the bartender-owner cried out after seeing what had happened, with the effecting pallid appearance of Mr. Masterson.

Everybody took the drink and gulped it down, but Mr. Masterson stared at his drink before him—thinking that it was responsible for what had taken place. It made him sick every time he made an effort to take the drink.

"Go on—take the drink! You look like you need it—a whole bottle of it!" one of the men around him cried out.

Mr. Masterson slowly looked at each and every face around him. He looked at the drink, and it made him sick when he thought of the business he could have had. Then he looked again at the men around him, and they made him sick. He left the drink where it stood. Feebly and slowly, he slid off his stool, and he made his way out, feeling that he would faint at any moment. On his way out, the men laughed at him, and they joked about him. He had not a penny in his pocket, so he sat on the running board of an old taxicab. The taxi owner looked out and saw the sickly appearance of Mr. Masterson. He helped him into the cab and drove him home, where he collected the fare. Mr. Masterson went to bed, and there he remained without eating or sleeping.

Meanwhile, Johnnie rushed to Addie's house. He showed her the check, and she broke out into tears.

"It makes me so happy," she said, and she cried with more feeling than before.

He tried to comfort her, but she had to cry it out. Together, they went to a bank where Johnnie established a checking account for the amount at the check. From there, Addie showed him the way to the real estate office that had the mortgage on her farm. They arrived at the office after nine o'clock. The office was open till six o'clock. It was a little office—a one-man-and-secretary outfit. Addie knew where he lived, so they went to his house. It was a huge fourteen-room house with expensive reception quarters. Johnnie told him that he would like to clear the debt on Addie's farm.

The real estate man was taken by surprise, and he didn't know what to do or say to Johnnie.

"Errr, seeing as it's after office hours," he said to Johnnie after giving it some thought, "you better come to my office tomorrow morning."

There was nothing else for them to do but to bid him good night and return to the office in the morning. It was a long and sleepless night for both Addie and Johnnie. He was supposed to go to school the following day, but he didn't. He went to the real estate office with Addie instead. At the office, they were greeted cordially by the real estate man, but when Johnnie brought up the subject of clearing the debt on Addie's farm with a checkbook in his hand, the man's attitude had changed to the unpleasant.

"I'm sorry," he said. "Yesterday was your last opportunity for payment."

"But we tried to pay you!" Johnnie and Addie spoke up at almost the same time.

"I could only transact business during business hours—that is why I stay open till six o'clock every night," he said in a sarcastic way.

"Couldn't I pay it today?" asked Johnnie with a mixture of hope, anger, and sorrow.

"It is too late. The foreclosure proceedings go through today. I must ask you to be sure to vacate my premises by half past two o'clock this afternoon," he said with an arrogant tone.

"What happens at two thirty?" Johnnie asked sharply in anger.

"At half past two o'clock this afternoon, I shall be there with the sheriff, who will throw you out into the street—or into jail, if you prefer," he said.

Johnnie could see no point in staying any longer. He took Addie's arm and helped her out of the office and into the car.

"Don't worry, Addie," he assured her. "We're not licked yet. We still have the title to the property."

They returned to Addie's house, where they pondered over the problem. It was hours before Johnnie thought of turning to the insurance company for help. One day they had come to him for help; now it was his turn or their opportunity to help him. He telephoned the president of the insurance company, and the president put one of their ablest lawyers on the telephone. Johnnie told him the story, and the lawyer said that he could do nothing since Addie had signed the paper turning the property over to the real estate man if she could not meet the requirements of the debt within one year, and yesterday was the last day of that year.

Johnnie mentioned the fact that they had been at the real estate man's house yesterday, but the lawyer replied that a businessman could not be compelled to transact business after office hours against his will.

That was the end of that from the insurance company. They knew the laws and the legal procedure, so there was nothing left for him to do but to prevent the eviction of Addie from her home. The time was nearing two o'clock. So he went to his house and came back with the submachine gun under his arm.

Addie was frightened at the sight or it because her imaginations went the wrong way. She thought that with it, he was going to eliminate the real estate man and the troubles he was causing. Johnnie finally calmed her down and told her of his plan, so they were ready for the real estate man when he came with the sheriff. Addie answered the door while Johnnie was hiding in the kitchen. She invited them in, and they were seated comfortably before the sheriff could mention his purpose of being there.

"Ahem!" The sheriff cleared his throat, breaking their silence since Addie was doing all the talking. "I wonder if you know the reason why I am here," he asked. "But that doesn't matter. You see, if you sign a contract, you have to carry out the provisions of the contract. Since you have agreed to leave your property in the hands of the mortgagee upon failure to clear the debt within the one year, it is my duty to tell you that the said year has expired yesterday, and it is my duty to see that you turn the property over to the mortgagee."

"But I won't leave this house! This is my home, and this man is trying to cheat me out of all my possessions. It is your duty to take him and to lock him up in jail, from where he won't be able to cheat any old woman like me anymore!" She turned upon the sheriff with full force.

The sheriff, in turn, looked out the window and waved his arm, and in a few minutes, two of his men came into the living room.

"Don't worry, ma'am," said the sheriff. "We'll take you straight to the poorhouse, and they'll take good care of you. There's lots of old women like you up there."

"Sure, there's lots of old women like me up there—that's because you put them there. Don't you come near me! Don't you even touch me!" she screamed, and Johnnie came out with the submachine gun ready. He had a cloth in his hand as if he were polishing the barrel.

The sheriff and his two men made a quick move for their guns, but they were stopped by Johnnie's command before they could draw the guns.

"Don't!" Johnnie yelled out, and they froze in their movements. "Don't do that!" he repeated. "You make me nervous." He had the gun pointed at them while he was pretending to polish the barrel at the same time.

"You'll pay for this." The sheriff winced.

"For what? For polishing my gun? I'd say it might go off accidentally if I should get excited," said Johnnie.

"This is a holdup," the real estate man meekly stated to the sheriff.

"It will be a holdup," Johnnie corrected him, "if you just try to take this kind old helpless lady's home from her. Anybody who as much as touches her against her will is involved in rape, and this gun speaks for itself, whether it be a sheriff or anyone else. This kind lady will leave only after due process of the law and only by her own free will."

"This is the process of the law," the sheriff said. "I saw the papers, and this lady has no more right here than you have."

"This lady stays here until the highest court of the land decides that she must leave—that's how far we're going to fight this crooked dealer. And if you want to start something now, then just reach for your guns," he warned.

"That's a submachine gun," Addie told them as if they didn't know what it was. "And he knows how to use it," she boasted proudly while Johnnie kept polishing the barrel. "He's the one who shot up that whole warehouse full of thieves, burglars, and robbers like that real estate man over there." She pointed to him.

"He did?" The sheriff gasped.

"Yes, he did—with that submachine gun too!" Addie cried out with pride.

"Something is beginning to smell about this eviction case." The sheriff gave the real estate man a cold stare. "All right, men—we haven't got anything to do here," he said to his men, who were shaking with fear and holding their hands high above their heads.

"I'll see you in court about this, and I'll show you every letter of the law. You're making a terrible mistake, and it's going to cost you plenty," the real estate man threatened Johnnie.

"It's too bad you don't have sense enough to settle for the debt alone. Your greed is driving you beyond your limits of decent human relationships," Johnnie replied, biting into him so deep that he left with anger.

On seeing them leave, Addie turned to Johnnie with a strong feeling of admiration. He was like a faithful son to her, as far back as she remembered, and now she looked at him as a hero.

"Where did you get those big words—'due process of the law,' 'highest court of the land,' and a few other things you said?" She grinned.

"I must have heard it on the radio program." He laughed.

"For a while, I thought you were a lawyer. That stuff was strong enough to twist the nose of the sheriff," she remarked, to his delight.

"You better dig up every paper you have that concerns your property, regardless how insignificant it might be," he advised. "I would like to look through the entire history of the property."

She took him to her safety deposit box at the bank, where he emptied all its contents into a cardboard shoebox. It almost didn't fit into the shoebox, which he wound with a heavy string. At home, she opened the wall safe where she had some more papers of less importance. They were looking through the different papers and sorting them out on the dining room table when Mary burst in without knocking or sounding the door chimes. She was angry and looked upon Johnnie with contempt.

"I hate you, Johnnie! I hate you!" she cried out. "I hate you with all the bitterness of my heart! You have poisoned my father with your evil ways. He can't eat, he can't sleep, and he can't speak to anyone. First, you give him something that brings him happiness, and then you take his happiness away. He sits at home like a living corpse. I will hate you for this the rest of my life. You have poisoned his heart—I hate you to the very last of my mental efforts."

She ended with a firm stare at him, and then she left as she had entered before he could find something to say. Her actions, he could not understand, but that did not interest him because he never did understand her actions. Yesterday she was feeding him marshmallows, and today she was hating him for the rest of her life. How had he poisoned her father's heart? How had he taken her father's happiness away? Something brought happiness to her father, something that he had given him . . . *The check!* It came upon him with a cold feeling creeping over his body to the top of his head, where it tightened his scalp. Of course, she was talking about the check. He was so engrossed with the papers laid out before him that her surprise visit and her speech confused his thoughts, and it took so long to clear things up.

He watched her retreat to the door without making any effort to follow her. What could he say to her if he caught her in his arms and stopped her?

"I'll have to go and see her father," he said, rising from his chair.

283

"Would it take much longer to look through the papers?" she asked, knowing that his attentions should be centered on Mary if he hoped to marry her.

"It wouldn't make any difference to her whether I see her father today or tomorrow. She's going to be hating me just as much tomorrow as she does today. That's what she said . . . She will hate me today, tomorrow, and the rest of her life. I think we better finish with the papers, and then we can both go to see Mary and her father," he said, sitting back at the table again.

"I'm sorry to be so much trouble to you. If I didn't take up so much of your time, you could have had that much more time for Mary," she said.

"Where do you get thoughts like those? You are a comfort to me like my mother always was, and Mary is my trouble. If it weren't for girls like you and Mary, the world would stand still," he said, smiling to her.

"It's too bad that Mary doesn't know you as well as I do." She smiled back.

XXIX

Collaborators

They spent another two hours looking through, sorting, reading, and discussing the papers before he found something that swirled his head around with the flattery of success.

"What's this?" he asked, showing her the paper. "Some kind of deed made out in my name?"

"Yes, I signed everything over to you soon as the doctor told me I was going to die in sixteen months. Then you went to war, and I forgot all about the will," she explained. "How could I remember with that villain hovering by my door?"

"But this is all you need to beat him away from your door forever! This is a recorded deed, and it went into effect the same day you have been living on my property," he remarked in glee.

"My property, your property—the good Lord only knows what I've been doing," she said.

"Don't you see? Evidently, the real estate man doesn't know about the deed."

"That's what you think—apparently, he's trying to pull a fast one," she corrected.

"Maybe you're right, Addie," he said. "We're going to keep that in mind and work accordingly."

They arranged all the papers in order and neatly put them away into the wall safe. Then she served a light dinner, and they were on their way to Mary's father. Johnnie could get the insurance company to help, but he realized this was his opportunity to smooth out his relationship with Mary's father, and that was so much more important since it would involve Mary too. Her father was a good businessman, and he would know how to handle the problem as well as any good lawyer. What troubled him was how he could face Mary's father after the grief he had caused him. He thought it over in many different ways while they were on the way. When they reached Mary's home, he asked Addie to remain in the car. While he was at the door, Mary answered, and she became infuriated by the sight of him.

"I would like to speak to your father," said Johnnie.

"I hate you. Therefore, you could not speak to my father," she said, and she shut the door sharply before him.

If he had only approached Mary, begging her forgiveness, he would have started a conversation with her that would lead to a conference with her father, but he was Johnnie, and his first thought was to undo the wrong that he had done.

It was dark already, and through the window, he saw Mary's father sitting at one end of the sofa in a statue-like, motionless way. First, now did he realize the error of his ways, but he had to do it if he was to save Addie from catastrophe. She was always like a mother to him. He had been blinded by the desire to help her. He returned to his car and explained everything to Addie. She understood the situation very well and asked him to remain in the car while she went to the door. Mary came to the door again, expecting to find Johnnie back again. She suspected that Addie had come with Johnnie, but she could not refuse Addie's request to see her father.

"Could you leave me with your father?" Addie looked to Mary, fearing that Mary would upset her plan.

When Mr. Masterson saw Addie come in, it made no change in his motionless state. Mary's mother and Christine were at the college play, and George was out as usual, so that was all the better. Addie talked to him without arousing any interest or replies. He was like a freak from the circus who advertised twenty-five dollars to anyone in his audience who could make him smile. He looked on through space with his cold, piercing eyes. His lips were firm with fear and sorrow, and in general, his face was covered with a mask radiating the symptoms of toxicosis.

It was discouraging, and the longer she talked to him, the more she felt the urge to help him. She felt the responsibility for his condition since Johnnie had reclaimed the check, dissolving their partnership to help her. Finally, she broke into tears, telling him how the villain was at her door, trying to cheat her out of her house and farm. Her heart struck a new beat when she saw him stir and turn to her.

"That is how I lost everything I had," he said.

"Are you going to let them do the same thing to me?" she asked in a pleading way.

"No," he replied. "Not to you—nor to anyone else. Let me see all your papers," he said, standing up and waiting for her to recover from her tears.

"Mary!" he called.

"Yes, Father?" She hurried in with surprise of the sudden change in her father.

"I'm going with Addie, and I won't be back for a few hours," he said.

"I must go too. Mother said I should remain with you at all times, and if I didn't go with you, I would have to stay home—all alone," she reasoned with her father.

"Very well. Then you may come along." He submitted to her wishes.

When they were getting into the car, Johnnie held the seat forward, while Addie motioned for Mr. Masterson to get into the back seat. Then when Mr. Masterson was seated, he saw Addie hold back Mary from getting into the back seat with her father, and Addie occupied the back seat with Mary's father, while Mary had to sit in front with Johnnie.

While they were starting on their way to Addie's house, Mr. Masterson burst forth with conversation, but Addie called his attention with a tug at his arm, and she put her finger over her lips. He took in the situation and began to see it all now. They rode in silence for a while before Mary couldn't stand it any longer.

"I'm sorry I acted the way I did this afternoon." She apologized to Johnnie since he had not spoken a word to her.

"There's no need for apologies—it was all my fault. I'm just a bungling fool," he replied.

Mr. Masterson listened to them while they ironed out their differences, and his head was cleared of its morbific condition. He was happy again—much happier than he ever was. Here were two of his friends—the only true friends outside the members of his family. He was beginning to experience the joy of life once more. When they reached Addie's house, he was amazed at the beautiful home she had. Eagerly, Addie brought out the papers again, and he became excited with the task laid out before him. While he and Johnnie started discussing the situation, Addie left them.

"I haven't washed my dinner dishes from yesterday," she said.

Naturally, Mary followed her into the kitchen and helped her with the dishes. Then they began setting the table for dinner when Addie brought out a cake she had baked.

"Don't tell a soul. This is Johnnie's favorite cake. I was going to take it to him at the hospital, and you didn't phone me that morning," she said to Mary.

"It looks delicious," Mary commented.

"Here's the recipe—you can bake one of these for Percival someday," she said, but she really meant Johnnie. Everything she said referred to Percival.

Mary looked at her with a puzzle in her mind. *Why does Addie speak of Percival instead of Johnnie?* She expected Addie to have Johnnie in most every sentence Addie spoke. She took the recipe with grateful reception and put it away into her purse.

Mr. Masterson went over the whole history of the house. Johnnie explained everything as he went along. Dinner was waiting for them before they were through, but the dinner could wait. When they were through with the papers, the dinner was cold but still waiting for them.

"The real estate man is making a terrible mistake, and we're going to sue him besides," said Mr. Masterson to Johnnie with a grin for revenge upon the shyster.

The case came up in court, and the real estate man was badly beaten with the skill of Mr. Masterson guiding the attorney furnished by the insurance company. Then the man was sued for the amount of the mortgage and settled for forty thousand out of court, all of which remained with Addie. Mr. Masterson and Johnnie wouldn't have a penny of it.

"It is my property now. I will settle the debt out of my account," said Johnnie, writing her a check for the amount of the suit they won since it was written from the debt of the farm.

"I never argue with a man I like," said Addie.

"How would you like to manage the farm for me?" Johnnie asked Mr. Masterson.

"I'd like it fine! I always was figuring on retiring to the country. There's nothing like getting down to earth and living on it," replied Mr. Masterson, realizing that it would bring Johnnie closer to Mary.

Johnnie moved from the rooming house to live with Addie, and he offered his home for the Mastersons to live in, but Mr. Masterson declined since Mary refused to leave Aunt Christine's house. Mr. and Mrs. Masterson could now see through Johnnie's propositions, and they sympathized with him. Mrs. Masterson was very grateful to Johnnie for the recovery of her husband, and Mr. Masterson was grateful to Johnnie for the new life that lay before him. He became more excited as the days went by and never touched a drop of any alcoholic beverage from the time Johnnie reclaimed the check. To iron out the wrinkles in his friendship with George, Johnnie presented his "delicate sunshine yellow" convertible to George. It acted as a psychological factor upon Mary since it reminded her of Johnnie and their moments of happiness.

"Mary," he would coax whenever they were alone, "let me return Percival's engagement ring to him."

"A promise is a promise, and I promised," she would reply.

"I'll pluck your heartstrings, Mary. I'll wrap your mind in poetry, and I'll give your body comfort and security. Leave him forever and come with me," he begged over and over.

"A promise is a promise, and I promised" was her only reply as tears blurred her eyes.

"The oyster had a secret—the secret of a pearl," he said. "I am an oyster, and you are my pearl. You must remain within my arms for all of my life."

She knew that she could never marry Percival because she was in love with Johnnie, but she felt that she could not marry Johnnie because of her sacred promise to marry Percival, so she was drifting helplessly into matrimony with Percival. Then came a day—just before Mary sent out the wedding invitations—when Johnnie came to Mary's house with a verse in his hand. He intended to turn the verse into a song.

"Mary, would you please, please help me write the music for this verse?" he begged.

"But I don't know how to write music," she said.

"You say that without even trying—come to the piano with me, and I'll tell you how it goes." He took her by the hand to lead her to the piano, where they sat down and worked on the song together.

They worked the music over and over till late into the night. The following day, Mary sang and played the notes on the piano from the morning hours till Johnnie returned in the evening. She worked the notes over and over while she sang the song until she thought it was the way she would like it to be. Immediately, Johnnie took the song to a talent scout. That was the reason why he had written the verse in the first place—because he had met the talent scout at the college and because popular music would get her in trouble with Percival.

When he came again to see Mary, Percival was there, but he paid no attention to Percival. He took Mary by the waistline and swung her around and around.

"Stop it! Johnnie!" she cried out.

"Mary, we made it! We made it!" he shouted.

"Made what?" Mary stood away from him to compose herself while Percival looked on.

"Our song will be recorded—and published too!" Johnnie cried out wildly in excitement.

"What is all this going on?" Percival finally worked up the nerve to cut in.

"We wrote a song and—" She never finished; she was so excited that she went to the piano to play it for him instead of telling him about it.

"Stop! I forbid it! I forbid it!" Percival cried out at the top of his voice.

"Something tells me you don't like it," Johnnie implied with cool sarcasm.

"I won't have you dabble in that trash. I forbid it," said Percival firmly.

"It's popular music. Johnnie wrote the verse, and I wrote the music," she explained.

"No matter what you call it, it's still trash, and I won't have it," said Percival.

"But I wrote the music—don't you understand, Percival?" Mary asked. "It's going to be recorded, and my name will be on every record," she added proudly.

"Oh my god! Have you made out the contract?" asked Percival, with his hands shaking from nervousness.

"No," Mary replied. "That will be taken care of in the following day or two."

"Well, you can't go through with it, and if you do, I'll have my ring back," said Percival, on the verge of having a nervous breakdown.

"Did you say you'll have your ring back, Percival?" Mary asked in cool seriousness.

"Yes, that's what I said," he replied, drawing his handkerchief while his lips quivered downward at the edges.

"Here you are, Percival," she said, taking the ring off and giving it to him. "I was so afraid that I would have to break my sacred promise of marrying you, but now that you have asked for the return of your ring, I feel that you have broken the bond between us. Therefore, I am bound to you no longer by any promise. You have always been and always would be my teacher, but Johnnie is my collaborator."

"But I don't want the ring back!" Percival protested in terror.

"But you said you did want the ring back, and I heard you say it with my very own ears, and I saw your lips move with my very own eyes while you said it," said Mary.

"I said I did and I didn't but that I would—if you didn't or wouldn't do as I say," he explained in fear and confusion.

"Maybe you did and you didn't, but you would because I must have the freedom to do as I please some of the time. Now that you have your ring back, you will not worry me anymore about taking it back," said Mary.

"Hurray!" yelled Johnnie.

"I'm all yours, Johnnie," she said, going to him.

He kissed her and swung her around again, but this time, she didn't say, "Stop it!"

Good fortune was the piper, and he danced to the piper's tune.

She held onto his neck while he held her at the waistline, and they waltzed around Percival's dumbfounded figure. Then they relaxed on the sofa to see Percival leave.

When Percival saw the engagement ring in the palm of his hand, his face turned a sickly pale color, and his mind failed to comprehend the full meaning of it until he saw Mary flee to Johnnie. When he saw Johnnie kiss her, he knew that it was time for him to move out since there remained no way by which he could restore the ring on her ringer.

After Percival left, Johnnie turned to Mary.

"Can you make twins?" he asked her.

"I can try." She smiled.

"You're supposed to teach me how to be like a gentleman," he reminded her.

"Wait," she replied. "Give me time. You're a tough job for a changeover. Once, you're a mad lover. Once, you're a poet. Once, you're an adventurer, and I don't know which one of you I like most of all—so be yourself, Johnnie."

"That won't be hard—if you can put up with me," he said, laughing it off.

Everybody made it a habit of going to the movies when Percival was at Mary's house. This time, when they came back, they were surprised into tears or happiness. Christine was the first to kiss Johnnie—the act that no one could understand besides Johnnie himself. It meant that he had cleared the way for her to work on

Percival, and there was no better time than now when he was down in a rut.

Johnnie had already telephoned Addie. He was happy as a bee with honey. Mr. and Mrs. Masterson were wild with joy over Mary's happiness, and before anybody knew it, someone was at the door. When Christine answered the door, Addie rushed in to offer her heartiest congratulations to Johnnie and Mary.

"You don't think I could stay home and wait for you to come?" she said, congratulating them.

Dinner was prepared in no time at all, with four cooks attending—Mrs. Masterson, Christine, Addie, and Mary—while Mr. Masterson and Johnnie stayed in the living room, discussing farm machinery. They all stayed up till two o'clock in the morning, when George came home to complete the celebration.

George was feeling fine with the odor of bottled spirits in his breath. When he heard the news, he had no control over his emotions. He had Johnnie's convertible, and now with Johnnie for a brother-in-law, he could get some spending money from Johnnie every now and then.

Everything worked out fine. Christine tightened her web around Percival, and he could offer no more resistance—which brought him to his senses.

"Mary said I would only be a teacher to her, and Johnnie would be her collaborator," he said.

"Well, you'd never be a teacher to me—you'd be my collaborator," she said.

"I would? I mean, I would!" Percival cried out, and then he laughed so vigorously, she became embarrassed.

"What is it?" she asked.

"Hold my hand," he said, and she did. "Now close your eyes," he said. He slipped the ring on her ringer while her eyes were closed.

She hoped it was the engagement ring, and it was.

"Why, Percival . . ." she said. "This is an engagement ring!"

"Uh-huh," he replied. "I should have had it on your finger fifteen years ago, but I didn't know until now that you are the one for me."

Christine threw her arms around Percival's neck, and she kissed him as though he had saved her from the fate that she dreaded most.

That was something that Mary had never done to him. Mary never kissed him, not even when he gave Mary the engagement ring. They were so excited with each other that Percival overcame his bashfulness for the moment, and he took Christine in his arms, and he kissed her in return. They decided to make it a double wedding.

The wedding day was the happiest day in Mary's life. She had no more troubles, no more confusion in her mind. She lived through her wedding day under the illusion that her life would be worthless without Johnnie. Late that night, when they were alone, Johnnie presented her with a napkin from the dinner table of the reception after the wedding. During the dinner, with his pen, he had written upon it,

> I listened to the angels—they told me not a thing . . .
> I gazed upon the stars, and I saw nothing . . .
> I looked into my algebra, I looked into my trig,
> I looked into my analytics, and I looked into my calculus—
> But I could not calculate . . .
>
> So I stared, and I stared into my crystal ball,
> And by guess and by gosh,
> Multiplied by two, divided by one-fourth,
> And taking one away—
> This is our wedding day!
>
> So my crystal ball says,
> "From this day on,
>   fill her heart with happiness."

The wedding day had passed by. The happy days of Christmas came to everyone, including George. With the yellow convertible he had gotten from Johnnie, he'd been making good time with the girl of his desires—Lorraine. Of course, Johnnie had been backing him with all the money George needed. When George had returned from the service to find his father penniless and his mother working for a salary, he suffered from the shock and the realization of starting all over from scratch and from the frustrations of the embarrassing situation in regard to his girl.

Lorraine was the only child in the home, and her father had one of the larger department stores downtown. When spring came along, George married his girl. Then he was given the responsibility of managing her father's department store, which he accepted with the utmost pride and happiness. A good businessman, like his father, George carried the responsibility remarkably well.

The summertime came. Then the harvest time came and with it the profits from the farm. Mary was so happy with everything at her hand that soon after the harvest, she went to the hospital, where her first child was born. It was a baby boy, and he looked like Johnnie.

"Have you decided what his name should be?" Johnnie asked when he came to her room at the hospital immediately after Mary and the child were ready for the father.

"Johnnie, of course," she replied with a smile.

He took a sheet of stationary from the bedside cabinet and began to write while she looked on, waiting patiently. When he finished writing, he folded the paper, handing it to her. She, in turn, unfolded and read it before his waiting eyes.

> I saw the saw to saw the wood.
> I would the saw to saw the wood.
> I would the wood a house of wood.
> I could if I would, and I would.
> I would and wooed a girl I could.
> I brought and wrought the girl I brought,
> And now I have a family.

Mary turned her eyes from the paper to Johnnie, and she laughed with him.

"Now all we need is a little one of you," he said.

Two years elapsed when Mary was again in the same hospital. This time, it was a baby girl, and it looked like Mary.

"What do you think should be her name?" she asked.

"Mary, of course," he replied with a smile.

Johnnie and Mary had gladdened the heart of Addie since she never was able to have children of her own. She took care of the little ones as though she were the grandmother. Johnnie and Mary lived with her from the day of the wedding. The Mastersons lived in Johnnie's house next door, but they spent most of their time at Addie's house; the other times, the members of Addie's house spent their time with the Mastersons.

George and his wife settled for a baby girl, while Percival and Christine wound up with a baby boy. Then came a day during the summertime when they all got together at Addie's house in a party-like celebration. The babies were able to get about by themselves on their hands and knees with the exception of Johnnie Jr., who was able to walk. While the party was going on, Johnnie was sitting in a corner of the living room. At that moment, he realized that not one of them had married without first going through some troubles of adjustment with their mates. He took out his pencil and a sheet of paper to picture what he saw, and it read,

> "We differ in more ways than one.
>> Agree with me, you ol' son of a gun."
> So she said to her boyfriend
>> In trying to straighten, to mend.
> "We argue about things and about dough.
>> Agree with me, you ol' so-and-so."
> So he said to his girlfriend
>> In trying to maintain, to bend.
> She didn't give in; she didn't care.
>> He didn't tell her his pockets were bare.
> It wasn't long, as the time goes,
>> Before he broke down to propose.
> Now it makes no difference where they go.
>> She takes care of the house and the dough.